She was His W...

THE

who Married Her

Three exotic and thrilling books by
three terrific authors:

Maggie Cox
Lynn Raye Harris
Meredith Webber

THE SHEIKH WHO… COLLECTION

On sale 5th July

On sale 2nd August

On sale 6th September

On sale 4th October

On sale 1st November

On sale 6th December

THE SHEIKH
who Married Her

Maggie
COX

Lynn
RAYE HARRIS

Meredith
WEBBER

MILLS & BOON

Mills & Boon, an imprint of Harlequin (UK) Limited, Eton House, 18-24 Paradise Road, Richmond, Surrey TW9 1SR

THE SHEIKH WHO MARRIED HER
© Harlequin Enterprises II B.V./S.à.r.l 2013

One Desert Night © Maggie Cox 2011
Strangers in the Desert © Lynn Raye Harris 2011
Desert Doctor, Secret Sheikh © Meredith Webber 2008

ISBN: 978 0 263 90736 0

026-1013

Harlequin (UK) policy is to use papers that are natural, renewable and recyclable products and made from wood grown in sustainable forests. The logging and manufacturing processes conform to the legal environmental regulations of the country of origin.

Printed and bound in Spain
by Blackprint CPI, Barcelona

ONE DESERT NIGHT

MAGGIE COX

Maggie Cox loved to write almost as soon as she learned to read. Her favourite occupation was daydreaming and making up stories in her head, and this particular pastime has stayed with her through all the years of growing up, starting work, marrying and raising a family. No matter what was going on in her life, whether joy, happiness, struggle or disappointment, she'd go to bed each night and lose herself in her imagination. Through all the years of her secretarial career, she kept on filling exercise books and—joy, oh, joy—her word processor with her writing, never showing anyone what she wrote and basically keeping her stories for her own enjoyment alone. It wasn't until she met her second husband, the love of her life, that she was persuaded to start sharing those stories with a publisher. Maggie settled on Mills & Boon as she had loved romance novels since she was a teenager and read at least one or two paperbacks a week. After several rejections, the letters that were sent back from the publisher started to become more and more positive and encouraging, and in July 2002 she sold her first book, *A Passionate Protector*, to Mills & Boon® Modern™.

The fact that she is being published is truly a dream come true. However, each book she writes is still a journey in courage and hope and a quest to learn and grow and be the best writer she can. Her advice to aspiring authors is, 'Don't give up at the first hurdle, or even the second, third or fourth, but keep on keeping on until your dream is realised, because, if you are truly passionate about writing and learning the craft, as Paulo Coelho states in his book *The Alchemist*, "The Universe will conspire to help you" make it a reality.'

To Ruth, who has the soul of a poet and a
heart made of love

CHAPTER ONE

'Who ever loved that loved not at first sight?'

The kingdom of Kabuyadir...

THE sound of crying came to Zahir on the wind. At first he thought he'd imagined it. But when he stepped out onto the balcony overlooking the mosaic-tiled courtyard he heard it again. The sound distracted him from the decision he'd already made to leave the party he was in no mood to attend and go home. He'd gone upstairs to his friend Amir's salon, to steal a few moments to himself away from the mundane chitchat he found it hard to respond to, and very soon he would seek out his host and make his apologies for quitting the party early. In light of what was going on at home, Amir would understand completely.

But now he found himself stepping out into the courtyard, easily bypassing the interested glances that sought to detain him by adopting a detached air that he knew not even the most courageous would disregard. Instead he embraced the kiss of the warm spiced air that stirred his senses as it never failed to do and glanced round him—for what? He hardly knew. Was it a child he'd heard? Or perhaps some small wounded animal? *Or was the gentle sobbing simply an imaginary product of a tired mind and heavy heart?*

The sound of splashing water pouring in a crystalline flow from the mouth of a mermaid into the magnificent shell-like fountain—an impressive centrepiece in the marble-paved courtyard—dulled his hearing for a moment. The only other noise carried on the soft night air was the steady high-pitched drone of cicadas.

Out of the corner of his eye Zahir spied a flash of pink. Narrowing his gaze, he stared hard into a dimmed corner, where there was a stone seat almost shrouded by the shiny dark leaves of a voluptuous jasmine plant. A pair of exceedingly pretty bare feet poked out. Intrigued, he moved forward.

'Who is there?'

He kept his voice low and unthreatening. Nevertheless it carried its usual air of authority. A sniffle, a soft intake of breath, and a long slim arm reached out to brush away some of the protective foliage that more or less kept the stone seat totally secluded. Zahir sucked in a breath.

'It's me…Gina Collins.'

The sweet-voiced announcement was followed by the sight of the most bewitching blue eyes he had ever seen. They all but equalled the light of the moon with their luminous crystal intensity.

'Gina Collins?' The name hardly computed in Zahir's brain. But the appearance of the fair-haired beauty that emerged from her hiding place to stand before him in an ankle-length pink dress with her feet tantalisingly bare could not fail to deeply stir him.

She was a vision of loveliness that no man would soon forget. *No wonder she hid out here, away from view!* Was there a red-blooded male living who *wouldn't* be tempted by such a vision?

Sniffing again, she stoically wiped away the damp smudges beneath her eyes with the back of her hand.

'I am none the wiser about who you are,' Zahir commented wryly, raising a brow.

'I'm—I'm sorry. I'm Professor Moyle's assistant. We came here to catalogue and study Mrs Hussein's books on antiques and ancient artefacts.'

Zahir vaguely remembered the wife of his friend Amir—Clothilde, who was a senior lecturer in art at the university—telling him about her intention to get some help with her library of rare and valuable books. But since his mother had died they had not met, and frankly there had been far more demanding things occupying his time.

'Is the work so distressing that it compels you to hide out here to conceal your dismay?' he mocked gently.

The enormous blue eyes widened. 'Not at all. The work is a joy!'

'Then I desire to know the reason for your tears.'

'I just—I just….'

Zahir found he did not mind waiting for an answer. Where was the need for impatience when his gaze was happy to linger in examination of exquisite features that suggested they had been created by a divine artist who clearly adored her? In particular her lush-lipped quivering mouth.

She sighed softly, and her reply had a tremulous break in it. 'I heard the news today that my mother has been taken ill and is now in the hospital. My employers have very kindly booked me on an early flight in the morning, so tomorrow I'll be travelling back home to the UK.'

A sympathetic wave of compassion and understanding rippled through Zahir. He knew only too well what it was like to have a beloved mother become ill, to watch her health deteriorate day by day and feel utterly helpless to do anything about it. But he was genuinely shocked at how disturbed he was at the notion that this beautiful girl was going home when he'd only just met her.

'I am so sorry to hear your sad news... But I must also confess my regret that you are going home before we have had the chance to become properly acquainted.'

A frown marred her clear brow. 'Even though my mother is ill, I wish I wasn't leaving. Do you think that's very bad of me? I would much rather stay here, if you want to know. I never realised what a painful wrench it would be for me to go, but there's a kind of magic here that's left me spellbound.'

Her response was so surprising that for a moment Zahir hardly knew what to think or say. 'So you like this part of the world? Then you must come back soon, Gina...very soon. Perhaps when your mother is fully recovered?' He folded his arms across his chest and his smile was benevolent and kind.

'I would love that...to come back again, I mean. I can't explain it, but this place has begun to feel more like home to me than my own country. I love it so.'

Her face glowed suddenly, as though lit from within, and suddenly he was not in such a hurry to leave Amir's gathering after all.

'But you must think me very rude for sitting out here on my own when everyone else is inside. Mr Hussein's nephew's graduation is meant to be a happy occasion, and I didn't want to bring things down by being sad. Suddenly I just couldn't seem to contain how I felt. It's difficult to talk to people and be sociable when you're upset.'

'There is not one soul here who would not understand and sympathise with your predicament, Gina. But it is good that you attended the party. It is the custom here to invite as many friends and acquaintances as possible to share in a family's joy when they have something to celebrate.'

'That's what I love about the people here. Family is really important to them.'

'And that is not so where you are from?'

She shrugged and glanced away. 'For some, maybe... but not for everyone.'

'Now I have made you sad again.'

'No...you haven't. I mean I'm sad that my mother is ill, but to tell you the honest truth our relationship is not the loving, affectionate one I could have wished for. My parents are devoted academics...they deal in facts, *not* feelings. To them, feelings just get in the way. Anyway, I've bored you with my troubles for long enough. It was very nice meeting you...but I think I should go back inside now.'

'There is no hurry. Perhaps you would consider staying out here for a while with me? Whatever is taking place in our lives, it is a beautiful night, no?'

Zahir's hand reached out lightly to detain her, and the vivid blue eyes grew round as twin full moons. But, aside from being mesmerised by her startled glance, the feel of Gina Collins's flawless satin-textured skin made him feel almost dizzy with want. He hadn't expected that. It was as though a hot desert wind had swarmed into his bloodstream. He could hardly take his eyes off her.

'All right, maybe I'll stay for just another moment or two. You're right—it *is* a beautiful night.' Folding her arms, she stepped back a little, as though suddenly aware that the distance that separated them was minuscule. 'Are you related to Mr Hussein's family?' she asked quietly, and Zahir saw the flare of curiosity in her limpid blue eyes that she couldn't quite quell.

'I am not related by blood, but Amir and I have been friends for a long time. I have always thought of him as my brother. My name is Zahir,' he volunteered with a respectful bow.

From beneath his luxuriant dark lashes he saw that she blushed. Was it because he had bowed, or because he had only delivered his first name? It might be the way they would have done things in the West if they had met informally at a party, but it was definitely *not* the way men of his rank conducted themselves here in Kabuyadir—especially not when they were destined to inherit the rule of the kingdom after their father!

'Zahir...'

She echoed his name softly—as though it were something wondrous. The sensuous sound caused a cascade of delicious shivers to erupt down Zahir's spine.

'Even the names here have a ring of mystery and magic,' she added shyly.

'Come,' he invited, his blood heating even more at the idea of having her to himself for a while. 'Let us walk together in the grounds. It would be a shame to waste such a glorious full moon on an empty garden with no one there to witness it, don't you think?'

'Won't you be missed if you don't go back inside soon?'

'If my hosts are troubled by my unexplained absence they will be too polite to say so. Besides, I do not have to give an account of my actions to anyone save Allah.'

The woman in front of him fell silent at that. Zahir glanced down at her small slender feet, with toenails painted the same captivating shade as her dress, and a frisson of disturbing awareness rippled through him.

'You will need your shoes if we are to walk together.'

'They're over by the bench.'

Moving back towards the stone seat, with its shield of glossy green leaves and intoxicating white-flowered jasmine, Gina collected her flat tan sandals and slipped them on. When she glanced up again at Zahir, a tendril of golden hair fell forward onto her brow. She brushed it away and smiled. A woman's smile had never had the effect of rendering him speechless before, but it did now. Clearing his throat, he didn't even think twice about extending his hand to take hers. When she wordlessly and trustingly placed her palm inside his Zahir lost all track of space and time, and the grief and turmoil he had been so racked with since his mother had died melted into the ether...

Studying the strong-boned face, with fathomless dark brown eyes and long glossily black hair that was parallel with his shoulderblades, Gina knew she was captivated. With his full-length dark robe—the *jalabiya,* as it was called—and his lean waist encircled by a light brown wide leather belt, he might have been an imposing inhabitant of a bygone court of a wealthy Caliph...a highly trained soldier or a bodyguard, perhaps? He was built as if he could take care of himself and many others besides.

It might be an entirely dangerous action, putting her trust in a man she had only just met, but since such an overwhelming compulsion had never seized her before Gina could only believe it was meant to be. *Kismet* as they often called it in this part of the world. Right then she needed the reassurance of a strong, understanding figure. Something told her that Zahir was a man who *did* understand feelings...the thought was quite intoxicating.

As they walked the meandering paved paths enclosed by a high stone wall that made the building very close to a fortress, with the shining moon benevolently following their progress, she wondered even more how she would endure the stultifying pattern of her day-to-day life when she got home.

When her mother recovered she had no doubt that its pattern would resume—just as though a false note had inadvertently been played, been quickly righted and then forgotten. But Gina couldn't forget or deny her growing yearning to connect with something deeper and more real in her life. She might have fooled herself for a long time that diligent study and adding more and more academic credits to her name, the perusal of dusty old tomes and cataloguing times long past was enough to engage her, to help her feel fulfilled, but since she had come to Kabuyadir she had started to question whether that was the right path for her.

Oh, she still loved her work, but travelling to the other side of the world, discovering a sensual paradise of sights, sounds and scents she had never experienced beyond the descriptive pages of a history book, had forged in her a restlessness and a desire that would never again be subdued.

Her parents—both professors in their chosen fields— had found academic study more than enough to fulfil them and to cement their relationship. Their marriage had come about through mutual interest and professional admiration, but they hardly ever expressed more profound feelings and emotions towards each other. They had raised Gina responsibly, protected her from harm and danger and done all the right things. It had been a given that she be steered towards a career in academia. Rarely had they told her that they loved her…

Now her mother was ill, and she knew in her bones that her father's way of dealing with it would be to retreat even more into the world of the intellect instead of feelings and emotions. Gina would sit awkwardly by her mother's hospital bedside and hardly know what to say or talk about. Yes, her heart would swell with sympathy, but she should have rebelled long ago against the path that had been laid out for her. She should have given academia and books a very wide berth. What had it done for her? She was *dull, dull, dull!* A twenty-six-year-old singleton who lived on convenience foods because she'd never learned how to cook—a pattern she'd inherited from her busily studying parents—and who had never had even one relationship with a man that meant anything.

She had a couple of similarly situated friends, who scorned the very idea of a meaningful relationship because it would undoubtedly be messy and distracting and take their concentration away from their studies. But since coming to Kabuyadir Gina knew that the 'distracting' and totally wonderful concept of a mutually loving relationship was crystallising more and more into a longed-for desire in her heart. So much so that she could no longer ignore it…

'Did you know that the ancient seers and astrologers used to track the destiny of kings through the stars?' Her companion pointed up towards the navy blue bowl of sky that was liberally arrayed with clusters of tiny winking diamonds.

A totally helpless shiver briefly convulsed Gina. Not only were Zahir's darkly handsome looks mesmerising, but his voice was imbued with power and magic, too. Coupled with the dreamlike atmosphere of a still-warm desert night, enchantment was being woven round her heart with delicate but unbreakable gossamer threads that would hold it willing prisoner for a long, long time.

'What about those of us who are merely ordinary, and not kings or queens or anybody special? Do the stars show us our destiny too?'

Gina's heart missed a beat when Zahir captured her free hand and turned both her palms upwards. His dark gaze looked to be deeply examining the fine lines—some with intricate little chains—that mapped her otherwise smooth skin. The playful caress of a soft breeze lifted a fiercely shiny coil of his hair and let it drop back against his cheekbone. Heat invaded her insides like a wild summer storm that plastered her clothes to her frame and ripped her hair free from its usual neat arrangement as though it wanted to free her soul, too.

'I do not believe you are ordinary in any way. Your destiny is beautiful, *rohi*. How could it be otherwise?'

'You're just being kind. You don't know me. Nothing extraordinary ever happens to me…apart from coming here, I mean.'

'It grieves me that you clearly have no sense of your own great worth, Gina…your incandescent loveliness.'

'No one has said such things to me before.'

'Then the people in your life must be blind…deadened to beauty and grace.'

She stared wide-eyed as he bent his head towards hers, with no thought of trying to struggle against a tide that now seemed inevitable. Her sadness and frustration with life was completely banished, to be replaced by the most ridiculous hope and longing as his large strong hands settled firmly on either side of her hips. The intimate contact was like a sizzling brand, burning through the thin material of her dress. When Zahir's mouth descended on hers, his lips were softer than down and more tender and erotic than Gina could have imagined.

He gentled her as though she were a nervous lamb, or a small bird he didn't want to scare or overwhelm with his powerful strength. Beneath his mindful gentle exploration a melting heat drowned her insides in a sea of sensuous honey. The dark trimmed hair that covered his chin and the space above his upper lip was far softer than she would have expected. It was a pleasurable sensation like no other. She would never forget it. As his masculine heat and scent invaded her blood like a drugging opiate, she sensed her knees tremble violently. It shocked her to realise that she wanted more…*much* more of this potent magic he was delivering.

'You are cold?' he asked concernedly, his hands still clasped round her hips as his eyes smiled down into hers.

'No, not cold… I'm shaking because I'm nervous, that's all.'

'I have overwhelmed you…'

When Zahir would have respectfully withdrawn, Gina reached out to lay her hand over his heart. The fine cotton of his robe was as sensuous to the touch as the most luxurious velvet. Beneath it she sensed muscles that radiated the masculine strength and energy of a trained warrior contract. The instant flaring of his inky-dark pupils easily confirmed just how he felt about her touching him. In a trice his arms came around her waist, and suddenly her trembling body was on shockingly intimate terms with the hard male reality of him.

Her thoughts careened into an abyss as pure compelling sensation took over. How could something she'd never even come close to experiencing before suddenly be as essential to her as breathing? If he let her go now she would have to *beg* him to keep holding her. She would risk everything— her pride, her fear, her very *heart*.

Just before his lips claimed hers, the mingling perfumes of jasmine, rose and orange blossom was carried on the air from the flowers that abounded in the garden, heightening moments that would be imprinted on Gina's mind and heart for an eternity. There was a sense of wildness—a raw, elemental hunger about Zahir's passionate kiss. The suggestion of bare control thrilled her, echoing as it did her own helpless urgency and gnawing need. As her mouth cleaved to his, their tongues swirling and entwining hotly, it made her cling to him to keep her balance.

He tore his lips away from hers, his breath ragged, his

glance molten. 'You are leaving tomorrow, and I…' He shook his head, his expression torn. 'I do not know how I can bear to let you go.'

'I don't want to go…but I have to, Zahir.'

'Must we part this way? On my honour, Gina, I have never felt like this with any other woman before… As if… as if she were a part of me that I never even knew I had lost until I saw her.'

Devouring him with her eyes, Gina felt her heart squeeze with anguish at the mere thought of them being separated. *Would people judge her as heartless—as cold and unfeeling—because she preferred to stay here with Zahir instead of going home to see her sick mother?* Right then she didn't care. How could she when she'd been so bereft of love—of warm, human touch—for too long? Why should she feel guilty and weigh herself down with painful responsibility when his impassioned confession echoed the heartfelt yearning in her to reach out for something wild, warm and wonderful beyond imagining?

'You are staying in one of the houses in the grounds, I presume?' He drew her with him beneath the shelter of a shady tree, glancing behind them as if to check whether they were being observed. But the shadowed fragrant garden was empty and still except for the hypnotic drone of the cicadas and the soft gushing of the water fountain.

Worrying her lip with the edge of her teeth, Gina nodded.

'Can we go there?' Zahir's thumb was stroking back and forth across the fine skin of her fingers, and the tension between them grew tight as a bowstring on the verge of snapping in two.

'Yes.'

They moved in silence towards the end of the garden, where a vine-leaved arbour led onto another paved area.

There sat a long, low adobe-style residence, with an arch-shaped entrance like the Ace of Spades. It was decoratively outlined by ornate gypsum, its walls inset with traditionally narrow windows to keep out the glare of the heat. Within the garden was a tranquil pond and a beautiful mosaic-tiled fountain. Because rainfall was more abundant up here in the mountains greenery thrived, and heavily perfumed blossoms were everywhere. The temperature was not so fierce, either. Occasionally they were blessed with distinctly cool breezes.

About two hundred yards away, secluded by magnificent date-palm trees, was another building. This was occupied by Gina's boss, Peter Moyle. But Peter was still at the Husseins' party, and she and Zahir could slip inside Gina's lodgings unnoticed.

Feeling daring and wild, as well as a little afraid, she knew her behaviour was unlike any she had displayed before. She'd thought of herself as staid and boring for so long that the uncharacteristic impulse to reach for something she yearned for with all her heart and not fear the consequences was utterly exhilarating. Reaching for the slim iron key that was in the pocket of her dress, she inserted it into the lock and gave it a twist.

The Moroccan lanterns she'd left burning softly cast a seductive glow round the wide decorative vestibule that led into the main living area. When Gina started to move in that direction Zahir caught her by the waist, and what she saw blazing in his eyes smothered every thought in her head to silence.

'Where is it that you sleep?' he asked, his voice low and imbued with the sensuous drugging heat of the desert itself.

Slipping her hand into his, she led him into the blissfully cool bedroom, with its marble floor, and to the bed that was graced with a silken canopy the colour of a dramatic burnt orange and red sunset. Brass wall lights and another softly glowing lantern rendered the interior warmly intimate.

Stepping in front of her, Zahir cupped her face between his hands—hands that were warm and capable and big. He had the hands of a protector, for sure. And his gaze…his steady dark gaze…was a benevolent silky ocean that Gina would willingly submerge herself in for the longest time.

Inside his chest, Zahir's heart drummed hard. His confession that he had never wanted a woman this much before was perfectly true. How could attraction be so instant and so…so *violent*? he mused. His every sense was irrefutably held captive, and he could barely think, let alone hope for some understandable explanation. He found himself intimately examining the arresting features before him. In contrast to the brightness of her golden hair, Gina's arched brows were dark and generous. They raised her exquisitely formed features to a visage far beyond merely pretty, stamping them with a beauty that was hard to forget.

It was, Zahir thought, perhaps the only night they could be together for a long time. Who knew how long Gina's mother would be in the hospital? How long before her lovely daughter could return to Kabuyadir? The idea made his insides lurch painfully. Why had fate brought him this treasure only to rip it away from him so soon…*too* soon?

'I never expected…'

Gina sucked in a breath, her lips visibly trembling, bringing home to Zahir how nervous she was. How to convey without the use of words—words that would surely be woefully inadequate—that he would never knowingly cause her hurt or bring her shame? Those same reasons had made him check to see if they were being observed just now in the garden. He would willingly shoulder all the blame if someone were to even *think* of judging her.

'Neither did I, *rohi*.' He laid the pad of his thumb across her plump lower lip and stroked it. 'And if all we are destined to have together for a while is this one night...then I will make sure it is a night that our bodies and souls will never forget. That is a promise I make to you straight from my heart...'

Three years later...

'Dad, are you there? It's only me,' Gina called out after letting herself in with her key.

She gathered up the stack of letters on the mat inside the door, frowned, and made her way along the rather gloomy hallway to the back of the three-storied Victorian house, where her father had his study. He was hunched over at his desk, staring at what looked to be an aged, yellowed document. Just then, with his mussed greying hair and his too-thin shoulders in a blue unironed shirt, he seemed not just preoccupied and isolated, but sad and neglected, too.

In Gina's heart a pang of guilt mingled with her sorrow. She'd been working hard at her new job at a prestigious auction house, had rung him nightly, but hadn't called in for a week.

'How are you?' Leaning towards him, she brushed the side of his unshaven cheek lightly with her lips.

He stared up at her with shock in his eyes...just as if he'd seen a ghost. Then he grimaced and forced a smile. 'I thought you were Charlotte. You're looking more and more like your mother every day, Gina.'

'Am I?' The comment surprised her, and made her heart skip a beat. It was the closest thing to a personal remark Jeremy Collins had made to her in weeks. He particularly avoided mentioning his wife, Gina's mother, if he could help it. Her death three years ago had hit him much harder than she'd ever envisaged it would. Gina was disturbed that he should bring her up now.

'Yes, you are.' Shrugging his shoulders, Jeremy laid down the yellowed document and tried for a smile. 'How's the job going at the auction house?'

'It's really testing my mettle, if I'm honest. I mean, just when you think you've got a handle on something you discover there's so much more to learn.'

'You sound as if you're learning some valuable wisdom along the way as well.'

'I hope so. No matter how many diplomas I've succeeded in getting, I still feel very much a junior in this trade, Dad.'

'I understand, dear. But don't be in such a hurry to get somewhere. This "trade," as you call it, is a lifetime's passion for most who enter into it, and you never stop learning and discovering things you didn't know before. You're still so young... How old? Remind me?'

'Twenty-nine.'

'Good God!'

His exclamation made Gina giggle. 'How old did you think I was?' she playfully challenged him. At least he wasn't looking so down and distracted now, she noticed.

The greying eyebrows made a concertina motion. 'In my mind I always remember you at round about five years old...reaching a sticky exploring little hand towards the papers on my desk. Even then you had an interest in history, Gee-Gee.'

Dumbfounded, Gina stared hard, 'Gee-Gee?'

'It was my pet name for you. Don't you remember? Your mother thought it highly amusing that a distinguished professor of antiquities and ancient history should have the imagination to come up with something like that.'

'Here.' There was a lump in her throat the size of an egg as she handed him the letters she'd found on the mat.

'What's this?'

'Your post…looks like it's been accumulating for days. Why didn't Mrs Babbage bring it in for you?'

'What?' The pale blue gaze was distracted again. 'Mrs Babbage resigned last week, I'm afraid. Her husband had to go into hospital for a major operation and she wanted to be able to visit him as often as she could. Under the circumstances, she couldn't keep her job here. Anyway, I shall need to interview for a new housekeeper.'

Reaching out her hand, Gina laid it briefly on his shoulder. She was shocked to feel how little flesh covered it beneath his shirt. 'That's the third housekeeper you've lost in a year,' she commented worriedly.

'I know. Must be my sparkling personality or something'

Ignoring the droll reply, Gina gazed at him, seriously concerned. 'What have you been living on for a week? Not much, by the looks of it. Why didn't you tell me about this when I rang you, Dad?'

For a moment the expression on her father's long thin face reminded her of a small boy who had been reprimanded by a teacher and told to stand at the back of the class. The lump inside her throat seemed to swell.

'Didn't want to worry you, dear… You're not responsible, you see. It's my own stupid fault that I never took the time to learn how to cope with the domestics… Head always in some book or other, you see. Since your mother went I don't seem to have the heart for much else. People thought I was a cold fish when I didn't cry at her funeral. But I cried inside, Gina…' His voice broke, and moisture glazed the pale, serious eyes, 'I cried inside…'

She hardly knew what to say—how to respond. It was as

though a stranger sat in front of her—not the remote, self-contained, preoccupied man who was her father. The man she would have been hard put to it to say had any feelings at all.

Patting his bony shoulder again, she gave it what she hoped was a reassuring squeeze. 'Why don't I make us both a nice cup of tea? We'll have it in the living room, then I'll nip out to the supermarket to get you some supplies for the fridge.'

'Are you in a hurry tonight, Gina?' The moisture beneath the pale eyes had been dashed away, and now his eyes glimmered with warmth...affection, even.

'No, I'm not in a hurry. Why?'

'Would you—I mean could you stay for a while? We could—we could talk. You could tell me a bit more about your work at the auction house.'

Was this some kind of breakthrough in their difficult and sometimes distant relationship? Why now, when it had been three years since she had lost her mother? Had it taken him that long to realise that he'd really loved Charlotte? That he loved his daughter?

Gina didn't know right then whether she felt hopeful or angry. Shrugging off her raincoat, she folded it over her arm, then crossed to the still open study door. 'I don't have to rush off. I'll go and put the kettle on. Why don't you go into the living room and make up the fire? The house is chilly.'

In the kitchen, staring at the peeling paintwork and the cupboards that she guessed were as bare as Mother Hubbard's, Gina filled the kettle at the sink and plugged it in. Before she realised it, her eyes were awash with tears. To find her father dejected, sad and reminiscing about her as a child was disturbing enough, but earlier on today her senses had received another jolt.

She'd been asked to work with a team of researchers on the provenance and history of a valuable jewel from Kabuyadir. Just the name of the place had the power to arouse the most potent of memories, and make her ache for a man whose skin was imbued with the scent of the desert, whose eyes burned with a passion that had consumed her from the very first glance—a man Gina had reluctantly had to say a premature goodbye to that magical, unforgettable night three years ago, because she'd been returning to the UK to see her mother in hospital.

When Charlotte Collins had passed unexpectedly away shortly afterwards, it had knocked Gina for six. It had also heightened her overwhelming sense of responsibility towards her father. So much so that when Zahir had rung her for the second time from Kabuyadir, in the days following the funeral, she had determinedly decided to put their night of wonderful passion and *kismet* behind her to focus instead on an academic career. Her father had told her that her mother would have wanted to see her make a resounding success of it.

With tears burning her eyes, and a lump in her throat the size of Gibraltar, Gina had declined Zahir's heartfelt pleas to return to Kabuyadir soon and told him she was sorry— what had happened had been wonderful, but the idea that they could be together wasn't remotely realistic. Now that she was back in the UK it was her career that had to be her focus, not some love affair she'd be completely foolish to trust in.

Even as she'd been speaking she'd felt as if a stranger had taken over her body and mind…a *despondent* stranger who certainly didn't believe in love at first sight or happy-ever-after. When more time had passed, she'd continued quietly, he would see it that way, too, she was certain.

Zahir's parting words had broken her heart. *'How could you do this to me, Gina…to us?'*

CHAPTER TWO

WALKING into the serene courtyard garden, where the air was heavily hypnotic with the perfume of drowsily alluring blossoms, Zahir saw his sister sitting on the long wooden bench beside the pretty ornamental pond. Her sad gaze was as far away as ever, in a land he couldn't reach.

Beneath his black *jalabiya*, Zahir's taut abdominal muscles clenched uneasily. They had always been close, but since Farida had lost her husband Azhar six months ago she had become withdrawn and uncommunicative, and all the joy had vanished from her almond-shaped dark eyes. Would he ever see it again? He hated to think he might not. There wasn't anything he owned that he wouldn't give to see her happy once more. With their parents gone all they had now was each other…

'Farida?'

Her glance barely acknowledged him before returning to its dreamlike examination of the pond.

'I am going into the city today on business, and I thought you might like to go with me? We could stay overnight at the apartment and have dinner at your favourite restaurant. What do you think?'

'I would rather stay here, if you don't mind, Zahir. I don't feel like facing the city crowds today—even if it is only from behind the tinted windows of your car.'

Zahir's responding sigh was heavy. Since he had lost his father and inherited rulership of Kabuyadir he was looked to—and indeed *expected*—to dispense wisdom, guidance and help to the people of his kingdom. But apparently not to his own sister. As far as that aspect of his rank and power was concerned he was all but useless.

'What will you do with yourself here all day on your own?' He tried hard, but couldn't quite keep the frustration out of his voice.

She shook her head and would not look at him. 'I will do what I usually do. I will sit here and remember how happy I was with Azhar, and know that I will never be happy again.'

'You should have had your marriage arranged, as is the custom!' Zahir flashed irritably, pacing the stone flags surrounding the pond. 'Then it would not have been such a blow to you when you lost your husband. This—this marrying for love was a mistake. Has our tragic history not taught you that?'

Now Farida *did* look up at him. 'How can you say such a terrible thing, Zahir? Our parents did not have an arranged marriage, and they knew the kind of joy and happiness that made them the envy of everyone. Have you forgotten how it was with them? Father told me once that loving our mother made him feel more complete and content than anything material this world could ever do.'

Folding his arms across his broad chest, Zahir came to a standstill beside her. 'And he was a broken man when she died. So broken that he followed her soon after. Have *you* forgotten *that?*'

'You have changed, Zahir, and it worries me just how much,' Farida told him sadly. 'Your rule of Kabuyadir is exemplary, and would have made Father proud, but your rigid rule over your heart has made you cold and a little bitter,

I think. Remember the prophecy of the Heart of Courage
that has been in our family for generations? It says that
all the sons and daughters of the house of Kazeem Khan
will marry for love—not for strategic or dynastic alliance.
Remember?'

Knowing he had already set plans in motion for the sale
of that cursed jewel, Zahir flinched a little. 'Yes, yes—I
remember. But I personally will *not* be adhering to that. In
fact my business today involves preliminary negotiations
with the Emir of Kajistan for the hand of his daughter in
marriage. She has just turned eighteen, so is eligible. It is
a good match, Farida…sensible.'

'You plan to marry the dull-witted plain daughter of
our neighbour? Are you mad? She will drive you crazy in
a matter of hours, let alone days!'

Her brother's eyes narrowed. 'Yes, but because it will be
a marriage of convenience I am not bound to spend every
waking hour with the lady. She will have her own interests
and I mine.'

'And what will they be, I wonder? Regularly visiting the
beauty parlours in the big city in the hope that they will
have some transformative elixir that will render her beautiful? I believe in the power of magic, brother, but I would
have trouble believing in a magic as powerful as that. It
would be like hoping for a powder to turn a mule into the
most elegant of Bedouin thoroughbreds!'

'Farida!' Zahir was quick to show his displeasure at this
insult to his potential bride, but underneath his admonishing glare his lips twitched in amusement. It reminded
him of how mischievous and playful his sister could be.
He threw her a final beseeching glance. 'Won't you come
with me today? When my business meeting is over I would
really welcome your company.'

'I am sorry, Zahir. But I have given you my answer and

prefer to be left here alone. However, I pray that you come to your senses and forget about making such a soulless marriage with the Emir's daughter. Have you never wanted to fall in love like our father did? Like our ancestors did… like *I* did, too?'

A pair of incandescent long-lashed blue eyes flashed in Zahir's mind, instigating such a powerful longing inside him to see their owner again that he fought to contain it and return to cold, hard reality instead. Icy reason told him that even to entertain such a hurtful memory was to go down a road made impassable by bitterness and disillusionment. The woman had rejected his entreaty to return to Kabuyadir and his arms outright. Never again would he risk his heart that way, or give his trust to a woman.

When he finally spoke his voice was gruff. 'The premise is pointless, and I am not a masochist willing to experience more pain and anguish than I have endured already. No, that is not a path for me. Now, can I bring you anything back from the city?'

'No, thank you. Just go safely and return home soon.' With the barest glimmer of a filial smile, his sister returned to her lonely musing over the clear still pond at her feet.

Gina had fought hard in her case to win the right to travel to Kabuyadir and examine the jewel she and her colleagues had been researching these past few weeks, and she'd won the battle. Still, it was a double-edged sword to go back to the place where she'd experienced her greatest joy and deepest pleasure and know that she'd foolishly trampled the chance she'd had to be with the man she loved into the dirt.

Now, as her colleague Jake Rivers drove them to the airport, she stared out of the passenger window of his small Fiat in silence, reflecting on returning to the place where she had lost her heart to a handsome, enigmatic stranger—a stranger she had dreamt about almost every night for the past three years. The dreams endlessly replayed that incredible night they had spent together under the desert stars.

'*Zahir.*' She murmured the name softly.

Not for the first time she wondered where he was and what he was doing. Was he married to a girl from his own land now? Was he father to a child that played happily at his feet and made him ache with pride? *Did he ever think of Gina and remember the incredible instant connection they had shared?* Or had he relegated it to a moment of madness he regretted because she'd callously rejected his invitation to return in preference to forging ahead with her career?

Chewing down hard on her lip, she felt her insides flip in anguish. She'd wanted to make her father proud and honour her mother's memory, but in doing so she'd sacrificed perhaps the one real chance of happiness she would ever have. Bad enough that she hadn't seen Zahir again after that one night, but to think that he might despise her for the choice she'd made was a psychological blow beyond cruel. *Please, God, no...*

'What did you say?'

Realising she had spoken out loud, Gina glanced round at her erudite bespectacled colleague, her face hot. 'Nothing... just thinking aloud for a moment.'

'I can't believe you've been to Kabuyadir before. What was it like?' Jake asked conversationally as he negotiated the route to the long-term car park.

Shutting her eyes for an instant, Gina felt it all come flooding back—the scent of exotic spices and incense, the sound of languages with their origins in ancient Persian and Byzantine empires, the vibrant glowing colours of the wares in the marketplace, and the fragrant perfume of the Husseins' garden that was hypnotically carried on the sultry wind.

Most of all she recalled Zahir's strong-boned face, and eyes so chocolate-dark that one arresting glance had been enough to steal her heart and keep it his for ever...

'Whatever description my words could give you wouldn't do it justice. Why not just see for yourself when we get there?'

He sent her a smile as he parked. 'All right, then. I will. By the way, how's Professor Collins doing? What's he working on at the moment?'

Jake's tone had both admiration and curiosity in it, and Gina kept her expression as neutral as possible. Usually she tried to stick to a policy of keeping her personal life well out of her professional one, but she supposed it was inevitable that her ambitious young colleague would be curious. He had confessed to her from the very first that he was Jeremy Collins's 'greatest admirer' because of what he had achieved in his long and distinguished career.

'I have no idea what he's working on, but he's been a bit under the weather lately, to tell you the truth. Thankfully I found him a new housekeeper, who seems very thoughtful and caring, so I'm trusting he'll be okay while I'm abroad.'

She hoped she didn't sound as anxious as she felt. Suddenly her father seemed worryingly forgetful and fragile, and her heart bumped a little beneath her ribs when she thought of him struggling with the daily chores most people found easy.

That was why she was so thankful that she'd found Lizzie Eldridge. As his new housekeeper she would be just perfect. A forty-something single mum of an eleven-year-old, she was down to earth and immensely practical, as well as kind. She and Gina's father had hit if off straight away. He was in safe hands, she thought as she wheeled her suitcase across the concrete to the dropping-off point for the bus that would take them to the airport entrance.

'I can't wait to see the jewel "in the flesh" as it were,' her companion enthused as he walked beside her. 'That central diamond—or *Almas*, as they call it—is quite something. The owner can't be short of a few quid, seeing that he's the local Sheikh an' all, so I wonder what's made him think of selling it?'

'That is surely none of our business?' Gina responded with an arch of her brow. 'All I know is that it's a tremendous privilege to study the history of such a jewel…a jewel that research had corroborated hails from seventh-century Persia.'

'Hmm…' Unrepentant, Jake grinned. 'I wonder what he's like, this "Sheikh of Sheikhs" as he's known? Can you believe we've been invited to stay at his *palace* instead of some local flea-bitten hotel?'

'I'd be careful about coming out with things like that when we're in Kabuyadir, Jake. It might be construed as disrespectful…which it *is*.'

'Have you always been such a good girl, Gina?' The hazel eyes behind the fashionable ebony glass frames were definitely speculative as well as teasing. 'Don't you ever let your hair down and just, well…*misbehave?*'

It was such an outrageous comment that Gina sensed herself flushing hotly. She had 'misbehaved' once—in Kabuyadir, as a matter of fact—but at the time it hadn't seemed at all as if she was doing wrong. Under the circumstances it had seemed like the most natural thing in the world, because it had been purely instinctive and *right*. She certainly didn't regret what others might regard as her moment of madness if they knew about it. Not even *once*.

Running her hand over her tidy French pleat, she felt the leap of intense longing to see Zahir again almost overcome her. 'I'm not perfect, Jake. I have my foibles just like anyone else. Let's leave it at that, shall we?'

There were moments in a person's life when the sheer wonder of a sight left an imprint on the heart and mind that would never be erased. Stepping into the vast mosaic and marble courtyard of Sheikh Kazeem Khan's ornately gilded palace was one of them.

Shielding her gaze against the dazzling sunlight that rendered the tall golden turrets almost impossible to look at for long, even with her sunglasses on, Gina glanced over at an equally mesmerised Jake and shook her head. Words seemed unnecessary.

Lifting her face up to the skyline again, she noted the impressive stone-built watchtower, hovering even higher than the golden pinnacle of the roof. Once upon a time this palace must have been the most intimidating and impenetrable fortress. It wasn't hard to imagine what it must have been like then. From the outside it appeared as if twenty-first century modernity had barely touched it at all.

A slim-built young man with watchful amber eyes, dressed traditionally in a *jalabiya* and a headdress with a colourful *agal* rope securing it round his head, stood waiting patiently as the two Europeans ogled a sight that for him was no doubt commonplace. His name was Jamal, and he was proud to call himself a servant of Sheikh Kazeem Khan, he told them. He had met them at the foothills of the city, where the taxi that had waited for them at the airport had left them, and had then accompanied them up the mountain in a cable car. From there, a comfortable horse-drawn buggy, with ravishing silk curtains and cushions, had transported them to the palace.

Gina was tired, travel-worn and melting in the heat, yet an undeniable excitement thrummed in her veins, making her not want to miss anything if she could help it.

'We must not linger here in the afternoon heat. We should go inside now. This way.' Jamal made a sweeping motion towards a vaulted sandstone passageway. 'Another servant will show you to your rooms, where you can rest for a while. Then, later, you will make preparations to meet with His Highness.'

Gina's tiredness vanished completely when she was shown to her guest quarters. She'd been absolutely charmed by the comfortable adobe style house that she'd lived in when she'd stayed with the Husseins, but *this*...this was like walking into the sumptuous boudoir of an eastern princess. The furnishings were lush, with ravishing silk brocades of every imaginable hue and colour, and floor-to-ceiling voile drapes fell in a sensuous sunburst from two slim windows. An azure-coloured blind was partially unfolded behind the curtains, to keep out the heat and glare of the sun, and the floor was made from blissfully cool white marble. A generous-sized Persian rug picked out in sensuous gold and bronze threads was spread out at the foot of the bed...*the bed*.

If Gina had been inclined to write poetry she would have composed a veritable sonnet to such a bed. It was vast in every sense, with the broad-clawed feet of a sphinx and intricate Arabian carvings inlaid in a rosewood head-board that appeared magical and ancient at the same time. It practically drowned beneath a sea of silk and brocade cushions of every conceivable shape and colour.

Throwing herself down amongst them, she sighed with pleasure. A delicious if bittersweet daydream about Zahir drifted into her mind. *Was there some way she could get to see him?* she wondered. *Was she crazy to even hope he might agree to a meeting?*

She would have broached the subject to Mrs Hussein on that morning before she'd left for the airport to return home—asked her hostess if she could elaborate on who he was and where he lived. But Clothilde had seemed busy and preoccupied, and it just hadn't felt right or proper to ask about the charismatic male guest that Gina knew simply as Zahir.

He'd left early the next morning, even before she'd risen to dress for the airport. His parting embrace had filled them both with intense longing all over again, but she'd given him her phone number and he'd promised to call her the very next day. It had been the hardest thing she'd ever done to kiss him goodbye and then watch him walk away, with the only remaining evidence of his presence the scent of warm aroused male he'd left on her body and the tingling ache between her thighs. She had surrendered her innocence to him—surrendered it with full heart and a fervent pledge to love him for ever…no matter what.

It was said that a woman never forgot her first love. In Gina's case her *only* love. That was why she could never give up her precious memories of that night. But she'd made sure all she would ever have was memory when, incredibly, she'd rejected Zahir's invitation to go back to Kabuyadir and be with him. Even now she couldn't believe she'd done it. Grief over her mother and worry over her father must have temporarily made her lose her mind. The thought of the pain and disbelief in Zahir's proud voice had gone round and round in Gina's head for three impossible years.

Turning her face into a plump silken pillow, she felt stinging tears of regret and longing wash into her eyes as she whispered his name…whispered it like a *prayer*…

* * *

At last Farida had retired to her quarters, and Zahir could safely entertain his guests from England. She would only become agitated and tearful if she knew of his intention to sell the Heart of Courage—the jewel that she seemed convinced was possessed of some kind of prophetic power when it came to their family's marriages. But when sufficient time had passed and she was more like herself again he was certain he could persuade her that the sale was for the best.

They had had a tumultuous time of late. Their parents had left this world one after the other, and then Azhar—Farida's husband—had lost his life in an automobile accident in Dubai. The only thing his beloved sister needed right now, Zahir believed, was peace and plenty of time to heal. The presence of a family heirloom that he privately thought of as a curse would not help her achieve that. And for him it would only act as a painful reminder of all he had lost. It mocked his once fervent belief in it himself. *He'd rejected the prophecy when the woman he had fallen in love with callously turned down his plea for her to be with him...*

The money he received from the sale of the jewel he would give to Farida, to do with what she willed, he decided. *He certainly didn't need it.*

There was plenty of evidence in palace records to vouch for the authenticity of the jewel, but as he planned to sell it abroad he'd needed to have that evidence corroborated by a respected independent source. The auction house in Mayfair had an internationally respected reputation. His two guests were a male historian and his female colleague who specialised in the study of ancient artefacts. Zahir hadn't seen their names—he'd left the details to his personal secretary and lifelong friend Masoud, who had now unfortunately been taken ill—but he had ensured that out of respect and deference the female would have one of the best staterooms in the palace.

Now, as he waited in the main salon where he received visitors, he didn't know why but an odd sense of foreboding gripped him. Telling himself that he was becoming as bad as his sister, believing in all kinds of supernatural phenomena, he impatiently shook away the unwelcome frisson that shivered down his spine. Lifting the sleeve of his *jalabiya,* he glanced down at the linked gold watch circling his tanned wrist. The ornate twin doors at the end of the long stately room suddenly opened and his servant Jamal appeared.

'Your Highness.' He bowed respectfully. 'May I present Dr Rivers, and his colleague Dr Collins?'

Already walking forward with his hand outstretched, Zahir felt his footsteps come to a frozen standstill. Beside a slim-built man with sandy-coloured hair who wore glasses stood a woman with elegantly upswept blonde hair, her svelte figure dressed in a long, flowing silk kaftan in stunning aquamarine. But it was her beautiful face and riveting long-lashed blue eyes that made his heart almost stop.

Gina... Was he dreaming?

He could hardly believe it. Everyone was staring at him, waiting for him to speak, but just then to him that was akin to growing wings and flying. Clearing his throat, Zahir moved towards the man first. Even as he was shaking his hand his mouth dried and his chest tightened. He knew he would slip his hand into Gina's next. She was clearly as shocked and startled as he was. Her cool, slim palm trembled slightly beneath his touch. Their gazes locked, and it was as though the room and everyone else in it apart from the two of them simply melted away.

'Dr Collins,' he heard himself intone gruffly, 'I am honoured to meet you.'

Only too aware that they were being observed, Zahir withdrew his hand and gestured towards the rectangle of Arabian couches positioned round a carved dark wood Moroccan coffee table a few feet away.

'We should sit and make ourselves comfortable. Jamal, you may serve coffee and refreshments now.'

'Of course, Your Highness.' The servant bowed and moved smoothly back towards the double doors, careful not to show his back to Zahir as he did so.

'Your rooms are comfortable and to your liking?' Moving his gaze from Jake Rivers to Gina, then back again to the man, Zahir settled himself on one of the longer couches and hoped the smile he'd arranged on his face was polite and relaxed—that it did not give rise to suspicion that he and Gina had met before and that the mere sight of her had all but undone him.

It was a most delicate predicament, and he would have to draw upon all his powers of diplomacy and tact to deal with it, he thought. But every time he found his glance returning to hers he wished they could be alone together, so that he could demand to know the real reason she had rejected him. *Had it been because there was someone else waiting for her back home in England?* How many times had he tortured himself with that thought over the years? *Too many.* One thing Zahir was certain of: before she left he would know *everything...*

'The palace is truly amazing, and our quarters more than comfortable—thank you,' Jake Rivers answered, linking his hands across his knees as he sat next to Gina. *How old was he?* Zahir wondered. He'd imagined that someone expert in their field, as he was supposed to be, would be older and more distinguished-looking. He could almost hear Farida teasing him. *That's because you watch too many old films where every English professor is a caricature,* she'd say. A sigh escaped him.

'That is good. As to the palace's origin, we believe it was erected in the ninth century, when the Persian and Byzantine wars were over. For the people of this region it has always been a powerful stronghold, and a symbol of strength to see off any foe. They have always helped maintain it, and take a pride in its beauty as well.'

Helplessly and hungrily, his gaze moved back to Gina. *What was she thinking?* he wondered. Was she shocked to learn his true identity at last? Would she curse her folly in turning him down? It was a bitter straw he would willingly grasp—a salve to his wounded pride that he'd never thought he'd receive.

'And your expertise is in antiquities, is it not, Dr Collins?' he asked. He saw her take a breath in and out again, then briefly fold her hands in her lap as if to compose herself.

'Classical antiquities and ancient artefacts... My colleague Dr Rivers is the historian in our team, Your Highness.'

'So you are equally qualified?'

'More or less.' Jake shrugged, throwing Gina an easy smile.

A stab of jealousy seared through Zahir's insides, his spine stiffening in protest at the envied familiarity. 'So Dr Collins is not your assistant?' he remarked, with a touch of mockery in his tone.

'My *assistant?*' Now the young man's lips split into a wide grin. 'I mean no disrespect, sir, but she is far too independent and bossy for that!'

'Is that so?' Zahir leant forward, his glance falling into a slow, leisurely examination of a pair of flawless china-blue eyes. 'How interesting...how interesting indeed...'

CHAPTER THREE

IF THEY had been with anyone but the Sheikh of Kabuyadir, Gina would have elbowed Jake in the ribs hard for his inappropriate teasing. He was developing into quite a brilliant historian, but he scored very few points for tact. Still, it really wasn't Jake at all who interested her in *this* discussion.

How could it be? It was the astounding discovery that it was *Zahir* who was 'His Highness'—handsome Sheikh of a historically once powerful Arabian kingdom and owner of the ancient and beautiful Heart of Courage. Never in her wildest dreams had she envisaged that that title belonged to *him*.

Why had he not told her the truth about who he was that night they'd spent together? And afterwards, when she'd returned home, he'd had ample opportunity to tell her when he phoned—but he hadn't. Had he feared that her decision to return would be swayed only by his exalted position and *not* the incredible man that he was?

'Dr Rivers and I are a team, Your Highness.' She blushed when she said his title, because it felt so surreal, yet her eyes hungrily cleaved to his strong tanned face and the long ebony hair that swung round his shoulders when he moved. He was dressed in traditional male clothing, and it was easy to see that the materials were much finer than anybody less privileged could afford. With his broad shoulders and natural air of command Zahir was every inch the esteemed ruler of his people, and seeing him again was like receiving a fresh supply of oxygen—as if for so long her ability to breathe freely had been compromised and Gina hadn't even known it.

'And we hope that our individual fields of expertise complement each other when it comes to undertaking our research,' she finished with a strained smile.

Making no immediate comment, Zahir continued to steadily hold her gaze. *Gina prayed that he couldn't see the longing, regret and dashed hopes reflected there.* Thankfully she heard the doors open behind her and guessed that Jamal had returned with their refreshments.

As he placed the large handmade brass tray down on the coffee table, the air was suddenly filled with the tantalising aroma of cardamom-spiced coffee. It was a delicacy that Gina had enjoyed when she was previously in Kabuyadir. Beside the small gold-rimmed cups, next to the coffee pot known as a *dallah,* on an ornate brass dish was an array of appetising-looking sweetmeats. One by one, Jamal served them their coffee. When he would have gone to Zahir first, his esteemed boss redirected him to Gina.

'We have lots to tell you about the Heart of Courage, Your Highness,' Jake piped up as Jamal bowed to Zahir, then discreetly left them to talk.

'Positive things, I presume?'

'Without a doubt… Its history is incredible. It's not every day that a historian is privileged enough to research an artefact that has its roots in the ancient Persian Empire.'

'So your own enquiry into its history has corroborated what I already know to be true about its origins? Then I am gratified that you welcomed the opportunity to research it. Were you similarly pleased, Dr Collins?'

'Of course… It's the chance of a lifetime for someone in my profession. The kind of thing we all dream of. To finally see the jewel for myself will be something I'll never forget, I'm sure.'

'Well, that will not be for a few days yet. You have both come a long way, and I would like you to relax and enjoy the hospitality of my palace first. The journey here was not too arduous for you?'

'Thanks to your kindness and generosity we travelled first class, Your Highness. I've never travelled in such luxury before. The trouble is, given the opportunity I'm afraid I could get used to it!' Jake answered, smiling.

'You have spent many weeks researching the jewel's history and provenance on my behalf, and you have travelled far to tell me what you have found. To make sure that you journeyed in comfort was the least I could do.'

'Once again, we thank you,' Gina said quietly.

A wave of heat submerged her when Zahir didn't seem to want to break his gaze from hers. *How was she supposed to bear this?* she wondered. How was she supposed to endure being so close to him when his high rank prohibited any possibility that they could enjoy a relationship again, even if they both desired it?

'Drink your coffee and take some refreshment, both of you. We will have plenty of time for our first discussion on the matter of the jewel tomorrow, after breakfast.'

When he turned his glance towards Gina again, Zahir's expression was hard to read. A wall had definitely descended, she intuited—a wall that had clearly been erected to prevent her from seeing too much.

'However, I am afraid I will not be able to join you for dinner tonight. There is a personal matter that takes me away from the palace for a while. I will direct Jamal to show you to the dining room when it's time, and also show you where to go for breakfast in the morning.'

She soaked in the deep Arabian bath, and scented herself with the exotic oils supplied. A long, lazy bath was a pleasure Gina didn't allow herself very often. Where had she learned the idea that she must *earn* the right to personal pleasure? That work must come first? *Thinking of her parents, she didn't need to search hard for an answer.* But blaming them wasn't to be considered—not when the way she wanted to live was in her own hands now.

Sighing, she realised that she'd lingered in the warm scented water a little too long. The water had started to chill and goosebumps dotted her slim upper arms. She stepped out onto the marble-tiled surround to dry herself with a luxurious bathtowel that could have gone round her slim frame twice. Dinner earlier had been impossible. All she'd been able to do was watch Jake tuck into the feast that had been prepared for them with gusto. How could she eat when her stomach kept on roiling and lurching whenever she thought of Zahir?

He'd left them in the salon alone to enjoy their coffee, departing from the room without so much as a backward glance. At dinner, sensing Jamal's hawk-eyed gaze on her at every turn as she sat at the beechwood dining table inlaid with exquisite mother-of-pearl, Gina had wrestled with double misery at the idea her lack of appetite would cause offence to the household in any way. She'd been utterly relieved to finally escape to her room.

Wrapping herself in the generous white bathrobe she'd found hanging behind the door, she moved back into the bedroom, freeing her hair from its tidy French pleat to let it tumble in buttery blonde waves down to her shoulders as she went.

The knock on the door made her gasp. It was after midnight, and she could only surmise that it was perhaps a maidservant, wanting to find out what time she would be down for breakfast.

Drawing the edges of the voluminous robe together more securely, and tightening the belt, she drew back the door—only to be confronted by the tall, imposing figure of Zahir. In the corridor behind him all the lamps were turned down low, and the soft lighting created an even stronger warrior-like cast to his handsome features—particularly his eyes. They seemed to burn with the intensity of stoked flame as he stared down at her.

'My apologies for calling on you so late... As I told you earlier, something took me away from the palace for a while and I have only just returned.'

Clutching the sides of her robe tightly to her chest, Gina hardly knew what to think, never mind say. It didn't help that she was trembling from head to foot.

'May I step inside for a moment?'

Silently, she held the door wide, then closed it behind him. Glancing round the beautifully appointed room, Zahir sniffed the air and smiled. The gesture reminded her of the first time they had met in the Husseins' garden. The kindness she'd seen in his eyes then had prevented her from being afraid of him. But right now it wasn't kindness she saw reflected. There was an edge about him tonight that made her wary.

'You have been taking a bath?'

'I had no idea that you were Sheikh Kazeem Khan. It was such a shock to learn that it was you.' Her voice had a distinct quiver in it. 'I know it was three years ago, but I take it you haven't forgotten me?'

'Of course I haven't forgotten!' His glance was pained, his deep, resonant voice clearly irritated. 'Did you think I could ever forget that night? But to discover that the antiquities expert I hired in London is you is not exactly a delight to me... No, it is not. How could it be when you deceived me so callously?'

Twisting her hands in front of her robe, Gina felt like crying. 'Deceived you...how?'

'I fell in love with you that night...I thought you felt the same. I counted the days until you would return. You promised you would. When you told me on the phone that you had changed your mind, that returning was not realistic and you preferred to focus on your career, how do you think that made me feel? It was like a bomb exploding in my face!'

'It wasn't just because I wanted to focus on my career. My mother died unexpectedly just a couple of days after she was taken into hospital... I told you, remember? My father needed me to stay at home after that...to give him some support. We were both grieving...I hardly knew what I was doing. Kabuyadir seemed like a dream...'

Observing the harshness of Zahir's expression, Gina decided right then wasn't the time to tell him that her father had pleaded with her to stay in the UK and focus on her career in memory of her mother...told her that she shouldn't trust that life in Kabuyadir, living in a strange culture with a man she barely knew, could yield something better. Gina had buckled under the pressure of guilt and responsibility and agreed to stay, even when it had meant denying her desire to return to Zahir and the extraordinary passion they'd shared.

Now she was reeling at his confession that he'd fallen in love with her. There was a big part of her that could hardly believe such a handsome, charismatic man could truly have cared for her like that. To hear him say the words after all this time, compounding what a colossal mistake she'd made in not coming back to him, was like having her insides scraped raw with a sharpened blade.

'Whatever happened, clearly you thought my regard for you wasn't important enough to make you come back to Kabuyadir. Knowing that, I wonder that you have decided to return now three years later? If I had known that *you* were the antiquities expert I'd hired to research the jewel I would have taken steps to prevent your coming and hired someone else. My secretary Masoud would normally have acquainted me with such details, but he was suddenly taken ill and had to return to his family, otherwise I would have realised.'

'So...how are we to proceed from here on? Do you want me to act as though I never met you before?'

He abruptly turned away for a moment, as if to gather his thoughts. The sudden motion made the midnight-blue *jalabiya* he wore swirl round his leather-booted calves. 'What I want...what I wish...is that you had vanished off the face of the earth, if you want to know the truth! Then I wouldn't have to deal with the fact that you live and the possibility that you have chosen some other man to spend your life with rather than me.'

Gina gasped at the bitterness and passion she heard in his voice. 'There is no other man, Zahir...there never was. That's the truth.'

When he turned his gaze on her again his eyes regarded her with such disdain that she curled up inside. Somehow, no matter how hard she tried, she seemed to have great difficulty in inspiring love in the people closest to her.

'It is of no account to me any more. It is all too late now.'

Distressed and dry-mouthed at the bleakness in his tone, she darted out her tongue to moisten her lips. She wrapped her arms tightly round herself to subdue the pain that vibrated inside. 'Why didn't you tell me who you were?' she asked quietly. 'Have you any idea how hard it is for me to see you again and discover that you're practically a—a *king?*'

'I was not the ruler of Kabuyadir when we met. I knew I would inherit the mantle of Sheikh when my father died—I was trained to do so from a boy—but I was still just Zahir when we were together. I had thought to share some carefree time with you before that happened. When we met that night at the Husseins I, too, was grieving. My mother had died just a month before. To meet you and feel the way I did so instantly…it gave me hope—hope that life *would* get better despite my losing my beloved mother. However, you declined to come back to me. Just days after I spoke to you on the phone my father's health started to rapidly deteriorate, and he too died. Any prospect of carefree time had gone. I was now Sheikh of the kingdom and my life would never be the same again.'

Gina's heart contracted with sorrow at what Zahir had suffered. *No wonder her decision not to return had hit him like a hammer-blow.* 'So you've ruled this kingdom for three years? Did you marry?'

The taste of the question was bitter on her tongue, but Gina desperately needed to know the answer. She had kept her promise to her father and for the past three years had totally dedicated herself to work. There had been no other man in her life since that night with Zahir—she'd even acquired a reputation as 'uptight and frigid' with some of her less than gracious male colleagues. To think that Zahir might have married and relegated their precious time together to the far corners of his mind, rarely to be recalled or examined except maybe to remind himself of how deceitful she'd been in turning him down, stung worse than a thousand cuts.

'No. I did not.'

Her heart missed a beat. 'Why not?'

He folded his arms, immediately drawing Gina's hungry gaze to the impressive width of his chest. 'When it comes to marriage, a man in my position has a duty to marry for the utmost strategic and dynastic benefit. Believe it or not the neighbouring kingdoms are not exactly overflowing with available and eligible women. That is why I have not married yet.'

Falling silent for a moment, Gina couldn't help dwelling on one disturbing flaw in Zahir's reasoning. Lifting her troubled blue glance to his, she breathed in deeply. 'What about the Heart of Courage's prophecy? That the descendants of your family are destined to marry only for love?'

'What about it?' His tanned brow furrowed warningly.

When she'd discovered the story Gina had been utterly transfixed by it. It was so unbelievably romantic that she hadn't been able to help hoping that the jewel's current owner had also fulfilled the prophecy and fallen in love with a woman of his choice, instead of having to marry for convenience. Now she had learned that *Zahir* was the jewel's owner and custodian she felt as though she was caught in the eye of a fierce storm that would batter her to the ground, leaving her unable to rise to her feet ever again.

She swallowed hard. 'Doesn't it mean anything to you?'

'The jewel is a curse! For generations our family has fallen under the spell of that damned legend, which is why I want to finally be rid of it.'

Gina stared. '*That's* why you're selling it? Because you believe it's a curse?'

'The last people it cursed to a doomed marriage that ended in early death were my parents and my sister's husband Azhar. He was killed in a car accident just a few months ago. The toll of unhappiness and disaster just gets worse and worse, doesn't it? Now Farida goes about the palace like a wraith, hardly eating or sleeping, not engaging with anyone but me and the servants. Do you honestly think I would want to keep the jewel after that?'

'I'm really sorry that you and your sister have had to endure such terrible tragedy, Zahir.' Without realising it she used the name she knew him by, instead of his far grander title. 'But I'm sure you know that the jewel is priceless… *beyond* value. The whole world will be bidding for a chance to purchase it if you put it up for sale, and what about your own descendants? Your children and your sister's children, should she marry again? Won't you be depriving them of an important family heirloom, not to mention an artefact of peerless history and beauty?'

'Forgive me…but I thought I had merely hired you for your expertise in assessing the jewel's provenance? Not to give me your opinion about what I should and should *not* be doing with it!'

He strode to the door, his whole body bristling with formidable rage. If that rage could have been transmuted into matter, Gina would have seen dazzling sparks of flame shooting into the room, she was sure.

'I'm sorry…' Moving towards him, she felt distress deluge her. She could see he was in pain—both at the loss of his parents and at the disturbing way his beloved sister had withdrawn from the world—not to mention in shock upon seeing Gina again after she had rejected him. It made her yearn to be able to reach him, to comfort him in some way. 'If I've caused you offence…if I've hurt you by word or deed…I honestly regret it. Can you forgive me?'

With his palm curved round the gilt handle of the door, he stilled. The dark eyes grew even darker, but within their mesmerising reflection Gina saw a spark of haunting gold light.

'Forgiveness where you are concerned is not an easy matter. But I would ask that when you meet Farida, my sister, you do not mention the jewel under any circumstances. It would only distress her if she learns that I plan to be rid of it.'

'But what will I say if she asks me why I'm here?'

Zahir sighed. 'The palace is full of beautiful artefacts. You may tell her that you and your colleague are doing an inventory of the most valuable ones for me...as you did for Mrs Hussein's books.'

'I will do it because you ask me to, but I want you to know that I'm not comfortable with lying.'

To Gina's alarm, Zahir came closer. Her space was suddenly disturbingly invaded by the subtle but intoxicating scent of a cologne with hints of sandalwood and agarwood. She knew that particular essential oil was highly prized in the region.

Reaching out, he lightly curled his fingers round the tops of her arms. 'When I first saw you peeping out from behind the leaves of that jasmine I believed that you were a trusting innocent, incapable of deceit or subterfuge. To my bitter cost I have since learned that is not true. Apart from your undoubted beauty, Gina, there is nothing about you that could elicit my attention or regard again. You may as well tell me if there has been any other man in your life since we last met, seeing as it hardly matters to me now.'

'I told you the truth—there's been nobody else.' Her answer was as direct as the challenging look she gave him. 'And neither am I interested in another man. A relationship isn't my focus. I prefer to devote my time and attention to my work. Sometimes the paths it leads me down don't deliver exactly what I expect, but…unlike most men…it never disappoints me.'

Suddenly the grip on her arms grew tighter, and Gina bit back a gasp. 'When did I disappoint you? When I took you to bed? I have a photographic memory, *rohi*. I easily recall how incredibly responsive and eager you were in my arms that night. Yes, *eager*…even though you were untouched. Did you not think I'd realised that? Tell me, has there ever been another man in your life who has pleasured you longer or more ardently?'

Even though shock and embarrassment flooded her, she took heart at the distinct jealousy in Zahir's tone. He'd said she would never elicit his attention or regard again, but something in his possessive and furious manner told her that that might not be entirely true. Her senses clamoured and her pulses raced at the idea there might be a chance— even if that chance hung by the slimmest thread—that she could make things right between them.

Holding his hot and angry gaze, she breathed out slowly. 'You just told me you knew I was untouched when we went to bed…so the answer is no, Zahir. There has never been another man who has made me feel like you did that night.'

He abruptly released her. Dark eyes glittering, he silently surveyed her. 'For now, even though it is a hard thing for me to do, I will have to take your word on that. Tomorrow I will hear your presentation on the jewel, so please be well prepared. Goodnight, Dr Collins. I will see you in the morning.'

She stood frozen as he spun on his heel and exited the room, fervently wishing she had a magic spell to make him look at her fondly again instead of disparagingly…

* * *

Zahir's eyes burned from lack of sleep. When he had managed to doze a little, in his vast bed with its black silk sheets, he'd been tormented by only too real images of an alluring blonde angel with eyes bluer than a clear desert sky. He couldn't seem to get the scent of her out of his blood, either...

Frustrated beyond endurance, he dressed and went outside. In the sultry stillness of the perfumed night his footsteps led him to his own private garden—a sanctuary where the only other person allowed to enter was his gardener. Arriving at the Bedouin tent that was always kept ready for his use, Zahir took off his boots and unwound his broad leather belt. He laid a match to the dry tinder of the cooking fire and, sitting cross-legged before the flickering flames, placed the waiting coffee pot in the centre. As the tempting, comforting aroma of delicious Arabian coffee filled the night, Zahir rubbed the back of his hand across his tired eyes and stared out into the distance.

Apart from the crescent moon and its accompanying tapestry of bright stars the night was deep as an ocean and blacker than the wing of a raven... But he never at any time found it threatening. On many sleepless nights he had come out here to his private sanctuary and found that the enfolding darkness acted as a balm for the sorrow he'd endured daily since the death of his parents and since Farida had lost Azhar. *He'd also sought solace from the knifing hurt Gina had caused when she'd told him she wasn't returning.*

Stoking the fire a little with a stick, he watched the sparks crackle and spit, erupting into the air like tiny fireworks. *Gina...* He couldn't even erase her name from his mind, let alone her taunting image. Seeing her standing there in her bathrobe, all flushed skin and tousled golden hair, had been the most colossal temptation. He'd burned to hold her close again—so much so that his body had all but vibrated just because she was in the same vicinity.

For the past three years he had tormented himself almost beyond bearing that she was with another man. *Had she thought him a fool for trusting her so implicitly? For believing she would love him and only him for ever?* The thought had him gritting his teeth and clenching his jaw. Could anyone blame him for believing a part of her very being would always be his when it was to *him* that she'd given the gift of her innocence that night? It was true what he had told her—he *had* known she was a virgin. A fact that had made their instant passionate connection all the more sacred and special. At least that was what he'd thought then.

The Heart of Courage's taunting prophecy had not proved true in his case, Zahir reflected bitterly. *The sooner he was rid of that blasted jewel the better...* Before he started to believe its prophecy had some hold over *his* heart, too...

Reaching for the nearby folded checked cloth that lay in the sand, he wrapped it round the handle of the coffee pot and poured some of the rich aromatic brew into a waiting cup. Then, turning carefully, he crawled into the entrance of the large cloth tent and sat just inside, staring out at the fire's dancing kaleidoscope of flame as he thoughtfully sipped his drink.

Later—much later—he lay down on the silk cushions and woven rugs and slept a little. But not before seeing the spectacular rays of the dawn seep through the intricate weave of the dwelling's fabric-made walls...

Jake and Gina were having their breakfast on a canopied covered mosaic terrace. In the distance the sound of someone playing the *oud*—a stringed instrument that produced a haunting sound not unlike a Spanish guitar—floated hypnotically on the air.

The two colleagues were not alone. Jamal appeared at regular intervals, issuing curt instructions to two young housemaids to frequently hand round dishes piled high with fresh chunks of *khubuz*—the local bread—earthenware bowls of fat glistening black and green olives and dishes of *labneh*—a strained cream cheese that resembled yoghurt.

At the same time as Gina carefully opened the stopper on a slim bottle of olive oil, to drizzle it on her bread, she sensed a warm bead of perspiration sluggishly meander down her back. The sun was already high and hot in the azure sky, and the thin full-length yellow and gold kaftan she was wearing felt more like a winter coat beneath such unforgiving heat. She hadn't been able to resist sitting outside—not after enduring one of the longest and bitterest winters back home—but she was far from at ease. How could she be at ease after the way Zahir had left her last night?

He'd been so accusing and angry…a million miles away from the tender, beguiling man who had so easily swept her off her feet at first sight. Again, her heart ached to make things right between them, but how?

Adjusting her sunglasses, she watched Jake lift a generous chunk of bread that he'd liberally covered in slices of cucumber and wedges of dazzling red tomato to his lips and take a large bite. When he'd chewed and swallowed the food, Gina smiled. 'You've certainly got a healthy appetite.'

'That's true. But then I need to eat a lot to keep the old grey cells replenished!' he joked, grinning back at her.

This morning he was dressed in a wildly patterned Hawaiian-style loose shirt, which probably wouldn't have looked out of place on the beaches of Majorca or Corfu, and it definitely made him look eccentric. All he needed to top the outfit off was a knotted folded handkerchief on his head.

'Are you ready to present your notes on the jewel to His Highness?' he asked her.

'Ready as I'll ever be.'

Gina's mouth tightened. Just the thought of sitting in front of Zahir to discuss that amazing jewel with its heart-rending prophecy was akin to the prospect of walking across a bed of hot coals. She'd never been so nervous or so mentally under siege. Perhaps she shouldn't take it so personally that he now scorned the legend of marrying for love, but God help her she *did*.

After absenting himself for a while, Jamal reappeared on the terrace. 'After breakfast you are both summoned to see His Highness. I will wait here to escort you.'

Nervously scanning the food that yet again she'd barely touched, Gina met the far-seeing gaze of Zahir's personal servant and forced a scant smile as her insides churned and apprehension dried her mouth. 'Thank you.'

With a polite bow, and his hands behind his back, Jamal moved away to stand by the wall and wait.

CHAPTER FOUR

THE Sheikh of Kabuyadir's office was enormous—almost like a small ballroom, with its marble floor and exotic octagonal brass lamps with little coloured windows hanging down from the rafters of the high ceiling. A desk was definitely present. How could they ignore the six-foot-long burnished table that stood in the centre, with carved and cushioned antique chairs surrounding it? But Gina's eye was immediately drawn to the circle of colourful patterned cushions round a hand-woven blue, red and gold rug, to the right of the impressive desk, where Zahir sat, chin in his hands, crossed-legged and thoughtful.

He wore another broad leather belt round his long hooded black robe, and this one had an attachment that crossed over his chest and shoulder. It looked as if it might have accommodated a hunting knife or scimitar at some point, but right then the slim holster was empty. The image of Zahir as a brave ancient warrior was never far away, it seemed—*at least to Gina*. For three long years his striking visage had fuelled her fantasies and stoked her longing for him to an inferno at times—especially when she reflected on what she had lost by letting him go.

As they approached Jake gave a respectful nod, and under Jamal's hawk-like stare Gina did the same.

'You have breakfasted well, I trust?' Zahir's questioning

dark gaze encompassed both of them, but definitely lingered longer on her.

'Very well indeed, thank you.' This from an enthusiastic Jake.

'That is a nice shirt, Dr Rivers. Very…shall we say *colourful?*'

'I'm glad that you like it, Your Highness.'

'Sit down, please. We should make a start on the matter of the jewel.' Sweeping an extravagant hand round the circle of floor cushions, Zahir was suddenly all business.

His lightly mocking comment about Jake's shirt woke Gina to the unsettling fact that he had a sense of humour. Seating herself on the cushion the furthest in distance from their host, she spied a gleam which might have been amusement in the depths of his hypnotically brown eyes. It made her self-conscious and uncomfortable as she opened the slim leather document holder on her lap and carefully withdrew her notes. A couple of feet away from her, Jake did the same.

'I will start with you, Dr Rivers, if I may? Tell me what your historical research says about the jewel.'

Jake's enthusiastic report was followed by some intense discussion between the two men. Gina took the opportunity to observe Zahir at her leisure—starting with his voice. It was undoubtedly strong, yet he kept it modulated, varying the tone from time to time as his gaze focused unwaveringly on her colleague, and managing to give not the slightest indication of his private thoughts about what was being discussed at any time.

Now and again Jake shifted a little nervously—as if overwhelmed by where he was and who was quizzing him—but by and large he gave a good account of his painstaking research, and as the discussion ended, the merest

smile touched the edges of Zahir's well-cut lips. At least
he *appeared* pleased with what he had heard.

Then it was Gina's turn.

As Zahir directed his glance back to her, she had the
panicked idea that his eyes were like the high-power lens
of a high-resolution microscope, illuminating a specimen
on a slide for detailed examination. *Right now she was the
specimen.*

Fumbling with her papers as she cleared her throat to
speak, she saw a few of the A-4 sheets slide off her lap and
onto the patterned rug. She was mortified. Not exactly the
best start, she thought, as she hurriedly gathered the papers
and tidied them.

'Are you ready to proceed with your presentation now,
Dr Collins?'

Hearing the sardonic edge to his tone didn't exactly help
Gina's case. 'Yes, Your Highness.'

She made herself look him straight in the eye to give
herself courage. After all, she was an expert in her field—
not some nervous schoolgirl making a presentation for a
class project.

'I thought I would start by discussing the fascinating
legend that has grown up around the Heart of Courage.'

Where had that come from? It wasn't the first thing she'd
intended discussing at all! The papers had got mixed up
when they'd slid off her lap, and the sheet that had been
at the bottom of the pile was now somehow on top. There
was a sudden drop in temperature in the sultry air. Gina's
glance collided with Zahir's. It was the iciest look she'd ever
received. For a couple of excruciating seconds her breath
was strangled inside her throat.

'I think not, if you don't mind, Dr Collins? I prefer
to stick to verifiable facts right now. Speculation about
any kind of mythical legend can only detract from a more

important discussion about the authenticity and provenance of the jewel's origins. So we will stay with what is important and not go off on some insignificant tangent...agreed?'

After such an unprepossessing beginning, Gina felt she made a hash of the rest of her presentation. By the time it came to an end, and Jamal had appeared with a tray of the delicious cardamom-scented coffee for their refreshment, she just wanted to flee back to her quarters and liberally splash her burning face with ice water.

'Dr Collins? May I have a private word with you?' Soundlessly, Zahir had materialised at her side, and was holding out his hand to help her up from the floor cushion. As she automatically slipped her hand into his, he turned briefly to Jake. 'Dr Rivers, you should take your coffee outside on the terrace and relax for a while. Later, Jamal will give you a proper tour of the palace.'

'Thank you, Your Highness. I'll very much look forward to that.'

When the twin doors had closed behind Jamal and Jake, Zahir put his hands behind his formidable back and paced the floor a little before turning back to Gina. There was no mistaking the anger that transformed his breathtakingly handsome features into an intimidating mask.

'What did you think you were doing, trying to make a fool of me like that?'

'What do you mean?'

'Bringing up the legend...that's what I mean!'

'I—I had no intention of trying to make you look a fool. I just got my notes muddled up and—'

His face was suddenly bare inches from hers, and the sensation of her blood roaring in her ears blotted out any others.

'Why should the tale of that cursed legend even be

amongst your notes when I have already told you I will have none of it?'

Hearts pounded a lot in romance novels, and now Gina knew *why*. She released the painful breath she'd been holding and nervously smoothed her hand down the side of her dress. 'In my search to establish the truth about an artefact I would hardly ignore anything that came up time and time again in the research—however unimportant or inconvenient a client regards it to be. My father taught me to fearlessly examine everything.' She unconsciously jutted her chin.

The man in front of her sighed heavily and rubbed his forehead. 'Your father?'

'He's a professor of antiquities and ancient history back home.'

'Ah, yes... The man you deemed more important than coming back to me.'

'He's my only remaining family,' Gina said miserably. 'He needed my support.'

Zahir's hot temper dissipated as abruptly as sometimes a sandstorm in the desert came to an end. How was a man with healthy red blood coursing through his veins supposed to ignore the tempting vision before him and resist? Especially when the vision was all glittering blue eyes, flushed cheeks and quivering coral-glazed lips—the lower slightly fuller than the upper, and so divinely shaped that they would drive a sane man *mad?*

'When it comes to his work he's very diligent and—and...' the big blue eyes were staring at him as though transfixed '...thorough. He doesn't leave any stone unturned.'

The space between them seemed to thrum with electricity.

'Is that so?' Zahir responded softly.

Before Gina had a chance to answer him, his mouth

claimed hers. His possession was clumsy and rough at first, because of his desperation to taste her again, but then he pulled her to him, and her slim body sagged against his, so that he felt every undulating curve and dip, and he kissed her more slowly and seductively. Kissed her and sampled her intoxicatingly addictive flavours until the heat in his blood consumed him like an inferno—until he wished he had the power to make the rest of the world go away, simply to forget about affairs of state, and the threatening insurgence in a local mountain region that would command the rest of his day, and take her to bed. And when he got her in his bed he would ravish and pleasure her until she was quivering in his hands...until she wept and swore she wanted only him—that any other man she had ever known since they met was erased from her mind and heart for ever.

His hands were in her hair, his fingers massaging her scalp, when he finally raised his head to look down at her. Aware that he was breathing hard, he smiled unabashed. 'You taste even more delectable than I remember. I had not foreseen the end of our meeting finishing like this, Gina, but I suppose after what happened between us the first time we met it was inevitable.'

She tried to prise herself free from his arms, but Zahir was having none of it. Right then he didn't even care if Jamal or one of the other servants walked in and saw him. They had sworn their fealty to him at his coronation, and no tittle-tattle would leave the palace—he was certain of that.

'Let me go, please! We can't—we shouldn't—'

'There is nothing to fear. There will be no stain of dishonour on you should we be seen together, Gina. This is *my* palace, remember? I am the law-maker in this kingdom.'

'I'm not worried about what anyone else thinks if they

see us together, but I *am* concerned about how I conduct myself while I'm here. I came here for professional purposes only, to present the results of my research. I'm not here as a personal friend of yours. I'm also here with a colleague.'

'You are concerned about what the diminutive Dr Rivers with his tasteless loud shirts thinks?'

'He may not have your stature or standing, or indeed your *dress sense,* Zahir, but he is a good man—a man who might be hurt if he finds out I knew you from before and didn't tell him.'

He muttered a well-used Kabuyadir curse and released her abruptly. 'Why should he be hurt?' he demanded, his heart hammering wildly inside his chest. 'Are you telling me that you two are having an affair?'

Gina appeared slightly dazed by the question. 'Me and Jake…? No, of course not!'

'Then why should you care what he thinks?'

'Out of respect—nothing more.'

Owning to feeling thoroughly dissatisfied with her answer, Zahir gave her a distinctly cool glance before turning away and striding across to the large desk. Pulling open a hidden drawer, he retrieved a small ornate knife with a high-polished blade that was pointed at the end. He slid it into the previously empty leather sheath on his belt and once more swung round to face her.

'I have to go out, so our business is at an end for now.'

'Where are you going? And why do you need that weapon?'

'There's a band of lawless rebels in the mountains who have been visiting local villages at night and causing trouble. They have received warnings from my council before, but still they continue to make a nuisance of themselves. Now I need to go and address them personally.'

Gina walked towards him a few steps, her expression alarmed. 'Isn't that dangerous? You're not going there alone?'

Liking the feeling that she cared about whether or not he might get hurt, Zahir allowed himself a lazy smile. 'I am not Zorro, Gina. I will of course be accompanied by a small detachment of trained soldiers.'

'But still…' She twisted her hands in front of the gold and yellow kaftan that so fluidly fell to her feet, caressing her shapely but svelte body underneath on its way. 'Please be careful.'

'I have too much at stake here to take unnecessary risks… My beloved sister, for one.' Aware that he sounded aloof and distant, and that he'd made a point of telling Gina it was his sister he cared most about in the world above anyone else, Zahir knew he was feeling anything *but* aloof towards the lovely woman who stood in front of him. Whenever he was near her molten heat seemed to beat an urgent path to his loins, and now was no exception.

'Of course.' She dipped her head.

'Later, when I return,' he continued, 'there is another matter that I would very much like to discuss with you. Even if it is late you should make yourself available. Do you understand?'

The prettily shaped chin that he could cup in one hand if he had a mind to jutted forward in surprise. The big blue eyes sparkled defiantly. 'Is that some sort of royal command?'

Her rebellious stance stunned Zahir. *It also aroused him.* His hands itched to touch her, sweep her high into his arms and carry her to his private apartments to do with as he willed. Knowing he could not, because even now his detachment of soldiers awaited him in the courtyard, he promised himself that he would teach her the most exquisite lesson later…

'Yes,' he bellowed, then swept past her to the twin doors, 'it *is!*'

Feeling on edge and restless, knowing that Zahir might possibly be in danger and that there was nothing she could do about it, Gina made a poor effort at eating lunch that day. *At this rate she'd return home to England looking like a bag of bones!* But how was she supposed to eat when fear that she might never see him again all but made her crazy?

That incendiary kiss they'd shared earlier had irrevocably reminded her why he was the only man in the world she could ever love. The warm pressure of his mouth and the hot silken tongue that had passionately invaded her had left an indelible tingling imprint, and she longed to experience more of the same.

She decided to try to distract her mind by asking Jamal if she could explore the palace grounds a little on her own. He immediately offered to escort her, as he had done Jake earlier, but she persisted in her request to go unaccompanied. With obvious reluctance in his expressive amber eyes, he agreed.

There were several paved paths—some extravagantly shaded—meandering into the lush gardens. Birdsong abounded. Various enchanting scents hung in the air. Gina detected jasmine, orange blossom and heliotrope amongst others. Everywhere she glanced there were ornate fountains and stately stone statues—presumably of ancestors of the illustrious Kazeem Khan family? If her mind hadn't been so distracted with worry about Zahir, and if she'd known for certain that he was safe, Gina might have allowed herself to investigate the statues further, indulge her love of history and genealogy together and truly revel in the discoveries she made. But under the circumstances, that was easier said than done.

She was almost level with the slight, black-robed veiled figure sitting on a bench before she realised she should probably retrace her steps in case she was intruding on someone's peaceful contemplation. It was a woman—a young, elfin-faced woman—with the prettiest brown eyes and yet perhaps the saddest expression Gina had ever seen.

'Who are you?' the woman asked, first in her own language and then, when Gina didn't immediately respond, in English.

'I'm so sorry if I disturbed you. I'm Dr Gina Collins, and I'm here to help make an inventory of the palace artefacts for His Highness.' She bit her lip after this announcement, feeling more than just slightly guilty as she did as directed and supplied her alleged reason for being there.

'My brother did not tell me he intended to make such an inventory.'

'Forgive me…your *brother?*'

'I am Farida, and the Sheikh of Kabuyadir is my brother…although lately he is becoming more and more like a stranger to me.'

This was followed by a heavily troubled sigh. Standing stock still, Gina half expected to be waved away and told not to intrude on this particular part of the garden again. But to her surprise, Farida turned up her face and smiled.

'It is nice to see another young woman about the place—someone from England, too. Zahir and I both went to university there—did you know that?'

Feeling a jolt of surprise, Gina shook her head. 'I didn't. Where did you study?'

'We both went to Oxford—he to Pembroke College, to

study politics and economics, and me to Lady Margaret Hall to study English and modern languages.'

'You're clearly both very bright. I'm afraid my grades weren't good enough to get me to Oxford.'

'Zahir's mind is like a rapier. Mine is a little slower, but I get there eventually.'

'And you liked it at Oxford?'

'It is a fascinating city. Full of stunning architecture and history and learning and all the things I love—especially books. I was always the family bookworm. Whatever the time of day, I could usually be found with my head in some fascinating tome even before I went up to Oxford. But all that changed when I met Azhar...' Her words trailed off, her expression became subdued, and she was clearly lost in thought again.

Gina's heart squeezed tight as she remembered Zahir telling her that Farida's husband Azhar had died in a car accident. She was so young...*too* young to be a widow.

Before she'd realised her intention, she dropped down onto the bench beside her. 'Azhar was your husband?' she said gently.

Farida nodded sadly. 'He was the love of my life. I have been so lost since he died. I don't really know what to do with my life any more. I don't believe I have anything left to offer anyone—even the brother I have always adored. Everything just seems futile.'

'For a long time after he lost my mother, my father told me he felt like that, too. His method of coping with his grief was to lock himself away in the house and bury himself in his work. I didn't really know how strongly he felt about her until recently. Their marriage always seemed more of a pragmatic arrangement than anything else. I honestly thought that their relationship was more a meeting of minds than hearts. But lately—lately I've started to believe I was wrong about that.'

Farida's soft brown gaze studied Gina for a long time before she finally spoke. 'I believe that love is everything… that no relationship or marriage can survive for long without it.'

'And I believe that true love can never die. Wherever your beloved Azhar is now, he watches over you and only wants the best for you. I firmly believe that he would want you to enjoy the rest of your life and live it to the full, with his blessing.'

To Gina's surprise, the other woman laid her hand over hers. 'Thank you, Gina. I may call you that? You have said something very important to me that will help me sleep a little easier tonight. How long do you stay in Kabuyadir?'

She flushed a little. A buzzing insect flew by her ear and she brushed it away. 'I'm not sure. It depends how long the work I've been hired to do takes. I'm here with a colleague, by the way…Dr Rivers.'

'I hope it takes a long time.' Farida smiled. 'For I feel that I have just made a new friend.'

Unbearably touched, and because she feared the same debilitating grief would be visited on her should anything happen to Zahir, Gina found her blue eyes misting over for a second. 'The feeling is mutual…you're very kind.'

The loudly insistent tattoo beaten on her bedroom door that night woke Gina from an already far from serene sleep. She hadn't bothered undressing because Zahir had told her to make herself available to talk when he returned. Even though she'd resented the command at the time, now she prayed he'd live to shout another one.

Shoving off the exotic silk counterpane, she got hurriedly to her feet.

'Dr Collins—His Highness desires your presence in his chambers immediately!' Looking as if he'd run all the way through the palace to reach her, beneath his dark red fez Jamal's forehead was lightly coated with glistening sweat.

Light-headed with shock, Gina held on to the doorframe to anchor her for a moment. 'What's happened? Has he been hurt?'

'Come.' Jamal gestured impatiently. 'No questions. Please come now.'

Not bothering to turn back and put on the pretty sequinned slippers she'd left by the bed, she pulled the door to and followed Zahir's officious servant down the marble corridor barefoot.

CHAPTER FIVE

BARELY registering the vast bedroom she was shown into, Gina's focus was on the strongly built man whose long dark hair was spread out against a bank of plump pillows on the emperor-size bed where he lay. His impressive bronzed chest was bare apart from the stark white bandage encircling his ribcage. A spectacled man with a neat black beard, she could only assume was the court physician, attended him. She bit back a gasp when she saw the spreading red stain beneath another neatly applied bandage round his hard-muscled bicep. The physician was just withdrawing a hypodermic needle from Zahir's uninjured arm, and both men glanced round immediately as Jamal opened the door and ushered her inside.

'Dr Collins…you have me at rather a disadvantage, I am afraid. Come closer. I won't bite you. I hardly have either the energy or the strength for that right now!'

How could he joke at a time like this? Gina thought as she hurried forward towards the bed. 'You're hurt. What happened?'

'Some foolish rebel leader thought he'd make a name for himself by killing the ruler of Kabuyadir—that's what happened! Luckily his ill-timed bullet only glanced against my arm and side. Do not look so worried, Dr Collins…my doctor has already assured me I'm going to live.'

Again the jokey manner. She could hardly understand it. Did he really take the fact he'd almost been killed so lightly? 'That's not funny. Don't you have a bodyguard or someone looking out for you when you do this kind of thing?' Because she was worried and upset, it was hard to control the quaver in her voice.

'My bodyguard took a bullet in the leg and is now being taken care of in hospital.'

Zahir's voice was full of frustration, and for a moment she saw regret and anger in his glance. She suddenly wished that Jamal and the doctor would leave them alone together, so that she could ascertain for herself how he was really feeling. Something told her he must be putting on a front of some kind. But then his rich dark gaze turned surprisingly warm as he surveyed her. To add to her surprise, he reached for her hand and possessively held it—clearly unconcerned that his physician and servant bore witness to the gesture.

They watched in silence as the doctor collected the tools of his trade and returned them to a bulky leather case. He spoke briefly in their shared language to Zahir, and his patient nodded as he listened. Then the man respectfully bowed, before backing away towards the door. Jamal held it open for him.

Catching his servant's eyes, Zahir said in English, 'You may leave us. I will be perfectly all right now. Shortly I will take the good doctor's advice and get some sleep. Make sure news of the incident does not reach my sister's ears before I get the chance to tell her myself.'

'Yes, Your Highness.'

The door quietly closed, leaving them alone.

Staring down at the small slender hand he still clasped in his, Zahir raised it to his lips and planted a tender kiss there.

Biting her lip, Gina felt tears spring to her eyes. 'You shouldn't take such terrible risks,' she murmured, and she didn't care that he was a ruler of a kingdom. To her he was just a man—a man whose welfare she cared about more than any words could possibly convey.

'I do not like this—that I make you weep,' he said gently, brushing away the damp trail that wet her cheek. 'And trust me—this is *not* how I'd planned to spend the night with you.'

She did a mental double-take as his provocative words registered. Tugging her hand free from his clasp, she stared. 'Spend the night? What are you talking about, Zahir?'

'Do you *really* not understand me?'

'I told you already that I am here in a professional capacity only—that I—' She couldn't continue, because sudden self-consciousness had robbed her of the power to keep talking. The man lying atop the great bed, in black silk pyjama bottoms that fastened at least an inch and a half beneath his belly button, clearly did not share her problem. Tearing her gaze away from his perfectly taut stomach and slim bronzed hips, she found her body flooded with disconcerting heat.

His sculpted lips curved in the most licentious smile. 'You can assume your professional capacity—whatever that means—during the day, but what is to stop us being together during the night? I know you are not immune to my attentions, even though you might hide behind the cover of your professional role.'

'Look…I know you're hurt, and you're probably just looking for some kind of comfort, but I'm not jumping into bed with you just because—because it happened before.' *If you could honestly forgive me for my mistake in not coming back,* Gina thought anguished. *If you really believed in the love I thought we shared that night we were together…*

then nothing could stop me sharing your bed. But I know because of what you now feel about the Heart of Courage's prophecy—and because you think I rejected you without a single regret—that that's not the case.

'I have a proposition for you.' His dark-eyed glance didn't waver. 'That's what I wanted to see you about.'

'And that is?'

'I am not going to waste time play acting and pretending I don't desire you, so I will get straight to the point. Many wealthy and powerful men in my position take a mistress. I haven't done so yet because I have never met a woman to meet all my requirements in every way. That is not until you came into my life again, Gina. I would like you to stay here in Kabuyadir. If you stayed you would not want for anything...*ever.* Anything you wanted that it was within my power to give you, you would have.'

She didn't know whether to laugh or cry. Beneath her robe her heart thudded painfully. Moving away from the side of the bed, she tucked a loose tendril of shining blonde hair back. 'I gather I'm meant to take such an offer as a compliment?'

'At least it shows I am not rejecting you as you so easily rejected me. At least I am being honest about the fact that I want you in my bed again.'

'Lust is a poor substitute for genuinely caring about someone, Zahir.' She wouldn't say the word 'love' in his presence...not yet. Not while he was clearly intent on some-how making her pay for not returning to him three years ago. Still she would not close the distance between them, and a soft sigh escaped her. 'Do you think I should settle for that because you feel I owe you in some way? Anyway, I can't stay here indefinitely. Once I've given you all the information I have on the jewel—and seen it for myself— I'll be heading home again. I have a job to get back to—a job that I've wanted for a long time and worked hard to get. I also have a father who hasn't been very well lately, so I'm afraid you'll just have to find someone else to fill the position of Sheikh's mistress.' She started to walk across the marble-tiled floor towards the door.

'Gina!'

His call stopped her in her tracks. Alarmed, she turned to see that Zahir had moved to the edge of the bed and was getting to his feet. She saw him sway a little, and dashed back to his side.

'What do you think you're doing? For goodness' sake, get back to bed before you do some irreparable damage to yourself!'

'What do *you* care?' he retorted sulkily, reluctantly allowing her to help him lie down and rest his head against the stack of plump pillows again. 'You would leave on the first plane home without caring whether I lived or died.'

'Don't be ridiculous.'

'You sound just like an old spinster teacher of mine. Of course you don't look like her in any way. Do you know what torment it is to me to have you so close, to smell your perfume and not be able to touch you the way I long to? It is a double agony for *this* to have happened to me today. Now not only am I sexually frustrated but I'm in physical pain from a blasted bullet wound, too! It will take more than a strong sleeping pill to make me sleep tonight.'

The strong bronzed brow crumpled a little in obvious pain, and Gina tenderly pushed back the hair from his smooth unlined forehead and frowned. 'Why did you have to go and deal with this trouble yourself? I wish you'd sent someone else instead—the captain of your army perhaps? Someone used to dealing with these volatile situations?'

'You think I am incapable of dealing with a physical threat from a few hot-headed rebels?'

'I'm not questioning your ability for combat, Zahir. You certainly look intimidating and strong enough. But it seems like a reckless thing to have done when you didn't have to.'

He tensed and gave her a fierce glare. 'And how would *you* know what I do and don't need to do? I am not just some useless figurehead or cardboard cut-out prince who sits in the palace issuing orders. I am a politician and diplomat, too, and after many months of this rebel faction employing their bullying tactics on peaceful villages it was time to step in and demonstrate once and for all that my kingdom is not going to simply sit back and accept it! Who better to bring that message home to them but the ruler himself?'

'Please don't get so worked up. I'm afraid you'll re-open your wounds if you get too upset.'

'You can go now.'

'What?' Taken aback by the curt dismissal, Gina froze.

'You are both a painful distraction and an annoyance, and what I need right now is some peace and quiet to contemplate the situation and recover.'

'All right, then. I understand.'

Just as she made to leave Zahir reached for her, curving his big hand round the back of her neck to pull her face down to his. His angry kiss was hot, hard and passionate, with no pretence at being anything other than punishing.

Gina stumbled, her tongue flicking to the stinging spot on her lower lip when he suddenly released her.

'Now you can go.'

His glittering dark-eyed glance made her limbs feel heavy as lead. Reaching the door, she exited the sumptuous room hardly knowing how she managed it...

* * *

A wounded bear was said to be dangerous. The following morning, walking alone in his private garden, Zahir felt his wounds throbbing and painful, and reflected on the crazy rebel who had inflicted them on him and his bodyguard. He was hurt, angry, and liable to lash out verbally at anyone who dared to come near.

Thankfully his servant Jamal intuited his moods well. The man's patience and understanding seemed to silently embrace even the most unpredictable and sombre shades of his employer's personality. Earlier he had brought Zahir coffee. Thinking of Gina—and how he had treated her last night—he had irrationally flung the small brass tray across the courtyard. Everything had landed in the previously calm waters of the ornamental pond, but Jamal had immediately hurried to retrieve it all and clean up the mess without batting an eyelid.

In an hour's time, after he had been examined again by his physician, Zahir was due to address a meeting of his council regarding the uprising by the rebels. But right now the topic that consumed him even more than that was definitely *Gina*. He had offered her a situation that most women would have grabbed at—but, no. Not *her*. Instead she preferred to put her job and her ailing father back at home before him…*again!*

While he privately had a grudging admiration for her loyalty to both her job and her family, it didn't stop him from feeling intensely jealous and aggrieved that he still clearly featured so low on her list of priorities. But he could not let her leave so easily. He had to find a way of making her stay in Kabuyadir for longer than just a few short days. After seeing her again he knew he would not easily get her out of his blood a second time—no matter *how* angry he was.

'Zahir!'

A slight, dark-robed figure was hurrying towards him along the paved pathway, arms extended. As his sister reached him, she all but stole the breath from his lungs when she threw herself into his arms. Zahir couldn't stop the grunt of pain he emitted as her body collided with the inflamed bandaged wound at the side of his ribcage.

As she stepped back in alarm, he saw the damp smudges beneath Farida's pretty eyes—evidence that she'd already been weeping.

'I couldn't believe it when I heard that you'd been shot. Why didn't somebody tell me? Was it because you ordered them not to? I'm not some little child you have to constantly protect, you know. I was a married woman until recently, and I won't fall apart if I hear bad news—even if it frightens me. What on earth possessed you to travel into the heart of the brigands' stronghold with just a handful of soldiers and a bodyguard?'

Zahir could hardly believe his ears. Here was another woman chastising him for doing his utmost to resolve a situation that was bringing fear and suffering to his people! Had his *father's* actions been questioned with such doubt and disbelief? He didn't think so.

The scowl on his face was inevitable. 'I had to try and talk to their leader. He's a hot-headed egomaniac, seeking to gain power by getting a band of similar unthinking idiots to rob and intimidate the villagers. In the end—when I saw that reason simply did not compute with him—I gave him a warning that if there was any more trouble I would imprison the lot of them for life. We were just about to make our return home when he pulled out a pistol and started firing.'

'You could have been killed!'

'Yes, but I wasn't.' He rubbed a weary hand across his eyes. 'Please do not fear for my safety so much, little sister.

I would hate to think that you were fretting every time I set foot outside the palace walls!'

'But somebody *shot* you, Zahir. Do your wounds hurt badly?'

Seeing the loving concern on her dear face, Zahir retrieved his sense of humour. 'Not badly. They're *inconvenient,* more than anything.'

'What do you mean?'

A stirring image of Gina fleshed out nicely in his mind—one in which she was wearing only her bathrobe, her golden hair all mussed and sexy, her cheeks flushed from a steamy bath and the scent of exotic oils clinging to her exquisitely soft skin. Straight away the thought acted as a flaming torch, igniting his blood.

His ensuing smile was almost painful. 'I only mean that I will probably not be as active as I would like for the next few days.'

'What about the man who shot you? What happened to him?'

'Right now he is languishing in a prison cell in the city. He was taken there last night by my guards.'

Farida patted down the silk *hijab* that covered her hair, neck and shoulders, and looked perturbed. 'There is no chance that one of his men will try and seek revenge and hurt you again, Zahir?'

'If they dare, my punishment will ensure they will never pick up a firearm or a weapon again. Not in this lifetime!'

But even as he contemplated such a repugnant reality, a wave of doubt and concern rolled through him. *Had he made a huge error in judgement, thinking that he could reason with such a lawless band?* Now wasn't the time to consider such a disturbing notion—not when Farida was so clearly worried and upset.

He laid his arm reassuringly round his sister's slender shoulders. 'The palace is a steadfast fortress that has stood the test of time. No amateur trigger-happy fool is going to get at me here. They would be crazy to even try. Now, enough talk about that. Let us discuss more pleasant things, hmm? What are you planning on doing with yourself this day?'

They were walking back along the shaded pathway, and the balmy agarwood scented air seemed to ease Zahir's troubled mind with its rich and mysterious fragrance as they walked.

'I hope to spend some time with Gina Collins, actually.'

'You have met Dr Collins?' Stopping dead in his tracks, Zahir stared at his sister in surprise.

'Yes, I have met her, and I like her very much. She said something rather wonderful to me about Azhar that gave me great comfort. I don't have many girlfriends around my own age, so it's very nice to have someone like Gina staying at the palace for a while. As you have employed her to make an inventory of some of the more important family artefacts, I thought I might be able to assist her? What do you think?'

The little speech she had just made was so surprising, so unexpected, that it took Zahir a few moments to digest it properly. It was the first time since Farida had been so tragically widowed that she'd shown even the slightest interest in anything other than her own misery. If Gina had been able to effect such a dramatic change—even in the short time she'd been here—what else might her presence be able to achieve? Zahir's mind raced with something that felt very much like hope.

'I am sure that if I speak with her on your behalf she

would be only too happy to have your help. Do you by any chance know where she is now?'

'I was just about to go and look for her.'

'Let me do that. Why don't you stay out here for a little while in the shade and relax? When I've discussed your suggestion with Dr Collins I will send Jamal to come and fetch you, okay?'

'She is very pretty, brother…don't you think?'

She is beautiful beyond imagining, his mind answered immediately. But Zahir curbed the words that hovered on his tongue for something a little more measured. After all, he didn't think it wise to alert Farida to his deepening interest in Gina—or the fact that he had asked her to become his mistress!

'Yes.' He allowed the briefest smile to touch his lips. 'She is very pretty…clever, too.'

He turned away before he had the urge to elaborate further on all Gina Collins's very appealing attributes…

On returning to her luxurious rooms the previous night, Gina had known that sleep would elude her for the rest of the night-time hours. After her encounter with the man who set her heart racing like no other, finding him injured and then *furious* when she refused his offer to become his mistress, she'd been both distressed and heartbroken. It shocked her that he had such apparent disregard for his own safety—so much so that he would venture into a lawless region of his kingdom to deal with some gun-toting rebels. Did he not realise how much the people close to him cared for him?

But she was hurt, too, because all he seemed to be interested in as far as she was concerned was appeasing his lust. Had she imagined the tender words and fervent feelings he'd declared when they'd first encountered each other in the Husseins' garden? Then she'd been so sure of his mutual love and affection that she'd given him her most precious gift. Had that meant *nothing* to him?

At breakfast out on the terrace, she ate very little. Her obvious lack of appetite even prompted Jake to comment.

'Are you feeling all right, Gina? You've got dark circles under your eyes and you've barely touched your food.'

'I'm fine,' she murmured. 'Just a little tired.'

'The heat can do that. Best take things easy today,' her companion responded consolingly.

Beckoning Jamal over to the table, after Jake had returned to his rooms to locate a book, Gina nervously enquired about Zahir's condition. The taciturn servant told her that His Highness was 'comfortable' and back on his feet, but she should be prepared for the possibility that she might not see him at all that day. His physician had told him that he must rest.

She then politely asked if she could use the palace library. Informing her that he was instructed that she and her colleague Dr Rivers should be aided wherever possible to undertake their work, he agreed. If the man had any thoughts about why the Sheikh should have summoned her last night to his private rooms when he had just been injured, neither by word nor deed did he give them away.

A library had always represented a comforting safe place to Gina. Often, during her childhood, she had taken refuge there when life had felt hard and there hadn't seemed to be a lot of love or affection going round. Books were her friends—constant loving companions that didn't let her down.

Zahir's library took her breath away. It was a repository for the written word that only the richest and most devoted imagination could conjure up. Shelf upon shelf of books ancient and modern confronted her, practically reaching up to the sky. Amid the shelves of books were sumptuous couches and chairs in which a browser could relax and peruse the book they'd selected. The ambience was not unlike that of a breathtaking cathedral, with a high-vaulted ceiling made of sandstone and granite interspersed with mosaic.

Gina had a plan. She was going to try and delve more deeply into Zahir's family, going right back through as many generations as possible. There must be hundreds of history books on the region here, chronicling the dynasty through the centuries. If luck was on her side she might even come across old family journals...*they* would be her primary sources. She wanted to discover as much extra information as she could on the family's association with the famed Heart of Courage, but she had to be discreet. If Zahir found out what she was doing he could very well put her on the next plane home and forbid her from visiting Kabuyadir again...

'There you are'

Immersed in the pages of a fascinating book she'd pulled from a shelf, Gina spun round in shock at the sound of Zahir's voice. He was as imposing as usual, in his dark robes and broad leather belt, his ebony hair like a velvety dark river rippling down over his shoulders. Straight away she noticed there was a light sheen of sweat on his brow, and she realised he must be in pain.

'What are you doing up and about? Shouldn't you be resting after what happened?' Anxiously she clutched the dusty volume she'd been examining to her chest. A ray of sunlight beamed in through the cathedral-like narrow windows and warmed her back.

'I've been walking in the garden, getting some air. I cannot stay confined to my bed for twenty-four hours a day just because I took a couple of small flesh wounds. Jamal told me I would find you here. What do you think of my library?'

'It's truly magnificent. A person could spend a life-time in here and barely get through the books on even *one* shelf.'

Her comment drew the hint of a smile to his lips. Moving towards her, he moved his hand briefly to his side.

'Are you hurting?' she asked. The distressed catch in her voice sounded loud to her own ears.

'That question is a double-edged sword. The truth is that my pride is stinging just as much as my physical wounds.'

'Why's that?'

'I…' He seemed to swiftly reconsider what he'd been going to say and lightly jerked his head towards the book Gina pressed to the white silk of her blouse. 'What have you got there?'

'It's a history of the Byzantine empire.' She sent up a silent prayer of thanks that he hadn't discovered her with an incriminating family journal, but she still couldn't help colouring guiltily.

'A little light reading, eh?' he joked, brown eyes twin-kling.

Her insides melted like butter over a hot stove. Staring back at him, she fell into a hypnotic semi-trance.

'I am sorry I treated you as I did last night,' he mur-mured, 'my behaviour was reprehensible.'

Now he was tipping up Gina's chin, gazing at her as though he, too, was hypnotised.

'You were hurt and angry… I understand, Zahir. I under-stand and I forgive you. But right now you clearly should be resting—not up and about like this, putting a strain on your wounds.'

She held her breath as his fingers moved across her cheek and into her hair. 'Could any man blame me for wanting you so much?' he said, and his usually strong voice sounded distinctly unsteady.

CHAPTER SIX

THE spell he cast was so profound, so intense, it was as if the rest of the world suddenly ceased to exist. There were no boundaries or walls any more—just Zahir and her, suspended in a weightless loving universe where who you were and the roles you assumed in life—whether antiquities expert or sheikh—ceased to matter. All there was were two souls recognising each other and silently rejoicing.

Her eyelids drifted closed as every cell vibrated with anticipation, waiting for the kiss that was bound to come.

It felt as though everything in his life had been teetering on the brink of disaster for a long time. Now, studying the entrancing beautiful features before him, Zahir thought that here was one thing that was right...that made him feel good...after talking to his sister *even* hopeful.

From his head to his feet his body yearned for this woman. He could scarcely think of anything else but losing himself inside her. His longing overrode even the unholy biting sting of his gunshot wounds. *And then he saw it...* A slightly raised scarlet abrasion on the plump pink flesh of her lower lip. Her mouth was naked this morning— free from make-up—so it was plain to see. Instantly he recoiled—the memory of the savage kiss that had been his parting shot last night dousing the heat that enveloped him like ice-water.

'I did this?' He winced as he stroked the pad of his thumb over the lightly swollen wound.

The incandescent long-lashed eyes appeared startled. Realising what he meant, she coiled her slender fingers gently round his wrist. 'You didn't mean to.' Her tone was warm and whisper-soft. 'It's nothing to be concerned about.'

'I meant to make you pay for my frustration, and that is not the action of a man who is honourable. A thousand apologies, Dr Collins…it will not happen again.'

He made himself withdraw in every way—physically, psychologically, mentally. It was agony, but Zahir had to do it.

Her face was a picture of confusion. 'It's nothing to feel guilty about. It happened in the heat of the moment.'

'Even so…' Inside, he was thinking, *I do not deserve her forgiveness. I acted like an arrogant fool.* 'The reason I came to find you,' he continued, 'is to ask something of you that will mean a lot to me.'

'Tell me.'

'My sister Farida informs me that you have already bumped into each other. It appears she has taken a great liking to you. It's the first time she has shown an interest in anyone or anything outside of the palace since she lost Azhar, so naturally I want to encourage it. She wants me to ask if she can help you with your inventory of some of the more important palace artefacts. I know I have not officially asked you to undertake such a project, but I am asking you now. Will you do it? Both conduct an inventory and allow Farida to assist you?'

She stroked her palm down over her hip in the pearl-coloured silk harem pants she'd matched with a tunic in the same delicate hue. Her troubled glance told him she was mentally regrouping—trying to make sense of his request.

'There must be countless important artefacts in a palace this size. Such a project could take months and months. What about my job at the auction house back home?'

'I have no doubt your employers would see it as an honour for one of their staff to undertake this task. There is no doubt in my mind that they will jump at my offer. If you are in agreement with the plan, I will make sure the remuneration you receive is generous.'

'It's not a question of money. What about Jake—I mean Dr Rivers? Do you want to employ him, too?'

A flash of annoyance assailed Zahir that she should mention her colleague. Mockingly he raised his eyebrow. 'No. It is *you* who is the antiquities expert, is it not?'

'I also told you that my father isn't well. I can't just disappear for months on end with no contact.'

Biting back a jealous retort at yet another show of consideration for her father rather than him, Zahir breathed in deeply. Such a response was beneath him.

'You can telephone him and talk to him all you want. I perfectly understand that you need to do that. If he needs a nurse, go ahead and hire one. The palace will foot the bill. As far as Farida is concerned, would you be willing to utilise her help?'

Looking torn, Gina lightly shrugged her shoulders. 'If I undertake to do the inventory, I'm sure her help would be invaluable. Her knowledge of your family treasures must be considerable, having lived with them all her life.'

'Good. Then you agree to do this?'

Zahir could hardly contain his impatience as he waited for her answer. His sister's enthusiasm for Gina's presence had unwittingly given him a legitimate reason to keep her there longer. Now that reason had entered his head he refused to entertain the possibility that his request might be denied.

The big blue eyes still mirrored doubt, but at last she nodded slowly. 'For someone in my profession it's obviously a great opportunity to deepen my knowledge, as well as a privilege—so, yes…I will do it.'

'*Inshallah*… I will make the necessary phone call to the auction house, letting them know what we have agreed.'

'What about the Heart of Courage?'

'Be assured, everything will take its course as it should in that regard. When I have had some time to recuperate we will discuss the rest of your findings concerning the jewel. Now I will send my sister to you here in the library. After that I must go and rest. My doctor will not be happy when he discovers I am not in my bed, where he left me!'

He spun on his heel, grimacing as the sudden movement made him feel as though a sharp-bladed knife had sliced through his ribcage…

It gave Gina a real lift to see less hopelessness and grief in Farida Khan's engaging brown eyes. To be Gina's assistant would give her a purpose, she'd confessed, and knowing that she was helping her beloved brother Zahir, too, would be doubly satisfying.

After the two women had met again in the library, and discussed a plan on how to proceed, Farida had disappeared for a while to locate the necessary keys—keys that would open some of the cabinets that were kept locked. They moved from room to room and floor to floor. She was showing Gina some of the palace's most prized treasures—possessions that were usually only seen by family and close friends. This was to be only a preliminary tour—the work of cataloguing everything would come later—but as she accompanied Farida on her mission to reveal the palace's most revered objects Gina was all but stunned into silence by what she saw.

She knew already how opulently decorated and sumptuous the interior of the palace was—nevertheless room after room seemed to outdo the one before with the riches it revealed, and everywhere she gazed the architecture was a dream. And that was *without* the abundance of extraordinary artefacts hidden away that she was privileged to be shown. Aladdin's Cave had *nothing* on the palace of the Sheikh of Kabuyadir.

Zahir was never far from Gina's mind as she trailed after Farida. *Whenever she thought about his gunshot wounds, she winced and bit her lip.* It was torture to imagine him in pain. Earlier, she had wanted to weep when he didn't kiss her as she'd believed he would. But she'd also been moved that the vivid evidence of his passion the night before had caused him to believe he'd both hurt and offended her. That he cared about that gave her hope. *She didn't want him to forget that they'd shared the most extraordinary connection three years ago that went far beyond mere desire...*

After learning that Jake had gone on a tour of the old part of the town for the evening, Gina ate dinner with Farida. Both women confessed to feeling tired afterwards, so retired to their quarters early.

After reading over her notes, then taking her evening bath, Gina tucked her legs beneath her on the opulent bed and let down her hair. Then she rang her father in the UK. They were three hours ahead here time-wise, so he would still be up and about—in his study working, most likely.

'Professor Collins.'

'Dad, it's me—Gina.'

'What a lovely surprise! How are you getting along in

Kabuyadir? Does it still have the same magic for you that it held last time?'

A little taken aback, she smiled. 'I'm afraid it does—so much so that I've agreed to stay on quite a bit longer than I'd planned. The Sheikh has offered me a job cataloguing some of the more important palace artefacts, as well as presenting my findings on the Heart of Courage.'

'You must have impressed him. That's quite a coup for the auction house as well as you personally.'

'He thinks so, too.' Her comment was wry.

'What's he like...His Highness?'

Gina struggled to find adequate words—especially when all she could really think of was that Zahir was hurting. Was he resting as he should? Might his wounds get infected? Her insides clenched anxiously. But she also had a confession to make.

'I met him once before, Dad,' she admitted softly. 'When I was here the last time. He's the man I told you about—though I didn't know at the time that he was going to inherit his father's title of Sheikh. He's the man I wanted to come back to before Mum died.'

At the other end of the telephone, apart from a few long distance connection crackles, all was silent. 'Dad?'

'Well, well...' he said, and Gina could imagine him rubbing his hand round his jaw and shaking his head in bemusement. 'Do you still care about him, Gina?'

'Yes.' Staring down at the receiver in her hand, she sighed with relief that she'd been able to admit the truth. 'Yes...very much. But he's still angry with me for not coming back when I said I would, and now I don't think he'll ever trust me again.'

'But he's asked you to stay on to catalogue the artefacts? That doesn't sound like a man who has no trust in you, my dear.'

'I'll just have to wait and see how things pan out, won't I?'

She could almost hear her father thinking hard. 'It was selfish of me to stop you going back, Gina. I was distraught about your mother, and fearful of the future without her. Yes, I wanted you to pursue a rewarding career—but I took advantage of your innate kindness to get you to stay at home. I was afraid of losing you to a man thousands of miles away from me. I've since realised what a dreadful thing I did. Now I need to ask *your* forgiveness.'

Tracing one of the swirling patterns on the bed's silk counterpane, Gina swallowed hard. 'There's nothing to forgive, Dad. You needed me, and I chose to stay. Perhaps it just wasn't meant to be...me and Zahir. Anyway, how are *you* doing? Do you mind if I'm away for so long?'

'Mind?' Her father sounded surprised that she would even think it. 'Of course I don't mind! This is a great opportunity for you to make a bit of a name for yourself as well as to advance your career—*if* that's what you want. And if you decide it's Zahir that you want then that's fine, too, and you have my blessing.'

His words stunned her. *He was definitely changing,* she realised. 'Thank you. By the way, how's your new house-keeper working out?'

'To tell you the truth, Lizzie has been an absolute god-send. Not only is she a marvellous cook, but history is one of her passions, too. She's a bright girl...extremely intelligent—and a very good mother to that son of hers. He, by the way, is very bright as well. He's already sorted out that hiccup I had with the computer. Yes, we all get along like a house on fire, so there's no need to worry, Gina. Just give me a ring from time to time and let me know how things are going with you, will you? And don't hesitate to call if you need anything...anything at all.'

Struggling to swallow across the lump in her throat, Gina nodded. After spending many years believing that he scarcely regarded her at all, it was almost overwhelming to hear such love, concern and acceptance in her father's voice. Especially when she considered that she was so far away, and it might be quite a while before they saw each other again.

'I will, Dad.'

'Well, goodbye for now, dear. We'll speak again soon.'

'Bye.'

Drawn to his balcony by the great glowing ball of orange fire that was the sun going down, Zahir experienced the familiar quickening in his blood that was always a given when he witnessed the phenomenon. It made him feel that he was part of much, much more than the mere sights and sounds that daily met his eyes. The realisation humbled him, and he silently gave thanks.

Then the incandescent moment passed and the ache in his side brought him back to more earthly matters—back to the frustration he felt at the thought of being confined by his discomfort for even the shortest time.

Right now he longed for the freedom and vast open spaces of the desert…longed to be pounding along the sand on his beautiful Arabian stallion with the warm wind in his hair and the sun on his back…to forget he was ruler of Kabuyadir for a while. Into his daydream came another tempting facet. On the stallion's back in front of him—his arms keeping her safe—was a woman: the woman who for the past three years had nightly haunted his dreams, the woman who by an incredible quirk of fate was now staying in his palace.

He hadn't written off the idea of making Gina his mistress, despite the fact that he'd said he wouldn't allow his desire to transgress her sense of safety or honour. Tomorrow he would continue his campaign to persuade her—to help her see that it was a natural solution to the inflammatory attraction that gathered force whenever they were together. *If she were to become his mistress he wouldn't have to risk his heart as he had done before,* he told himself. In a way he could hold her at arm's length except for when they were in bed together. Fear of her letting him down again would always ensure he would not wholly trust her.

Even so, his tension lessened a little at the idea she wasn't far away, and that soon—*very* soon—they would share a night together. Zahir released a long slow breath.

'Jamal!'

'Yes, Your Highness.' The loyal servant appeared almost instantly from one of the connecting rooms where he waited on Zahir's instructions—even all through the night.

'I'm going downstairs to the *hamam*. After my bath I will have my usual massage, then I'll need the physician to attend me to rebandage my wounds. Arrange it for me, will you?'

'Straight away, Your Highness.'

Rising shortly after dawn broke, when a full sun had burned away the night and heralded a new day, Gina washed and dressed, then made her way straight to the library. She'd promised to meet Farida after breakfast to make a start on the inventory of palace artefacts, but for now her time was her own.

Browsing the stacked shelves with an intuitive as well as professional nose, she retrieved four heavy volumes of history of the area and carried them to the long varnished table beneath a row of narrow windows. The air echoed with the spine-tingling sound of the Muezzin, calling the faithful to prayer, and Gina shut her eyes for a moment to absorb the ancient chant more fully. Then she opened the first great book in the pile she'd laid on the table.

Moroccan-style brass lamps on the walls were still glowing softly from the night before, and even though the sun was already blazing, the extra light definitely helped illuminate the hushed cathedral dimness of the area. There were several interesting references to Zahir's dynastic family, and what she read kept Gina enthralled for at least a couple of hours. Finally realising the time, she quickly returned the books to the correct shelves and all but fled back down the maze of lofty gilded corridors to the terrace, where she'd breakfast with Jake.

'Morning, Gina... I heard you were hobnobbing with the Sheikh's widowed sister yesterday. What's she like? Is she as striking in appearance as her imposing brother, or did she get the short straw in the looks department?'

'For goodness' sake, Jake, where are your manners? What if Jamal heard you?' Gina looked daggers at her tactless colleague, then anxiously swept her gaze round the terrace to see if Zahir's faithful man was nearby. Thankfully, he wasn't. Only the two girls who served the food stood silently by the sandstone wall, waiting to be of assistance.

Already helping himself to the colourful generous repast that was arranged on the table, Jake returned an unrepentant glance. 'It's only natural that I should be curious. I gather the general consensus in these parts is that she'll never marry again. Something to do with that prophecy that so fascinates you—she was head over heels in love with her husband and won't give her heart to anyone else. Not in this lifetime anyway.'

At this reminder of the prophecy, Gina's own heart seemed to turn over in her chest. It wasn't hard for her to understand Farida's vow, should it be true. If she couldn't be with Zahir then she, too, would probably live out the rest of her days alone.

'Seems a terrible waste, though, doesn't it?'

'What does?'

'I think this place is hypnotising you! You've increasingly got that faraway look in your eyes. It's going to be hard when you return to good old Blighty, isn't it? Back home to the *real* world.'

Falling silent, Gina helped herself to some bread and a few olives. Soon she would have to tell Jake about the extra job Zahir had asked her to do—but not yet. She wanted the chance to complete her presentation on the Heart of Courage first. When Jake's work was also completed, and he was thinking about travelling home, then she would tell him. The man was so ambitious that for all she knew he might be funny with her because she'd been asked to undertake the inventory and he hadn't. It definitely wasn't above him to be jealous and petty about her perceived good fortune.

'It is another world here, isn't it?' She forced herself to be sociable and friendly.

'By the way, there's the most bizarre rumour going round that the Sheikh was shot by some rebels the other day when he went to try and make peace with them. He wasn't killed, obviously, just wounded. This place is like some kind of paradise lost, but I still get the feeling that anything could go off at any time, don't you? I didn't see him at all yesterday. Do you think the rumours are true?'

Schooling her expression to stay calm, Gina swallowed some food, then delicately touched her napkin to her lips. 'I don't think we should speculate about it. If it is true then I only hope the poor man is resting and recuperating as he needs to, so that he can heal.'

'I don't like to think we won't be able to finish our

presentations if he really is laid up with a gunshot wound. We've both worked hard these past two months. I don't want it all to be for nothing.'

Finally Gina lost patience. Pushing to her feet, she glared at the man, who was dressed in another inappropriately garish shirt this morning. 'Don't you *ever* think about anybody but yourself? The palace has paid for you to travel first class, and we've been waited on hand and foot, as well as receiving a generous advance for our research on the Heart of Courage. I'd hardly call that "nothing", would you?'

Throwing her napkin on top of her plate, she marched away, leaving the two sweet girls who had been assigned to serve them staring at her as if she was a species from another planet.

In his study on one of the upper floors, the sound of girlish laughter reached his ears. Frowning in puzzlement, Zahir moved across to the sandstone and mosaic embrasure and glanced out. There were two women seated at the marble inlaid table in the intimate courtyard below, where a silk canopy protected them from the fierce midday sun. One wore the traditional black garb of a widow, and the other a long coral silk dress with a loose white overshirt and an incongruous straw hat that made him smile.

Seeing them together, clearly enjoying each other's company, was a revelation. *Rarely had a sight and sound given him more pleasure.* Without knowing he'd intended it, he found himself outside, approaching the table where they sat. When the women started to rise from their seats he gestured for them to stay where they were.

'I was beginning to fear I would never see you smile or hear you laugh again, my sister.'

'It is all Gina's doing. See how good she is for me? Not

only is she clever and kind, but she has a wicked sense of humour, too.'

'Is that so?' Immediately Zahir's interested glance moved from his sister to the fair-skinned woman seated by her side. Her lovely blue eyes had been brimming with humour just a few moments ago, but now, beneath his scrutiny, her expression turned serious. He didn't know why, but it grieved him.

'Good afternoon, Your Highness,' she murmured.

'You are looking very well, Dr Collins.' He smiled. 'Like a rose plucked from an English country garden and planted out here in the desert.'

'Such a rose probably wouldn't survive in this heat.'

'If it was tended and looked after by an expert gardener, I have no doubt it would blossom.'

Helplessly, he fell into a trance, his skin prickling hotly with languorous need. He ignored the fact that his sister was staring at him speculatively. Then Gina reached out to gather up some papers that were strewn across the table, and Zahir snapped out of the hypnotised spell that had overcome him.

'I will let you get back to your conversation. I apologise for disturbing you both,' he muttered, then turned abruptly and strode away.

As his dark robes flew out behind him, his booted footsteps ringing out across the paved courtyard, Farida frowned. 'My brother does not seem at all like his usual self this morning. It could be that he has suffered a sleepless night because of his wounds. You know he was wounded in a skirmish with some rebels the other day?'

'Yes…I heard what happened. It was a shock.' Lowering her lashes, Gina tried to scan some of the notes she had made with regard to the inventory that was underway, but all she saw on the screen of her mind was the disturbing heat in Zahir's riveting dark eyes. It made her press her thighs together beneath her dress, because suddenly she ached to the very core of her being for his ardent lovemaking.

Inevitably, she remembered the night she had surrendered her virginity. The erotic electricity their bodies had generated had been so powerful, so magnetising, that when he had penetrated her she hadn't experienced the slightest pain or discomfort. Their bonding had been so perfect, so natural, that she had no doubt it had been written in the stars...

Realising that Farida was waiting for her opinion, Gina strove for a reassuring smile. 'Your brother...His Highness...is clearly a very strong, fit man, and I've no doubt that he'll make a full and speedy recovery.'

The other woman shrugged. 'That is what I tell myself, too. But no matter how strong he is, he is not infallible. No one is. This house has known too much death of late. It needs new blood to revitalise it and give us hope. Perhaps it is a good thing that Zahir intends to marry soon. Even if I cannot agree with his bride of choice.'

Feeling as if her breath had been seared inside her lungs, Gina stared in shock. 'The Sheikh is getting married?'

Farida sighed and nodded. 'His intended is an Emir's daughter. She is plump and plain, and I'm sorry to say not very clever. Thank Allah he is not looking for scintillating company, because he won't enjoy such a thing with her. No... He has only seen the girl once or twice, but her family rule a great kingdom, too. It is a marriage of convenience my brother has planned, and I see nothing but pain and unhappiness ahead for him should he go through with it.'

It was hard for Gina to speak because of the dryness in her throat. 'But what about the Heart of Courage's prophecy that all your family will marry for love, not dynastic advantage?'

'You know about the jewel?'

She'd forgotten she wasn't supposed to mention it to Farida. Her heart raced as she quickly sought to explain. 'Knowing I was going to undertake an inventory of the palace artefacts, I did some research before I came and discovered the existence of the jewel. It's got quite a history.'

Leaning forward, Farida grabbed Gina's hand. 'I totally believe in the prophecy! One cannot and should not argue with fate. As soon as I set eyes on Azhar I knew it was meant that we should meet and fall in love. In fact I loved him from the very first moment, and I will not stop loving him for the rest of my life—even though he is gone from me. My heart keeps him alive. Do you understand?'

'I do… I believe everything you say, Farida. But your brother…? He doesn't believe in the prophecy?'

'He does not. I have tried to talk to Zahir many times about it, but he will not listen. Because my parents married for love, and my father pined for my mother so much when she died that he himself passed away shortly after, and then I sadly lost Azhar, he is scared to experience a love so profound in case he will be a broken man if he should lose it. There is no convincing him otherwise. He can be very stubborn at times—especially when he thinks he is right!'

'So he would rather marry someone he barely knows or cares about instead?'

The other girl sadly dipped her head. 'It would seem so.'

Walking in a semi-daze down the corridor later, her notes clutched to her chest, Gina didn't even register a door opening until a deep male voice uttered her name.

'Gina.' Holding the study door wide, Zahir commanded her with his piercing dark gaze.

'Don't you mean Dr Collins, Your Highness?' It was almost impossible to keep the hurt from her voice when all she could think was that he was marrying a woman he hardly knew, purely for dynastic alliance. Of all the things she had ever suffered, surely this was the hardest to bear of all?

CHAPTER SEVEN

'I WISH to speak with you.'

'I'm sorry, but I can't spare the time right now. I have too much work to do.'

Gina barely knew where she found the temerity to speak to him like that, but she supposed hurt and anger instigated it. The fiercely warning glance Zahir gave her in return was enough to quell the courage of Ghengis Khan himself, and she couldn't deny that her legs weren't shaking.

'How dare you address me in such a manner? Such disrespect would be enough to have you incarcerated. In future I would advise you to think twice before succumbing to it. Come into my study...*now*.'

Closing the door behind them, Zahir gestured to Gina to take a seat. *She was glad of it.* Laying down her papers on a lavish brocade-covered couch, she folded her hands in her lap, took a deep breath, then made herself meet his glowering gaze.

'I apologise sincerely if I was rude, Your Highness. It won't happen again. What is it you want to talk to me about?'

Hands behind his back, he paced the marble floor, his handsome profile ominously formidable as his boot heels rang out against the stone. When he came to a stop, but still didn't speak, a jolt of fear zigzagged through her.

'What's wrong? Are you in pain?' she asked.

A curse violently left his lips. Striding up to her, he hauled her to her feet. Suddenly finding herself on the most personal and intimate terms with his flashing eyes, warm breath and steely strength as he gripped her arms, Gina was shocked by how faint with longing for him she was.

'Yes, I *am* in pain! I am in pain not because of a gunshot wound but because I have had to endure not having the taste of your mouth whenever I desire it, not having your body naked beneath mine! Can you even imagine what I am going through because you deny me these things? Or are you so heartless that you don't even care?'

'Zahir, I do care. I—'

Any words she had been about to say were cut off by the hot pressure of his mouth on hers. Groaning, Gina wound her arms round his neck, and he was like a rock or the trunk of a tree she could hang on to for dear life were she in danger of being swept away by a hurricane.

In turn, Zahir held her fast as his tongue tangled hotly with hers, moving his hands up and down her back as he tried to position her closer, even closer, until there was no space between them and they were but one passionate beating heart. Reaching up, he freed her hair, and it spilled curling and golden round her shoulders.

He had said that *he* had had to endure surviving without the taste of her lips, the intimacy of her body against his… Gina didn't even know how to *start* telling him she felt the same. All she could do was demonstrate her wildly hungry feelings by matching him kiss for ravenous kiss, her hands as greedy for the touch of his skin as his for hers. His body was hard as iron beneath his flowing robes, his mouth a passionate burning brand that left her heart no choice but to be enslaved by him for ever.

Breathing hard, he broke off the kiss to cup her face

between his hands. 'I must have you in my bed tonight... After this, can you still deny me?'

Thinking was hardly possible right then, while Gina's body still throbbed from the delicious intimacy of Zahir's passionate embrace, and her senses were frustrated at not having her craving for him completely fulfilled. But, like a serpent in paradise, an unhappily wounding thought reared its dangerous head and wouldn't be ignored.

'Release me.'

'What?' Confusion and not a little frustration filled his eyes.

'You have to let me go. I—I need to sit down for a minute.'

As soon as Zahir set her free Gina sank down onto the brocade couch, her mouth drying uncomfortably at the question that had reared commandingly inside her head—a question she desperately needed an answer to.

'Your sister told me today that you are soon to be married. She said it is to be an arranged marriage to an Emir's daughter. Is that true, Zahir?'

His glittering gaze considered her bleakly for a moment, then he spun away to pace the floor again. A couple of feet away from her he stilled. A shaft of sunlight beaming in through a narrow window alighted on the mane of long hair that spilled across his shoulders, and the copper lights deep within the fiercely glossy ebony strands glinted like dark fire. In her wildest dreams Gina couldn't have dreamed up a man more magnificent—or more *unattainable*.

'It is true... But what has that to do with us? I am not marrying her for her beautiful body, or her wit and charm, so there is nothing to be jealous about if jealousy is what you feel—not when you possess all those attributes in abundance. It is, as you say, merely an arranged union for dynastic purposes only. The arranged marriage is common enough amongst titled landowners in these parts.'

'The last time you explained about that you hadn't found anyone suitable. Obviously things have moved on quickly since then?'

'Look…whether I marry this woman or not has nothing to do with what *we* share. Absolutely nothing! Why can you not see that?'

Capturing a strand of the bright hair that drifted round her shoulders, Gina coiled it round her finger, then let it spring free. 'Why can't I see that?' A soft, wounded sigh escaped her. 'Perhaps because I firmly believe that marriage should be one man for one woman, and that the relationship should have love as its foundation…not convenience or—or sex!' Gathering up her scattered papers from the cushion beside her, she pushed to her feet. 'If you'll excuse me, I must get on. I've promised to meet up with your sister again, and I need to pop up to my room for a book first.'

Zahir was back in front of her in an instant. A myriad of passionate emotions swirled and flickered in the silken depths of his long-lashed eyes. 'Know this…I do not ask you to become my mistress because I do not care for you. Even though you hurt me with your false promise to return, there is no other woman I desire or want to be close to but you, Gina.'

Biting down on her lip, she resisted the strongest urge to touch her hand lovingly to his high-contoured cheekbone. She hadn't forgotten that he'd recently been shot at and might have lost his life. 'I believe you, Zahir.'

'Then why shut me out as you clearly *are* doing?'

'Because even though you say you care for me, it's not enough to persuade me to either share your bed again or become your mistress. I don't want to play second fiddle to another woman, even though you might not hold her in high regard and your marriage would be just a formality…a convenience. I would be betraying my own integrity *and* hers if I do that, and that's important to me. I'm sorry, Zahir, but that's just how I feel.'

Leaving him standing there, his expression stunned and sombre, she moved across to the door and went out.

After Gina had so shockingly deserted him, Zahir bellowed for Jamal and gave him orders to get his Arabian stallion saddled up, ready for his immediate use. Less than half an hour later, ignoring his concerned manservant's plea to not ride too far lest he tear open his wounds, he mounted the magnificent ebony steed and rode off into the hills.

What else could he do with all the restless and unsatisfied desire that thrummed through his veins? He had to burn some of that raging fire in him away or else he would certainly go mad. And he couldn't abide staying at the palace and twiddling his thumbs for the afternoon just because his doctor had advised him to rest…not after Gina's unbelievable rebuff.

Why was the woman being so stubborn? It seriously perplexed him. There was an old saying: *patience is beautiful*… Right now he was far too frustrated and furious to contemplate the wisdom it was no doubt meant to impart. What would entice her to become his mistress, to realise it would give her far greater access to his body and his time than any plain, unimaginative eighteen-year-old wife, who would rather giggle with her girlfriends and feed her face than learn how to pleasure a man?

When Zahir glanced round to see a palace bodyguard following him on another steed, he let loose an oath. Giving the horse his head, he stirred him into a brisk canter. Then, when they were out in more open country, into a full heart-pounding gallop…

* * *

'Turn around.' Farida's look of quiet concentration was endearing as she watched Gina model the black *hijab* and dress that she'd loaned her, so that she could accompany herself and a male servant to the market.

After that emotional scene with Zahir in his study earlier, the unexpected trip Farida had suggested was the perfect antidote to the melancholic feelings that kept washing over her. It hurt deeply that she was apparently good enough to be Zahir's mistress but *not* his wife. Yet, underlying the sensation of despondency, she held on to the fact that he had at least declared he cared for her. Maybe that knowledge would give Gina something to work with? Thinking of the personal search she had started in the library, she yearned to get back there soon.

'From behind you will look just like any other young woman visiting the marketplace. It is only when people see your fair skin and sapphire-blue eyes they will know you are not a native from Kabuyadir.'

'I rather like the anonymity these clothes give you,' Gina remarked thoughtfully, running her hand down over the smooth black silk. 'Back at home women are bombarded daily by the media with what we should look like, what size we should be and what clothes we should wear—usually revealing ones. It's a refreshing change not to worry about that for once.'

'Well, I am glad they make you feel more at ease. We will have a good visit… You will enjoy it and so will I. This will be my first outing for a long time. Now, if there is anything you want at the marketplace—for instance souvenirs or a length of silk or brocade to make a dress— let my servant barter for you. That is how it is done here, and it will ensure you get a good price.'

The marketplace was a sensation overload. Turning her head this way and that, Gina endeavoured to absorb as much

of the sights and sounds as possible. When she was back in
the UK, doing her weekly shop at the supermarket or visiting some soulless shopping mall for some so-called 'retail
therapy,' buying clothes she didn't really want that would
disappear amongst similar impulse buys in her wardrobe,
she would certainly long for Kabuyadir and all the fascinating goods that made the market so much more exotic and
appealing—so much more *authentic,* somehow.

Staying close by her side, Farida was the best guide she
could have had. As well as pointing out various stalls that
might be of interest—whether their vendors were selling
colourful silks, yarns and brocades, handmade rugs or the
beautifully crafted ceramics that so many visitors made a
beeline for—she often added humorous little anecdotes
that made Gina smile.

After about an hour of negotiating their way through
the melee of people, with their colourful clothes and many
languages littering the sultry air, Farida thankfully suggested they take a break for some refreshments. Coming
upon a group of chairs and tables beneath a tall date palm
tree, she despatched her servant Hafiz to the stallholder
who was serving drinks and sweetmeats.

'Is there anything you have seen that you like enough
to take home?' her companion asked as they sat together
with their backs to the refreshment stall.

'I noticed a vendor selling essential oils… I'd definitely
be interested in taking some agarwood oil home—the scent
is divine. It will always remind me of Kabuyadir.' *And
Zahir,* she thought with a bittersweet tug.

'We will visit his stall after our refreshments—but I
will only allow you to purchase the oil if I know it is of the
highest grade.'

'Thanks. You've been very good to me, Farida… I just
want you to know how much I appreciate it.'

''Nonsense! You have been like a breath of fresh air to me, Gina, and I thank you for agreeing to spend time with a dull and sombre woman like me.'

'You are not dull *or* sombre…you mustn't put yourself down like that. I wish I had as good and bright and engaging a friend as you at home. When I eventually return there you'll always be welcome to visit and stay with me at any time.'

'That pleases me very much—but do not talk about leaving Kabuyadir yet, I beg you!'

'I'm not in a hurry to leave at all, as I'm sure you—' Gina didn't finish the sentence. An arm that felt like iron had grabbed her round the neck from behind, and the smell of stale masculine sweat enveloped her.

A strangled yelp left her throat as she was dragged violently from her chair, even as Farida screamed for Hafiz. Her hands fastened on the coffee-coloured forearm of the man she now realised with sickening shock was trying to abduct her, and pure adrenaline-fuelled reaction—and not a little indignant fury—made her sink her teeth into the smooth hard flesh and bite him hard. Immediately he let her go, cursing loudly. By then Hafiz was on the scene, along with a crowd of shrieking, excitable onlookers, and the well-built servant and another man grappled the assailant to the ground and held him fast.

'Gina! Are you all right?'

Farida was as stunned and shaken as she was. Even though her answer was an affirmative nod, Gina sensed the violent aftershocks of her assault roll through her, and she couldn't stop shaking. It was hard to believe that such an out-of-the-blue frightening occurrence had happened here in broad daylight, in a busy marketplace.

'I'm okay…I think. But I—I do need to sit down.'

A chair was quickly positioned behind her, and someone

pushed through the crowd to put a bottle of water into her hand with the halting instruction. 'Please do drink.'

Instantly Farida took the bottle, opened it, and sniffed the contents. 'It's okay. You can drink it—it will help.' She returned it to Gina.

With Farida's encouragement she downed the water in one, and the dryness in her mouth, as well as her shock, eased a little.

Someone had yelled for the security forces, and as if by magic officers peeled out of nowhere into the crowded market, swarming round the man who had dragged Gina from her chair. The assailant was young, but she blanched when she saw the seriously lethal-looking sharp-bladed knife that was retrieved from beneath his long robes.

'Who is he?' Her voice was decidedly shaky as she met Farida's concerned brown eyes. 'Why would he do this?'

'I don't know, my friend. But you can be sure of one thing…my brother will find out who he is and who put him up to this before you can blink an eyelid!'

Hafiz returned. Bowing courteously to both women, he turned his worried gaze specifically on Gina. Clearly frustrated at not being able to converse with her in English, he turned back to Farida, addressing the Sheikh's sister rapidly and urgently in their own language.

She sighed and said, 'Hafiz is distraught that he did not protect you better, Gina. I have told him it was not his fault. None of us was remotely aware of any danger as we made our way through the market.'

'You're not to blame, Hafiz. There's no need for an apology, really.'

'It is *I* who is to blame,' Farida insisted. 'My brother will go crazy when he learns that I took you to the market without taking a bodyguard with us. I can't have been thinking clearly. In the light of what happened to Zahir I should have realised that it might not be completely safe. But, Gina, you were so brave—biting the attacker like that. If you had not, I shudder to think what might have happened.'

'You're not to blame, either, Farida. And I prefer to deal with what *is* than speculate on what might have been. I'm okay, aren't I? I'm still here—alive and kicking.' Injecting some firmness into her tone, Gina even made herself smile—the last thing she wanted was the other woman berating herself for the incident, even if the truth was that her nerves were as scrambled as if she'd leapt from a fast-moving train.

'You remind me of Zahir when you say that. He had a similar reaction when I told him that he could have been killed by that gunman. "But I *wasn't*," he said...' Eyeing Gina with a definitely speculative glance, Farida stood in front of her and held out a hand to help her to her feet. 'I will talk to the public security forces and then we will go directly home.'

The hard ride on his stallion had partially torn open the wound on Zahir's side. Biting back a soft curse as his disapproving physician put in fresh stitches, he was nonetheless unrepentant. The ride had not only helped divert some of his frustration and restless energy, but had also helped clear his head.

As much as his proud, fiercely masculine nature and privileged position made him want to demand that Gina share his bed, he sensed that that was definitely *not* the way to go about achieving his goal. After all, he didn't want to alienate her or make her hate him. No...instead he would employ a charm offensive that she couldn't resist.

To start with he would give her a private showing of the Heart of Courage—even before he let her colleague Dr Rivers see the artefact. Then he would organise a special dinner for two in the palace's grandest dining room, where she would marvel at the opulence and grandeur of the furnishings and—

'A thousand pardons, Your Highness.' The double doors flew wide and Jamal strode purposefully into the room. His urgent tone and agitated expression immediately applied the emergency brake to Zahir's distracted train of thought. He'd been lying back against the luxurious satin pillows on his bed whilst his doctor snipped the thread from the last stitch he'd applied, but now he sat up abruptly. 'What is it? What's happened?'

In a heated rush, Jamal told him. It was as though he'd been punched in the stomach by an iron fist. *Gina...* For a disturbing few seconds his thoughts were so distressed by the idea she might be hurt that Zahir was paralysed. Then, as Jamal continued to regale him with the story of how Dr Collins had almost been abducted in the marketplace, where she'd gone with Farida and his sister's servant Hafiz, he swung his muscular legs to the floor and grabbed the long black robes he'd been wearing from the end of the bed—deliberately ignoring his physician's plea to wait until his wounds were rebandaged as he hastily dressed.

Inside his chest his heart mimicked the heavy thud of a steel hammer against stone. *Had he visited this latest calamity on his family by thinking he could apply reason to his dealings with the rebels?* It had already been demonstrated what a deluded belief that was! Would his father have simply sent in the military to sort them out, giving them no chance to state their grievances whatsoever? Had Zahir's arrogance in believing his way was right diminished his wisdom?

Shutting out the bittersweet memory of his father—a man who had been affectionately admired by officials and the public alike for his wisdom and fairness when dealing

with matters of governance—he hurried out through the
door at a mile a minute, with no mind to Jamal who, although young and fit, panted a little in his bid to keep pace
with him.

The women were in a private downstairs salon, where
they were drinking tea. On entering the lavishly decorated
room, with its long gold-coloured couches and antique furniture, Zahir let his anxious glance deliberately overshoot
his sister to dwell first on the slender, fair-haired woman
seated at her side. Her usual tidy French pleat was a little
awry, and escaping curling tendrils framed the delicate
beauty of her face to give her the same vulnerable look that
Zahir remembered from their first meeting in the Husseins'
garden. His breath caught in his throat.

In contrast the plain, traditional long black dress she
wore hardly seemed fitting for such incandescent loveliness.
He guessed it belonged to his sister. His first desire was
to go straight to Gina, but because Farida and her servant
Hafiz were both present he didn't.

'What is this I have been hearing about an assault on Dr
Collins in the marketplace?' he demanded, not bothering
to temper his outrage.

Both Hafiz and his sister flinched. 'It happened so
quickly, Zahir. There was nothing we could—'

'Nothing you could do?' he interrupted furiously, uncaring in that moment that Farida looked distraught. 'Why
didn't you take a bodyguard with you? In fact, why did you
not take two—one for each of you? Have you forgotten
what happened to me just the other day? For the love of
Allah, what possessed you to go to the market in the first
place? If you had wanted something specifically you could
have sent your servant!'

'I'm sorry, Your Highness, but I can't sit here and let

your sister take the blame for something that happened totally out of the blue.'

Having risen to her feet—a little shakily, he noticed with alarm—Gina all but pierced Zahir's soul with the fiercely protective glint of her blue eyes. She continually astonished him. No more than now, as she refused to let him berate Farida for undertaking a trip she hadn't needed to make in the first place, thereby putting them both at grave risk.

'As lovely as it is, we both needed to get out of the palace for a while. When Farida suggested a trip to the marketplace I jumped at the chance. So if you're intent on blaming your sister, then I want you to know that I am equally to blame.'

'Did the assailant hurt you?' He couldn't help the catch in his voice. Right then he didn't care who noted it, either. It was hell to stand there and pretend his concern was only that of a respectful host for a guest who had suffered some accident or mishap whilst under his roof when all the while he wanted to hold Gina in his arms and ascertain for himself whether she was hurt or not.

'The man grabbed Gina from behind and dragged her from her chair. I am certain his aim was to abduct her, but fortunately she reacted quickly and bit him. He cursed and let her go,' Farida explained, colouring slightly.

'You *bit* him?' Was it possible for this woman to amaze him any further? Arms akimbo, Zahir stared.

'It was purely instinctive. I'm no heroine, I assure you.'

'The law enforcement officers found a dangerous-looking knife under the man's robes.'

His sister glanced at Gina with what looked to be an apologetic shrug, but it was too late. Zahir's mind had already delved into the most horrific scenarios at news of the attack *without* the information that the assailant had been carrying a knife.

'And the officers interviewed you for details of the assault on Dr Collins?' His voice sounded strangely disembodied to his own ears, as shock and mounting fury spilled through his veins.

'They did. They'll be here shortly to have a meeting with you, Zahir. Do you think it was anything to do with the rebels?'

'I do not doubt it.' Scowling, Zahir dropped his hands to his hips. Helplessly, he returned his concerned hungry glance to Gina. Her skin had turned the sickly pallor of oatmeal, and suddenly, frighteningly, it was clear to him that she was having trouble keeping her balance.

'Gina!' Rushing forward, he caught her slim body in his arms just before she hit the marble floor.

CHAPTER EIGHT

As HE kicked open the door of Gina's bedroom, to carry
her across to the emperor-sized bed with its purple silk
counterpane, Zahir realised he had an entourage. His sister,
two servants—not including Jamal—and finally Dr Saffar,
the personal physician he had commanded Jamal to fetch
straight away, followed him.

Laying his precious cargo carefully down on the bed,
he personally removed her shoes, then sat on the edge of
the counterpane beside her, the tension inside him building
excruciatingly every moment her eyes stayed closed. Taking
her hand in his, he could not hide his shock at how cold
it was. Moving to the other side of the bed, his physician
lightly slapped Gina's pale cheeks.

Realising they were being watched, Zahir irritably waved
his audience away. 'Go. Leave us!'

'May I stay?' His sister had tears in her eyes.

'Of course.' He didn't apologise for his clipped-sounding
tone. His whole being was focused on one thing and one
thing only...*Gina*.

As he turned back the doctor was cradling her head and
moving a bottle of smelling salts back and forth beneath her
nose. Her eyelids quivered then opened thankfully wide to
reveal dazzling blue irises.

'What happened?'

'You fainted, my dear.'

The physician's avuncular tone surprised Zahir. The only person he had addressed quite as kindly before was his sister Farida.

'It can happen sometimes after a bad shock.'

'I've never fainted before.'

'There is a first time for everything, and it is nothing to worry about.'

The man smiled again, and Zahir was almost jealous that he was the one to comfort and reassure Gina. But then her worried glance collided with his, and this time he made sure it was *his* smile she was the recipient of.

Cupping her cold hand, he lightly stroked it. 'You frightened me,' he said simply.

Pursing her lips, she didn't attempt to speak, but he sensed her hand curl deliberately into his palm and his heart leapt.

'Now, I am afraid that you will have to leave us for a while, Your Highness… I need to properly examine Dr Collins.' The physician was opening his medical bag. Peering over the rims of his spectacles, he looked straight at Farida across Zahir's shoulder. 'You may stay and assist me, Your Highness.'

Outside in the silent corridor, Zahir crossed his arms over his chest and paced, grim-faced. A wind was getting up outside. Through the apertures in the narrow windows, it disturbed the glass and brass lanterns hanging from the ceiling and made them tinkle like windchimes.

After what seemed like an interminable period, Farida opened the door. Her smooth forehead was disturbed by a somewhat sad frown. 'Dr Saffar says you may come back in now.'

'Is she hurt?' he demanded.

His sister's frown deepened. 'She has some bad bruising

either side of her neck and on her collarbone, but the doctor has given me some salve I may apply to help soothe the soreness. I don't think she registered she was hurt at the time…it was more the psychological shock that affected her. But, Zahir…'

'What is it?'

'I think whoever did this may have mistaken Gina for me. We were both sitting with our backs to the refreshment stall—we are of similar size, and she was wearing one of my dresses and a *hijab*. We were with Hafiz, who had the palace insignia on his tunic, and I am known in Kabuyadir and she is not. What reason would the rebels have for taking *her?*'

'None that I can immediately think of.' He fisted his hands and swore. Rubbing at his temples, he stared at the woman in front of him. 'It sounds to me like this was a totally opportunist act—not one that was orchestrated. Else why did the assailant act alone in the middle of a crowded marketplace? No… He must have seen Hafiz with the two of you, noted the palace insignia on his tunic and aimed to ingratiate himself with his leader by trying to kidnap you to get at me. The idea of someone abducting you sends a shudder though my soul, but I am equally furious that they hurt Gina—who is, after all, an innocent bystander.' The wheels of Zahir's mind were rapidly spinning with thoughts of what to do next.

'She will make a good recovery I am sure, brother. She is strong, and today I have seen for myself she's a *fighter.*'

Even though he privately concurred with his sister's summation, it didn't prevent his insides from twisting agonisingly at the thought of that uncouth rebel half strangling her. As sure as Allah's will reigned supreme he and his leader would pay and pay *dearly.* And so would anybody associated with them. This time Zahir would neither be in the mood nor the market for reasoning—in any shape or form...

'Your Highness, the captain of the security forces is downstairs, waiting for an audience with you.' As he walked hurriedly towards them, from the other end of the lofty corridor, Jamal's usually calm demeanour was a little flustered.

'Tell him I will be with him shortly.' Giving his servant the barest glance as he snapped out the instruction, he gestured to his sister to precede him back into Gina's room. 'First I must ascertain for myself how Dr Collins fares.'

Zahir had said little to Gina when he'd returned to see her after her examination. How could he when they'd had an audience of his sister and Dr Saffar? But his eyes—those deep, dark, silken orbs—had spoken *volumes* as they'd studied her. In turn she had felt as if she was developing an incurable fever—a fever that no medicine could cure because the only cure for her malady was *him*.

He'd indicated that he was going crazy, not being able to be alone with her, and she echoed the feeling with every fibre of her being. Even more so now, after she'd been grabbed by that madman in the marketplace! Now she wanted to grab onto Zahir—to have him exhibit his passion in the most uninhibited feral way—so that she could convince herself she'd survived that attack—still lived, still breathed—and that someone *cared,* truly cared, that she had.

In a deeply luxurious armchair in a corner of the room Farida sat silently, absorbed in some intricate-looking embroidery. At any other time the simple, peaceful movements of needle and thread going in and out of the gold and white silk runner she was sewing would have lulled Gina into relaxing.

Sensing her glance from where she lay, resting on the bed, the other girl lifted her pretty mouth in a smile. 'Are you okay? Do you need anything?'

Gina shook her head, with the barest of smiles back. It was such a loaded question. What else could she do when what she needed most of all was Zahir? 'I feel ridiculously pampered and spoiled, lying in bed like this, so—no… there's nothing I need right now, Farida…thank you.'

'You must be the most undemanding patient in the world, Gina. After what you suffered this afternoon you could ask for anything and Zahir and I would try to get it for you.'

'Talking of your brother—His Highness—will he join us for dinner tonight?'

'I'm afraid not, Gina. He has some important business to attend to. He left in a bit of a hurry with the captain of the security forces and told me he didn't know when he would be back. In the meantime he left strict instructions that you were not to lift so much as a finger. Dr Saffar suggested you should have a tray brought up to your room rather than endure a more formal dinner, and I agree with him. We all want to make sure you are fully recovered from your ordeal before even the slightest demands are made of you.'

Swallowing down her crushing disappointment that she wouldn't see Zahir for the entire evening, Gina drew her knees up beneath the counterpane, then wrapped her arms round them. 'And what about Dr Rivers? Did anybody tell him what happened?'

'Yes, he was told. He was very shocked. He told Jamal to tell you that he would see you when you felt more recovered.'

She grimaced at that. It was typical of Jake not to disturb himself with hearing the details of what had happened to her, and also not to want to see her in case she was distressed. He wasn't the kind of man who could cope with

any kind of display of female emotion. But in a way Gina
was relieved. Spending time with her colleague when she
was fit and well was taxing enough, never mind when she
wasn't...

In the light of the single brass lamp beside the bed Gina
drifted off to sleep after another meal she had barely
touched. In the far distance the strains of some haunting
melody played on an *oud* reached her ears. Eventually it
lulled her to sleep. But the dreams that visited her were not
the kind of dreams that ensured her rest was peaceful.

When the memory of a cruel strong arm round her neck
replayed itself with frightening clarity, she bolted upright
with shock. As her gaze adjusted to the dim lighting she
saw that Farida was no longer ensconced in the armchair.
Someone else had taken her place. It was *Zahir*...

Her heart thudding, she tried to rub the sleep from her
eyes to focus better on the dark, haunting face that was
almost in complete shadow.

'I could not stay away, *rohi*. Did you think I could?'

He got up from the chair and came to the bedside. To
Gina's captivated senses his shoulders seemed extra wide
tonight, and he was tall—so tall. His hypnotic dark eyes
and disturbingly handsome features had never been so powerfully affecting and beguiling. With his unbound ebony
hair and the black robes that covered his strong masculine
form he resembled nothing less than a mythical prince—a
prince who had perhaps reigned here at the same time as
the necklace that held the Heart of Courage was created.

'I'm glad you came,' she whispered.

The tips of his fingers softly grazed her cheek. 'I want
to take you somewhere. Are you up to making a small
trip?'

'A trip where?'

'Not far.' Gentle humour briefly stretched the corners of his mouth.

Needing no second bidding, Gina swung her legs over the side of the bed. Some time between her eating her meal and falling asleep Farida had helped her into one of her long white cotton nightgowns. The material clung to her bare body underneath, then fell away down to the floor as Zahir helped her to her feet.

'You will need your slippers,' he instructed, smiling. He held her hand as she reached down for the soft sequinned shoes beside the bed and slipped them on.

They walked beneath the shadowed light of a crescent moon through the gardens. The powerfully drugging scents of jasmine and orange blossom infiltrated Gina's blood as they moved silently beneath grand mosaic arches towards a destination that was unfamiliar to her.

Ahead of her, in an enclosed private garden, an open fire glowed fiercely, hissing sparks like the forge from a smithy. Just behind it an imposing Bedouin tent rose up. Above them the inky night sky was peppered with a million, zillion stars…too many to count.

She glanced sidelong at Zahir. His hand still firmly held onto hers. 'Who sleeps here?'

There was a glimpse of strong white teeth amid the dark shadow of his face. 'I do.'

At his instigation, Gina preceded him inside the tent. She gasped at the wondrous atmosphere that greeted her invitingly—an atmosphere created by the hand-woven walls and ceiling, the medley of satin and silk pillows liberally scattered, and the colourful, intricately patterned hand-stitched rugs that covered the floor. Apart from the glow of the open fire, a single Moroccan lamp with a flickering candle burning inside was the only illumination. The shadows it threw onto the material walls mesmerised and danced like ghosts.

Moving across the soft rug-covered floor, she turned to rest her back against one of the sumptuous pillows. 'It's so beautiful…' Her voice was respectfully hushed, as though she had sneaked inside a church in the middle of the night. 'Magical.'

Saying nothing, Zahir reached for the topmost corner of the tent flap and closed the opening that had been there previously. Then he took off his long leather boots and, briefly opening the tent flap again, put them outside. Crawling over to her on all fours, he carefully, silently removed Gina's slippers and laid them aside. Then, bending his dark head, he reverently kissed her feet.

That simple, astonishing act released the flood of emotion she'd been desperately trying to hold back for days, and when he raised his gaze to hers she could hardly find her voice to speak. Instead, she simply held out her arms for him to fill them. His kiss when it came was satin and fire, summer heat and electrical storm. It was pure undiluted heaven.

When his lips left hers, to bury themselves against her throat and then the shoulder his hand had left bare by tugging down the sleeve of her nightgown, her body was so restless for his possession that she had to bite her lip to quell a desperate plea for him to simply just *take* her. But Zahir's burning eyes told Gina that he knew what she needed, what she ached for in the deepest core of her being, and he knelt in front of her, lifted her gown above her head and let it fall softly against the rug.

Lightly shaking his head, he sat back on his heels to survey her nakedness with something that looked like wonder. 'You are ravishing. I am all but stunned to silence at seeing you like this. One thing I know for sure…your beauty is beyond compare,' he uttered, low-voiced.

The tips of Gina's breasts prickled hotly, as though glanced by a burning brand. They seemed to grow hotter and harder still beneath his uninhibited hungry examination. When he put his mouth first to one and then the other to suckle Gina dragged her hands through the glossy strands of his hair greedily, to keep him there, moaning softly as the edges of his teeth nipped her. By the time he hauled her against him, she sensed his desire was at breaking point.

'Undress me,' he ordered huskily.

Almost crying with need, Gina started to carry out his order. But when he was bare-chested her busy hands grew still for a moment. Her gaze had fallen on the wound at his side, covered with a clean white dressing.

Cupping her face between hands that were warm and calloused, suggesting that he wasn't unfamiliar with hard physical graft, Zahir dismissively shook his head. 'Do not be concerned that you might hurt me. I have waited too long for this moment to let anything stop me now. You are in my blood like a fever, *rohi*. I am like a starving man at a banquet, seeing you like this. Now I will wait no more.'

The sheer beauty of his sculpted masculine physique made Gina gasp. Bare, his shoulders, torso, abdomen, hips and long well-shaped legs were pure hard muscle and bone, shielded by supple bronzed flesh, and on his chest swirled dark soft hair. Here and there were healed nicks and cuts that confirmed her opinion that he was a man who revelled in the physical challenges of life—whether it be riding his stallion through the hills and plains, as Farida had told her he liked to do, climbing high into the mountains to fearlessly confront a band of rebels, or practising sword-fighting with his guards.

But any further thoughts were stemmed as he laid her down amongst the satin pillows, passionately stroked his warm tongue into her mouth and kissed her. The deeply stirring caress had the effect of an incendiary device imploding inside her. As she reeled from the impact, molten heat like lava flowed through her bloodstream. She couldn't bear to have her body apart from his for another second.

Moving her hands from the firm flanks between his ribs and hips down to the proud, silky manhood that nudged against her belly, Gina hungrily clasped him. Zahir couldn't suppress a groan, and his answering smile was lascivious and knowing.

Paying her back in kind, he boldly prised apart her thighs, to plunge his fingers inside her moist silky heat. Her breath was all but punched out of her lungs for a moment, and dizzyingly she voraciously welcomed the bruising urgency of their mouths, teeth and tongues as his deeply rhythmic exploration took her higher and higher, winding her so tight that she almost couldn't bear it.

When her violent release came she collapsed, shuddering beneath him, emotion swamping her like an unstoppable tide. Hot, helpless tears streamed down her face, and Zahir gathered her into his arms. As he held her his lips rained kisses on her mouth, cheeks and unbound hair, until the tearful spasms slowly died away. 'It is all right. There is nothing to fear any more, my angel. I am here with you, and I will hold you and keep you safe all night.'

Hiccoughing, Gina laid her head against the warm silky hair on his chest and sighed. Through the weave of the fabric tent walls the dance of bright flame from the fire outside gradually dimmed. Inside, here in Zahir's strong arms, she realised she'd never felt safer. An intense feeling of calm suddenly came over her. The spectre of the man who had sought to abduct her faded away. He wouldn't haunt her dreams any more—not tonight at least.

Her hand drifted idly down over Zahir's flat taut abdomen, then lower still. If she'd thought that her desire had been spent in that wildly emotional release just now, she realised how wrong she'd been. It had merely been simmering, and just the touch of her lover's warm hard flesh would stir it into flame again.

Clasping her head, Zahir stared down soulfully into her eyes. Silently she transmitted her emphatic answer to the question she saw there. Reaching into a hidden pocket of his discarded robe, he sheathed himself with the protection he retrieved, then, returning to Gina's waiting arms, swept her down onto the pillows again.

Joyfully, her spirits soaring, she welcomed him inside her. His thrusts were strong, deeply possessive, and they took her body, mind and spirit into another realm. His demanding masculine possession made her ache even more to have him with her always. She almost cried again when she was reminded he couldn't be...

As soon as he entered her scalding satin heat, Zahir remembered vividly the first time he had taken this woman—remembered how their passionate joining had spun his whole world into another orbit and how it had left him reeling for days, months, *years* afterwards. That world was spinning into another sphere now. It was as though they had never been apart.

With her golden hair spread out on the silken scarlet pillow behind her, her lovely face and extraordinarily crystal blue eyes dazzling him more than the finest gemstones to be found anywhere, he jealously vowed he would never let her go again.

His heart was full and hot as he thrust deeper and harder. The emotions that flooded him were overwhelming, and so was the pleasure. There was not one other woman he had ever experienced this kind of incredible connection with… only Gina.

Her long slender legs anchored themselves round his middle, and he held back the almost overpowering temptation to just let go, to simply allow the force of his great need to overflow. As his lips fastened onto a softly rounded breast and suckled hard on the rigid nipple he knew she was close to coming apart, so he waited…

Her soft moans of pleasure turned to near cries as he took her over the edge, and they filled the tent. Then and *only* then did Zahir let go and spill his seed…

'Gina…'

The sensuously husky whisper in her ear, followed by a warm kiss nuzzled at the side of her neck, woke her from the deliciously restful sleep she'd been having. It was joy unparalleled to wake up and find Zahir's arresting handsome face smiling down at her. The last time they'd been together intimately like this seemed like eons ago.

'Good morning.'

There wasn't a place on her body that didn't throb from the delights and ecstatic release of their unrestrained lovemaking, but for some reason she couldn't fathom she suddenly felt self-conscious about finding herself naked in his arms.

'Are you blushing?' he teased, gently brushing her hair back from her face.

'No… What made you think that?'

The heat that seared her cheeks made a liar of her, but Zahir was staring at her throat as if hypnotised. The breaking dawn seeping through the stunning elaborate weave of the tent clearly illuminated his shock.

'That bastard really hurt you,' he breathed.

Unable to deny it, Gina sensed her heart bump a little beneath her ribs. 'Let's not talk about that right now.'

'At least he is behind bars now, with his no good brother. No more for *them* the comfort and hospitality of family and friends. Instead they will have to get used to the very different kind of hospitality of a high-security prison—because they will both be there for a long time!'

'I don't understand, Zahir. Who is this man's brother?' She sat up, dragging the soft wool rug that had covered them up to her chest.

His expression was formidably fierce for a second. 'He is the leader of the rebels who shot me. His brother sought to avenge his incarceration by abducting my sister when he saw her in the marketplace. Yesterday evening, in front of the captain of my security forces, he confessed everything. Because you were wearing similar clothes to Farida and had your back to him he mistook you for her. You cannot know how much I regret what happened, Gina. But the fact is my sister made a bad judgement in visiting the marketplace without adequate protection. I was speechless when I found out she'd gone there with just a servant. Especially when I had already been wounded by a crazed gunman's bullet.'

'Farida's intentions were completely good. She's slowly emerging from the pain of losing her husband and wanting to live again—to do the normal, everyday things she used to do before she lost him. Don't you think that's encouraging? She told me everything felt futile before. I thought the visit was a good idea, too, and nobody could have possibly predicted what happened.'

Concerned that if he blamed his sister for the shocking incident that had occurred it might set her recovery back even more, Gina reached out to soothingly touch Zahir's hard-muscled bicep.

'Don't be angry with her. I know how much you love her.'

'It is because I love her that I fear daily for her wellbeing and safety.' He glanced away for a moment, a muscle throbbing in his temple. 'If I were to lose her I would not—I don't think I could bear the pain.'

'I understand.' Keeping her hand on his arm, Gina yearned to reassure him. 'None of us ever want to contemplate losing the people we love. But, as hard as it is to bear, we all of us have to face loss in our lives. We can't live our lives constantly fearing it, because that's no way to live for anyone. By living in fear we only make ourselves suffer more, and we forget the tremendous privilege that life is. Don't torture yourself with thoughts of something bad happening to your sister. Just believe in the good things.'

Zahir shook his head as though amazed. 'And where did you acquire this great wisdom, I would like to know?' Heaving a sigh, he looked thoughtful. 'I extracted a promise from the rebel leader last night that there would be no more violence in retaliation for his imprisonment,' he confided. 'Some of my guards will go into the hills to make sure that promise is kept. They will see that his men go home to their wives and families. I told him things would go better for him if he lets it be known that he wants this, too, and he agreed. But be assured I will be taking no more chances. The fact of the matter is that being ruler of a kingdom means that you sometimes have to make difficult decisions in the name of the greater good. In light of recent disturbing events both you and my sister will have a regular guard. No more will I trust that I can reason with men who see violence as the only way to keep their families fed and clothed. Now, as much as I desire to stay here with you for the rest of the day, my tempting, beautiful Gina, I have my work to do, and you must return to your room and rest. I will give orders for breakfast to be brought up to you.'

'But I don't *want* to stay in my room and rest, Zahir. I want to get on with the inventory.'

'And what if you feel unwell or faint again?' he challenged, a flare of irritation in his glance.

'I won't feel unwell.'

'So you are a seer now? You can foretell the future, perhaps?'

That made Gina smile. 'Of course I can't. But I do know my own constitution, and I'm more resilient than I look.'

'Resilient and determined, I'd say…and clearly extremely stubborn!'

She lifted her shoulders in a shrug. 'I'd rather be occupied doing something that interests me than having time on my hands to frighten myself with thoughts of what happened yesterday.'

'Hmm…' Zahir tipped his head to the side. 'Maybe, in that case, it *would* be better if you occupied yourself with the inventory. All right, then, I will not stop you from carrying on with it if you want to do it—but only on the proviso that you are sensible and do not overtax yourself.'

Giving her a hard warm kiss on the mouth that could have turned lingeringly seductive if he'd willed it, he ruffled her hair with a rueful grin, then got out of their makeshift bed to dress.

CHAPTER NINE

JAKE RIVERS'S door was open as Gina passed by on the way to the terrace for breakfast. It was the first morning since she'd been at the palace that her hunger was really sharp. *Lovemaking with Zahir had certainly given her an appetite.* But that changed when she saw Jake's packed suitcase, lying open on his bed.

She rapped her knuckles lightly on the door, and he called out to her to 'Come in!' in a tone that was agitated and impatient.

'Jake? What's happening? You look like you're leaving.'

He adjusted his glasses on his nose, and his glance was preoccupied as he dropped a couple of folded Hawaiian shirts on top of the already packed clothing. 'You've got it in one. That's exactly what I'm doing Gina…*leaving!*'

'Why?'

'Do you even have to *ask* after what happened to you yesterday?' He jerked his head towards her disparagingly, clearly indicating the light pink chiffon scarf she'd looped and fastened gently round her neck to hide the bruising. 'First the Sheikh gets wounded by a gunshot, then you get half strangled by some maniac in the marketplace! I'm sorry, but I value my own neck far more than any kudos I might get researching the history of that blasted jewel—a jewel which, by the way, His Highness hasn't even had the decency to show us yet, after all our hard work!'

'The man who shot His Highness and the one who dragged me from my chair in the marketplace yesterday are both in a high-security prison now. It was just a localised skirmish, and the rebels are being helped to disband now that their leader has been imprisoned—no doubt they're probably worried about being thrown into jail themselves. Presumably they've all got families to feed. So there's no need for you to abandon your work and run away.'

'And how do you *know* these guys are in prison?'

Feeling her face heat, Gina crossed her arms over her chest. 'The Sheikh told me.'

'Did he, now?' Jake's tone was scathing. 'You two are getting very *cosy,* aren't you? Thinking of presenting yourself as a candidate for his harem, are we?'

'Don't be such an idiot!'

'I'm not an idiot, Gina. I've seen the way his eyes follow you around whenever you're both in the same room. But men in his position don't have serious relationships with women like you…no matter how pretty or intelligent they are. They only want you for one thing. I heard it rumoured that there might be an arranged marriage on the cards for our Sheikh…did you know *that?*'

It was the *last* thing she wanted to be reminded of—especially after the wonder and magic of last night. Desperately trying to quell the hurt that arose inside her, Gina took a long, steadying breath in. 'Have you told His Highness that you're intent on leaving today?'

Yanking down the lid of his suitcase and fastening it shut, Jake dragged his fingers back and forth through his already dishevelled sandy-coloured hair. 'Yes. I told him last night. He was in an all-fired hurry to leave the palace with the captain of the security forces. "Tell Jamal to arrange it," he shouted as he left, clearly not caring less. Well, I spoke to Jamal, and he made the necessary arrangements to get me out of here. Needless to say I won't be travelling home first class, as I'll just jump on any flight back to the UK I can get, but I'll willingly forego that particular pleasure to be back safe on home ground again. You should come with me, Gina.'

Not wanting to rub salt into the wound by confessing she'd taken on another job for Zahir, or let Jake see that she was in no way near ready to leave Kabuyadir, she slowly approached him as he stood by the packed suitcase on the bed. Just then he looked for all the world like some distressed and homesick boarding school boy, unsure whether his parents would turn up to collect him or not at the end of term…

'I can't go home yet. I came here to do a job, and I won't leave until I complete it. Besides…' She smiled. 'I really want to see the jewel.'

'Well, good luck with that. And what about your father? How do you think he'll feel about you staying here after you've been hurt, and with such unrest in the kingdom?'

The question made her insides jolt, as if at the impact of a heavy rock dropped into a river from a great height. 'That's none of your business. The unrest here has been quelled, and I'd seriously advise you against contacting my father to tell him I got hurt. I told you he hasn't been well.'

'It's your call, of course…'

'Yes, it is.'

'Well, I suppose I'd better be off, then. I've got a ride waiting to take me to the cable car.'

'Have a safe journey. I'm sorry that your trip had to end this way. Please give my regards to everyone when you get back to work. Tell them I'll be in touch soon, with a progress report.' Leaning forward she brushed her lips lightly over the side of his jaw. This morning he was unshaven, she noticed. It proved how rattled he was.

Grimacing at the gesture, he glanced uncomfortably away. 'Yes, well—you probably think I'm a terrible coward, don't you?'

Feeling suddenly sorry for him, Gina moved her head, indicating no. 'Only you know what's best for you, Jake. It's not up to me to make judgements.'

'For what it's worth, I think the Sheikh would be damned lucky if you were to grace his bed...*damned* lucky.' Smiling awkwardly, he dragged his hefty suitcase off the bed and left.

'I thought I might find you out here.'

Gina hadn't seen Farida all morning, so had got on with work on the inventory by herself. Now, taking a walk in the gardens to get some fresh air, she found Zahir's sister seated on the same bench in the courtyard garden where they'd first met a few days ago. Even before she reached her she had a strong inkling that the other woman's mood was low. The beautiful gardens, with their flowers, sculptures, myriad fountains and blue skies overhead, emitted tranquillity and calm, but Farida's sad-eyed demeanour did not.

'I'm sorry I didn't come and find you this morning, Gina. I have had a lot on my mind. How are you feeling today? You are not in any pain, I hope? If your bruises are still sore I can apply some of that salve.'

'Don't worry about that. I'm fine.' She absently touched the chiffon scarf round her neck. 'Mind if I join you?'

The other woman moved a bit further down the bench with the briefest glimmer of a smile. 'Please do.'

Out of the corner of her eye Gina saw a palace bodyguard dressed in a dark *jalabiya* and traditional headgear, observing them from the mosaic tiled archway that led into a more formal garden. At the end of the hall, where her room was situated, another similarly dressed bodyguard had been stationed by the narrow window. *Zahir had clearly meant business when he'd promised that she and his sister would have protection.* Right then Gina didn't know whether she welcomed the idea or not. The presence of a bodyguard might act as an unwanted reminder of the incident in the marketplace. She didn't want to walk round glancing over her shoulder every five minutes.

'What's the matter Farida? You look sad this morning.'

Her companion sighed. 'I did a wrong thing, taking you to the marketplace yesterday. Not only did you get hurt because that man mistook you for me, but now Zahir is furious with me. I fear I have alienated him, when he is the last person in the world I want to be alienated from.'

Automatically Gina reached for one of the slim small hands folded in the lap of the black dress and squeezed it gently. 'I doubt that you could ever alienate your brother, Farida. His love for you is unconditional and devoted. If he blames anyone for what happened I think it's more likely he blames himself.'

The almond-shaped dark eyes before her widened. 'How do you know this?'

A niggle of alarm fluttered through Gina's insides. She must be more careful about revealing her opinions on the man known as His Highness. Farida had no idea that they were having an intimate relationship, that they'd met before, or that her brother had revealed certain fears to her about his sister.

She wouldn't be so indelicate as to suggest that she'd received the information from him personally. It might cut her to the quick that Zahir was happy to take her as his mistress and not his wife, but that was between the two of them and as far as Gina was concerned would remain a strictly private matter.

She retrieved her hand to run it over the blush-pink dress she had donned that morning. 'I'm just guessing, that's all—though I can clearly tell that you're the most important thing in the world to him. It can't be easy being ruler of a kingdom…being responsible for so many important decisions. That's what I meant. Your brother obviously takes his duties very seriously, and it must grieve him when things go awry.'

'It does.' The other girl's gaze was clearly examining her as she kept it trained on Gina. 'I pray I don't offend you by saying this, Gina, but I have noticed that my brother takes a particular interest in your wellbeing…not just as someone he has hired to do a professional job for him, but as someone he seems to care personally about. Yesterday, when he knew you were hurt, I could see that he was distressed—more distressed than I have seen him for a long time, I think. Am I wrong to suspect there might be something between you…something more than just a strictly professional association?'

There was nowhere to hide. As much as she wanted to be careful and diplomatic, Zahir's sister had become a friend, and Gina wanted to respond with the same open and honest approach that she had extended to her.

She grimaced a little. A small trickle of perspiration slid down between the valley of her breasts. 'I met His Highness once before…when I first came to Kabuyadir. It was three years ago, and I had been hired to make an inventory of Mrs Hussein's rare book collection. I had just heard that my mother had been taken ill and was in hospital, and I was due to fly home the next day to see her. The Husseins were having a graduation party for their nephew, and your brother ran into me in the garden. I was upset and he was kind to me. I had no clue at the time who he was.'

Glancing round, in case Zahir himself suddenly appeared, Gina sighed and then carried on. 'We had—we had an instant connection. The kind of once-in-a-lifetime thing that you read about. I'd never, ever experienced anything as strong or profound as I experienced with—with Zahir that night.' Her cheeks flushed with heat for a moment. Farida's glance was growing more and more interested.

'Anyway, we parted after I promised him I would return…just as soon as my mother had recovered. When he rang me the first time I fully intended to do just that. I could think of little else but him. But the second time he rang my mother had died.' She made a movement indicating disbelief. 'My father seemed to age overnight, and I could see that he really needed me. When I told him about Zahir he pleaded with me to stay in England, to carry on with my career and be around so that he could see me. He was worried that I was being completely rash and irresponsible in wanting to be with a man so far away…a man I barely even knew. His argument was so convincing that I questioned my own reason for wanting to go back. All kinds of doubts and fears crept in. Kabuyadir seemed like a dream then, and England harsh reality. So when I talked to Zahir on the phone I told him I wasn't coming back after all…that my father needed me since my mother had died, and wanted me to stay and pursue my career in memory of her wishes. I think it was the hardest, most distressing conversation I have ever had. Even as I said the words to him I felt my heart break at the thought I would never see him again.'

'And how did my brother receive the news that you were not coming back?' Farida's tone was hushed, considered.

'He was…' Gina flinched. 'He was very upset.'

'Three years ago our father died, too. Then Zahir became

Sheikh. I remember at the time that he seemed to turn in on himself, as if he was strictly guarding his emotions from any possibility of further hurt. I thought it was just because we had lost our parents. Now I know he must have been grieving at losing you, too, Gina. How is it that you've come back here now, three years later, to do the inventory?'

Linking her fingers, Gina breathed in the warm spicy air for a moment. 'I changed jobs. I went to work for an auction house and the palace approached it for someone to…' She coloured guiltily as she remembered not to mention the Heart of Courage—the *real* reason she'd returned to Kabuyadir. 'Someone to do an inventory of its artefacts. It was a great shock to discover that Zahir was the ruler.'

Restless suddenly, as a sea of desperately suppressed emotion threatened to rise up and engulf her, Gina pushed to her feet.

Farida did likewise, her expression concerned. 'And now?' she asked bluntly.

'What do you mean?'

'Has Zahir not discussed the two of you getting together at last?'

Embarrassed, Gina dropped her gaze to the ground. *Why did things have to be so excruciatingly difficult?* How was she supposed to tell her lover's sister that in the future all he wanted was for her to become his mistress—and after last night hadn't she already complied? As far as Zahir's long-term plans were concerned, he seemed intent on going ahead with an arranged marriage. 'No. Not as such.'

'Why not? If he cares for you, then surely that is the next step?' Throwing her hands up in obvious frustration, Farida shook her head.

Gina was astonished that the other woman seemed to accept the idea of her having a relationship with Zahir so easily. She supposed she'd been half-afraid she might think that she was aspiring way above her station. 'Your brother intends to marry for dynastic alliance, so I hear. The very idea of a more—a more loving relationship doesn't seem to feature in his thinking at all.'

'You love him?'

She'd revealed so much already. How could she deny the one truth that disturbed her every waking moment? Gina thought. 'I do.' Her steady blue-eyed gaze was un-flinching.

One minute Farida was clasping her hands in front of her chest in wonder, the next she'd thrown her arms around Gina to hug her tight. 'You love my brother—truly love him? This is the best ever news I could have heard. It is just what he needs—to have a woman who loves him only for himself, and not because of his status or wealth. It is just as the Heart of Courage prophesised—that all our family's descendants would marry only for love.'

Heart thumping, Gina stepped out of the spontaneous embrace, her distress mounting alarmingly. 'No, Farida. You mustn't assume any such thing where Zahir is con-cerned. He is his own man, and he has to make his own decisions about what he wants. Feelings on both sides have to be taken into consideration.'

'I love Zahir dearly, but it does not blind me to his faults. He is too unbending for his own good sometimes. But if he believes he can somehow subvert his destiny then he is deluding himself. He simply cannot go through with this marriage to the Emir's daughter when it is you that he loves, Gina!'

Shocked and taken aback by the assumption, Gina gasped. 'If he ever did love me he doesn't any more. He's too angry with me for deserting him. Farida, what we've discussed must stay just between us—I'm imploring you. Please don't mention any of this to your brother.'

'Don't upset yourself, my friend. I would not dare blunder in and tell him what's best for him...even if he needs to hear it. Sometimes subtlety is the way. No, I will not betray your trust in me, Gina—I promise. For now let's get back to work on the inventory, hmm? I will do my share with much more dedication now that I know the truth about you and Zahir.'

Unable to keep her worry about the situation totally at bay, Gina accompanied the other girl thoughtfully back into the palace. Glancing behind, she noted that Farida's well-built bodyguard moved that way, too...

He had been gone from the palace for most of the day. Zahir and his small entourage of guards had travelled into the city, where he'd visited his wounded bodyguard in hospital, then gone on to see his secretary Masoud, who had been laid low with a virus. To his relief, both men were healing well. By the time he returned home, all Zahir really wanted to do was take a shower, then go and find Gina.

The library was where he finally located her. In the glow of several softly burning lamps, she was seated behind a long table, reading. He paused for a few moments, just for the sheer pleasure of observing her. Her beautiful eyes were locked onto the opened pages of her book, and she absently curled a drifting gold strand of her hair round her finger and let it spring free again. Zahir's avid glance honed in on the delicate pink scarf round her neck. His gut contracted almost violently at the sight. There was no doubt that he felt personally responsible for her horrific experience in the marketplace, and there was a great desire in him to somehow make it up to her for his appalling lack of care.

It hadn't been easy to think of much else but her today. Even when he'd been conversing with his injured bodyguard in the hospital, and then his secretary at his house, thoughts of Gina had drifted into his mind with increasing regularity. Their lovemaking last night had lifted his spirits and definitely renewed his energy. And this morning he had deepened his resolve to be a compassionate, fair and strong ruler, like his father before him, and make his descendants proud. That meant that he would not hesitate to make tough decisions when it came to what was best for the kingdom, even if it meant sacrificing his personal happiness. But, in truth, last night had only temporarily sated his desire for Gina—a desire that seemed to be growing in its demanding intensity rather than decreasing. The erotically charged memory ensured he had not lingered overlong in the city.

'It is getting late. And yet I find you here still working.' He moved towards her with an indulgent gentle smile.

Startled, she hastily shut the book she'd been so absorbed in and shot to her feet. Her softly pale cheeks coloured prettily. 'It doesn't feel so much like work as indulging a genuine passion,' she answered.

'Still…you have surely done enough for one day, no?'

'I suppose I have.'

She started to gather up her book and some papers from the table, and Zahir couldn't help noticing that her hands shook a little. Immediately his concerned glance swept her features for signs that she'd overtaxed herself. 'Have you rested at all today?' he demanded, knowing that he sounded gruff.

'I've been absorbed in doing something I enjoy…that's as good as resting.'

'I should have left stricter instructions with the doctor and my staff to make sure that you had some proper time off today—specifically to rest in your room.'

'I'm not a child, Zahir.'

Her resentment was evident. *He liked the way she*

pouted... Her full plump lips were the perfect vehicle for a little sexy pouting, even if she wasn't aware of it.

'If you ignore your needs and carry on regardless then you are indeed like a child—who does not know the pitfalls of her own reckless behaviour.'

Gina bit back what he guessed was an irritated reply, then with her book and papers clutched to her chest made to sweep past him.

Chuckling softly, Zahir reached out to gently but firmly waylay her. 'I did not seek you out to upset you, *rohi*. I have been thinking about you all day.'

Some of the rebellion he'd seen in her flawless blue eyes ebbed away. 'Where have you been?' she asked, and her voice had a soft catch in it. 'You weren't at breakfast, lunch or dinner.'

'Are you saying that you missed me?' he taunted.

She blushed deeply.

'I went to visit the bodyguard who got injured by that foolish rebel the other day.' With provocative deliberation Zahir's fingers tipped up her chin. 'And then I went to see my secretary, Masoud. He is recovering from a virus. When he returns to the palace I very much want you to meet him. You'd like him, I think.'

The pad of his thumb pressed into her fulsome lower lip. Along with the provocative sensation of her vulnerable soft mouth beneath his thumb, the heated little gasp that feathered over him hardened him instantly.

'Will he...will he be back soon?'

'Masoud? I hope so... Maybe in another week or two.'

As much as he respected his loyal employee and friend, Zahir was in no mood to discuss him any further.

He lowered his hand to retrieve the book and papers Gina still clung onto so avidly. 'Why don't you put these down for a while, hmm?'

She released them reluctantly, and he laid them back down on the table. Then he gathered her face between his hands so that he could examine her lovely features at close quarters. The quiver that he sensed went through her reminded him of a delicate rose petal, shivering in the wind. Not able to resist the temptation of that seductive yet innocent mouth any longer, he lowered his lips to hers. The sensual meeting was like a dizzying conflagration— an explosion of feeling, need and want like no other. If a tremor had ruptured the earth right then beneath his feet, Zahir could not have felt as shaken.

His palms slid over her shoulders down to her breasts. Catching the burgeoning nipples between thumb and fore-finger, through her dress and the delicate lace bra she wore underneath, he mercilessly provoked the already rigid tips to grow harder still. With the softly velvet whimpers that sounded in his ears inflaming him, he moved his eager hands down to the seductive womanly curve of her hips, then her delightfully shaped bottom. The thin, clingy silk of her dress was hardly any barrier at all to his fevered exploration.

The scalding heat all but flooding his loins practically rendered Zahir mindless. He was a mere breath away from dragging Gina down to the conveniently long library table and taking her in the most basic, feral way when she wrenched her lips free from his and flattened her palm against his chest. His breathing a hotly ragged rasp, he stared into her languorous blue eyes in shock.

'We can't be crazy like this. Have you forgotten that there's a bodyguard outside? A bodyguard that *you* insisted follow me everywhere.'

The thought hadn't even entered his head, even though he'd passed the man in the hallway before he'd entered the library. Zahir immediately dismissed her concern with unconcealed irritation. 'So? He is trained to be discreet as well as to defend and protect.'

He would have pulled Gina back into his arms if not for the fact that she was already moving away from him. Looking as if her mind was already made up as to what she would do next, she collected the book and papers he'd lain on the table and once more held them against her chest. Her features were flushed, her clothes sexily disarrayed—and so was the golden hair that threatened to tumble free from its clasp at any moment.

Inside his chest, Zahir's heart thumped in an agitated blend of frustration and pure unadulterated lust. 'Where are you going?'

She lowered her gaze. 'I'm feeling tired all of a sudden. You're right…I think I should go and rest now.'

'You cannot be serious?' He stared at her as if she'd taken leave of her senses. Did she have any idea how much *pain* he was in right now? And he wasn't referring to the flesh wounds he'd received, either.

'I'm not pretending. I really *am* tired.'

'You would rather sleep than stay and finish what we started? Didn't you enjoy our lovemaking last night?'

Gina went very still for a moment. 'Of course I did. It was incredible. But I'm trying to be respectful—to you and to myself. There's a time and a place for everything, and… like I said…there's a bodyguard outside.'

Dragging his fingers through his long unbound hair, Zahir could hardly contain his mounting frustration. 'If you are worried that we might be overheard, then we can retire to my quarters instead.'

'Not tonight, Zahir. I'm not trying to deliberately frustrate you, but it's been a tiring day and I *am* going back to my rooms now. I'll see you in the morning. Goodnight.'

Her head held high, and more regal than any princess

he had ever met, Gina walked past him and out of the room. Shaking his head in dazed disbelief, Zahir kicked a nearby chair and sent it skidding noisily across the marble floor. Instantly he heard the running footsteps of the alert guard race towards him from outside in the corridor, and vehemently cursed under his breath.

CHAPTER TEN

INSTEAD of seeking out the relaxing steam of the *hamam* bath, followed by a massage, Zahir had stormed back to his quarters the night before, and immersed himself in the longest cold shower known to man. Afterwards he'd turned and tossed as though he were in the grip of a fever, and had barely slept a wink. Gina's unexpected rejection of his amorous attentions in the library had left him feeling aggrieved, ill-treated and sore.

How dared she rebuff him like that? Reminding him that the bodyguard he'd instructed to watch over her waited outside had been just an excuse. Why did she now seem wary of the passion that erupted between them whenever they were together? She was a young, vibrant woman, with needs just like any other woman, and Zahir was a fit and healthy male with a strong libido. Why couldn't she simply allow herself to enjoy fully the opportunity for them to be together and receive the sensual pleasure that he was more than willing to provide? Was she afraid that he would just use her and forgo all respect for her?

Furious at the fact she'd left him frustrated, and unwilling to explore the unsettling thought that his feelings for her might run a little deeper than having her as a convenient bedmate to assuage his lust, Zahir set out early that next morning to travel with a small entourage into the neighbouring kingdom of Kajistan. It was a day and a half's journey, so he'd be gone for at least three days. *Three days for Gina to reflect on what a mistake she'd made in so foolishly turning him down.* At least that was his hope.

He determinedly cast the irksome thought aside. He was making the journey to Kajistan—because after the recent distasteful events with the rebels—Kabuyadir needed to make an outward demonstration of stability. How better to achieve that than by his marrying, and aligning the ruling dynasty with another great house? A cause for celebration would help to reassure everyone.

And so it had come to him, in the sleepless early hours of the morning, that perhaps it was time to run a more serious gaze over the Emir's marriageable daughter...

'Gina! Gina, I have to talk to you.'

Lost in a world of her own in the library yet again— she'd gone there in search of peace and consolation after a torturous sleepless night during which her thoughts had been consumed with Zahir—Gina glanced up in surprise to find the Sheikh's pretty sister bearing down on her, her expression distressed.

'Is something wrong?' *She prayed it didn't concern Zahir.*

She'd seen the look of hurt and frustration on his face last night, when she'd declined his suggestion of going to bed with him, but she'd honestly been emotionally drained after the incident in the marketplace, and had needed to retreat and lick her wounds a little. She also didn't want him to think she would sleep with him at the drop of a hat just because of their night together in the Bedouin tent.

Perhaps they both needed some space and time to reflect and assess the situation? But right then the idea that some harm might have come to him filled her with icy dread.

'Zahir left the palace early this morning to travel to Kajistan.'

'Kajistan?'

'Remember I told you about the Emir and his daughter?' Farida dropped down into the chair across the table from her a little breathlessly. 'He's gone there to consolidate his marriage plans.'

A silent hurt scream echoed despairingly round the chambers of Gina's heart. Keeping her hand on the opened yellowed leaf of the journal she'd been studying, she fought hard to conceal her distress, but knew she failed miserably.

'He has?' She knew she looked as devastated as she felt.

Farida plucked her hand from the book and held it warmly. 'We can't let him ruin his life like this, Gina—we just can't! When he returns you must tell him that you love him.'

'No.' She firmly tugged her hand free. 'He's made his decision about what he wants from a relationship, Farida, and it's not a woman who loves him. If making your dynasty stronger by aligning himself with the emirate of Kajistan is what's important to him, then so be it.'

'So be it? Have you lost your mind, Gina? Don't you believe in fighting for the man you love?'

'I won't fight for a man who doesn't love *me*, Farida... What would be the point? I might keep him for a while, as long as he desires me, but what happens when he finds somebody else he likes more? I'd be utterly devastated. If Zahir doesn't believe in love, then I can't *make* him believe in it.'

'So you'd rather just stand by and let him marry the dull, boring daughter of the Emir of Kajistan?'

'I didn't say I'd rather do that.'

Despondent, Gina sighed with private terror. Now she regretted abandoning their lovemaking in the library last night. How terrible if her hurt pride had stood in the way of allowing Zahir to be close to her once more. Especially if after his return from Kajistan it turned out to be the last opportunity she'd ever had!

'Have you completely forgotten the prophecy of the Heart of Courage? The prophecy that states every descendant of the house of Kazeem Khan will marry for love?'

The other woman's beautiful almond eyes were imploring. Taking a deep breath before she replied, Gina knew she had to be honest about something at last—something that had seriously been troubling her since she'd been asked to keep it secret. 'Farida...I didn't come here purely to do the inventory. The auction house I work for in London was approached by your brother to corroborate the research and provenance of the Heart of Courage. He plans to sell it, we were told...because he thinks of it as a curse on his family.'

'Are you serious?'

'I'm afraid so.'

'I have heard him talk about it as a curse before, but I had no idea that he planned to sell it...to be rid of it for good. In truth, I am utterly shocked to hear this.'

'I'm so sorry I've had to be the bearer of such disturbing news. It's because your parents died so close to each other and then you lost your beloved husband in the accident. Zahir thinks that in marrying for love you were cursed— not blessed by the prophecy associated with the jewel.'

'His mind must have slipped into temporary madness!' The other girl's skin turned abnormally pale for a few moments. 'How could he contemplate selling such an important piece of our family's history? He is just scared, that's all...scared that if he should fall in love that love would be ripped away by some awful tragedy and he would never get over it. I have always considered my brother to be one of the bravest men I know, but now I see that when it comes to one of the most important things of all in life he is a coward.'

Gina wanted to respond—but how? Words seemed terribly inadequate right then. But now she felt as if she understood why Zahir would seek an arranged marriage rather than a love-match.

Her hand idly but carefully turned over a couple of the journal pages in front of her. Inside her a little flame of hope lit and wouldn't be doused. 'For what it's worth, Farida, I was captured by the jewel and its wonderful prophecy from the moment I heard about it. It's practically all I can think about. And I may have an idea,' she said, indicating the book on the table.

'What do you have there?'

'It's an old family journal I found. It must be a couple of hundred years old at least. The only problem is my knowledge of your language is nowhere near good enough to understand it. I can make out some odd words and phrases, but that's all.'

'Why don't I help you?' Zahir's sister leapt up from her seat to move round the table and join her. 'I don't think I've ever seen this.' Her fingers stroked the intricately embroidered cover patterned with silk flowers in wonder. 'Where did you find it?'

Gina flushed guiltily. 'It was tucked away on one of the higher bookshelves. When I spotted it I guessed it must be a personal record of some kind. To tell you the truth I've been looking for evidence of marriages in the dynasty that have fulfilled the prophecy and continued happily right up until the end.'

After perusing the contents with their beautifully

scripted writing for a few moments, Farida glanced back at her companion with excitement brimming in her eyes. 'This is my great-great-grandmother's journal, and in it she mentions the Heart of Courage! She's bound to have mentioned her own marriage at least, and if it was happy or not.'

Daring to stay with the hope that had been ignited inside her, Gina silently shook her head in wonder, even as the edges of her teeth clamped down anxiously on her lip…

For three years Gina had been bereft of Zahir's presence. But now, having seen him again, and knowing for certain that she had never stopped loving him and never would, the three days of his absence from the palace was like being slowly tortured.

Oh, she filled her days well enough with the job of the inventory, and Farida had been the kindest and best hostess and friend…but every cell in her body *ached* interminably to see Zahir again, and hopefully get the chance to show him just how much she cared. The idea of him returning with news of his upcoming wedding was like an approaching violent storm about to tear down her house, but Gina told herself she would *not* leave Kabuyadir without expressly telling him exactly how she felt once and for all. She *would* fight for the man she loved, and if after that he still rejected her then she would just have to accept that it wasn't her destiny to be with him after all.

Zahir was glad to finally arrive back at the palace. The sight of the turrets blazing like molten gold in the afternoon sun filled his heart with both pride and joy. It was good to be home. He'd spent most of the journey there and back again from Kajistan consumed with concern about Gina and his sister. Having given instructions that their personal bodyguards were to be extra-vigilant and stay close to them at all times, as well as posting extra guards round the palace and in the watchtower, he was still not totally reassured they were safe.

The uprising might have been quelled with the imprisonment of the rebel leader and his equally hot-headed brother, but after the incident Gina had suffered in the marketplace he knew there was no such thing as being *too* careful. On his way to Kajistan he had wrestled painfully with the wisdom of what he intended. He had almost turned back... *almost*.

'Zahir!' Farida ran towards him as he strode down the hallway towards his personal quarters. She hugged him hard, then stood back to survey him. She appeared a little nervous, he thought, and his brow furrowed in concern. 'I'm so glad you're back,' she said.

'All is well here?'

'Yes, everything's fine—absolutely fine. How was your trip?'

Her small hands twisted restlessly in front of her black silk dress, prompting a quizzical smile from Zahir. 'You are sure?'

'Perfectly sure.'

'Well, my trip was fine, too. The Emir's hospitality was second to none, as usual.'

'And what of his daughter?'

'She was...' He concentrated hard for a moment on how much to tell. 'She was very well.'

Suddenly brother and sister were like two awkward strangers, trying to make conversation at a party neither had wanted to attend. Zahir regretted that, but there would be time enough to make amends. Right now he was anxious to get out of his travelling clothes and take a reviving shower. But there was one subject he had to touch upon before he left.

'And Gina…how is she?'

Farida's answering smile was broad. 'She's good. We've been working hard on the inventory. She's upstairs in one of the galleries, surrounded by books and papers, researching the history of a pair of ancient urns from Persia—you know the ones I mean?'

She saw by his raised eyebrows that he did.

'She absolutely loves the work. It's a joy to spend time with her. I've learned so much about our own family's heritage through Gina. By the way—I've arranged a special dinner tonight for your return, so we can all convene then and hear each other's news.'

'That was thoughtful of you. Right now I would like to shake off the dust of my travels, have a shower and change into some fresh clothes. I will see you this evening at dinner.' Briefly Zahir touched the side of her face, then continued on down the long corridor to his private domain.

Not hearing the soft tread on the carpeted hall floor, Gina chewed thoughtfully on her pencil as she perused the delicate urns on the plinth in front of her. She had been trying to date them. Her training and intuition led her towards believing they were two of the finest examples of some of the earliest glazed pottery in the world—probably from the Achaemenian era of the Persian Empire, she thought. Sitting back on her heels, she silently admired their incredible artistry—particularly the figures of some archers, with their still dazzling gold and silver swords.

'The inventory is keeping you very busy, I see. I fear I am working you too hard, Dr Collins.'

The gently teasing warm male voice from behind made Gina grow still. Slowly, she turned, and the imposing sight of Zahir dressed in his fine robes, dark hair shining fiercely even in the half-light of the evening, and his eyes glinting in mocking merriment, made her heart race madly. He was home. *At last...*she thought feverishly.

Removing the pencil she'd been absently chewing, she smiled helplessly shy—because all of a sudden it was as if she was meeting him for the first time. 'Like I told you before…it's not like work when it's a genuine passion. Did you have a good trip to Kajistan?'

On the last word Gina lowered her gaze, because she didn't really want to know if his trip had been good if 'good' meant that he'd become officially engaged to the Emir's daughter.

'If you are asking if I had a safe and uneventful journey, then the answer to that question is yes. As for the hospitality of the Emir—that lived up to its famously high standard, as always, and did not disappoint.'

Making a slow, measured approach, Zahir was suddenly in front of her. His leather boots were buffed to a mirror-shine, she noticed, and just as her eager glance travelled upwards to examine the rest of him he dropped down to his haunches, so that their gazes were level. The fine calf leather of his boots creaked a little as he lowered himself, and the arousing scents of agarwood and sandalwood made a potent assault against senses that were already under siege.

It was all Gina could do to keep her fingers laced together in her lap and not reach out to touch him.

'I'm glad that you're back safe,' she said softly.

'I confess it is good to be home again. You have a pencil

smudge at the corner of your mouth. Here...' He leaned forward and gently rubbed at it.

Gina all but held her breath. 'It's a bad habit of mine, I'm afraid,' she murmured. 'Chewing the end of pencils, I mean.'

Smiling into her eyes, Zahir withdrew again. 'Those urns were two of my father's favourite pieces,' he commented, nodding his head towards them.

'Were they? Your father must have had impeccable taste, then, as well as being a bit of a historian. *Was* he interested in history?'

'He was, as a matter of fact. How could he not be when he lived amongst so many incredible historical treasures in this palace?'

'What was he like? Will you tell me?' Again Gina almost held her breath. As yet he had never shared with her any personal details of his family, or how the loss of his parents—particularly his father—had affected him. She knew how a son's relationship with his father and the example he'd had from his first and most important male role model shaped their future.

'He was definitely the authority figure in our home, but he was never cruel or unfair. He loved us all very much and showed it daily. He was also revered by our people. Trust me...' he grimaced ruefully 'he was a very hard act to follow. It devastated me when he died not very long after my mother. Sometimes I imagine I can still hear the deep rumble of his laughter, or the firmness of his voice instructing the guards echoing round the palace walls. Anyway... he is gone now.'

Gina said softly, 'You must miss him very much, Zahir.'

'Every day.' He quickly shielded the emotion that she had briefly detected in his tone. 'I came to find you not just to say hello, but to inform you—at my sister's request—that dinner will be served in the dining room in about one hour. See how she makes me useful? Perhaps you should finish what you're doing and go and get ready? Farida tells me it is a special meal to welcome me home.'

'Of course… I completely forgot the time.' Getting herself ready to stand, she was taken by surprise when Zahir stood up first, then reached out his hand to help her. He held on to her for several long seconds as his dark eyes roamed her face.

'I never knew that just three days away from the people I care about could seem like a lifetime, but it did…' His voice was suddenly pitched sensually low. 'It did.'

Desperate to ask him what he meant by 'the people I care about', Gina nevertheless remained silent. Was he including her in that exclusive little group? If so, what about his engagement to the Emir's daughter? It was so frustrating not to know what he intended. Didn't he realise it was all but *killing* her to imagine him married to someone else?

'I'd better go and get ready for dinner. I know Farida's been busy organising the menu with the kitchen staff all day,' she murmured.

'Do you have anything else in *this* colour?' Zahir nodded his head towards her silky aquamarine kaftan. 'If you have, I would like you to wear it. It complements your eyes and reminds me of a too rare glimpse of the sea. I like it very much.'

It wasn't exactly easy to mentally assess her wardrobe right then, when he'd made such a surprisingly personal request, but Gina managed a shrug and answered, 'I think I might have something else in the colour. I'll check when I go back to my rooms.'

'Good. I will look forward to seeing you at dinner, then.'

He was walking back down the corridor, his long robes swirling round his booted calves, before she could even think to move and gather up her papers from the carpeted floor...

They were dining in a room Gina had not had the privilege of seeing before, but once seen it would be hard to forget. Above the long burnished table at which they sat was a vaulted ceiling, with a stunning circular dome made up of several different sections of vividly coloured glass. On the walls were lavishly painted murals of scenes depicting days of a powerful empire long gone, and a theme of arabesque patterning could be seen throughout, inlaid to particularly stunning effect in the marble floor. The space was lit tonight by softly glowing candles encased in lanterns—both on the walls and on the beautifully laid table. With the scent of spices and incense hanging in the air, it was like walking into a magical scene from the country's magnificent past.

After they'd washed their hands in a ritualistic vessel filled with warm water, they sat in silence as the servants passed various aromatic dishes of food from guest to guest.

Relieved to find it was just to be the three of them tonight, Gina tried hard to relax—but it wasn't easy with Zahir sitting opposite her, his darkly hypnotic glance frequently locking with hers and making her insides jump.

Of the three of them, it was Farida who seemed most at ease. Tonight her pretty face was literally glowing with pleasure at having her brother safely home again.

The servants departed—including Jamal, at Zahir's express request—and Farida raised her glass of fruit juice in a toast. 'To Zahir, in honour of your safe return from Kajistan after what has been a difficult time for us all...and for your steadfast, dedicated and wise rule of the kingdom. Our father would have been more than proud.'

He seemed taken aback. Was that a flush of hot colour beneath his bronzed skin? 'I have only ever wanted to honour his great memory by doing justice to his faith in me,' he murmured. 'And if I can do that even in a small way I should be very glad.'

'To Zahir.' Gina flushed as the handsome recipient of the toast glanced her way. *Should she have said Your Highness, instead of addressing him so personally?* But he was smiling, and for a moment she breathed a little easier.

'Thank you, my sister…and you also, Gina. Like I said earlier, I am very glad to be home again. I've returned with some important news.'

Gina's reprieve from anxiety was not yet over. Her insides tightened painfully. Was this where he announced that he was officially engaged to the Emir's daughter? If so, was she willing to remain in Kabuyadir as his mistress, knowing that he would never wholly be hers? Returning her glass to the table, she nervously brushed an imaginary piece of lint from the long sleeve of the aquamarine top that matched her long silk skirt.

Her expression equally concerned, Farida's voice was falsely bright. 'Perhaps we should enjoy our meal before you tell us your news, Zahir?'

He frowned. 'It is most unlike you not to want to hear my news straight away, Farida.' Narrowing his gaze, he silently assessed her for a moment. 'I think you must have undergone a serious change of character while I've been gone if that is the case.'

'Not at all. I have simply been much more at peace with Gina here to keep me company. I've very much enjoyed working alongside her on the inventory. It has really helped me find some purpose at last. These things have occupied my time and my mind much more than idle speculation about what news you might bring from Kajistan.'

'So to ponder on the news I bring from that place is "idle speculation"?' He grinned. 'You really know how to deflate a man's ego, my sister! Well, whatever else is happening, it is very good to learn that you are in a much better place and that your spirits have lifted. Now—regardless—I will tell all.'

With her tummy full of fluttering butterflies, Gina held onto her drinking glass as though it was an anchor in wildly stormy seas. Again, her appetite for any sustenance other than Zahir's drugging, passionate kisses fled.

'As you know, I had talked about the possibility of marriage with the Emir's daughter.'

'And I believe I told you I did not think that was such a good idea,' the girl at Gina's side piped up accusingly.

At the side of Zahir's bronzed cheekbone a muscle ticked irritably. 'As always, sister, your views are never kept hidden from me. In a strange sort of way I suppose I should appreciate it that you care enough to share them with me.'

The corners of his mouth were duelling with a smile again, and Gina wondered how that was possible when he was just about to break her heart into a million shattered pieces.

'All right, Zahir. Just put us out of our misery and get on with it, will you?'

Now his sister's voice was petulant. In answer, Zahir wiped his hands on his fine linen napkin, then let it drop back down onto the table again. 'My news is that I will *not* be getting engaged to the Emir's daughter after all.'

'You won't? I mean, you're not?' Farida's brown eyes were twin mirrors of stunned surprise.

Meanwhile, after the unbearable tension of waiting for his announcement, Gina almost crumpled with relief.

With a heartfelt sigh, Zahir studied both girls. 'The most surprising thing happened. I learned that the Emir does not want to relegate his beloved only daughter to a love-less marriage—no matter how influential or beneficial. It seems he is much influenced by the legend attached to our infamous family jewel, and is breaking with his family's tradition by now believing that she should only marry a man who adores her. Also, he does not believe it would be a good thing for a descendant of my father to go against the prophecy and marry merely for convenience or dynas-tic alliance. He admitted he fears possible "supernatural" repercussions if I were to go against it. So...' an intriguing but puzzling little half-smile played about his lips '...it seems there will be no dynastic marriage to bring our two powerful kingdoms together after all.'

'That's wonderful!'

At her brother's reproving glance Farida blushed, then quickly tried to play down her obvious delight.

'I don't mean it's wonderful that our kingdoms will not benefit from a marriage between our houses. I just mean that it's great that the Emir believes his daughter should only marry a man who adores her. I am happy for her... that's what I meant. Underneath her dull exterior she's a sweet girl, and deserves to be in love.'

'You are happy for her, are you? What about your poor brother?' Zahir's silky dark eyes belied his reprimanding tone. They were positively twinkling...

'Perhaps...perhaps you could revise your opinion about the jewel and open your mind to the possibility of being with someone that *you* adore as well, Zahir? It's not outside the bounds of feasibility that a woman—a *lovely* woman—might fall in love with you.'

His powerful shoulders lifted in what might have been a resigned shrug. 'Maybe… It is definitely a consideration.' The smile now touching his lips grew wider. 'In fact, it would not be a lie to admit that I am coming round to believing that perhaps it *is* completely the right thing to do after all…to marry a woman I adore and cherish.'

As he finished speaking his dark chocolate gaze was drawn to Gina. And as her hungry eyes were magnetised by his she felt them well helplessly with tears.

'Gina and I found our great-great-grandmother's journal, and in it she mentions the Heart of Courage,' Farida related eagerly. 'She affirms that she had total belief in the truth of the prophecy because *all* our ancestors before her had enjoyed very happy, successful marriages, and most of them died of natural causes. There was no mention of any terrible tragedies being visited upon them.' She took a deep breath, and her smile was wistful and sad for a moment. 'It was a terrible blow for me to lose Azhar…but I will not rail at the heavens for it. I think that would be sheer arrogance— because clearly I do not know the mind of the Divine, or for what reason Azhar was taken from me so young. But just because that happened to me, Zahir, it does not mean that it will happen to *you*. You mustn't spend your whole life dreading such a thing. As for our parents—we already knew that Father had a weak heart. It simply gave way because Mother died. It was his time…'

Reaching across the table, Zahir tenderly covered his sister's small hand with his own much larger one. 'You are very brave, Farida… I am truly blessed to have such a one as you as my sister. I know Azhar was the love of your life, but perhaps, given time, you might open your heart to the possibility of loving again? You are young yet, and have too much to offer to be alone.'

Relaxing back in his chair, he almost immediately moved

his attention to Gina again. His intense examination of her gave her goosebumps. It made the hope rising inside her almost bubble over—just as though she had imbibed too much champagne. She felt quite heady with joy. Yet an old fear that she might not get her heart's desire after all dampened it down a little. *Whoever heard of a boring academic marrying the handsomest Sheikh in the world?* it mocked.

Determined to ignore it, she pulled her glance determinedly away from the strong, handsome face at the opposite side of the table, to contemplate the delicious selection of food on her plate instead.

'You are hungry, Gina?'

Zahir's tone was teasing but she found she didn't mind it…didn't mind it at all. 'I am as a matter of fact,' she admitted shyly.

'Then, seeing as I do not want to be responsible for my treasured guest fainting with hunger, please go ahead and eat. You too, Farida.'

The grin hijacking his wonderful features elevated his handsome face to the most stunning male visage Gina had ever seen, and for a few moments it was all but impossible for her to look anywhere else.

'Let us enjoy this wonderful feast that my sister has organised for us,' he continued. 'There will be plenty of time for conversation afterwards.'

'A thousand apologies, Your Highness.' The twin doors opened abruptly, and Jamal appeared. He went straight up to Zahir.

'What is it?'

'A telephone call from the house of Masoud.'

The rest of the servant's explanation was in their own language, and both Gina and Farida tensed as Zahir stood up from the table and threw down his napkin. As he surveyed them, his dark eyes were fever-bright. Was that *fear* she saw reflected there? Gina thought anxiously.

'I have to go out, I'm afraid,' he said. 'My secretary Masoud has taken a sudden turn for the worse. Please try and enjoy your food without me, and I will see you both later.' Turning to Jamal, he laid his hand on the other man's shoulder. 'I am charging you to look after my sister and my guest,' he said clearly.

As he swept towards the door, his handsome profile grimly resolute, Gina shot up from her seat and rushed round the table towards him. 'Zahir!' She stopped him in his tracks, and for a jittery moment wondered at her own audacity.

'What's wrong?' he asked, not without a hint of impatience.

'Let me go with you.'

'That is out of the question.'

'Please… I've heard in your voice how highly you regard Masoud, and I thought—I thought I might be able to be of some help.'

'Help? How? A medical doctor is what I need right now—not an expert in antiquities!'

Ignoring the barbed retort, Gina pressed on. 'I don't like the thought of you keeping a lonely vigil. At least if I was there you'd have someone to share your thoughts and concerns with. Please, won't you change your mind and let me go with you?'

'No. I want you to stay here with Farida. Like I said before, I will see you both later.' And with that he swept through the double doors and was gone.

CHAPTER ELEVEN

It had been a long night—a night during which his loyal secretary and friend Masoud had literally been fighting for his life.

The medical staff at the small exclusive hospital that Zahir had had him flown to by helicopter had worked like Trojans to keep him alive. Earlier that day another virus had taken hold of him, leaving him dangerously ill, but in the early hours of the morning the senior doctor in charge had at last given him the all-clear, and informed Zahir that the man was over the worst. Only the days to come would tell whether he had enough strength left in his compromised immune system to pull through completely.

Grey-faced and anxious, Zahir returned to the palace. In his room he collapsed on the bed, and stared up at the gently whirring blades of the ceiling fan. Like his friend Amir, Masoud had been to school with him. He, too, was like a brother. To see his gaunt face and black eyes staring blankly up at him from a hospital bed, his body wired up to countless tubes and drips, had left him in a state of mounting fear and despair. *Was he to lose yet another person he cared about?*

He had no doubt he was being tested by Allah—although it felt more as if he was being mocked. Just when he'd decided to give love a chance, he had again been shown how precarious his future with Gina might be if he should lose her. He was strong, but not *that* strong. If she should die young—either by some dreadful accident or through an illness of some kind—he honestly didn't think he could bear it. With his heart and mind in turmoil, Zahir shut his eyes and prayed harder than he had ever prayed before...

It seemed as though Zahir had retreated from her in every possible way. Gina had got over the abrupt way he'd told her that he needed a medical doctor, not an antiquities expert, telling herself it was because he'd been so distressed on hearing the news about Masoud. He had been so curt— and it had wounded her when he'd so brutally dismissed her offer of help.

More troubling behaviour was to come.

The morning after he'd rushed to Masoud, Gina saw him on the way to his rooms. His handsome, unlined face was haggard.

'Zahir.' She hurried after him. It appeared that he was reluctant to stop even for a moment to talk to her.

'What is it?' he asked wearily, rubbing his hand across his eyes.

Her heart knocked hard against her ribs. 'How is Masoud?'

'Right now it is touch and go, so I am told. To speak the truth, I don't really want to discuss it. All I will say is that the next few days are critical. If you need anything, talk to Farida or Jamal, will you?'

'I don't want to annoy you, Zahir, but perhaps the next time you go to the hospital I *could* go with you? I know I can't make your friend better, but I could be a support and someone to turn to for you, instead of you sitting there alone worrying about him.'

'To be frank, your presence would be an unnecessary

distraction rather than a support. Right now I need to focus on what has to be done for my friend—not be fussed over by a woman like some needy child!'

Biting back a hurt retort, Gina felt her face burn at having her offer of help again so bluntly refused. 'Well...' She twisted her hands in front of her and shrugged. 'If you change your mind at any time I just want you to know that I'll be here for you...that's all.'

'Hmm...' His distant gaze withdrew from her even before he turned and continued down the corridor.

Frozen into a statue, Gina stood staring after him.

Every time Zahir came into contact with her after that morning he deliberately kept their exchanges to the minimum, then made himself absent as soon as possible. After the high hopes of his homecoming dinner, it was a painful knock-back.

He was travelling back and forth to the hospital to visit Masoud on a regular basis. One day the news was good, the next not so good. Frequently his expression bordered on the haunted.

Gina had tried to reach him with words, with warmth, with an understanding look, but his self-protective shutters had definitely slammed down as hard as a heavy portcullis, and nothing seemed to make an impact. She had no choice but to bide her time. Even now, when he seemed so distant and the possibility of them being together seemed ever more remote and impossible, she vowed she would not give up on her love for him.

Masoud becoming ill had shaken him to his core—she knew that. She also knew that he feared losing his friend as he had lost his parents and then his brother-in-law. He feared the pain that it would bring. Farida's plea that he should not spend his life dreading the loss of those he loved had apparently been forgotten.

'Do not despair,' the other woman had consoled her. 'Masoud's health will return, and so will Zahir's belief in love.'

Not allowing herself too much time in which to speculate on what would happen if Masoud *didn't* recover, Gina kept her gloomy thoughts at bay by working on the inventory. But underlying everything she did was her hope and prayer that Zahir would come back to himself and *her* soon.

Five nights after Zahir had left his homecoming dinner to rush off to his friend's bedside, they learned that Masoud was emerging from the nightmare of his illness with flying colours. The medical staff had removed the drips, and he had even had his first taste of solid food for days. Zahir was in much higher spirits, even seeking Gina out in one of the galleries where she was working to speak with her.

'I am off to the hospital again. I feel like I'm taking up residence there, if you want to know the truth.'

His smile still looked tired, Gina thought as she studied him, but the haunted expression was thankfully gone. She was very moved that he would be so dedicated to the care of a friend that he would put him before everything else... even duty...yet inside she was wrestling with the agonising idea that he didn't want to be with her at all. That she was, as he had said, just an *unnecessary distraction*.

'When I return later tonight I want to see you,' he declared. 'I want to tell you things—' He broke off to arch a rueful dark eyebrow. 'I have not been the best host or the kindest and most understanding friend to you in the past few days, Gina... But I promise I will make it up to you.'

'You don't owe me anything, Zahir—honestly. I'm just very glad that your friend is getting better and that consequently you won't be so worried.'

'Yet still I feel I have neglected you.'

'I assure you, you have not. Like you, I'm not "some needy child" who needs constant attention or fussing over. At the end of the day I merely came here to do a job. When that job is ended I'll go back home again, and you won't have to give me another thought.' Her throat swelled and tightened as she finished speaking, and hot, despairing tears weren't far away.

'You think I would never give you another thought if you should return home?' The tanned brow furrowed in not just concern, but confusion and annoyance, too. 'Have I been so remiss in my care of you that you would leave and dismiss me as if my feelings were of no account whatsoever?' he demanded.

'Forget what I said, Zahir.' Having great difficulty in containing her spiralling emotions, Gina forced a smile to her lips. 'You need to focus on your friend, and I understand that—I really do. When you return I'll still be here, working on the inventory. I promise.'

Not looking entirely convinced, nonetheless Zahir briefly gathered her hand in his, then raised it to his lips to deliver a tender kiss across the fine skin of her knuckles. His eyes watched her carefully as he did so, almost as if he expected her to bolt like a rabbit. 'I pray that will be so, *rohi*.' His rich voice was husky and warm with feeling. 'When I return I will come straight away to see you no matter what the time is.'

Almost faint with the mixture of relief and hope that had swirled through her at his words, after he had gone Gina took some time out from doing the inventory with Farida. She simply went to her rooms to try and calm the nervous excitement that had suddenly turned her brain to mush and her limbs to sponge…

'You are still up? I was hoping you would be.'

Farida had gone to bed quite a while ago, he'd learned,

and at last…*at last* Zahir had an opportunity to have Gina to himself. *If* she was still awake, that was. He'd knocked on her door, half expecting her to be fast asleep in bed. It was, after all, past midnight. But she'd answered his knock almost immediately, her shy glance lit up by an equally unsure smile.

'I waited for you. You said you wanted to tell me things.'

'I did, didn't I?'

'How was Masoud today?' she asked, her expression concerned but wary.

Breathing out a long sigh, Zahir nodded his head. 'He has made a miraculous recovery, and is looking even better than before. Two or three more days in hospital to recuperate and he will be home again. Take a walk with me, will you?'

'A walk where?'

'Not very far.'

They moved slowly down the lamp-lit corridor and both fell silent. Dressed in a soft white tunic and skirt, her bright hair arranged behind her head with a pretty floral clasp, the woman at Zahir's side made his heart soar just looking at her. But it had taken a ruler wiser than he—a ruler who *did* listen to his heart—to make him finally acknowledge the depth and breadth of his feelings. Masoud's illness had set his hopes back for a while, Zahir silently admitted, but only because he'd feared his friend might not survive. Now he realised that even if he had *not* life would go on, *Zahir* would go on, and his great hope now was that he would do so with Gina by his side.

'I want to show you something.'

He caught her by the hand, then pushed open a door to the side of him. The small salon was barely furnished, but that was for a good reason. Inside there was a single glowing lamp, and on the wall a stunning landscape of the desert. The painting had been one of his mother's own works. She'd loved to paint, and her favourite subject had been the diversity and beauty of this incredible land they lived in. Beneath the picture was a beechwood cabinet with a clear glass top, so that whatever was laid inside there could be viewed to its best advantage. It was the reason there was so little else in the room—so nothing could detract from its incredible beauty and presence.

Placing his hand gently at the small of her back, Zahir urged Gina towards it. 'You have been so patient, *rohi,* and this is your reward. You are looking upon the Heart of Courage.'

The jewel seemed especially lovely tonight, as it lay on its bed of black velvet, he mused. With a buttery-yellow gold chain, the stunning pendant was made up of a circle of rubies and sapphires—and at its centre, dazzling the eye, was the *Almas*...a pure diamond whose colour was the flawless hue of a midnight desert sky shaped into a breathtaking heart. It radiated not just beauty, but magic, too.

It had been a long time since Zahir had even glanced at it, let alone studied it. But with its imagined connotations of visiting tragedy on his family he hardly needed to ask himself why. Hearing about the discovery of his great-great-grandmother's journal, and learning that the previous love-matches of his family had—as far as they were aware—been happy and successful, he now felt reassured to follow his heart.

Yet even if the history had not been good, Zahir knew it wouldn't have affected his decision... His arrogance had indeed diminished his wisdom when he'd sought to circumvent his destiny, but after his visit to Kajistan a few days ago, and hearing the wise thoughts of the Emir, he knew he would never be so foolish again as to think he even had a say in the matter.

'Oh, Zahir…' Turning towards him, Gina knew her lovely blue eyes glistened with tears. 'To be standing here, gazing at such an incredible sight… I feel utterly awed and privileged. Jake would have been beside himself to see the jewel as I am seeing it now.'

The sickening flash of jealousy that slashed through Zahir's insides was like having his legs kicked away from under him. 'Then how unfortunate that he so rashly decided to cut short his stay and go home,' he murmured, unable to keep the sarcasm from his voice.

'Yes…it was.' Her expression confused, Gina dipped her head.

'Are you sad that he left?'

Her head whipped up again. 'No! Why do you say that?'

'Because for you to mention that insignificant man at such an important time as this displeases me greatly, and it also has me thinking that perhaps you care for him more than you have admitted.'

'That's absolutely not true. He's a colleague—that's all. A colleague who worked as hard on researching the jewel as I did, and longed to view it for himself.'

'Then he should have stayed longer, instead of running away and insulting me by believing his very life was jeopardised by staying at the palace!'

His temper spilling over, Zahir stalked away from the cabinet to move across to the door. He could rationalise his emotionally charged response by telling himself he was still a little overwrought at all the events that had recently unfolded, but this was patently *not* the way he'd imagined the scene when he finally showed Gina the jewel and told her how he felt. A turbulent mix of anger as well as despair twisted his gut, and his mind took him down an even darker road.

'If it is not Jake you honour with your interest, what about the other men you must have met since we parted that night three years ago?'

'What other men?' The blue eyes widened indignantly, like dazzling twin lakes. 'I never had an intimate relationship with any other man except *you*, Zahir—not in three years. I already told you that.'

'Even so…my fear is that you are merely *saying* that so as not to disappoint me.'

'I wouldn't lie to you. I want you to know that after we were together that night even the mere thought of being with another man that way was repugnant to me.'

Zahir sucked in a steadying breath. To learn that Gina had been intimate with him and *only* him rocketed his previously sinking spirits to the moon and back. He ventured a smile. 'Can't you tell how jealous I have been at the idea you had slept with other men after surrendering your virginity to me? If I've handled it badly and offended you, I sincerely apologise.'

She crossed her arms in front of her chest and sighed. 'I accept your apology… But, like I said, after we were together I simply wasn't interested in any other man but you, Zahir. And while we're still on the subject of my colleague Jake,' she continued, 'he simply couldn't *help* being fearful. He's an urban man who lives alone, and he has had no experience of much other than his books and his work. There's an old church near where we work, and every time its clock chimes the hour he practically jumps out of his skin. It's just not in his nature to be brave, Zahir. He's not like you. Some people confront their fears head-on, and others find themselves retreating to protect themselves because they can't cope with anything shaking them up.

Are you going to condemn him for what is, after all, quite a common human weakness?'

Clenching his fists down by his sides, Zahir shook his head. '*You* didn't run away. You even bit the man who assaulted you to get away from him—yes, *bit* him—without knowing how he would react and possibly risking more harm to yourself!' Unable to contain the great tide of strongly felt emotion that washed over him, he moved swiftly back to Gina's side. 'I die a thousand deaths every time I relive that scene in my mind and imagine that you could have been killed or maimed for life.'

'But I *wasn't* killed or maimed.' Her plump lower lip trembled. Shakily she moved her hand to brush back her hair.

The tumult inside Zahir's chest slowly started to subside. But it was replaced by an even stronger emotion. He sighed. 'I am in awe of your incredible bravery…at what you did that day. Not one in a hundred women would have had the presence of mind to do what you did. Not to put too fine a point on it, the man who attacked you is a trained fighter…a mercenary. He lives high in the mountains, where he and his brother believe themselves to be outside the realms of any civilised law made to curtail their more base instincts and reckless activities. Yet, not knowing the danger, you fought back. You are quite a remarkable woman, Gina Collins.'

'Not really,' she murmured softly, gazing up at him. 'But sometimes…sometimes certain strong feelings can give you the courage to be stronger.'

'And what strong feelings would those be…hmm?'

'When you—when you care for someone deeply you don't want to leave them…you want to stay with them for the rest of your life, and you'll do anything you can to prevent being parted. I truly regret not coming back to you three years ago, but when my mother died I was overwhelmed with fear. I wasn't courageous enough to trust that it was right to return. When my father put doubts in my head about it, I listened to him rather than to my heart. It's true what they say, you know…about what happens when you're in serious danger. My life *did* flash before me when that man grabbed me at the marketplace, and I promised myself in that same moment that if I survived I would tell you exactly how I feel.'

Zahir stilled, yet his heart thudded hard. 'You said that gazing at the jewel made you feel awed and privileged. I could say the same thing about looking at you, *rohi*.' His voice was now helplessly infused with the warmth that was growing powerfully inside him. Tenderly, gently, he laid his palm against her cheek. 'I want to hear what you have to say, my angel. But first I have a question. There is an inscription on the back of the jewel's fastening…do you know what the translation of it is?'

Her smile was instantaneous, but shy. 'I could recite it in my sleep,' she confessed. 'It means *Transcend fear to find the courage to follow your heart and love without reservation*. I know I've had to do just that, Zahir.'

'And my heart echoes it.' Moving his hands to the small, feminine waist he could span with just his hands, Zahir drew Gina towards him, his blood pounding through his veins like a turbulent river as he examined her exquisite features and shining eyes. She was like rare perfume, or some intoxicating elixir that he had inadvertently drunk—he would never get over the effects…*not as long as both of them lived and breathed.*

'Yes, my beloved… For a while I confess that I could not find the courage to love you unreservedly—not as long as I feared losing you. In my confused thinking I thought if I made you my mistress that would be a way of keeping you here, but at the same time I would not have to completely surrender my heart. It was the most colossal self-deception. Having found you again, I realised that to live without you would be the worst pain I could ever envisage. It is simply not an option. From the first moment I saw you, it never was. I love you, Gina. I want you not just because you are an incredibly beautiful and lovely woman and I desire you, I want you as my friend and companion as well as my lover…I want you to be my *wife*.'

Was she dreaming? Gina thought dazedly. Had her longing for this man at last turned her mind to madness? But, no, Zahir's love was blazing down at her like a fierce undaunted sun that would never set. She wanted to bask in that sun for the rest of her life.

'Are you sure, Zahir?' she asked quietly, afraid even at this incredible longed-for moment that she might somehow have misheard or misread him.

His glance was definitely perplexed. 'Am I *sure?*' he echoed in disbelief. 'I have just told the loveliest girl in the world that I want her to be my wife and she asks me that? Of *course* I am sure. Never again will I speak anything but the truth where my feelings for you are concerned.'

'It's just that right now I feel like I've somehow wandered into a dream. Nothing looks remotely the same any more. Everything has a celestial light shining on it. Seeing the jewel at last, and…' She lowered her lashes, overcome with shyness all of a sudden. 'I've dreamt of being with you, of becoming your wife for so long. Since that very first time we met, in fact. I knew then that you were the one I'd been waiting for all my life. But when I came back to Kabuyadir to find that you were ruler of the kingdom, no less… Well, I thought I had been dreaming a dream that was totally impossible. Forget it, I told myself. But I couldn't… I *couldn't*—because I love you so much. You mean the world to me, you know.'

He tipped up her chin so that she could not mistake the love that poured from his eyes…from his *heart* into hers.

'I told you when we first met that I had never felt as strongly about a woman before—as if she were a part of me that I never even knew I had lost until I met her… I still feel that way. In fact the feeling has deepened beyond measuring. But when you came back to Kabuyadir I was a different man from the one who spent that incredible night with you, Gina. After my father died, and then my sister's husband, I lost faith in love. All I seemed able to see was the pain it caused—because if you loved someone it was *beyond* agony when you lost them. I didn't want to suffer that pain again if I could help it. So I thought to bypass love completely. I fooled myself that I could marry purely to make an alliance that would benefit the kingdom. But I was wrong…*so* wrong. Just seeing you again taught me that. There are no words to describe how much your love for me thrills and fulfils me. Of all the things I have achieved it is your love, *rohi*, that will always be my greatest achievement.'

'You have called me that from the beginning…*rohi*. What does it mean, Zahir?'

He pressed a lingering warm kiss to her delectable lips, then gently drew away. 'It means "my soul" and that is what you have become.'

'I love that,' she breathed on a wistful sigh. 'I love the way that word sounds on your lips. I will *always* love it.'

'Well?' Reaching behind her head, Zahir opened the clasp that held her hair back, then threaded his fingers through the silken gold locks that tumbled unhindered onto her shoulders.

'Well, what?'

'I have just asked you to be my wife, have I not? I would very much like to hear your answer.'

'Yes!' Her arms went lovingly and firmly round his waist, and although her tight embrace made him wince because of the still tender wound at his side, Zahir had no intention of asking her to ease it. 'Yes, yes, *yes,*' she uttered passionately. 'A thousand times yes!'

She moved over him in the flickering shadows reflected by the burning candle in the lamp, and her skin was pale as new milk and softer than the finest silk. Zahir released a groan that scraped over gravel as he thrust up high inside her, his sex hardening like hot steel.

'I love you,' he murmured as he filled his hands with her velvet-tipped breasts. 'I love what you do to me… I love how you make me feel.'

Gina's bewitching blue eyes smiled provocatively down at him in the half-light of the Bedouin tent, her unbound hair gleaming gold fire across her pale slender shoulders. 'How *do* I make you feel? Tell me—and you can be as poetic and romantic as you like, my love.'

'Poetry right now is perhaps a tall order.' His aroused grin was rueful. 'But being inside you like this makes me feel like I'm going to die from the sheer pleasure of you, my Sheikha.'

'Sheikha…doesn't that mean the Sheikh's wife?'

'It does.'

'But I'm not your wife yet, Zahir.'

His hands fell to her softly rounded hips and cupped them possessively. 'But you soon will be,' he declared fiercely, emotion making him thrust harder.

'Oh, my…' She shut her eyes, as if to fully absorb the power of their incredibly passionate union, then opened them again to gently rock her hips forward and back. 'I soon will be.'

'And soon after that…' He held her still for several moments, so that he was acquainted with her body more intimately than he had ever believed possible, until he felt every pulse and contraction inside her as though they were his own. They had literally become one—together and indivisible—in a true connection that was not just of the body but of the heart and the spirit, too. The sensation was definitely transcendent.

'Didn't anyone ever tell you to finish your sentences? *Ohh!*' Gina's head fell back as her climax burst upon her, carrying her away to a state of bliss he was eager to join her in. She had never looked more radiant.

'Soon after we are married you will be carrying my child, *rohi*.' Zahir's fingers curled into the soft flesh of her hips as he deliberately kept her exactly where she was. Seconds later his seed spilled hot and unconstrained inside her.

CHAPTER TWELVE

GINA had hardly been able to stop shivering all day. But it was excitement not fear that had given her tremors. From the moment she had seen Zahir in his magnificent black and gold robes, looking like a powerful warrior from ancient times, from the moment she had uttered her vows in taking him as her husband, and from their entry into the palace's grand hall for the reception afterwards, where a huge gathering of friends and extended family waited to greet them, she had been beside herself with joy.

But there was one guest she was anticipating seeing more than anyone else. Her father Jeremy had flown in from London late the night before, and apart from greeting him enthusiastically and making sure he had everything he needed she hadn't really had a chance to talk to him yet.

He had not arrived unaccompanied. With him he had brought his new housekeeper Lizzie Eldridge, and now, when Gina saw him waiting patiently, away from the tight knot of well-wishers and friends who waited to greet the bride and groom, she noticed with a small leap inside her stomach that he was holding the attractive brunette's hand... holding it rather *possessively,* too.

Leaving Zahir's side, Gina rushed over to him. Opening his arms, her father tightly embraced her. *Was that a new aftershave he was wearing?* He looked very smart, dressed in a trim ecru-coloured suit, and his greying hair had had a decent cut, she noticed. Was this Lizzie's doing? Clearly the woman had wrought more changes in his life than simply easing the burden of housework for him. Gina was more than glad. She knew now that she loved her father dearly, and more than anything she wanted the second half of his life to be as fulfilling as the first had been with her mother.

'You look utterly radiant, my darling—like a princess from the court of one of the caliphs,' Jeremy enthused, still gripping her hand when their embrace was over. 'Does your young prince of the desert know how lucky he is?'

Gina gasped as Zahir came up behind her and drew her back against him. She adored it when he held her like that. Sensing his hard, indomitable male strength made her feel safe, loved and protected.

'He does indeed, Professor Collins. Believe me, I count my blessings every day that I have found the greatest love of my life, and I thank you from the bottom of my heart for giving her to me in marriage.'

Flushing a little, the older man smiled. 'Just take good care of her, will you? She means a lot to me...always has and always will. During her growing up I was sometimes remiss in telling her that I loved her, but now that I'm older and wiser, and have realised what a great gift she is, I hope I can make up for that.'

'You will always find a welcome here at the palace,' Zahir told him warmly.

Feeling her throat swell tightly, Gina leaned forward and kissed her father on his cheek. 'I love you, too, Dad... very much.'

When she stepped back, Zahir drew her possessively to his side again, as if staking his claim and saying, *I'm the one who will take care of her now.*

'Many congratulations to you both.'

The expression in Lizzie Elridge's clear grey eyes was a little nervous for a moment, and who could blame her? One minute she was in London, housekeeping for a professor still grieving for his wife, then the next she was in Kabuyadir, at the wedding reception of an imposing sheikh and the very ordinary British girl he incredibly wanted to marry! If Lizzie were in her shoes, she would wonder if she hadn't inadvertently rubbed Aladdin's lamp while she was doing her household chores and conjured up a scene from a fairytale.

'Thank you,' Gina and Zahir replied at the same time.

'And I'd just like to say thanks to you, Lizzie, for helping my dad,' added Gina. 'I feel so much happier being away from him knowing that he has someone like you in his life, helping take care of him.'

'You're more than welcome. Your dad's made such a difference to my life, and my son's, too, Gina. The truth is I never trusted men very much until I met Jeremy, so us getting along so well has been a lovely revelation to me. He's a real gentleman, your dad is.' Beneath the carefully applied blusher she'd applied to her softly plump cheeks Lizzie blushed even more. 'And if you're ever worried about him, please don't hesitate to call me and have a chat.'

'I will.'

'Did you have that sensational outfit specially made?' the older woman asked, politely changing the subject and gently touching her fingers to the red, bronze and burnt ochre-coloured silk skirt and matching jewel-encrusted fitted jacket that made up Gina's bridal dress.

'I did, yes.'

'Well, it's absolutely gorgeous. You look just like a goddess.'

'Thanks, Lizzie... I don't know about a goddess, but I

must admit I feel a little like royalty in this outrageously glamorous ensemble. I've promised my husband I won't let it go to my head!'

'You are allowed to behave like royalty on your wedding day, *rohi.* because that's what you are. And, knowing you, you will very quickly revert back to the shy, unassuming, but secretly *feisty* Gina I adore.'

'Would you call me feisty, Dad?'

'You're your mother's daughter, Gina. Charlotte was a dedicated academic, but that doesn't mean to say that she was boring, or didn't have a temper, or didn't like to have her own way from time to time.'

'Oh…'

'That took the wind out of your sails, my princess, didn't it?' Zahir grinned.

Gina made a face at him.

After that, the couple were drawn away by other patiently waiting well-wishers—first and foremost Farida. For their wedding, and at Zahir's carefully worded request, she had eschewed her familiar black dress for a set of midnight-blue regal robes, and with her elfin face and glossy dark hair caught up high behind her head she was the one, in Gina's eyes, who appeared every inch the royal princess.

'Gina—my dear, dear sister.'

The two women hugged affectionately, and when they broke apart, it was Zahir's turn to be embraced.

'I was wrong about the Heart of Courage, my sister.' He smiled fondly. 'And you were right about it being a blessing all along. I swear to you I will never again think of getting rid of it. In future I will listen to the wisdom of the women in my life where such important matters are concerned, rather than riding roughshod over their opinions.'

'If you do that, my brother, then you will indeed be a truly wise ruler!'

'Pardon me...' A slim, dark-haired man with the most intense ebony eyes presented himself.

'Masoud!' Zahir embraced his friend fondly.

When he was set free again, the man turned his gaze on Gina. 'Your love and beauty have transformed my friend His Highness into the happiest of men.' He smiled. 'I would like to thank you for that. There is no man who deserves the joy you bring more.'

'Thank you, Masoud. I know that your friendship means a lot to Zahir and always will.'

Late into the night, when the party was over and the guests had disbanded, Gina and Zahir drank aromatic coffee with Farida, Gina's father and Lizzie in one of the many beautiful salons that abounded in the palace. Together they reflected on the incredibly happy event that had taken place that day.

Snuggled up next to her new husband on a sumptuous couch, pleasantly tired and secretly longing for the moment when they could retire to bed together, Gina reflected on how happy it had made Zahir to be reacquainted in a much more joyful scenario with his friends Amir and Masoud. He was so loyal and devoted to those he cared about that she was certain they all felt blessed to count him not just as their ruler, but as a firm and constant friend, too.

Seated opposite them in the intimate arrangement of seats, her father leant forward from the gold-coloured embossed couch he shared with Lizzie to address Kabuyadir's handsome and impressive ruler. 'Sheikh Kazeem Khan—' he began politely.

Next to Gina, her husband held up his hand. 'Call me Zahir,' he said. 'You are my father-in-law now, and I do not want formality to be a barrier to our friendship.'

'Zahir,' Jeremy Collins said, an embarrassed little quirk

to his lips, 'I hope I am not being presumptuous by raising the topic right now, but I was wondering if you might in the future consider bringing the Heart of Courage to London. Perhaps to be exhibited in the British Museum? I have no doubt it would excite much interest amongst not only historians and those interested in ancient artefacts but in the general public, too. Especially because of the way it inadvertently brought you and my daughter together.'

'What do you think, Gina?'

She was a little taken aback when her handsome husband asked her opinion. Clearly this was a new side to him that she would have to get used to. He had barely let go of her hand since the ceremony, and even now, as they sat informally with family, he still held it. Glancing into the gaze that definitely reflected the tender feelings of his heart on this most special of all the days since they had met, Gina nodded lightly. 'I agree with my dad that it would definitely excite interest. But the point is…would you be prepared to bring it to London to be shown, Zahir? It is, after all, a family heirloom first and foremost.'

'Why not?' He touched his palm gently to her cheek. 'It might be nice to go to London in a few weeks' time, when it can be arranged. We still haven't reached a solution about a honeymoon because you will not make a decision on where to go.'

'I like it here,' Gina confessed, dimpling, 'I like it so much that I don't want or need to go anywhere else for quite a while.'

'Well, if we go to London you can show me the sights and give me a personal guided tour. When I was at university in Oxford I was too fond of my studies to go there very often. I confess I have a great desire to experience the view from the top of the London Eye.' He turned back to his father-in-law. 'So, my answer to your question is, yes, Jeremy. I *would* be prepared to take the jewel to London.'

Gina and Zahir—accompanied by a sturdily built palace bodyguard—swept by the eager queue that had formed outside the small private gallery where the Heart of Courage was making its much anticipated debut. With her handsome attentive husband holding her hand all the way, Gina felt as if she was on the set of a movie—her role that of the very fortunate heroine, and Zahir's the devastatingly gorgeous and strong hero. Every female in the audience would breathe a collective sigh of longing when they saw him.

The whole scene had a very dreamlike quality to it, but in truth all she had to do was glance up into Zahir's mesmerising dark gaze to learn that it was no dream or illusion. It was real, and it was true.

They had been married for three months now, and every day and night felt like a honeymoon. Every morning when she woke up in their bed, either in the palace or in the beloved Bedouin tent that they continued to visit often, Gina would find some exquisite gift left by her husband on her pillow—each one more beautiful and precious than the last.

Now, as she stood beside him to gaze again at the breathtaking jewel that had brought them together, arranged in pride of place at the centre of a collection of ancient Persian artefacts that included items from both temples and tombs as well as from royal houses, Gina found herself pulled gently against Zahir's side. Dressed in his now familiar robes, his luxuriant hair loose round his powerful shoulders, as he wore it in Kabuyadir, he might have been some dark exotic bird in the middle of an aviary of sparrows, she thought, smiling. Such was his imposing presence. The head curator of the gallery, a tall, slim redhead with glasses, looked as if she'd won the Lottery every time Zahir so much as glanced her way.

When they turned round, there was a bank of photographers, eager to take their pictures—Zahir, Gina and the famous jewel. With no time to prevaricate, Gina tugged her husband's hand to get his attention.

'What is it?' he whispered urgently, his intense dark gaze mirroring faint alarm.

'I'm pregnant.'

'What?'

'I was going to tell you tonight at dinner, but suddenly I...' She felt herself blush hotly. 'Suddenly I just couldn't wait.'

'Are you sure? How long have you known this?'

'I've been having symptoms for a while now, but I didn't want to say anything in case I was wrong. I'm about eleven weeks along...so Dr Saffar thinks.'

'My own physician knew about this before I did?'

'Don't look so put out,' Gina teased, brushing an imaginary speck from the front of his dark blue robes. 'Of course he knew before you. He's *my* doctor as well now—remember?'

Zahir shook his head. He was trying to pretend he was annoyed, but the edges of his well-cut lips kept tugging upwards and betrayed him. 'You are a little minx, giving me this news at such an awkward time.'

'Why is it awkward?'

'Well, if you don't mind me demonstrating my pleasure to you in front of an audience of interested strangers, then just say the word.' He purposefully lowered his head towards her, and there was a distinctly lascivious gleam in his eye.

Gina put her hand against his chest to stop him. 'Perhaps this isn't the best time,' she agreed, feeling suddenly hot.

Zahir's expression turned serious for a moment, prompting her to hurriedly enquire, 'You don't mind…about the baby, I mean?'

'Mind? You know it is the news I have dreamt about hearing ever since you agreed to be my wife—the news every man who loves the woman in his life beyond reason hopes to hear… But you certainly know how to choose your moments, my love!'

'Well…' She let him tug her closer into his side. 'You delight in surprising *me*…now it's my turn. So you're pleased, then?'

She almost held her breath as his glance became serious again. Yes, she knew how much it meant to him for them to have a child together, and wanted it as earnestly as Zahir, but sometimes the doubts of the past would occasionally surface and threaten to take away her happiness. Bit by bit she'd resolved to ignore those doubts and simply dwell on her good fortune instead and be glad.

Zahir was smiling warmly down at her again, and the depth of that incredible smile chased away all Gina's doubts. When her husband utilised that smile it was as though blazing sunshine appeared from behind a bank of stormy grey clouds and lit up the world.

'Pleased?' he answered. 'I am almost speechless with happiness. I just have to take it in for a moment. How you now expect me to give a talk about the Heart of Courage after hearing such news, I do not know.'

'You'll be fine.' Grinning mischievously, Gina stood on tiptoe to plant a tender kiss at the side of his mouth. 'You faced a horde of unruly rebels without a blink… If you can do that then you can easily talk about your family heirloom to a crowd of curious visitors. It'll be a piece of cake!'

'Sheikh Kazeem Khan!' someone called out from

behind them. 'Can we have a picture of you and your lovely sheikha now?'

They turned together to face the sea of flash-popping cameras. Zahir slipped his arm protectively round his wife's still slim waist. 'The sooner we return to Kabuyadir and relative anonymity, the better I will like it,' he whispered low in Gina's ear.

She glanced up at him and her blue eyes were infinitely tender, and somewhat teasing, too. 'Even if you weren't the Sheikh of the kingdom, you couldn't be anonymous if you tried, Zahir. You're far too imposing for that!'

'Imposing, but friendly,' he joked, and kissed her there and then on the lips, for everyone to see...

* * * * *

STRANGERS IN
THE DESERT

LYNN RAYE HARRIS

Lynn Raye Harris read her first romance novel when her grandmother carted home a box from a sale. She didn't know she wanted to be a writer then, but she definitely knew she wanted to marry a sheikh or a prince and live the glamorous life she read about in the pages. Instead, she married a military man and moved around the world. She's been inside the Kremlin, hiked up a Korean mountain, floated on a gondola in Venice and stood inside volcanoes at opposite ends of the world.

These days Lynn lives in North Alabama with her handsome husband and two crazy cats. When she's not writing, she loves to read, shop for antiques, cook gourmet meals and try new wines. She is also an avowed shoeaholic and thinks there's nothing better than a new pair of high heels.

Lynn was a finalist in the 2008 Romance Writers of America's Golden Heart® contest, and she is the winner of the Harlequin® Presents Instant Seduction contest. She loves a hot hero, a heroine with attitude and a happy ending. Writing passionate stories for Mills & Boon is a dream come true.

You can visit her at www.lynnrayeharris.com.

In memory of Sally Jo Harris, beloved aunt-in-law, intrepid adventurer and amazing human being. I can't believe I will never get to talk about books, travel, great coffee and fabulous food with you ever again. You brought joy wherever you went and you left us too suddenly. We miss you.

CHAPTER ONE

"…THE possibility she is still alive."

Adan looked up from the papers his secretary had given him to sign. He'd been only half paying attention to the functionary who'd been speaking. Since his uncle had died a week ago, there'd been so much to do in preparation for his own coronation that he often did as many things at once as he could. "Repeat that," he ordered, every cell of his body revving into high alert.

The man who stood inside the door trembled as Adan focused on him. He bowed his head and spoke to the floor.

"Forgive me, Your Excellency. I said that in preparation for your upcoming nuptials to Jasmine Shadi, we must investigate all reports that reach us in regards to your late wife, since her body was never recovered."

"It was never recovered because she walked into the desert, Hakim," Adan said mildly, though irritation spiked within him. "Isabella is buried under an ocean of sand."

As always, he felt a pang of sadness for his son. Though Adan had lost a wife, it was the fact Rafiq had lost his mother that bothered Adan most. Theirs had been an arranged marriage, not a love match. While he hoped that Isabella had not suffered, he could drag up very little emotion for her.

Isabella Maro had been beautiful, but she'd been unremarkable in every other way. Quiet, lovely and well-suited to performing the duties of their station, she'd been exactly what his wife should have been. And though he hadn't been the heir to the throne then, he had no doubt she'd have made a lovely queen.

A lovely, bland queen.

It wasn't her fault. Though she had been half-American, she'd been raised by her father as a traditional Jahfaran woman. He would never forget that when he'd met her shortly before their wedding, he'd asked her what she wanted out of life. She'd told him that she wanted whatever he wanted.

"There has been a reported sighting, Your Excellency."

Adan gripped the pen he'd been signing papers with and spread his other hand flat on the desk. He needed something solid to hold on to. Something to remind him that he wasn't in the middle of a nightmare. In order to ascend the throne formally, he needed a wife. Jasmine Shadi was to be that wife, and he was marrying her in two weeks time. There was no place in his life for a phantom.

"A *sighting*, Hakim?"

Hakim swallowed. His nut-brown skin glistened with moisture, though the palace had been modernized years ago and the air conditioners seemed to be working fine.

"Sharif Al Omar—a business competitor of Hassan Maro's, Your Excellency—recently returned from a trip to the island of Maui. He says there was a singer in a bar there, a woman who called herself Bella Tyler, who resembled your late wife, sire."

"A singer in a bar?" Adan stared at the man a full minute before he burst into laughter. Isabella had survived the desert and now sang in a bar on a remote Hawaiian island? Impossible. No one ever survived the burning Jahfaran desert if they weren't prepared.

And Isabella had not been prepared. She'd wandered alone into the deepest wastes of Jahfar. At night. A sandstorm the next day had obliterated every trace of her, though they'd looked for weeks. "Hakim, I think Mr. Al Omar needs to see a doctor. Clearly, Hawaiian sunshine is somehow more brutal than our Jahfaran sun."

"He took a picture, sire."

Adan stilled. "Do you have this picture?"

"I do, sire." The man held out a folder. Mahmoud, his secretary, took the file and set it on the desk in front of Adan. He hesitated only a moment before flipping open the cover. Adan stared at the picture for so long that the lines started to blur. It could not be her, and yet...

"Cancel all my appointments for the next three days," he finally said. "And call the airport to ready my plane."

The bar was crowded tonight. Tourists and locals alike jammed into the interior and spilled out the open walls onto the beach below. The sun had just started to dip into the ocean, and the sky was turning brilliant gold when Isabella walked onto the stage and took her place behind the microphone. The sun sank fast—much faster than she'd ever believed possible when she'd first arrived on the island—and then it was gone and the sky was pink, the clouds high over the ocean tinged purple and red with the last rays.

It was a brilliant and beautiful sight, and it always made her heart ache and seem full all at once. She'd grown accustomed to the melancholy, though she did not know from where it sprang. She often felt as if a piece of her was missing, but she didn't know what that piece was.

Singing filled the void, for a brief time anyway.

Isabella looked out at the gathered crowd. They were waiting for *her*. They were here for her. She closed her eyes and began to sing, losing herself in the rhythm and feel of the music. On the stage, she was Bella Tyler—and Bella was completely in control of herself and her life.

Unlike Isabella Maro.

She slid from one song into the next, her voice wrapping around the words, caressing them. The lights were hot, but she was used to the heat. She wore a bikini and a sarong for island flavor, though she did not sing many island songs. Her eyelids felt weighted down beneath the makeup she wore. She always applied it thickly for the stage, or it wouldn't show up in the bright lights. Around her neck she wore a white puka-shell necklace. A matching bracelet encircled one ankle.

Her hair had grown and was no longer twined in the sleek knot she'd once favored. It was heavier, blonder and wild with seawater and sunshine. Her father would be horrified, no doubt, not only at the hair but also at the immodesty of her dress. She smiled into the microphone, thinking of his reaction. A man in the front smiled back, mistaking the gesture. She didn't mind; it was part of the act, part of the personality of Bella Tyler.

Except that Bella wouldn't go home with this man. Or any man. It didn't feel right somehow. Had never felt right since the moment she'd come to the States. She was free now, free from the expectations and duty her father had raised her with, and yet she couldn't shake the idea she had to save herself for someone.

"Bella Tyler, ladies and gentlemen," the guitarist announced when she finished the last song. The bar erupted in applause.

"Mahalo," Isabella said as she shoved a strand of damp hair behind her ear. "And now we're going to take a little break. We'll be back in fifteen."

As she left the stage, she grabbed the glass of water that Grant, the club manager, held out for her, and headed into the back for a few minutes' rest. The room she went to could hardly be called a dressing room, and yet it was where she stowed her stuff and applied her makeup for the evening. She flopped onto a chair and propped her bare feet on a bamboo trunk that served as a coffee table.

Laughter and disembodied voices from the beach came to her through the thin walls. The rest of the band would work their way back here eventually, if they didn't grab a cigarette and head outside to smoke instead. Isabella tilted her head back and touched the icy glass to her collarbone. The coldness of it was a pleasant shock as moisture dripped between her breasts.

A few moments later, she heard movement in the hall. She could sense the moment when someone stopped in the doorway. The room was small, and she could feel that she was no longer alone. But people were always coming and going in Ka Nui's, so she didn't open her eyes to see who it was.

But it wasn't a waitress grabbing something, or one of the band members come to join her, because the person hadn't moved since she'd first sensed a presence.

But was the visitor still there—or was she imagining things?

Isabella's eyes snapped open. A man stood in the entry, his presence dark and overwhelming. Raw panic seized her throat tight so that she couldn't speak or cry out. At first, all she saw was his size—he was tall and broad and filled the door—but then she began to pick out individual features.

A shiver slid down her backbone as she realized with a jolt that he was Jahfaran. Dark hair, piercing dark eyes and skin that had been burnished by the powerful desert sun. Though he was dressed in a navy blue shirt and khaki pants instead of a *dishdasha,* he had the look of the desert, that hawklike intensity of a man who lived life on the edge of civilization. She didn't know why, but fear flooded her in waves, liquefying her bones until she couldn't move.

"You will tell me," he said tightly, *"why."*

Isabella blinked. "Why?" she repeated. Somehow, she managed to scramble to her feet. He was so tall that she still had to tilt her head back to look up at him. Her heart thundered in her breast as she realized he was terribly, frighteningly angry.

With her.

His gaze skimmed down her body. When his eyes met hers again, they burned with disgust. "Look at you," he said. "You look like a prostitute."

The cold fear that had pooled in her stomach began to boil as anger stirred within. How typical of a Jahfaran male. How absolutely typical to think he had a right to criticize her simply because she was female, and because he did not understand her choices.

Isabella drew herself up. She thrust her chin out, propped her hands on her hips and gave him the same thorough once-over he'd given her. It was bold, but she didn't care. She owed this man nothing.

"I don't know who you think you are, but you're welcome to get the hell out of my dressing room and keep your opinions to yourself."

His expression grew lethally cold. "Don't play games with me, Isabella."

She took a step back, her pulse thrumming in her throat at breakneck speed. He'd used her name—her given name—and it stunned her, though perhaps it should not have. Clearly, he knew her father, and he'd recognized her somehow. Perhaps they'd met in the course of her father's business dealings. A party, a dinner…

But no. She didn't recognize him. And she was sure that she'd never have forgotten a man like this if she'd met him. He was too big, too magnificent—and much too full of himself. He would have been impossible to ignore.

"Why would I play games with you? I don't even know you!"

His eyes narrowed. "I will know how you came to be here, and I will know it *now*."

Isabella drew herself up. How dare he question her as if he had a right? "You're bright. Figure it out."

He took a step into the room, and the room shrank. He overwhelmed the space. He overwhelmed her.

Isabella wanted to back away from him, but there was nowhere to go. And she would not cower before this man. It seemed vitally important somehow that she did not.

"You did not do this alone," he said. "Who helped you?"

Isabella swallowed. "I—"

"Is everything okay here, Bella?"

Her eyes darted past the stranger to Grant, who stood in the door, his fists clenched at his sides. The stranger had turned at his entrance. Grant's expression was grave, his blue eyes deadly serious as he tried to stare the man down.

She could have told him it wouldn't work. The man stared back at Grant, his expression not softening in the least. The last thing she wanted was a fight, because she did not doubt that Grant would try to defend her. She also didn't doubt that he would lose. There was something hard and cold about this man. Something fierce and untamed.

"I'm fine, Grant," she said. "Mr...um, the gentleman was just leaving."

"I was not, in fact," he said, his English oh-so-perfect. The cultured tone of his voice proclaimed him to be from an elite family, the ones who usually sent their sons to be schooled in the United Kingdom.

"I think you should go," Grant said. "Bella needs to rest before she goes back on."

"Indeed." The stranger turned back to her then, and she felt the full force of his laserlike attention. "Sadly, she will not be returning to the stage. Isabella is coming with me."

Fury pounded through her. "I am *not*—"

He reached out and grasped her arm with an iron fist.

His fingers didn't bite into her, but they were firm and in control. Commanding.

Shock forced Isabella to go completely still as her body reacted with a shudder at the touch of his skin on hers.

But it wasn't revulsion she felt. It wasn't terror.

It was familiarity. It was heat and want and, underlying that, a current of sadness so deep and strong she wanted to sob.

It stunned her into immobility as she tried to process it.

Why?

"Hey," Grant protested. "Let her go!"

At the same time, Isabella looked up in confusion. "Who *are* you?"

A shadow passed over his face before it hardened again. "Do you really expect me to believe you do not know?"

Anger and despair slashed through her in waves. It made no sense. And yet he hated her. This man *hated* her, and she had no idea why. Somehow, she found the strength to act, wrenching herself free from his grip.

Isabella hugged her arms around her torso as if to shield herself. She couldn't bear to feel the anger and sadness ripping through her a moment longer. Couldn't bear the currents of heat arcing across her nerve endings. The swirling confusion. The crushing desperation.

Grant had disappeared, but she knew it was so he could fetch one of the bouncers. He'd be back at any moment, and this man would be thrown out on his arrogant behind. She was going to enjoy that.

"Of course I don't know you," she snapped.

"On the contrary," he growled, his dark eyes flashing hot, "you know me *very* well."

Her heart pounded at the certainty in his voice. He was insane. Gorgeous, but insane. "I can't imagine why you would think so."

"Because," he replied, his voice laced with barely contained rage, "you are my *wife*."

CHAPTER TWO

SHE gaped at him like a fish. There was no other way
to describe it. If he didn't know better, he'd think she
truly was shocked. Adan's mouth twisted. Who'd have
thought that little Isabella Maro was such a fine actress?
He'd had no idea, or he'd have paid her much closer
attention.

Because, clearly, she'd duped him. Duped them all.

And he was going to find out why.

She hadn't acted alone, of that he was certain. Had
she had a lover who'd helped her to escape?

The thought lodged in his gut like a shard of ice.

What a cold, cruel woman she was. She'd abandoned
her baby son, left him to grow up motherless. She'd
cared more for herself than she had for Rafiq.

Adan hated her for it.

And he hated this stirring in his blood as he looked
at her. It was anger, yes, but it was something more, as
well. His gaze slid over her nearly naked body. She was
wearing a red bikini with a tropical-print sarong tied
over one hip. Her nipples jutted through the meager
fabric of her top, drawing his attention. He remembered,
though he did not wish to, the creamy beauty of her
breasts, the large pink areolas, the tightly budded nipples

in their center. He remembered her shyness the first time they'd made love, the way she'd quickly adapted to him, the way she'd welcomed him into her bed for an entire month of passionate nights.

He'd stopped going to her bed because she'd fallen pregnant. Not because he had wanted to, but because she'd become so sick that lovemaking was out of the question.

"Your wife?" She shook her head adamantly. "You're mistaken."

Behind him, he heard the heavy stomp of footsteps. And then the man she'd called Grant—the man who'd looked at her with his heart in his eyes—was back, a large Samoan by his side.

"I'll ask you once more to leave," Grant said. "Makuna will escort you out."

Adan gave them his most quelling look. He had a six-man security team outside. Not because he'd expected trouble, but because he was a head of state and didn't travel without security. One signal to them, and they would storm this place with guns drawn.

It wasn't something he wanted to do, and yet he wasn't leaving without Isabella. Without his wife.

"It's okay, Grant," he heard her say behind him. "I'll talk to him for a few minutes."

Grant looked confused. But then he nodded once and tapped Makuna on the arm. The two of them melted away from the door, and Adan was once more alone with Isabella.

"Wise decision," he said.

She sank onto the chair she'd originally been sitting in. Her fingers trembled as they shoved her riot of dark golden hair from her face. Her heavily made-up eyes stared at him in confusion.

"Why would you think I'm your wife? I've never been married."

Anger clawed at his insides. "Deny it all you like, but it won't make it any less true."

Her brows drew down as she stared at him. "I don't know why you're telling me this, or why you think I'm your wife. I've never met you. I don't even know your name."

He didn't believe it for a moment. "Adan," he said, because arguing about it was pointless when she insisted on carrying through with her fiction.

"Adan," she repeated. "I left Jahfar a long time ago. I think I'd remember a husband."

"I won't play this game with you, Isabella," he growled. "Do you really expect me to believe you don't remember? How stupid do you think I am?"

She frowned deeply. "I never said that. I said I didn't know you. I think you've confused me with someone else. It's not unusual for men to try and get close to me in this business. They see me sing and they think I'm available for an easy hookup. But I'm not, okay?"

Adan wanted to shake her. "You are Isabella Maro, daughter of Hassan Maro and an American woman, Beth Tyler. Nearly three years ago, you and I were wed. Two years ago, you walked into the desert and were never seen again."

He couldn't bring himself to mention Rafiq to her, not when she was so obviously trying to play him for a fool.

She blinked, her expression going carefully blank. And then she shook her head. "No, I…"

"What?" he prompted when she didn't continue.

She swallowed. "I had an accident, it's true. But I've recovered." Her fingers lifted to press against her lips. He noticed they were trembling. "There are things that are fuzzy, but—" She shook her head. "No, someone would have told me."

Everything inside him went still. "Someone? Who would have told you, Isabella? Who knows you are here?"

She met his gaze again. "My parents, of course. My father sent me to my mother's to recover. The doctor said I needed to get away from Jahfar, that it was too hot, too…stressful."

Fury whipped through him. And disbelief. Her parents knew she was alive? Impossible.

And yet, he'd hardly seen Hassan Maro since Isabella had disappeared. The man spent more time out of the country these days than he did in it. Adan had chalked it up to his business interests and to grief over the loss of his only daughter, but what if it were more? What if Maro were hiding something?

Was the man truly capable of helping his daughter to escape her marriage when he'd been so thrilled with the arrangement in the first place?

Adan shook his head. She was lying, playing him, denying what she knew to be true simply because she'd been caught. She'd survived the desert, there was no doubt, and she could not have done so without help.

But whose help?

"I have never heard of selective amnesia, Isabella," he growled. "How could you remember your parents, remember Jahfar—yet not remember me?"

"I didn't say I had amnesia!" she cried. "You did."

"What do you call it, then, if you say you know who you are and where you come from, but you can't remember the husband you left behind?"

"We're not married," she insisted—and yet her lower lip trembled. It was the first sign of a small chink in her armor, as if she knew she'd been caught and was desperate to escape.

Adan hardened his resolve. She would not do so, not until he was finished with her. She had much to answer for. And much still to pay for.

She clasped her hands in front of her body. The motion pressed her breasts together, emphasized the smooth, plump curves. A tingle started at the base of his spine and drifted outward.

No.

Adan ruthlessly clamped down on his libido. Was he so shallow as to allow the sight of a woman's half-naked body to arouse him, when the woman was as treacherous as this one? When he had every reason to despise her?

"Let's turn this around, then," she said, worrying her bottom lip with her teeth. "Assuming for a moment that you're correct, that we *are* married—where have you been and why didn't you come for me sooner?"

"I have been in Jahfar," he ground out. "And, as you very well know, I believed you to be dead."

Her face grew pale beneath her tan. "Dead?"

He was tired of this, tired of the caginess and obfuscation. He'd flown through several time zones and had had no sleep in his quest to learn if the picture were true, if the woman holding a microphone and peering up at the camera as if to a secret lover was indeed his wife. He'd told himself it wasn't possible. She could not have survived.

But then he'd walked into this bar and seen her standing there, her face so familiar and so strange all at once, and he'd known the truth.

And he was done being civil. "You walked into the *desert,* Isabella. What you did after that is anyone's guess, but you did not come back out. We searched for weeks."

She shook her head. "It's insane, absolutely insane."

"Is it?" Adan tucked his hand under her elbow and pulled her out of the chair. She rose surprisingly easily, as if she were distracted. He pointedly ignored the current of electricity that zapped through him when he touched her bare skin.

She looked up at him, her dark, smoky eyes full of emotion. "I don't remember."

He would not be moved. "Gather your things. We're leaving."

Married.

Isabella shook her head. It was impossible. But a knot of fear lodged in her stomach like a lump of ice. She had a few fuzzy spots in her memory, it was true, and yet, how could this man be a part of it? How could she possibly forget something as *monumental* as a husband?

She could not. It was out of the question. Besides, her parents would not have kept this from her. Why would they do so? What terrible thing would make them do so?

There was one way to clear this up. Isabella turned and grabbed her purse, digging through it for her cell phone.

"What are you doing?" Adan asked.

She whipped the phone out and held it up triumphantly.

Her hair was in her eyes, stuck to the lipstick on her mouth, but she didn't care. She knew she looked wild. She felt wild.

Crazy.

He'd said she was dead—that everyone in Jahfar believed she was dead.

But her father knew she wasn't, so how could that be?

When she'd asked questions about her accident, he'd told her it was better if she did not know the specifics. She'd been in a wreck, and she'd fallen into a coma. There were drugs, pain meds, and they were making her memory fuzzy. It was nothing, he'd insisted.

Nothing.

Her mother, typically, hadn't known anything about what Isabella's life in Jahfar had been like. Beth Tyler had been gone from the country for ten years, and though she'd seemed pleased when Isabella came to stay with her, they'd both been a little relieved when Isabella had moved on.

But if she'd been married, wouldn't her mother have known about it? Wouldn't she have attended the wedding?

Now, Isabella looked up, into the hard, handsome face of the man standing so near. He didn't look like *nothing* to her. Isabella gave her head a little shake. No, her parents would *not* have lied about this. There was no reason for it!

"I'm calling my father," she said as she began to scroll through the phone's contacts. "He'll know the truth."

Adan stiffened as if she'd slapped him. "Do you

mean to tell me that your father really does know you're here?"

Isabella frowned. "I already said so, didn't I?"

He swore in Arabic, a vile curse that shocked her with its vehemence and profanity. She'd been in the States for more than a year now—was it closer to two?—and she'd heard a lot of foul language. But she wasn't accustomed to hearing it in Arabic. In Jahfar, she'd been cosseted and protected—a lady who had been bred to marry a powerful sheikh someday.

Until her accident changed everything.

He grabbed the phone out of her hand. "You will not call him."

Isabella reached for the phone, but he held it just out of range. She folded her arms and glared at him. She should be relieved. "Then I guess you're lying to me about being married. Because my father could expose the lie, right?"

"If it amuses you to think it, by all means do so." He tucked the phone into his breast pocket. She tried not to let her gaze stray to the hard muscle exposed by the open V of his shirt. If she'd seen him on the beach, she'd have thought he was magnificent. No doubt about it.

But he was hard and cold, and she had no business finding him attractive. Not to mention, he was lying.

"If that's not what you're worried about, then why can't I call him?" she challenged.

"Because I intend to deal with him myself, when we return to Jahfar."

Isabella's blood ran cold for reasons she couldn't begin to articulate. Jahfar. The desert. The hard, harsh landscape of her father's heritage. It was her heritage, too, and yet there was something primitive about it that she couldn't quite make her peace with. The idea of going back caused a wave of panic to rise like bile in her throat.

"I'm not going with you."

His dark eyes slid down her body, back up again. "And just how do you propose to stop me from taking you, Isabella?"

"I'll scream," she said, her heart thudding a million miles an hour.

"Will you now?" He was so cool, so smug, that a knot of fear gathered in her stomach and refused to let go. He would throw her over his shoulder and haul her bodily out of here. He was big enough and bold enough to do it.

"They won't let you take me. My friends will help," she said with as much bravado as she could muster.

His laugh was not in the least bit amused. "They are welcome to try. But Isabella, I have my own personal security. If anyone touches me, they will assume it is an assassination attempt. I cannot be responsible for the measures they might take."

Ice coated the chambers of her heart. He was every bit as cold and cruel as he seemed. And she had no doubt he would take delight in hurting anyone who attempted to stop him.

"It's no wonder I can't remember you," she said bitterly. "You're a tyrant. Being married to you would be hell on earth, I'm sure. Any woman would do better walking into the desert to die than staying with you."

The corners of his mouth tightened. "Would to God that you had truly done so and saved me the trouble of dealing with you now."

She couldn't say why, but her heart constricted. Why

did she care? He meant nothing to her. She didn't even like him.

"*If* we are married, then why don't you save us both a lot of trouble and divorce me? You're a Jahfaran male. The power is yours," she said as coldly as she could.

Would to God that you had truly done so and saved me the trouble…

His cruel words echoed in her head. She meant nothing to him. She was a problem, an embarrassment. An issue to be dealt with.

It was too much like her childhood, when she'd felt like an object that her parents fought over after the divorce. An issue they would never solve. She'd tried to be good, tried to be so good and perfect for them both. But she could not please them, no matter how she tried.

Isabella swallowed angry tears. She was finished with trying to please anyone but herself.

"If only it were that easy," he growled. "But circumstances have changed, and we must return to Jahfar."

"You can't simply expect me to leave with you when you've given me no proof. To me, you're a stranger. I don't know you, and I'm not going anywhere with you."

His eyes hardened. "What proof would you have me give you? Shall I tell you that we met only a week before we married, and that you were as frightened and meek as a lamb? Or perhaps you'd like to hear that the wedding feast went on for three days and cost in excess of a half-million American dollars? Or that your father was supremely pleased that he'd managed to wed you to a prince?"

Isabella's stomach went into a free fall. "A prince? You're a prince?"

"I was," he said, and though she didn't know what he meant by that, she didn't ask.

She wiped damp palms across her sarong. It simply couldn't be true. Status was everything in Jahfar. If her father had managed to arrange a marriage with the royal family, he'd have been so proud. He would not have lied about it.

"Tell me something about me," she said, apprehension fluttering inside her belly along with the first swirling current of doubt. "Tell me something no one else knows."

"You were a virgin."

She stamped down on the blush that threatened. *Was* a virgin? "That wouldn't have been a secret. Tell me something I might have told you, something personal."

He flung his hands wide in exasperation. "Such as? You weren't very talkative, Isabella. I believe you once said that your single goal in life was to please *me*."

"That's ridiculous," she answered, her voice little more than a whisper. Because she *had* been raised to please a man, to be the perfect wife, and it was exactly the sort of thing she would have been expected to say. But to actually have said it? To *this* man?

"Enough," he said, slashing a hand in the air before reaching into his khakis and pulling out a cell phone. "We are leaving."

"Wait just a damn minute," Isabella cried, closing the distance between them and grabbing his wrist before he punched the buttons. He wasn't *listening* to her, and she wasn't about to meekly accept his decree.

Heat sizzled into her where she gripped him. So much heat. Her fingers couldn't span his wrist.

He gazed down at her with glittering dark eyes. His

sensual mouth was flat, hard. She wondered what he looked like when he smiled. Black stubble shadowed his jaw, so sexy and alluring that she wanted to reach up and feel the roughness against her palm.

His gaze settled on her mouth, and she suddenly had a picture in her head of him kissing her. The image was shocking. And she didn't know whether it was a memory or a desire.

Yet her body responded to the very real longing it called up, softening, melting, aching. The moment spun out between them until she felt as if they must have been standing this way for hours.

He swore softly in Arabic, and then he broke her grip on his wrist and tangled both his hands in her hair. Something dropped and hit the woven rug beneath their feet. Her heart thundered in her chest, her throat. He took a step closer until he was inside her space, dominating her space. She wanted to pull away, and yet she couldn't do so. She didn't like men who tried to dominate her—

And yet…

And yet…

Hands still tangled in her hair, he tugged her head back, exposing the column of her throat. He was so much taller than she was. She should feel vulnerable and afraid, but she did not.

"See if you *remember* this," he growled.

His head descended and her eyes dropped closed without conscious thought. He was going to kiss her, and she realized with complete shock that she wanted it. How could she want it when she didn't even like him?

But she did. And she knew she would hate herself for the weakness later.

His mouth didn't claim hers, however. Instead, she felt the touch of his lips—those hard, sensual lips—in the tender hollow of her throat. She gasped as sensation rocked her, throbbed deep in her core.

His tongue traced the indent of her collarbone. He pulled her head back farther, forcing her to arch her body against his. Her breasts thrust into his chest, into the warmth and solidity of him. Her nipples were aching peaks against the thin cups of her bikini. Surely, he knew it, too. She was embarrassed—and not embarrassed.

Her hands tangled in the silk of his shirt, clinging for dear life as his mouth moved up her throat, his kisses stinging her with need.

And then he claimed her mouth. She opened to him, let him sink into her, met him as an equal. The ache inside her chest was new, and not new. She thrust away thoughts of a possible past she couldn't remember and tried to focus on the now.

On the way he kissed her as if she was the only woman in the world. The heat between them was incredible. Had she really been chilled only moments ago? Because now she wanted to tear at the layers of clothes between them, to remove all barriers, to quench this fire the only way it could be quenched: by opening her body to him, by joining with him until the fire burned itself out.

If what he said were true, then how many times had they begun just like this? How many times had they lost themselves in each other's embrace after a scorching kiss? She couldn't ever remember being with this man—being with any man—and yet her body knew. Her body *knew*.

One hand left her hair, spanned her rib cage, his

fingers brushing beneath her breast. She couldn't stop the little moan that escaped her as he gently pinched her nipple through the fabric. The sweet spike of pleasure shot through her, connecting to her center. Liquid heat flooded her, so foreign and familiar all at once.

She became aware of something else then, as her body ached for more touching, more soft exploration. Of something thick and hard pressing into her abdomen. The first ribbon of unease rippled inside her. This couldn't be a good idea.

She couldn't give herself to him. She simply couldn't. She'd already let it go too far.

She should have never touched him. She didn't understand it, but it had been like setting a match to dry tinder.

She could feel an answering change in him, as if he too were confused and wary about what was happening between them. Before she could push him away, he stepped back, breaking the contact between their bodies.

The loss of his mouth on hers was almost a physical pain. She wanted to reach for him, pull him back, but she would not do so. She could not ever do so.

He looked completely unaffected as he bent to pick up his phone from where he'd dropped it when he'd shoved his hands into her hair.

Her lips tingled, her skin sizzled and her breathing wasn't quite the same as before he'd kissed her.

"Why did you do that?" she asked, her voice thick. It would have been so much easier if he had not.

He looked at her then, his golden skin so beautiful, his eyes still hot as they slipped over her. How many women had melted under the force of that gaze? How many had taken one look at that face and body and burned with need?

Hundreds. Thousands.

Her included.

"Because you wanted me to," he said.

She shook her head to deny it, but stopped abruptly. What would be the point? She *had* wanted him to kiss her. But she knew what it felt like now, and she would never be so weak again. "Now that you have, I'd like you to go," she said firmly.

"You and I both know that's not going to happen, Isabella."

Isabella drew in a sharp breath. The man had a hearing problem. "You can't force me to return to Jahfar. I'm an American citizen, and there are laws here that prevent such things."

He looked so coolly elegant, in spite of his casual clothing, in spite of the way she'd crushed his shirt in her fists and wrinkled the fine silk.

"Nevertheless, you will go—"

"There's no reason," she insisted.

"There is every reason!" he thundered, the fine edge of his temper bared at last. "You will cease being so selfish, Isabella. You will do this for Rafiq, if for no other reason."

Isabella hugged herself as a river of ice water poured down her spine. She was tired and confused and ready for this to be over. "I'm sorry you think I'm being selfish, but I've told you the truth. I don't know you. And I don't know who Rafiq is, either."

Adan's eyes were so cold in his handsome face. Like black ice as he gazed at her with unconcealed contempt. He was angrier than she'd yet seen him.

He pronounced the next words very precisely, each one carefully measured, each one like a blow to her subconscious as the full effect landed on her with the force of a sandstorm whipping through a purple Jahfaran sky.

"Rafiq is our son."

CHAPTER THREE

THE interior of Adan's private jet was sumptuous, but Isabella hardly noticed. She'd been in shock since the moment he'd told her they had a child. It had felt as if someone was slicing into her heart with a rusty knife. How could she have given birth to a child and not know it?

It was surreal.

But as much as her mind kept telling her that everything he said was impossible, her heart whispered doubts. Her heart said that something had happened to her two years ago, and that a car wreck didn't explain it nearly as well as she would like.

She'd gone with him then. She'd let him take her back to her condo where she'd packed a suitcase and called the landlord to tell him she would be gone for a couple of weeks. Adan had stood by impassively, not saying a word as she'd readied herself. He'd looked around the small living space as if it were completely foreign to him. As if he were horrified she would live there.

Which, she supposed, he probably was. He was a prince of Jahfar. Princes did not live in studios that weren't much bigger than a large shoebox.

They'd ridden to the airport in silence, then boarded

the sleek Boeing business jet and taken off shortly thereafter. Now they were somewhere high over the Pacific Ocean, and Isabella sat in a large reclining leather chair and stared out the window at nothing but blackness. On a small table in front of her was an untouched glass of papaya juice. She shivered involuntarily. She'd put on a pair of jeans and a T-shirt and grabbed a light jacket, but still she was cold.

"Would you like a blanket, ma'am?" one of the flight attendants asked.

"Thank you, yes," Isabella replied. Her voice sounded scratchy, distant, as if she weren't accustomed to using it. The attendant returned with the blanket and a pillow. Isabella wrapped herself in the plush fabric. This wasn't one of those cheap excuses for a blanket used on major airlines these days. It was thick and soft and smelled like spice.

A few moments later, Adan sank into the chair across from her. She hadn't seen him since shortly after they'd gotten airborne. He'd said he had business to attend to and had disappeared into his private office. Now, he clutched a sheaf of papers. His gaze was disturbing. She wasn't sure if it was because of the kiss they'd shared in Ka Nui's, or simply because he caused something to tighten inside her every time he looked at her.

Or maybe it was because he despised her.

"You haven't touched your drink," he said.

"I'm not thirsty." She dropped her gaze, conscious suddenly that she was still wearing heavy stage makeup. She hadn't thought to wash her face in the rush to grab her suitcase and change clothes. He hadn't rushed her, but she'd felt as if she had to hurry. As if the answers were thousands of miles away and she needed to get there as soon as possible.

"I thought you might like to see these," he said, holding out the papers.

She took them cautiously, not really certain she did want to see them, but knowing she had no choice but to look. For herself. For her sanity. Not because he was forcing her to, but because she needed to know.

Her heart began to thrum.

She looked at the first sheet. It was an article from *Al-Arab Jahfar*.

Prince Weds Daughter of Prominent Businessman.

There was a photo of her and Adan. He was so handsome in his traditional clothing, with a ceremonial dagger at his waist. He looked solemn, as if he were performing a duty.

Which he no doubt had been. *We met a week before the wedding...*

She was smiling, but she didn't look happy. Her dress was a beaded silk *abaya* in a deep saffron color. She wore the sheerest *hijab*, the fabric filmy and beautiful where it skimmed her hair.

She glanced up, saw Adan watching her closely. He was sprawled in his chair like a potentate, one elbow propped on the armrest, his index finger sliding absently back and forth over his bottom lip. His dark eyes gave nothing away.

Isabella slid the article to the bottom of the pile. The next one sent her heart into her throat.

It was a birth announcement. Rafiq ibn Adan Al Dhakir, born April fourth.

Tears pressed against the backs of her eyes. She wanted to sob. She bit her lip, hard, to stop the tears from coming. She wanted to shove the papers at him and tell him to take them away, but gritted her teeth and told herself she would do this. She would look at them and she would survive it.

Because everything she'd known, everything she'd believed—about herself, about her parents—was shattered and lying broken at her feet. She wasn't who she thought she was.

She was this woman, this Princess Isabella Al Dhakir, who had a baby and a husband. Who should have had a perfect life, but who was sitting here broken and alone.

She uncovered the next article with trembling fingers.

This one proclaimed her missing. From her father's house, where she'd gone to visit after the birth of her child. Evidence suggested she'd walked into the desert. A sandstorm had stopped the rescue effort for three days. When it resumed, there was no trace of her.

She thought of her father's house at the edge of the wilds of Jahfar. He loved to tame nature. He had a pool, fountains and grass on the edge of the hottest, starkest land imaginable.

And she had willingly walked alone into that desert?

The fourth article made the numbness creep over her again. It was small, a quarter sheet, the words stark against the white background.

Dead...

She quickly flipped to the next page. A marriage

contract, spelling out everything her father and Adan had agreed to. She didn't read it. She didn't need to.

She closed her eyes and dropped the papers on the table between them, then clasped her hands in her lap so he wouldn't see them shaking. She was his wife. The mother of his child.

And she couldn't remember any of it. Isabella tried so hard to conjure up an image of a baby in her arms, but she couldn't do it.

What was wrong with her? How could a mother forget her own baby? She turned her head away on the seat back and dug her fingernails into her palms. She would not cry. She could not cry in front of him. She couldn't be weak.

"Do you still wish to deny the truth?" Adan asked.

She shook her head, unable to speak for fear she would lose control.

"Why did you do it, Isabella? Why did you leave your baby son? Did you not think of him even once?"

It took her several moments to answer.

"I don't remember doing it," she forced out, her voice barely more than a whisper. "I don't remember anything about that...that night. In the newspaper."

She thought he wouldn't believe her, that he would demand to know the truth, demand she stop lying. But he blew out a breath and looked away before turning to pierce her with his dark stare again. "Tell me what you do know, then. Tell me how you got to Hawaii."

She wanted to be defiant, but she was too mentally drained to conjure up even a hint of strength. "I was in Jahfar, and then I was at my mother's house in South Carolina," she said, hugging the blanket tighter. "I don't remember when I left, or how I got there. My father says it's because of the accident. Because I hit my head in the crash and was in a coma for five weeks. I don't remember the accident, but the doctor said that was normal.

"After, I spent time recuperating at my mother's before I moved out on my own."

"You didn't want to return to Jahfar?"

"No, not really. I thought of it from time to time, but my father told me to stay in the States. He said he traveled a lot now, and there was no reason for me to return yet."

"Hawaii is rather far from South Carolina," he mused.

It was, and yet she'd been pulled there by homesickness. "I missed the sea, and the palms. I went there for a short vacation but ended up staying."

"Why did you change your name?"

"I didn't change it. Bella Tyler is a stage name," she said, not wanting to admit that she'd wanted to be someone else, that calling herself by another name had been an effort to make her feel different. More confident. Less alone.

"And why were you singing in a club, Isabella? Did you need money?"

He no doubt thought so based on the size of her condo, but it was perfectly adequate for Maui. And more expensive than he might imagine.

"No. My father sent me plenty. But I sang karaoke one day, for fun. The next I knew, I was performing."

A disapproving frown made his sensual mouth seem hard. "A lounge singer."

Isabella felt heat prickle over her skin. "I *like* to sing.

I've always liked to sing. And I'm good at it," she said proudly.

"I never heard you sing before tonight."

"I sang plenty growing up, but it was for myself. If I never sang for you, then I suppose I was afraid to. Afraid you would disapprove."

"I might not have," he said softly.

"I must have thought so."

"Perhaps you did." He was unapologetic.

Isabella clutched the blanket in a fist. This was such an odd conversation. She was married to this man, and yet he was a stranger to her. They were strangers to each other, if this conversation was anything to go by.

"We must not have spent a lot of time together," she ventured.

"Enough," he said, his eyes suddenly hot, intense.

Isabella dipped her head, hoping she wasn't blushing. Clearly she wasn't a virgin, and yet she couldn't remember anything about her first sexual experience with him. About *any* sexual experience with him.

"How long were we married before…the baby?"

"You were pregnant the first month. And you disappeared only a month after Rafiq was born."

She pressed a hand to her stomach beneath the blanket. It was so hard to imagine she'd ever been pregnant. "So we weren't together a year."

He gave his head a shake. "Not quite, no."

She was trying so hard to process it. Because they *were* married. He hadn't faked a bunch of documents to prove it to her. These were printed copies of actual newspaper articles.

Far more likely—and harder to understand, quite honestly—was the fact her parents had lied. Oh, she didn't really expect that her mother had orchestrated this fiction Isabella had been living with—or that she'd had a problem going along with it. No, it was her father who'd done so.

And Isabella couldn't figure out why.

Was Adan abusive? Had her hurt her? Was her father simply being protective?

She considered it, but she didn't believe that was the case. Because Adan had been very angry with her, yes, and he'd been arrogant and presumptuous. But he hadn't for one moment made her feel physically threatened. If he had, she wouldn't be here.

Or at least not willingly.

She was uncomfortable with him—but not because she feared him.

Isabella pressed two fingers to her temple. It was so much to process.

"Does your head hurt?" Adan asked suddenly.

She was surprised at the answer. "Yes." She'd been so focused that she hadn't realized her temple was beginning to throb. Soon, the headache would spread to the other side. And she'd left her migraine medicine on the kitchen counter. She didn't get them often, but when she did, they weren't in the least bit pleasant.

Adan pressed a button on his seat and a flight attendant appeared. He ordered a glass of water and some ibuprofen. When it arrived, she gulped down the tablets, though she didn't expect they would do any good.

"Perhaps you should sleep," he said. "There's a bedroom at the back, and a bathroom where you can wash your face."

She should sleep, and yet she couldn't quite yet. "Do you have a picture of him?" she asked quietly.

The corners of his mouth grew tight. Then he pulled out his cell phone and pressed a few buttons. When he held it out to her, the breath caught in her throat.

The little boy staring at the camera was adorable, of course. But it was more than that. She gazed at his face in wonder, searching for signs of her own features. She saw Adan easily in the dark hair and dark eyes. But the chin, that was hers. And the shape of the nose.

A tear slipped free and slid down her cheek. "He's two now?"

Adan nodded as he took the phone back. She wasn't ready to stop looking at the photo, and yet she couldn't ask him to let her see it again.

She'd missed so much. So damn much. His first word. His first step. She scrubbed a hand across her face. Her head throbbed. Her stomach churned. She wasn't sure if it was the headache or the heartache causing it, but she felt physically ill.

Isabella shot to her feet. Adan rose with the grace of a hunting panther, his brows drawn together. "What is wrong?"

"I have to—the bathroom."

Adan pointed and Isabella bolted for the door. She made it just in time, heaving the contents of her stomach into the toilet. When she finally straightened, she caught sight of her face in the mirror. She looked like hell. Like a girl who'd got into her mother's makeup and put way too much on in an effort to look more grown-up.

Isabella turned on the taps—bronze taps on an airplane, so much fancier than the usual airline bathroom— and began to scrub her face with hot water and soap. The tears started to flow as she scrubbed. She tried to stop it at first, but then decided to let herself cry. He would never hear her with the water running.

She scrubbed hard, as if she could scrub away the past two years and clean her memory free of the black curtain cloaking it at the same time. Her head continued to pound, but she cried and scrubbed until the makeup was gone and her tears were finished.

She hoped Adan would be gone by the time she returned to her seat—in his office, or sleeping in one of the staterooms—but she wasn't that lucky.

He looked up as she approached. His expression didn't change, but she was certain he hadn't missed a thing. She looked like hell. Her face was pink and her eyes, though not puffy yet, soon would be from the crying.

"You are ill?" he asked.

"It's the migraine," she replied, shrugging. "If I have my medicine, it doesn't get that bad, but without it…"

"You did not bring this medicine, I take it."

"I was a bit preoccupied."

"Tell me the name of this drug," he commanded. "It will be waiting for you when we arrive in Jahfar."

She said the name, then folded herself back into the reclining chair.

"You should lie down on a bed."

She waved a hand. "I'd rather not walk that far right now, if you don't mind."

He rose, and before she knew what he was about to do, he'd come around to her chair and reached for her. She started to protest, but her head hurt too badly to put up much of a fight as she was lifted against his chest.

He was warm, hard and so solid. She felt safe for the first time in years. *Safe*.

And yet it was an illusion. Now, more than ever, she needed to guard herself against emotion. Because she was emotionally raw right now, vulnerable.

She felt so much. *Too much.*

She could feel his heart beating strong beneath the palm she'd rested on his chest, could smell the delicious spicy male scent of him. He carried her toward the back of the plane and into a room that contained a double-size bed. The sheets were folded down already, and the lights were dim. Heaven for her throbbing head.

He set her on the bed and she lay back, uncaring that she wore jeans. Adan slipped her shoes from her feet and then pulled the blanket over her. She closed her eyes, unable to watch him as he cared for her.

Because he didn't *really* care for her, did he?

"Sleep, Isabella," he said.

"Adan," she said when he was at the door.

"Yes?"

She swallowed. Her throat hurt from crying. "I'm sorry."

He merely inclined his head before pulling the door shut with a sharp click.

Adan didn't sleep well. He kept tossing and turning, kicking off the covers, pulling them back again. In the next cabin, he imagined Isabella huddled beneath the blankets and sleeping soundly.

He had to admit, when she'd walked out of the bathroom earlier with her face scrubbed clean, he'd been gutted by her expression. She'd been crying, he could tell that right away. Her skin had been pink from the hot water she must have used, but her nose was redder and her eyes were bloodshot. She looked as though she'd been through hell.

And maybe she had. She'd seemed so stunned as she'd absorbed the news about their marriage, about Rafiq. About her *death*.

Adan pressed his closed fist to his forehead. He had no room for sympathy for her. He had to do what he'd come here to do. His country depended on it. His son depended on it.

He would not risk Rafiq's happiness. Isabella was his mother, but what kind of mother was she? She'd abandoned her baby. Even if she truly didn't remember doing it, she had. And she'd been in possession of all her faculties at the time. What had happened after, he did not know, but she'd chosen to leave.

Whether she'd truly walked into the desert or whether it was a fiction she'd cooked up to cover her tracks, he wasn't certain. But whatever the truth, her father had helped her.

He would deal with Hassan Maro soon enough.

Right now, he had to deal with Isabella.

Adan threw back the covers. There was no sense in lying here any longer when he could get some work done instead. After he'd showered and shaved, he dressed in a white *dishdasha* and the traditional dark red *keffiyeh* of Jahfar.

A new shift of flight attendants was busily preparing breakfast in the galley. When they saw him, all activity immediately stopped as they dipped into deep curtsies and bows. He was still getting used to it, really. As a prince, he'd received obeisance, but not to the level he now did as a king. It was disconcerting sometimes. He was impatient, wanted to cut right to the matter, but he realized—thanks to Mahmoud's tutelage—that the forms were still important to people. It set him apart, and there were still those in Jahfar who very much appreciated the traditions of their ancient nation.

"Would you like coffee, Your Excellency?" a young man asked.

"Yes, thank you," Adan replied. "Bring it to my office."

He went into the large space and sat down behind the big wooden desk. His computer fired up instantly, and he checked email. Then he brought up a window and typed in a search phrase: *selective amnesia*.

The coffee arrived, and Adan drank it while he read about dissociative amnesia, systematized amnesia and a host of other disorders. It was possible, though rare, for someone to forget a specific person and all the events surrounding that person. Did Isabella know it, too? Had she looked it up and decided to use it as an excuse?

And yet that would have required that she had known he was coming. Adan frowned. Whatever the case, he would have her examined by a doctor when they arrived.

He picked up the phone and called his assistant in Jahfar. Adan ordered the man to request that Hassan Maro come to the palace the next day, and then asked him to find a specialist in psychological issues.

An email from Jasmine popped into his inbox as he was finishing the call. He opened it and read her chatty missive about the fitting for her bridal costume and the preparations for their wedding feast.

A shaft of guilt speared him. He hadn't told her where he was going when he'd left.

He'd known Jasmine since they were children. There'd

never been a spark between them, but they liked each other. And she was kind, gentle and would make a good mother to Rafiq, as well as to their future children.

Jasmine was a *safe* choice. The right choice.

Adan worked a while longer, eating breakfast at his desk, and then emerged to find Isabella sitting in the same seat as last night, her bare legs stretched out and crossed at the ankles as she studied the papers in her fists. The papers from last night, he realized.

She looked up as he approached. There was no smile to greet him, as there once had been. She still seemed nothing like the girl he'd married. That woman had been meek, biddable and sweetly innocent. It hit him suddenly that she'd been as forgettable as a table or a chair, or any other item you counted on but didn't notice on a daily basis.

This woman was sensual, mysterious and anything but biddable. There was a fire in her. A fire he'd never observed before. And he couldn't stop thinking about it.

Her face without all the makeup was as pure as an angel's. Her hair was as wild as yesterday, dark gold with lighter streaks that didn't come from a salon. He'd only ever seen her with long, straight locks that she usually wore in a loose chignon. This was a completely bohemian, surfer-girl style that he wasn't accustomed to.

She was wearing a dress today, a blue cotton sundress that showed too much skin for his liking, and a pair of sandals.

"You slept well?" he asked.

Her green eyes were still smoky, though not as smoky as yesterday when they'd been surrounded in dark makeup. She looked troubled, not rested.

"As well as can be expected, I guess."

He understood the sentiment.

"We will arrive in Jahfar in another three hours or so," he said.

She set the papers aside. "And what happens then, Adan?"

"Many things, I imagine," he replied, purposely keeping it vague.

"When can I see...Rafiq?"

He noticed that she swallowed before she said his son's name. *His* son, not hers. Not anymore. She'd given up that right two years ago. And he would not subject Rafiq to any confusion, not when he was about to marry Jasmine.

"You cannot, I'm afraid. It is out of the question."

CHAPTER FOUR

ISABELLA stared up at him, wondering if the shock and
hurt she felt were showing on her face, or if it was only
inside that she was being clawed to ribbons. The pain
was immense, but she refused to cry. She was finished
with crying. She'd cried in the bathroom and she'd cried
in her bed in the night while the plane's engines droned
endlessly on, but she would not cry again.

Nor would she accept his decrees as if he were her
own personal dictator.

"Perhaps I shouldn't have phrased it that way," she
said. "It wasn't truly a question."

He looked so hard and handsome in his *dishdasha*
and headdress. His dark eyes glittered in that hawklike
face. His lips, no matter how they flattened or frowned
or grew firm with irritation, managed to be much more
sexy than she would like them to be.

"You cannot see him," he pronounced. "It will confuse him."

Anger burst in her belly like a firecracker. "He's two,
Adan. How will it confuse him?"

He blew out a hard breath. "You know nothing of
him. You will not presume to tell me what is best for
my son."

"Our son."

He got to his feet in a swirl of robes. Out of the corner of her eye, she saw one of the flight attendants backing away. Everyone treated him as if he were a god. As if he controlled their destinies and made the sun shine or the rain fall on their rooftops.

She would not do the same.

Isabella shot to her feet and faced him squarely. Everything she'd known about herself and her life was in the gutter now, and he thought she would meekly accept his decrees? Especially a decree that regarded her child?

"I'm his mother," she said before he could turn and walk away from her.

"You gave birth to him," Adan snapped. "But it takes more than that to make a mother."

She clenched her hands into fists at her side. Her heart pounded, and the remnants of her headache made her temples throb oh so lightly.

"I realize that."

"Do you?" he said, his jaw rigid with anger. "When, precisely, did you have this revelation?"

"Adan—"

"Did you consider it in the moments before you made your decision? Those last moments before you left your infant alone in your father's house?"

Every word was like a physical blow. And yet she could not back down. She had to be firm, had to stand up under the onslaught, or be crushed forever by his fury and derision.

"I left him alone? There was no one else in the house?"

His jaw flexed. "There were servants, but that's not the same as a mother."

Her heart hurt. Why had she done such a thing? *Why?* "And you would continue to deprive him of a mother now that you've found me?"

"He does not need you," Adan said, and her heart shattered anew.

"How do you know?" she flung at him. "Is this merely because you've decreed it must be? Or do you truly know what's in the mind of a child?"

"Don't test my patience, Isabella." His voice was a feral growl.

And she didn't care. She took a step closer, hands on hips, and glared up into his glittering obsidian eyes. "Then why in the hell am I here, Adan? What do you want from me?"

"You know what I want. You've already named it."

Her blood began to beat harder in her veins. Her head felt light suddenly. Dark spots swam in her vision.

No. She would not be so silly as to pass out simply because he wanted a divorce.

She didn't really know him. Didn't love him. His rejection shouldn't matter.

It *didn't* matter.

But the child did. Rafiq. Her baby. The baby who was also a stranger to her, but who was a part of her flesh and blood. He carried her DNA. He was half her. She would not give him up when she'd just found him.

"I won't divorce you," she said, her voice as low and hard as she could make it. It didn't even come close to his, however.

"You don't have a choice, Isabella. Have you forgotten that we are Jahfaran?"

She thrust her chin out and shoved her hair from her face. "By Jahfaran you mean that you hold all the power. No, I haven't forgotten that. But I don't intend to make it easy for you."

He blinked. "You," he said very dangerously, "don't intend to make it easy for me?"

And then he burst into laughter, startling her with the richness of the sound. It was funny, of course, because he was right: she had no power. There was nothing she could do, really.

Still, she didn't intend to go down easily. "I'll fight you. Whatever it takes, I'll do it. I won't let you take my child away from me before I've ever had the chance to know him."

He closed the distance between them, looming over her like a tall and menacing shadow. "You made your choice two years ago. You have nothing to fight me with."

They stared at each other for several moments.

And then he lifted his hand. She flinched, but refused to cower. His fingers touched her—so softly, so lightly. They stroked down her cheek, her neck, back up the other side to the opposite cheek. Rivulets of flame trailed in their wake. Her skin prickled with heat, cooled and then heated again.

Her lips parted, her tongue darting out to moisten them. His gaze sharpened, followed the motion.

"You had it all, Isabella," he said softly, so very softly. "A wealthy husband, a child and the possibility of more. But it wasn't enough for you. *We* weren't enough for you. Tell me why I would ever give you that chance again."

She swallowed. His eyes were full of emotion, though she wasn't sure which emotion.

A thought struck her like a lightning bolt. She could hardly believe it was possible, considering how he'd told her they'd barely known one another, but what if it was? What if it explained everything?

"Were you..." She swallowed again. "Were you in love with me? Is that why you're so angry?"

He looked surprised. But then he shook his head slowly, his eyes mocking her. "Not at all. It was you who loved me."

She stiffened beneath his touch, that soft stroking of her skin that she shouldn't be allowing and yet couldn't seem to pull away from. "How do you know that?"

This time the expression on his face was one of pity. "Because you told me so."

"I don't believe you," she said automatically. If she'd been in love with this man, wouldn't she have known it? Wouldn't she feel some sort of connection even now, even with her memory damaged?

"Believe what you wish, Isabella. It does not change the truth." His hand dropped away. She wanted to protest, wanted to ask him to keep touching her, but she did not. "And yet it was a lie, wasn't it? Because if you had loved me—loved us—you would not have run away."

"This is very convenient for you," she said, her soul aching. "If I protest or disagree, you simply tell me that I did this terrible thing, knowing I cannot argue with you. Knowing that I don't remember what truly happened." She put her fists on her hips and glared at him. "How do I know you weren't involved? What if everything *you* say is a lie?"

"There was a time long ago in Jahfar," he said, "when calling me a liar would have got you a death sentence."

"Well, thank God we live in enlightened times!" she snorted.

Behind Adan, another flight attendant had stopped with one foot in the air as if she had been arrested in motion. She pivoted and started to walk away.

"Oh, for God's sake," Isabella exploded. "Why does everyone tiptoe around you like you're about to chop off their heads?"

She hurried past Adan and caught up with the woman. "If you wish to speak to him, please come do so."

The girl bowed her head. "His Excellency is busy. I will come another time."

Isabella's blood boiled. She'd had it with his high-handedness, and she didn't care if he was the prince of the universe. People had jobs to do, and they couldn't do it with him carrying on like a wounded lion.

"You wished to ask if we wanted drinks? Food?"

"Drinks, Your Highness."

Isabella was taken aback at the title and almost corrected the girl.

Until she remembered. She *was* a princess, at least for the moment, and though the staff hadn't seemed to know it when she'd boarded, they certainly knew so now that she and Adan had been arguing so loudly.

"I would like water with lemon, please." She turned to look at Adan, who was still glowering in the same spot. "Your Worship, would you like anything to drink?"

She thought she saw his jaw grinding. "No."

"Very well." She turned back to the girl. "I'll just have that water, then."

"Yes, Your Highness." She dipped into a curtsey and was gone, hurrying toward the galley at double speed.

"I don't know how you live with yourself," Isabella

said. "Terrorizing women, demanding obedience and glaring at everything in sight. Wouldn't you like, just once, for someone to *want* to talk to you without being terrified about what you'll do or say?"

His expression was stone. "This will no doubt come as a surprise to you, but I don't terrorize anyone. They obey me because it is my due."

Isabella returned to her seat and sank down into it. "You are a deluded man, then. Because from where I'm sitting, you pretty much terrorize everyone."

"You don't seem terrorized," he remarked somewhat wryly.

"I'm trying very hard not to be."

The flight attendant returned with a glass of mineral water and a plate of sliced lemons. She set it on the table in front of Isabella and curtsied again. "Will that be all, Your Highness?"

"Thank you, yes."

The girl then asked Adan if he would like anything after all. He replied that he would not, and she disappeared into the galley.

Isabella squeezed a lemon slice into the glass and sipped the cool, bubbly water. It felt good against her throat, which was sore from a night of singing and crying. She pointedly ignored Adan, staring out the window instead. It was day now, and they were high over the clouds.

"You have changed, Isabella."

She looked up at him, her heart flipping at the heat and anger in those dark, dark eyes. "Everything has changed," she said softly. "It's adapt or die. I prefer to adapt."

"You will soon be returning to Hawaii, so do not adapt too much."

Her stomach tightened, but she refused to react. "You won't frighten me away, Adan. No matter what you do, you won't frighten me away."

"It would be unwise of you to plan for a future in Jahfar," he warned. "You will only be there as long as it takes to sort out the legal tangle of you being alive rather than dead."

"I will *not* be silent. And I will not fade away into the night like a ghost, no matter how you might wish it."

He considered her for a long moment. "And yet, that is not your choice to make."

Stepping off the plane onto Jahfaran soil was like stepping from a refrigerator into a blast furnace. The sun beat down on the white tarmac, reflecting light into her eyes. Isabella wore sunglasses, but she felt as if her corneas were burning nonetheless.

She'd forgotten how bright, how hot, how desolate Jahfar could be. Especially compared to the lush verdancy of Hawaii.

In the distance, date palms lined the runway. Farther away, stark sandstone mountains loomed in the background. It was home, and it was foreign.

Three black Mercedes limousines sat nearby, and a team of dark-suited men with earpieces waited stoically beside them. Several men in white *dishdashas,* wearing traditional *keffiyehs,* stood in a cluster near the bottom of the stairs. A red carpet had been rolled out from the plane to the cars.

Adan preceded her down the stairs. The men at the bottom sank to their knees and touched their heads to the ground as he approached. Isabella stopped short. This was the greeting given to the ruler, not to a royal family member.

Adan spoke with the men, and then they were standing and he was striding down the carpet toward the cars. She was stuck in place, trying to process what she'd just seen, and wanting more than anything to turn around and climb back up the stairs. Part of her—the small, scared part—wanted to rewind the past twenty-four hours and go back to the way it was before she'd known about Adan and their son.

Adan reached the car and turned to look at her. At that moment, something inside her broke loose, broke her foothold on the steps, and she was running down them and hurrying to his side. She would not let him leave her behind. She would not cower from this, or from the hard truths that awaited her when she spoke with her father again.

He stepped back to let her inside the car, then climbed in beside her. The door shut solidly behind them and then the car was moving.

Isabella ran a nervous hand along the skirt of her sundress. Where was her bravery of earlier? Where was the woman who'd stood toe-to-toe with him? Who had challenged him and threatened him?

She didn't know, but she did know she was having trouble catching her breath. Moisture pooled in the valley between her breasts. She should not have run in this heat. She'd been gone too long and she was no longer accustomed to it.

Adan reached down into what she realized was a small refrigerator and then thrust a bottle of cold water at her. "Drink this before you pass out."

Isabella twisted the top off and took a gulp. "I'd forgotten how hot Jahfar is," she said, hoping her voice didn't betray her unease. She wanted to appear calm, unruffled, though she was anything but.

"You seem to have trouble remembering quite a lot of things," Adan said coolly.

Isabella ignored the taunt. "That was the greeting for a king."

She couldn't see his eyes behind his mirrored sunglasses. But his lips thinned. "Precisely."

"You are the king? I thought the king was an Al Nasri." Her heart was beginning to throb. What had she walked into? What awful, tangled mess was this?

"My cousin and his family died in a boating accident last year. I became my uncle's heir, as I am the oldest of my brothers. My uncle died a little over a week ago."

Her breath stopped in her chest. It was too much. "I am not... I can't be..."

"The queen? No, you aren't," he said firmly. "Nor will you be."

"But if you are king?"

His mouth turned down. "I cannot be formally invested until I am married. It is the law. I am the acting king until the coronation."

Isabella resisted the urge to roll the cold bottle against her neck and chest. She would never be cool enough, especially now that her heart beat so hard and her skin prickled with the nearness of this man. "I'm afraid I don't understand. You *are* married."

He slipped the glasses from his face and tossed them down on the seat beside him. His eyes speared her, so hard and cold in the frame of his handsome face. And hot. How did they manage to be hot, as well?

"Twenty-four hours ago I was a widower. You have thrown a bit of a spanner in the works, as the charming saying goes—but we will take care of that shortly. Once we do, I can proceed with the wedding that you have interrupted."

"Wedding? You're getting married?"

"This is what I have said."

Hurt and fury warred within her. Of course he would have moved on, and of course he would have had to re-marry if he thought she were dead. But now that she was back? Now that she knew they had a child together?

"Are you in love with her?" she asked. Because if he was, if he'd found someone he adored who adored him in return, how could she stand between them?

And how could she *not,* when her child's future was at stake?

"That is none of your concern," he said shortly.

Her heart thrummed. "That means no, then. Because if you were, you wouldn't mind saying it."

His fingers drummed the leather seat. "You do not know this."

"I do," she insisted. "No one in love minds that question. Unless the relationship is forbidden for some reason."

His gaze sharpened. "Have you been in love recently, Isabella? Do you speak from experience?"

She dropped her gaze, unwilling to let him see even an ounce of her loneliness over the past couple of years. Her certainty that someone was out there for her, but that she had not yet found him.

"No."

He gripped her chin in his fingers and forced her head

up. His eyes searched hers. "You belong to me, *habibti*. I would not take it kindly if you have a lover."

"I don't see why it would matter," she said. "You can't wait to be rid of me."

Something flashed across his face—and then he abruptly let her go. "Yes, this is true. The sooner it is done, the better. It is time Rafiq had a proper mother."

It was as if he'd taken a hot dagger and thrust it through her heart. Isabella had to restrain herself from doing violence to him. He was insensitive, brutal, cold.

No doubt she'd be thrown into the depths of Port Jahfar's dankest prison, should she raise a hand to their king, and yet that wasn't what stopped her. It was the thought of her baby.

"You are the vilest person I know, do you realize that? Why did you bring me here? Why did you ever come find me if all you wanted to do was shatter my heart like this? You lied when you said I was in love with you. I could never, *ever* have loved a man like you."

"That's a very charming speech," he said. "But you know why you're here. If I had not come for you, I would be committing a terrible fraud when I take a new wife and queen."

"Of course," she said bitterly. "It's all about *you*. About your feelings and your wants. You could care less about mine. And you damn sure could care less about our little boy's!"

"Be careful what you say to me, Isabella," he growled. "Jahfar is not so modern as you might wish, and if you continue to push me, you will find out precisely how ruthless I can be."

"I think I already know," she flung at him.

"You really don't," he said silkily.

"What could be more ruthless than separating a mother and child?"

His eyes narrowed, the corners crinkling with years of sun and wind. She could see the harshness of the desert in his face, the struggle for survival that punctuated life in that wilderness. He was a king, but he wasn't tame by any standard—would never be tame.

She shivered, as if in premonition.

His words were coated in ice. "Abandoning a child to grow up without a mother is far more ruthless than anything I have ever done."

CHAPTER FIVE

ADAN sat at the large carved desk in his office and stared stonily at his private solicitor. "What do you mean, my divorce will take *some* time?"

The solicitor cleared his throat. "The marriage contract with Isabella Maro is very clear, Your Excellency. If she does not agree to the divorce, then only if she is barren can you set aside the contract. This is not an issue, clearly."

Adan's blood pressure skyrocketed.

"But there are extenuating circumstances," the man continued, "and those will be a factor in presenting our case that your marriage should be dissolved, with or without her agreement."

Adan tossed his pen down on the desk with a sharp crack. Damn her! She was proving to be nothing but trouble after all. He'd read the contract before he'd ever signed it, but, of course, nothing about it had been out of the ordinary. Though it was true that Jahfaran men had much of the power, women were not without protection. He could not divorce her for no reason.

He shoved to his feet and paced over to the window. "What about the coronation?"

The solicitor cleared his throat. "You are married and

can proceed. But no crowned king of Jahfar has ever divorced his queen."

Adan turned to look at the man. "But *can* it be done?"

He was determined that Isabella was not going to win this battle by default. She was not the sort of woman he wanted to mother his son. Rafiq's welfare was paramount. There was nothing more important to him.

"I am not certain of it, Your Excellency. There is no precedent to go by."

"Keep me informed," Adan said by way of dismissal. The solicitor bowed and Mahmoud showed him out.

Adan's gut burned with rage at the predicament he now found himself in. But there was something more swirling inside him, some other feeling that had an edge of…anticipation?

He shoved the thought aside. What was there to anticipate? Isabella infuriated him and the longer he spent in her company, the more he wanted to grasp her by the shoulders and…

Kiss her.

No. He wanted to shake her, not kiss her.

But you do want to kiss her. Everywhere.

No, he thought. *No.*

He'd kissed her once, and that had been enough. She was poisonous; he would not risk bringing her into Rafiq's life again. He did not know why she'd left them, but it was undeniable that she had done so. Just as it was undeniable that she now felt guilty for it.

Was guilt the only reason she wanted to see Rafiq, the only reason she claimed to want to be a part of his life? And what would happen when she realized that little boys were energetic and messy, that they needed love and discipline and parents who put their welfare first?

He would not take that chance. He knew what it was like to have a mother whose love you craved, but who would rather see you when you were cleaned and groomed and dressed like a perfect little boy so she could show you off to her friends.

Her friends would *ooh* and *aah* and pinch your cheeks.

And then you would be sent back to the nursery with your nanny, the woman who would clean your scrapes, wipe your tears and mitigate your fights with your brothers on a daily basis. The woman who really loved you and raised you as if you were her child, because your own mother claimed that children were too much for her delicate nerves.

He did not want that for his son. He wanted a woman who loved Rafiq with her whole heart, and who would never see him as an inconvenience or a burden. Jasmine was that woman, not Isabella.

Not only that, but he was also determined not to be forced into spending the rest of his life with a woman he didn't trust. A woman he despised.

A woman he wanted so badly he could taste it.

Adan swore under his breath. How could he want her? How could he feel this pull of attraction for her, but not for Jasmine? How could he want to strip that damn blue dress off her body and find her sweet feminine center with his fingers and tongue before plunging deeply into her body in order to slake this craving?

He had never been ruled by desire. Had never allowed his need for a woman to override his good sense. He remembered delighting in Isabella's body before, but they'd been newly wed and it was his duty to get her with child.

Liar.

It had been more than that, and he knew it. He'd wanted her then, and he wanted her now. In spite of her lack of personality back then, in spite of her unsuitability now.

He would not act on the compulsion, however, no matter how long the divorce took. There was nothing good that could come of it. He'd been weak when he'd kissed her in Hawaii, but he would not be so weak again.

For Rafiq's sake, he would not be weak.

Isabella didn't remember ever having been to the palace before, though for all she knew, she had been. The whitewashed sandstone was inlaid with gold and porcelain tiles until the whole structure seemed to gleam in the sunshine. But that hadn't been the most amazing thing.

The most amazing thing about the palace was the approach. The marble fountains and statuary, the palms, the lush tropical plants and the acres of green grass that were indicative of fabulous wealth in such a hot and water-conscious country. Port Jahfar sat on the Arabian Sea, but the water had to be desalinated before it could be used to care for plants. And it took massive amounts of water to make grass grow in Jahfar.

After their arrival, she'd been shown to a suite of rooms and left on her own for the past several hours, with the exception of a visit from a doctor who wanted to ask questions about her memory. She'd answered as truthfully as she could. He hadn't been able to enlighten her about her condition in any way, but he'd seemed satisfied by her answers.

She'd tried to leave her room afterward, but a servant had been assigned to her whose single duty, it seemed, was to keep her from doing so.

Finally, after exploring her quarters, she'd taken up residence in a window seat that afforded her a view of the sea beyond the palace's gardens. She was full of restless energy, and frustrated that she had no way to use it. There was no computer, no books, no television, nothing to occupy her time. There was a desk and some writing paper, and there were several seating areas with comfortable furniture, but nothing else of note.

Out of boredom, she decided to sing. First, she sang an old Jahfaran song that her father had taught her. Then she moved into the songs she'd sang at Ka Nui's. She ran through several of them, letting the songs reach deep into her and pull out the sadness and heartbreak.

This was the first time she'd sung with the knowledge that she was a mother and wife, and the hollowness that had always been there while she sang now made sense. She understood where that core of loneliness was coming from now, and she ached with the knowledge of what she'd lost.

She wanted her child. She wanted to see him and hold him. She didn't know what it felt like to be a mother, but she could think of nothing else now that she knew she'd had a baby. Always before, she'd been somewhat wary of children. She didn't know what to say to them, didn't know how to soothe them or amuse them.

But now, in the space of a few hours, she was surprised at how desperately she wanted to hold a child.

Her child. She wouldn't know what to say or do, but she would learn.

She *wanted* to learn.

And Adan wanted to deprive her of that. Anger welled up inside her, and desperation. How could she fight a king? She was here so he could divorce her, no other reason. He would hustle her out of the palace and back to Hawaii as soon as it was done. Tonight, perhaps.

She stood up and paced to the door in frustration. She knew she'd find a servant sitting on the other side, but what if he was gone? It might be her one and only chance to escape this room. Isabella jerked open the door—and froze, the song in her throat dying away.

The servant was indeed sitting beside the door, but it was the old woman standing in the corridor, holding a small child, that had Isabella's full attention.

The boy's eyes were fixed on her, his little mouth hanging open in surprise. Her eyes drank him in greedily. He had the black curls and eyes of his father—but he had her nose and chin. He was the most beautiful little boy she'd ever seen.

She wanted to reach for him, but he suddenly burst into tears.

"Oh, no, please, I'm sorry," she said, taking a step toward them with her hand held out. But then she stopped, her heart breaking as Rafiq continued to cry. She desperately wanted to hold him and soothe him, but he didn't know her. He turned his head into the neck of the old woman and wailed.

"It's not your fault, *sitt*," she said. "He wants you to sing. We stopped because of the singing."

Isabella bit back a choked sound that was half sob,

half laugh. Her heart ached, and yet it was swelling with love for this baby who was half hers.

"Of course," she said. "But why don't you come in, it will be more comfortable. And then I will sing for as long as he likes."

The woman's eyes narrowed, as if she were seeing Isabella for the first time. She ran her hand up and down the boy's back, crooning to him. Then she glanced down at the child in her arms and back at Isabella, as if she were considering something.

"Yes," she said after a long pause. "We will come."

Adan shoved back from his desk. It was time to call it a day. After the solicitor had left, he'd spoken with Jasmine and told her the truth of what was going on. She'd been so silent on the other end of the phone. And then she'd said, "Perhaps it is for the best."

"It is not what I want," he'd replied. "She is not what I want."

Jasmine's warm voice poured through the line like sweet honey. "She is still your wife, and the mother of your child. I think she has been brought back to you for a reason."

They'd spoken some more, about the wedding, about the necessity of putting any plans on hold and about the coronation. Jasmine was understanding, gracious, and he grew angrier and angrier as he talked to her. Not with her, but with the woman who was forcing him to go through this.

Because he wanted Jasmine to be a mother for Rafiq, and he wanted her now. He didn't know why he hadn't thought of asking her to marry him before, but the truth

was it hadn't occurred to him until he'd needed to wed
for the coronation.

He wanted Rafiq to have a mother, but not just any
mother. He'd convinced his old nanny to come out of
retirement to take care of his son, and he knew that his
boy was in good hands with her. Loving hands. But
Kalila was getting old and he felt guilty taking her away
from her retirement.

Still, Adan was there every night, spending time with
his son, playing with him, reading to him. Rafiq was
loved in a way that Adan never had been. His own father
had loved him, but he was a proud man incapable of
showing true affection to his sons. They were meant to
be hard men of the desert, not cosseted young men with
a sense of entitlement.

But Adan didn't believe Rafiq would be any less
manly because his father loved him and wanted him to
be happy. There was nothing on this earth better than
walking into the nursery each night and seeing that little
face light up with the purest love he'd ever seen.

Isabella had claimed to love him once. He hadn't
made that up, though she believed he had. He could
still remember her saying it, after they'd made love one
night. She'd been so young, so naive, and he'd pulled
away from her, troubled. He didn't know why.

Shortly after that, she'd learned she was pregnant.
And then the morning sickness took over and he'd left
her bed. He'd wanted her to rest, to be healthy, and he'd
felt as if his presence disturbed her sleep.

Adan frowned. Had he told her why he'd stopped
sleeping with her? Of course she'd known why they
weren't having sex—she'd been too ill to want it any-

way—but had she realized why he'd left her alone in her bed?

It bothered him to think he hadn't. But what difference would it have made?

The psychiatrist he'd had examine her upon their arrival today could tell him nothing he didn't already know. Isabella claimed to have no memory of her marriage or of her baby. It was an unusual case, but not impossible. In consulting Isabella's records, the doctor had frowned and said that she had shown signs of postnatal depression, though her symptoms hadn't been abnormal at the time.

Baby blues were common enough, he'd said, and resulted from the changing hormones in a woman's body. Sometimes, the depression got worse and could cause hallucinations or thoughts of harming oneself or one's baby.

Adan had been shocked. He hadn't realized that anything could be wrong with Isabella at the time. Then the doctor suggested that she might have tried to commit suicide. Her records up to her disappearance showed no antidepressant usage. If her doctor at the time had believed she was suffering from postnatal depression, he should have prescribed medication to mitigate it.

It was possible, too, that her doctor simply hadn't recognized the signs. And Isabella would have been more vulnerable to the effect of the hormones on her body without them.

Adan didn't quite know what to make of all the information, but as he reached the nursery, he firmly shoved thoughts of Isabella aside. All he wanted right now was to hold his son and spend time watching his toddler antics. Adan pushed open the door and went into the suite of rooms that was overflowing with toys and games.

"Kalila," he called, but no one answered. He went into the nursery itself, but Rafiq was not in his crib or playing on the floor.

He checked his watch. Kalila and Rafiq were usually here at this time of day. He stood for some moments, wondering, until, like a bolt of lightning, a thought shafted through him.

A terrible thought.

He'd had Isabella put as far from here as he could get her, yet these were still the family quarters and her rooms weren't on another planet. They were simply down another corridor. He'd stationed a servant to make sure she didn't leave her room, so it should not be possible that she'd somehow found Rafiq.

And yet he suddenly feared, with a terrible, dreadful certainty that ate a hole in his gut and sent him running down the corridors to her room, that it was possible. As he skidded to a stop at her door, the man he'd stationed there fell off his chair and began to babble, his face pressed to the floor.

Adan could hear singing. She was singing, the sound so rich and pure it wrapped around him like a warm blanket on a cold desert night. He shoved open the door, his heart beating so fast as he prayed he was wrong, that he'd got the time mixed up, that his intuition was merely superstition—

She sat on one of the low couches, her eyes closed as she found the note and held it. Kalila perched on another sofa, across from Isabella.

And Rafiq stood with his hands on Isabella's knees, his little face turned up to hers as she sang. Adan's world went red. Rage curled and twisted inside him like a coiling snake.

The rage he understood, but there was another feeling underpinning it. Loss?

How could he feel loss? Rafiq was his, no matter what. This was one moment, one regrettable moment, and it would not be repeated. Rafiq would not remember it. Ever.

She let the note go and opened her eyes to smile down at Rafiq. He bounced in place, laughing in delight.

Isabella finished the song and held her arms out. Rafiq stretched his up until she bent and caught him. And then she was holding him close and Adan was dying inside.

"What is going on here?" he said smoothly, despite the churning emotion inside him.

All eyes turned to him. Kalila climbed to her feet and curtseyed. He hated that she did so, but she'd always been particular about observing the forms with him. As she would be with Rafiq, as well. A mother, but not a mother.

Isabella stood. Rafiq had his arms around her neck. When he saw Adan, he crowed, "Papa! Sing, Papa!"

"Does your papa sing?" Isabella asked.

Rafiq nodded his little head.

"Put him down," Adan growled. He thought she would argue with him, but she simply bent to set Rafiq on the floor. He held on to her neck and refused to let go.

"No want down!"

His expression was militant and Adan knew he was fighting a losing battle. Somehow he found the ability to move again. He walked over to Isabella and held his arms out.

"Come to Papa," he said, and Rafiq stretched his arms wide. Relief flooded him. Isabella let the boy go easily enough, but he didn't miss the way her fingers tightened oh so briefly before relinquishing his son.

He had to stand close to her to take Rafiq, and now his senses were overwhelmed with her scent. She'd showered and changed again since they'd arrived. Her hair was every bit as wild as it had been back in Hawaii, and it smelled like tropical flowers. He wanted to close his eyes and breathe her in.

Instead, he turned away. "Come, Kalila. It is time we took Rafiq for his *b-a-t-h* and bedtime."

Isabella did not want them to go, and yet she knew there was nothing she could do to stop Adan from taking Rafiq away. She'd spent the past hour singing for her baby, delighting in his little smile and enthusiastic singing along with her. Nothing had cracked a memory open in her head, but she'd felt as though everything was right with the world in the short time she'd spent with her son.

She did not want it to end. She felt whole when he was near. It was not a feeling she was accustomed to.

She also felt lost, she had to admit, because she didn't automatically know what to do or say to him. Just because he was hers didn't mean she understood him. It saddened her that she didn't know how to be a mother, but she desperately wanted to learn.

And Adan wanted to keep her from learning. He wanted to keep Rafiq away from her. When he'd spoken and she'd looked up to see him standing there, the hatred and rage on his face was worse than anything she'd seen yet. He did not believe she had value of any kind for their son, and it hurt her at the same time as it strengthened her resolve not to give up.

But she understood why he was cautious. How could she not after meeting that precious little child? Adan's primary goal was to protect Rafiq. She couldn't argue with that. But she could argue that he wasn't being fair, that she deserved a chance to be a part of her son's life just as he deserved a chance to know his real mother.

"Adan," she said.

She didn't think he would stop, but when Rafiq said, "Lady sing, Papa," Adan stopped short of the door.

"Not now, Rafi. The lady needs to rest."

"Lady sing!" he insisted.

"No, Rafi," Adan said—and Rafiq's face screwed up in a frown. She knew what was coming next, even in so short a time of knowing her son. He burst into tears, his face turning red as he wailed.

Adan shot her a look over the top of Rafiq's head that was full of loathing before he disappeared through the door. Kalila followed, and the servant reached in and shut the door behind them.

Isabella stood in the center of her lonely room, listening to Rafiq's wails as they disappeared down the hall. She was numb. Whereas just a few moments before she'd been full of life, she now felt drained and dull.

The laughter was gone. The warmth. The love.

She pressed her fist to her mouth, chewing on the knuckles. She loved Rafiq. It had happened that quickly. Instantly. She'd fallen head over heels for her little boy.

Her poor little motherless boy.

What had she done two years ago? Why? Why had she left him in the first place?

As hard as she tried, she couldn't remember anything about that time. It was blank, as blank as it had always been. She'd awakened and been told about the accident. Then she'd gone to her mother's to recover. That was all she could recall.

The doctor she'd spoken with today had merely shrugged and said that the brain was a strange and sensitive organ. What had happened to her was not common, but her memory loss wasn't completely unexpected, either. When she'd asked if she would ever remember, he'd said it was possible, though perhaps not likely.

Another hour passed before a servant brought her dinner. She ate alone, then took her coffee and went out onto the balcony that overlooked the gardens below. The sun had set recently, so the heat was finally leaching out of the air. The sky was red-tinted—almost like Hawaii, and yet not—and the Arabian Sea slid to dark purple in the glow of the sky.

Port Jahfar glittered like a jewel in the dusk. Industrial ships crowded the harbor in the distance, bringing supplies to the kingdom or taking on loads meant for other destinations. Her father had a home along the coast, much farther from here, where the turquoise water caressed the white shore. She'd loved that home growing up most of all. It was why she'd been drawn to Hawaii.

As she drank her coffee, the night darkened, the red fading away until it was only a ribbon along the horizon. And then she sensed that she was no longer alone. She knew who it was without turning to acknowledge him.

"Come to shove me off the balcony and end your troubles, Adan?" she asked.

Behind her, he blew out a breath. "No."

She heard him move, and then he was standing beside her. He'd changed into a dark polo shirt and jeans. His head was free of the *keffiyeh*. She wasn't certain what disconcerted her more—his handsome face framed in the dark cloth, or the added distraction of his hair and the shape of his head to accompany his chiseled features.

How was it possible to forget a man like this? To forget making love with him, sleeping and waking with him, eating with him, talking with him?

"He cried for over an hour," Adan said without preamble. She could hear the emotion in his voice, the love he felt for his son. It was the only thing about him that made him redeemable to her. Adan truly loved Rafiq, and everything he did was for Rafiq's well-being. Understanding that didn't make it any easier, however.

"I'm sorry," she replied, a lump rising in her throat at the thought of her baby crying.

"He refused to eat because he was so upset. Kalila finally got him to sleep." He shoved a hand through his hair. "I don't know how she did it."

He turned to her, propping his elbow against the railing. It was a casual gesture, and yet everything about his presence was anything but casual. There was tension in the lines of his body, tension in the furrow of his brow and the intensity of his gaze.

"It's not easy raising a child," he continued. "They are fussy, independent, messy and a million other things you can't imagine one tiny person could be. It's a giant responsibility."

"I know that, Adan." Her heart thrummed at his nearness, at the way he stood so close to her and discussed their child. It was as if, for a moment at least, they were on the same side. As if they were two parents talking about their son.

She knew better, however.

He pushed a hand through his hair. She found herself wanting to smooth the crisp curls back into place, but she did not do so.

"He does not know you," he said. "If you insert yourself into his life, and then decide you can't handle the responsibility, you will hurt him because he will have grown close to you."

She gripped the coffee cup in her fingers. "I didn't do anything wrong. I didn't try to be anything to him—"

"I know." He let out a sharp breath. "Kalila told me what happened. She was taking a shortcut back to the nursery when he heard you singing."

Her temper sharpened. "Then why are you here, if not to chastise me? I know you would be happier if I didn't exist. But I do, Adan. And I want to know my child."

His eyes glittered hotly in the westering light. His mouth tightened. Her gaze settled on those firm, sensual lips. They'd been so masterful against her own. The wetness flowing into her inner core at the thought shocked her. She was angry with him, and yet her body reacted to him until the tingle of desire was soon a buzz in her veins.

How could she feel this way for him? How could she be attracted to him when he infuriated her so much? Was her body remembering what her mind had forgotten?

He took a step closer, then stopped as if he realized

he'd done so against his will. His voice, when he spoke, was low and determined.

"I am here, Isabella, because I have come to a decision."

CHAPTER SIX

ADAN was taking a risk. He knew it, and yet he was now convinced it was the only solution. When he'd carried Rafiq back to the nursery, the child crying all the way because he wanted the lady to sing for him, Adan had realized that he could not undo what had been done.

Not only that, but perhaps he'd been wrong to try and keep Isabella away from Rafiq.

Not because he believed she was suddenly going to make a fabulous mother. He wouldn't bet Rafiq's future on that shaky hypothesis. But, his son was still so young, and he would encounter various people who would be a part of his life for a short while before they were gone again. Teachers. Friends. Even Kalila, who suffered from arthritis that would soon make taking care of Rafiq more difficult as he grew bigger and heavier.

People moved on. It happened all the time, and Adan couldn't protect Rafiq from it.

Isabella was looking up at him, her green eyes so wary and sad at the same time. She held her saucer in her right hand, the fingers of her left hooked through the coffee cup that she hadn't drunk from since he'd joined her.

She still smelled like tropical flowers. Tropical flowers, coffee and the spicy sweetness of the cardamom seed that flavored the brew. He wondered if she would taste sweet and spicy if he kissed her.

"What is it, Adan?" she asked, her voice as smoky and rich as the coffee. He shook thoughts of kissing her from his head.

"I'm going to give you two weeks with us." Because he'd decided that the only way to convince her she was not cut out for motherhood was to let her spend time with Rafiq. She'd walked away before—for whatever reason—and she would do so again.

And he intended that she know it sooner rather than later.

She seemed so serene, and yet he hadn't missed the tiny gasp that had escaped her.

"Two weeks," he repeated firmly. "But you are not to tell him you are his mother. He does not need the confusion."

"But I *am* his mother," she said.

"That's the deal, Isabella. Take it or leave it."

She tilted her head. "What am I supposed to be to him, then?"

Adan shrugged. "A nanny. A caretaker. A teacher. Someone who will not be staying."

She set the coffee down on a nearby table. The delicate china rattled as she did so, betraying her nerves. Or maybe it was anger. He had to acknowledge that she was certainly capable of bypassing nerves and going straight for the anger.

"And what happens at the end of two weeks?"

"We'll decide when we get there." It was all he could say to her. Because if he told her that he hoped to be divorced from her at the end of two weeks, she would most certainly fight him.

But it's what he expected. Two weeks for her to decide she didn't want to be a mother after all, and she would agree to a divorce, assuming his solicitor hadn't managed to get the job done by then. The coronation wasn't scheduled for another two weeks anyway, because the laws of Jahfar required a minimum twenty-one-day period of mourning before a new king was officially crowned.

She bowed her head, as if she were thinking. Her arms crossed beneath her breasts, and an arrow of heat sizzled into his groin at the way they nearly spilled over her silky tank top. When she lifted her head again, her eyes speared into him.

"You know I'm going to accept. What choice do I have? I'll do anything to spend time with my baby. And, whether you believe it or not, I care about his welfare every bit as much as you do. I won't tell him I'm his mother."

He inclined his head. "Thank you."

"It's not for you," she snapped. "It's for Rafiq. Because you're right, he doesn't need the confusion right now. He's too young to understand what it means, and I won't use him as a pawn in our argument with each other. Until we settle our issues, his understanding of who is who in his life should remain the same."

She was so different than she'd once been. The woman before him now lit up like a firecracker, blazing sparks of outrage and righteousness, whereas the woman she'd been before would have nodded meekly, accepting whatever decree he cared to make.

Like Jasmine, he thought. *No.* Jasmine was perfect,

nothing like Isabella used to be—and nothing like her now. Jasmine would not blaze in the night. She would glow softly. She would not defy him.

But there would be no need, would there? He and Jasmine were friends. There was no reason for sparks between them.

"Very well," he said, "tomorrow we are moving inland, to the Butterfly Palace. There are fewer people there, as well as fewer questions."

Because it was best if her return to Jahfar wasn't widely known. His staff knew, of course, but they were discreet and loyal. He had so little privacy anymore, but this was one area in which he meant to keep his— their—personal business confidential. He and Isabella would not play out the last days of their marriage before the public eye.

She seemed to understand, as she only nodded.

"Adan," she said when he turned to go.

He stopped. "Yes?"

"I want to speak with my father." She bit her lip, that lush lower lip he wanted to nibble as he thrust deep inside her body. The image of him doing just that started the telltale tingle at the base of his spine. He clamped down on his libido before he embarrassed himself. *Focus.*

He could *not* keep thinking of her that way. It was counterproductive to his plans.

"He's the only one who knows the truth about what happened," she continued.

A wave of frustration rolled through him then. He very much wanted to speak to Hassan Maro, as well. He wanted to know the truth. "Your father is out of the country."

She seemed to sink in on herself then, her shoulders slumping, the fire inside her flickering dangerously. One breath, he thought, and it would go out.

"It figures." She sighed.

He suddenly found himself wanting to pull her into his arms and comfort her. But he would not. He couldn't afford to soften toward her, couldn't allow his judgment to be clouded or to make her think something more was possible between them.

Then why are you taking her to the Butterfly Palace and letting her spend time with Rafiq?

Because he had to get her to agree to a divorce. That was it, the only reason—aside from the issue of keeping her return a secret from the public, of course. They would be isolated, but he would have plenty to keep him busy. He had a nation to run. He would never be alone with her. Kalila would be there, and Mahmoud, as well as a small staff.

He would spend time with her and Rafiq during the day. At night, they would go to separate rooms. It was a good plan. A sound plan.

"I have left orders that he is to be brought to me the moment he returns," he said. "It is the best I can do."

She tilted her chin up as her strength returned. "Fine. And now, if you don't mind, I think I'll go to bed. It's been a long day."

"Of course," he said, sweeping his arm wide to indicate that she precede him inside. She didn't stop once indoors, marching straight to the hall door and holding it open for him. It wasn't until he was halfway back to his own room that he realized he'd just been dismissed.

Early the next morning, a team of tailors and their assistants arrived. Isabella had just finished breakfast when the knock on her door sounded. A moment later, a servant led the procession into the outer rooms of her suite.

"His Excellency says you are to have a new wardrobe, my lady," the head tailor offered by way of explanation.

The morning was filled with measurements, choosing from bright bolts of silk georgette, and standing still for fittings of a few readymade items the women had brought along. Isabella felt self-conscious. She wanted to protest that she did not need so much, but the truth was she had no idea whether she did. Adan had said two weeks, but of course she hoped for more. The clothing she'd brought with her wouldn't get her through much more than a week.

She already missed her life in Hawaii, and yet she missed it the way you miss something that happened in the past—not as if it was something she desired now. Because now that she'd met her baby, she couldn't imagine anywhere else she wanted to be.

She did not know how they would work this out between them, but she hoped to be a part of Rafiq's life for far longer than two weeks. She sensed this was a test and, as much as it infuriated her to have to take it, she was determined not to fail.

By the time Adan came for her later that afternoon, she had a suitcase full of clothes to take along. She'd dressed in a soft green *abaya* for the trip by car into the desert. The garment skimmed her form, suggesting curves rather than delineating them.

Adan stopped short when he entered the room and she stood up. His eyes slid over her appreciatively, but he banked the fire in them as he met her gaze.

"You are ready, then?"

"Yes," she replied, as coolly as she could manage.

The ride to the Butterfly Palace took just over two hours in the caravan of Land Rovers that rolled up and down giant red sand dunes. The desert was stark and beautiful, and yet it made her heart beat crazily in her chest.

Was it because she had walked into the desert alone, as Adan said? Whatever had happened to her had happened out here. And that made her nervous.

She sat stiffly in the seat beside Adan, her hands clasped together in her lap. She'd wanted to ride with Rafiq and Kalila, but there hadn't been enough room in their car.

"Why is it called the Butterfly Palace?" she blurted after they'd rolled down yet another steep dune. Beads of sweat broke out on her brow and between her breasts. The car was air-conditioned, but it wasn't cool enough to conquer the evidence of her nerves.

Adan glanced over at her. "It was built five hundred years ago for the favorite wife of a king. She loved butterflies and had a garden built for them. In the spring, it was said, hundreds of butterflies swarmed the palace. They perched on her shoulders and hair, ate with her and even slept with her. And when her husband eventually died and she was brokenhearted, the butterflies carried her to heaven to be with him—or so the legend goes."

"Are there any butterflies there now?" she asked, trying to imagine the sad queen and her colorful companions.

"I have never seen any," he said. "I think the climate has shifted as the desert has grown, and it's now too hot for them here. There are butterflies closer to the

sea, of course." He frowned and leaned closer to her.
"Are you unwell, *habibti?* Do you need your headache
medicine?"

Isabella swallowed against the tidal wave of nausea
that threatened to take her down if she didn't hold fast
against it. "It's not my head," she forced out. Tears
pricked the backs of her eyes. "It's just so hot."

Adan's frown deepened. He pressed a button and gave
an order to the driver in the front seat, and the blast of
air from the AC unit intensified. He picked up a stack
of papers he'd been leafing through earlier and fanned
her with them.

Isabella closed her eyes and leaned back against the
seat. "Thank you," she whispered.

"What is truly wrong, Isabella?"

His voice was soothing, and she had a sudden feeling
that she needed to share it with someone. That maybe
if she voiced her concerns, heard how silly they were,
the feeling would go away. "It's the desert. I...feel...as
if it's going to crush me beneath it."

She heard him sigh, and then she felt his arm around
her, pulling her close against him. He continued to fan
her with the papers. "You are safe with me," he said in
a low voice. "I promise you that."

She sat stiffly at first, but the rhythm of the Land
Rover, the soft breeze from the papers and the warm
body at her side lulled her into a doze. She drifted in
that half-twilight state between dreaming and waking.
She thought of her father's house near the sea, then the
one on the edge of the wildest part of Jahfar. Her father
and mother rose up in her mind, arguing, of course, and
then quickly faded away.

Then a man appeared before her.

A dark, dangerous man. Adan. He held his hand out and she slipped hers inside it. He pulled her to him and kissed her. She was wearing a deep orange *abaya*, heavily jeweled, and a veil covered her head. She was nervous, but he comforted her with soft words as he gently slipped the clothing from her body. Then he laid her on a bed and stripped off his clothes before lying down beside her.

She knew what came next as she gazed up into his face. That handsome face that had been so aloof all day, but was now intense and sensual. He caressed and kissed his way down her body, taking his time. He dipped his tongue into the wet seam between her legs and brought her to shattering bliss while she moaned and cried his name. Then he was on top of her, pushing at her entrance as the remnants of her pleasure ricocheted through her body.

As he pushed inside her, whispering hot words, she gasped out in pain and surprise—

Isabella blinked. The sun was bright and hot outside the car. Red sand spread as far as the eye could see in every direction. Beside her, Adan was frowning at her again.

"What is the matter, Isabella?"

Her body was hot, but not from fear this time. Oh, dear God. She'd been having an erotic dream about him—or was it a memory? She'd been wearing the dress from their wedding photo in the paper.

"I…" She swallowed. "I think I remembered something…with you."

His gaze sharpened. "You did?"

Isabella felt a fresh wave of heat wash over her. Why

had she told him that? Because now he'd want to know *what* the memory was.

On the other hand, what did it matter? Her desire to know if it was really a memory outweighed her embarrassment over the subject.

"I think it was our wedding night. I was wearing the dress from the photo. You undressed me before… before…your mouth… And then—"

Isabella closed her eyes. Dear God. Could it get any worse?

When she found the courage to peek at him, he was staring at her. His expression seemed distant, as if he, too, were thinking of that night.

Then he shook his head. "It's never going to work," he said more to himself than to her.

"What isn't?" Fear threaded through her voice, pitching it higher. Was he planning to turn the caravan around and take her back to Port Jahfar? Was he reconsidering allowing her to spend time with Rafiq? Dammit, *why* had she said anything?

"Adan," she said. Demanded.

He looked at her again, his dark eyes hot and intense. And then he kissed her.

It shocked her to realize that his mouth on hers felt right. That the sweep of his tongue, the hot thrill sliding down her spine and the explosive current of sensation pooling in her belly were familiar and welcome.

Her feminine core, already flooded with heat and moisture from the memory, ached with need.

Her arms drifted around his neck as he spread one broad hand against the small of her back and pulled her into his body so that she was half lying on his lap.

Reaching down, he hooked an arm around her legs and lifted her the rest of the way into his lap.

Her buttocks nestled against the solid hardness of his masculinity. When she moved, he groaned low in his throat, a sexy sound that made her want to press her hand against him just to see if the sound would get better.

He cupped her breast, his thumb caressing her sensitive nipple, rubbing so lightly and so expertly she thought she would scream. Her nipples were hard, tight points, and her whole body was attuned to every agonizing caress.

"I want you," he growled against her lips—and then he was kissing her throat, her collarbone, before claiming her mouth again.

Isabella couldn't stop the moan that rose in her throat. She'd kissed one man in the two years that she'd thought she was a different person, and she'd pulled back immediately because it hadn't felt right.

This did.

Incredibly, amazingly right. Which disconcerted her, because she had no illusions about Adan. He might want her physically, but he despised her. Perhaps he'd always despised her. Perhaps that's why she'd felt compelled to leave.

Feelings swirled in her head, her heart, until she couldn't untangle them. She felt happy—and sad. She felt cherished—and despised. She felt, with a certainty, that she had once loved him—but that he had not loved her. Sorrow rose up in a solid wave inside her and she suddenly put her hands against his chest and pushed.

It was too much.

He broke the kiss, confusion in his dark eyes as he

gazed down at her. His mouth—that beautiful mouth— was slick from kissing her, and she instantly wanted to press her lips to his again and forget her tangled thoughts.

"I—I'm not ready for this," she said, her voice thready. "It's too soon."

His expression cleared by degrees until he was once more the cool, unflappable ruler. He set her away from him and she smoothed her skirts self-consciously.

"You are correct, of course," he said. "Forgive me."

"It's not that I don't want…" Isabella swallowed. How could she say it? How could she admit that she did want him? It would be an acknowledgment of his power over her.

And she couldn't give him any more power than he already had.

"I don't know you well enough," she said softly. "I know we've had a child together, but what kind of man are you really? What kind of marriage did we have? Did we at least like each other?"

He leaned back on the seat and sighed. "We were good in bed," he said matter-of-factly. "Though we did not have much time together."

"Because you were so busy? Or do you mean because I got pregnant?"

"Both, I think. But mostly because you were ill during the pregnancy. We had one month, Isabella, before we began to live like roommates instead of lovers."

"Oh. Was it a difficult pregnancy, then?"

"Other than your nausea, no. Everything was normal."

She smoothed the fabric on her thighs again. "I wish I could remember. I feel…cheated."

Cheated because she'd carried her child for nine months and she could remember nothing about the experience. Cheated because she'd obviously shared her life—and body—with this man, and he was still a stranger to her.

Adan sighed. "You were very beautiful, in spite of your sickness. And you grew quite large. Rafiq weighed over nine pounds when he was born."

Isabella's jaw dropped. "He did? My goodness." And then she giggled, though it threatened to turn into a sob. She pressed her hand to her lips to stop it from doing so. "Maybe it's a good thing I don't remember."

Adan smiled. Her heart stopped. He was breathtaking when he did so. His face, already so handsome, became warm and open, almost innocent in a way. It was an odd thing to think about so hard a man, and yet it was the one word that popped into her mind. *Innocent.*

"You looked as if you'd swallowed three soccer balls," he said. "The doctor said it was only one baby in there, but I began to think he was wrong."

"Were you there when he was born?"

He shook his head and her heart sank a little at the sad expression on his face. "I was out of the country on business. You weren't due for another two weeks."

"I'm sorry you missed it, then."

He picked up her hand and kissed it. Shock raced in hot spirals along her nerve endings. "I am, too. I would have liked to have been there for you both. You had a difficult time with the labor and delivery, but Rafiq was healthy and you bounced back…"

His voice trailed off and she looked at him quizzically. "What, Adan?"

He shook his head. "Nothing. It's nothing."

"I *want* to remember," she said. "Even the hard parts. I want to remember every moment of our lives together. It's hard not knowing."

"Perhaps you will remember someday. You remembered our wedding night, after all."

"Did I? Or was it only a dream?"

One corner of his mouth quirked in a wicked grin. "No, you remembered it quite well. It was a long and pleasurable night."

Her heart pounded for an entirely different reason now. He was as tempting as sin. And she desperately wanted to take a bite out of the apple.

"Careful, Isabella," he growled suddenly. Except it wasn't an angry growl at all.

It was a passionate, sensual sound that stroked along her senses like a trail of hot candle wax.

"I don't understand," she managed.

He cupped a hand behind her head and pulled her in for a kiss. Just as quickly, he let her go again. "I'm a man, *habibti*, not a saint. If you keep looking at me like that, you're going to know me *very* well before we ever leave this car."

CHAPTER SEVEN

THE Butterfly Palace wasn't as ornate as she'd expected it to be. Nor was it anywhere near as big as the palace in Port Jahfar. Other than a caretaker and a housekeeper, there was no permanent staff. That was why, Isabella thought, they'd traveled in a caravan.

They still hadn't brought that many people along. A cook. Adan's assistant, as well as two extra office personnel. Two additional women to help the housekeeper and cook, and a couple of others whose functions she did not know.

Adan took a sleeping Rafiq from Kalila and carried him to his room, which was already prepared, while the housekeeper showed Isabella to her room. She wanted to go with Adan and Rafiq, but she told herself to be patient. They'd just arrived, and there was time to settle in. Besides, Rafiq was asleep and wouldn't even know she was there.

The room she was shown to was just a room, not a suite, but it was large and airy with tall ceilings, overstuffed couches, and an inlaid wooden armoire and dressing table. A large canopied bed occupied one wall, the mattress thick and covered with a cream duvet and a collection of pillows.

White curtains hung on either side of distressed wooden doors that opened to the outside. The doors were old and shuttered to let the light in, but glass had been fitted to the outer portion of the casement, so that the doors could be opened at any time and yet the room would remain cool due to the modern air-conditioning that had been added to the palace.

The doors were pushed partially to, but Isabella didn't open them to see what was outside. First, she wanted to unpack, and then she would explore.

While she was putting everything away, a maid brought refreshments—mint tea and a selection of cool fruit—and then hurried away again before Isabella could tell her she really didn't need anything.

"Is it to your liking?"

Isabella whirled at the sound of his voice. They'd only arrived a little over a half an hour ago—how could she already be so pleased to see him, as if they'd been separated for days instead of minutes?

"It's lovely," she replied.

Adan strode over and pulled open the wooden doors. "Come, let me show you something."

He held out his hand. She didn't even hesitate before joining him and slipping her hand into his, her skin sizzling where they touched. He stared down at her for a moment, as if he, too, were jolted by the contact, and then he was pushing open the glass and leading her onto a shadowed terrace.

Bougainvillea vines grew in profusion over the arbor that stretched the length of the terrace. A short sandstone wall ran along the back of the terrace, and beyond that was a small hedge that seemed to wind in a path, though she couldn't figure out the pattern.

"It's a labyrinth," Adan said, tugging her forward. "The Butterfly Queen had it built centuries ago. The original hedge didn't survive, but this one follows the path she had laid out."

They stopped at the entrance to the labyrinth. She could see the path meandering back and forth.

"You can see all the way to the center," she said. "I didn't think that's how it worked."

He grinned, and for the second—third?—time today, her heart went into free fall. "You're thinking of a maze," he said. "Two different things. A labyrinth is for meditation, among other things. The idea is to walk it and see what the path shows you. It's a personal journey, and it means something different for everyone."

She'd have never thought he was the meditating type. "Do you walk it?"

"I have."

"And?"

Again, with the smile. "Truthfully, I didn't get it the first time. I was impatient and wanted to reach the end. And then I realized that impatience is one of my faults, and the labyrinth could perhaps teach me something after all."

"Nooo," Isabella said disbelievingly. "Don't tell me you have faults. I can't imagine that to be true."

He laughed. "It's possible I have one or two."

Isabella grinned back at him. "Careful, Adan, or I might have to start liking you after all."

"I'll be sure to do something evil just to keep you on your toes," he replied.

She looked out over the labyrinth and the garden beyond and sighed. The sun was setting now, and everything was bathed in a soft ocher glow. It was peaceful.

So much quieter than Port Jahfar—or even Maui, with the tourists and the parties taking place so frequently along the beach.

"Did we talk like this before?" she asked. "Or did I merely bow my head and do or say whatever I thought you wanted?"

His fingers ghosted along her cheek, pushed her riot of golden hair away from her face. Her heart raced at the soft touch of his skin on hers. She had to stop this. Because every time he touched her or smiled at her, her heart opened just a little bit wider for him.

"You already know what the answer is, Isabella, even if you cannot remember it."

She looked up at him. His dark eyes regarded her with something that she thought might be appreciation. Not sexual appreciation, though there was that, too, but an intellectual approval that she was certain she'd not had from him when they were first married.

"Yes, I do. I did what I'd been raised to do, Adan. What my father expected from me. What you expected from me. I tried to be a good Jahfaran wife. I know that, even if I have no memory of it."

"And what would you do now?" he asked. "If the clock was rewound and you went into our marriage as the person you are at this moment?"

She bit her lip. Why was he asking her this? Was he fishing for an answer, trying to gauge her suitability to be his wife? If she said the right thing, did it mean she could stay with Rafiq forever?

She opened her mouth to say what she thought he wanted to hear.

And then she stopped.

She couldn't do it. She couldn't say what she thought

the correct answer was, because it wasn't what she knew to be true for herself. Was she still that girl who'd tried so desperately to please her feuding parents? Who'd said whatever they'd wanted to hear if only it would make them happy with her?

She wasn't, and she couldn't ever be again.

Isabella took a deep breath. It was filled with the fragrance of bougainvillea and the spicy scent of the man standing so near.

"I would be me, regardless of whether it pleased you or not," she said.

His smile was as sudden and unexpected as diamonds raining down from heaven. "I am very glad to hear it."

Dinner was served picnic-style, on a big mat under the stars in the garden with gas lanterns to light the night. There was tabbouleh salad, fresh hummus, roasted lamb with lemon and garlic, rice, and a variety of olives, cheeses, mangoes, figs and fresh hot flat bread that tasted amazing with everything.

Isabella sighed as she popped a bite of bread in her mouth. Rafiq sat beside her, his little head tilted up to watch her eat.

"Very good," she said. "Yummm. Does Rafi want a bite?"

He shook his head—but then he nodded, and Isabella laughed as she tore off a small piece of bread and fed it to him. He chewed so seriously, then got up to toddle toward his father on the other side of the mat. They'd long ago learned to make a path down the center. Dishes were arrayed to either end of the mat with a big swath in the middle for Rafiq to hold court.

Kalila sat in a chair beside them. She'd insisted on joining them on the mat, but Adan had told her no. At first, Isabella had thought he meant to send her away, but he pulled a chair from nearby and perched it there for her.

Isabella's heart did that melty thing again when she watched him help the old woman into the chair. He truly cared for Kalila.

Now, Rafiq climbed into Adan's lap and began babbling something. Adan's forehead wrinkled as he listened intently. Then he picked Rafiq up and hugged him tight, tickling him as the little boy laughed and squirmed.

Isabella bit her lip. Emotion swirled through her in sharp currents. She was happy—and sad.

She was confused—and frustrated. Hopeful—and hopeless. So many emotions, so many possibilities.

"Sing, Papa!" Rafiq exclaimed through his giggles.

"Ah, you want Isabella to sing? Perhaps you should ask her."

Rafiq turned his head to look at her. He stuck a finger in his mouth, chewing on it while he watched her with dark eyes. His father's eyes. Both sets of eyes stared at her now, waiting.

"Ask her," Adan urged.

"Bell sing?"

Isabella's heart swelled with love. It was the first time he'd called her anything besides 'lady.' It was progress, and she was ridiculously pleased.

"Of course I'll sing for you, sweetheart," she said.

"Go sit with Isabella," Adan said, and Rafiq toddled his way to Isabella's side. Then he plopped down in front of her and fixed those sweet eyes on her.

She started with a soft, slow island tune she'd learned on Maui, then sang a couple of Jahfaran songs. Rafiq watched her, mesmerized, until eventually his eyes began to droop. Isabella smiled, but she didn't stop singing. As he tottered, she pulled him close and he settled against her lap. When she looked across at Adan, he was watching her intently. His eyes were as dark and hot as always, but for once she wasn't thinking of how he despised her so much as she was thinking of how it had felt to kiss him in the car today.

Of how he'd caressed her body and told her that he wanted her. Was it possible they could work their way through this? It seemed odd to be thinking it, when she'd so recently sworn to one of the waitresses at Ka Nui's that she would never spend her life with a man who didn't love her—

But that was before she'd realized she was already married and had a child with this man.

Her fingers combed through Rafiq's soft curls. She would do anything, sacrifice anything, for this child. It was the oddest sensation, and yet it was the absolute truth. She knew it to the bottom of her soul.

She sang more quietly now, as Rafiq's eyes remained closed and his breathing evened out. A few more minutes and Adan nodded at her. She let the last note taper off and then it was quiet, except for the sound of the gas flames in the lanterns and the night sounds of locusts. Occasionally, there was a distant howl from a lonely jaguar hunting the dunes.

Isabella glanced at Kalila, who was shifting in her chair, and realized that the woman was probably uncomfortable by now. As much as she would love to continue to sit here with Rafiq asleep on her lap, she couldn't let Kalila be stiff from sitting too long.

"Perhaps we should take him to bed," she suggested, glancing at Kalila when Adan looked at her.

"Yes, I think you are right." Then he got up and came to take Rafiq from her. They progressed into the house while a servant began to clean up the dishes. This time, Isabella followed Adan all the way to Rafiq's room. It was packed with toys, of course, and decorated in cool blues and white. Connected to his room was another, and this was where Kalila stayed. Adan told her to go ahead to bed, his voice full of concern and gentleness. She curtseyed before going into the room and shutting the door.

Isabella thought that Adan stiffened, but then she decided she must have imagined it because he turned and laid Rafiq so gently into his crib. His hand ghosted over Rafiq's curls, and then he bent and placed a kiss on his son's forehead.

Isabella's eyes filled with tears. Every man, no matter how hard, could be brought to his knees by something. For Adan, it was love for his son that made him human.

Adan stood and turned to her. "If you want to…"

She shook her head. She desperately wanted to kiss Rafiq goodnight, but she was afraid to disturb him. She didn't know how to do all the things she wanted to do just yet. It saddened and infuriated her all at once, but she had to be patient.

Adan took her hand and led her from the room and back out onto the terrace where coffee had been set at a small table for two. He pulled her chair out and she sank onto it, her pulse pounding in her throat and temples as he stood so close.

And then he was sitting across from her and lifting his coffee to his lips as he turned to gaze out at the darkened garden.

"It is very peaceful here," he said after a few moments of silence. "I would stay for weeks if it were possible."

"I imagine it's been very hectic since your uncle died."

"I have been the heir for over a year now, but yes, it has still been quite an adjustment. There is much to do when one is responsible for an entire nation."

"But we have a parliament now. Surely that helps."

"I think it does, yes. But there is still much work to be done. Fortunately, wherever I am, I am connected. Imagine the days before we had computers and cell phones."

"A trip out here would have been a true vacation then."

"Yes. Now, it is simply another stop. A different location, but the world does not truly go away."

It occurred to her that she didn't really know anything about him. "I'm sure I must have known this before, but how many siblings do you have?"

"Three brothers and one sister, who came much later in life. She is ten now."

"I always wanted a sister. Or a brother," Isabella added. She'd been so lonely, with her books and tutors and no other children to play with.

Adan seemed to know without asking what she meant. "I would like siblings for Rafiq, as well. He would enjoy having other children to play with."

Isabella studied the steaming liquid in her cup. "I'm surprised you didn't remarry by now."

He shrugged. "Time passed faster than I thought. I don't think I realized it had been two years until very recently."

"Do your brothers have children?"

"Not yet," he said. "Only one of them has married. The other two seem to think playing the carefree bachelor in Europe to be more fun." His eyes narrowed. "What about you, Isabella? Did you find playing the bachelorette fun?"

A shiver crept over her, not only because the sun had gone down and the desert was cooling. "I didn't date, if that's what you mean."

"Why not? You are a beautiful woman. And you must have got lonely."

Her heart throbbed. "Did you?"

His eyes glittered in the half-light of the torches. "Ah, answering a question with a question. Classic avoidance. And yes, I did get lonely."

"So did I. But I didn't date." She sighed and told him the truth. "It didn't feel right somehow. But I did let a man kiss me once."

He looked as if he could bite a nail in two. A fresh wave of irritation flooded her.

"It's not like I knew about you," she said. "And it was only a kiss. I'll bet you can't say the same," she added defiantly.

"I'll bet I can," he replied coolly. "I've kissed no one but you since the day we were married."

Her mouth dropped open. "I don't believe it."

He set the coffee down. "Believe it, Isabella. I've had

a child to raise and a business to run—and then I had a throne to prepare for. There's been no one but you."

She blinked in surprise. "But you were getting married again!"

"Jasmine is an old friend."

"I—I don't know what to say." She really didn't. A man like him…celibate?

"There is nothing to say." He stood abruptly. "Perhaps it's time we called it a night, yes? It's been a long journey and it's getting late."

She got to her feet, too. "What's the point in getting angry with me? It's not my fault."

"Nothing is, is it?"

She clenched her fists at her side. "What do you want from me, Adan? I'm trying."

"And I'm not?" he asked dangerously.

Isabella blew out a breath. "That's not what I meant. I meant this is hard, for both of us, and there's not a lot we can do about the past now."

"I'm beginning to think this was a bad idea after all," he said softly, his gaze dropping briefly to her lips before spearing her again.

"We just got here. You promised me two weeks."

"Promises, as you very well know, are easily broken," he said. And then he stalked into the house, leaving her lonely once more.

CHAPTER EIGHT

ADAN couldn't believe he'd told her. He'd confessed to her that he'd had no lover since she'd gone away. It hadn't been intentional. After she'd been declared dead, he'd grieved her loss. But he hadn't been heartbroken because of it. He'd grieved because she was Rafiq's mother, because he'd been fond of her.

He'd taken her presence in his life for granted, and he'd regretted that immensely. But that wasn't what had stopped him from attending to the sexual part of his life after she was gone.

He'd always intended to take a mistress. Or another wife. It had just never happened. He truly had been busy, first with taking care of Rafiq and finding a decent nanny for him. Adan had fired three nannies before he'd finally begged Kalila to come raise his son.

After that, he'd been busy with his business interests and then with the aftermath of his cousin's death and becoming the heir to the throne. There'd been no time in his life for casual affairs. He'd missed sex, missed women, but he'd had little time to worry about it.

Now that he'd brought Isabella out here, all he could think of was sex. He'd intended to stay busy and stay away from her as much as possible. But then she'd told him in the car about her memory of their wedding night, and he'd realized the futility of that plan.

He wanted her. And as he'd sat with her tonight and listened to her sing, as Rafiq had fallen asleep on her lap, he'd realized that his intention was to take her to his bed at the end of the evening. He'd pushed everything from his mind but her.

Then she'd told him she'd kissed another man. Until then, he'd purposely avoided thinking about what she'd been up to for the past two years as a lounge singer.

Hearing it had made him crazy. It was ridiculous, because it was nothing really, and yet the knowledge of that kiss had sliced into him with the utter unfairness of it. He'd been celibate, and she'd been kissing another man.

It was nothing, and everything.

He'd wanted to pick her up and carry her to his room that very minute. He'd wanted to make her his. Irrevocably.

But it was wrong—wanting her was wrong—because in two weeks, when this was all over, he would wed Jasmine.

It was late when he shoved the covers aside and got out of bed. His body was heated and his brain wouldn't settle down. He was restless, like a caged lion. He padded naked to the en suite bathroom, then pulled on a pair of shorts, not really certain what he intended to do other than leave the bedroom.

Outside the window, movement in the garden caught his eye. And then he realized what it was: Isabella walking the labyrinth by moonlight.

The path was dark, but the moon gave enough light to make out the pattern. Isabella moved slowly through the labyrinth, wondering when illumination was supposed to happen. She walked closer to the inside, and then farther away again. Just when she thought she was almost there, another twist in the pattern took her to the outside of the circle.

She didn't know why she was doing this. She lifted her head to look at the dark walls of the small palace. A light burned in an upper window, but that was all. The torches had been turned out hours ago, and the garden was dark and still.

She'd gone to bed and slept fitfully, her dreams filled with Adan and Rafiq—but mostly Adan. She'd dreamed of lying in bed with him, of telling him she loved him and of him stiffening beside her. Then she'd dreamed of waiting for him to come to her bed and falling asleep in tears when she realized he wasn't coming after all.

The dreams had disturbed her. She'd wanted to know their meaning. It was silly to think that walking a dark path in the moonlight was going to teach her anything, but she'd been drawn out here by the idea that it would calm her.

She wasn't feeling calm so much as frustrated, however.

"This is ridiculous," she muttered as another turn took her away from the center. Then she stopped in the pathway. This wasn't working. It would be better simply to go inside.

She turned to leave, intending to step over the knee-high hedges, but gasped at the sight of a man standing at the edge of the labyrinth, watching her.

Adan.

"I couldn't sleep," she said.

He stepped over the first hedge. "Neither could I."

Then he stepped over another one. "You aren't giving up, are you, Isabella?"

He wasn't wearing a shirt. Dear God in heaven. His torso gleamed in the moonlight, all hard planes and ridges where muscle and bone melded to create something damn near to perfection.

Isabella swallowed. No, not *near* perfection. Definitely perfection. She'd seen enough muscled chests on the beaches of Maui for the past year to know perfection when she saw it.

"I'm not getting anywhere," she said, her pulse beginning to throb in her throat. And elsewhere.

Her body was reacting, melting, aching. The surge of moisture between her legs didn't shock her. Adan made her feel things that no man ever had. Hot, needy things. She wanted to roll with him in a bed, to feel his magnificent body inside hers, to see if the things she'd dreamed—remembered?—were as good as they were in her head.

"It takes patience," he said, stepping over another hedge, and then another one.

"I've waited too long," she said—and wondered exactly what she meant by that statement. He stepped over the last hedge, stopping in front of her. He was so near, his body radiating so much heat that she thought she might burn if she touched him.

"Sometimes waiting makes the culmination that much sweeter." His deep voice was a vibration of sound through her body. She felt the words as much as she heard them. "Finish the path, Isabella."

"Will you go with me?" Because it seemed it would be easier if someone was with her. Less frustrating.

Slowly, he shook his head. "You have to walk it alone. But I'll be waiting in the center."

And then, before she could stop him, he hopped the rest of the hedges into the middle. She wanted to do the same. She stood there, undecided for several moments. It was just a path, for heaven's sake, and yet it intimidated her.

"Trust me, *habibti*. Walk the path," he urged.

Isabella blew out a breath and started to trace her way through the path again. She didn't want to finish. She wanted to *be* finished. Frustration built inside her like a snowball, gaining layers on each turn. The weight of it pushed outward until she felt she would split apart if she didn't reach the middle. It urged her to just hop the hedges and join him.

No.

She was going to walk the damn thing at least once. She would not allow him to call her a quitter. She wasn't a quitter, no matter what he might think. She didn't know why she'd left her father's house in the night, alone, but she would be damned if she'd let this man continue to believe it was because she had no staying power.

She'd be damned if she'd let *herself* think it was because she had no staying power. Because that was her secret fear, she acknowledged. That she was somehow flawed and that Adan had been right. That she'd left because she couldn't handle the responsibility.

She circled toward the center again, then back outside, and then, just when she thought she was about to be directed to the outside yet again, the pathway spilled her into the grassy center. She stopped abruptly as a flood of emotion nearly overwhelmed her. And then the feelings of unworthiness, guilt and fear lifted off her shoulders—as if she'd been carrying a load of rocks that had suddenly fallen away.

It was shocking. Because all she'd done was walk a circular, twisting path into a small clearing. It was nothing significant. Nothing earth-shaking or life-changing.

And yet she felt as if she'd succeeded somehow.

Adan held out his hand and she took it, let him pull her into the center of the clearing. He turned her until her back was to him. She could feel his body pressed close to hers, feel the heat and hardness of him. He was so solid, so overwhelming.

And he'd made love to no one but her in three years.

Isabella shivered. Why had she thought of that, out of everything she could possibly think of at this moment?

His lips touched her ear. "It's surprising how it makes you feel, isn't it?"

She could only nod.

His hands were on her shoulders, burning into her. Then one slipped down, curved around her midsection and pulled her tighter to his body. His arousal was unmistakable, pressing into the small of her back, and she closed her eyes and took a shuddering breath.

Suddenly, she knew why she was here. Why they were here together.

"Adan...I want..." She couldn't finish the sentence. A lump rose in her throat.

"I know," he replied. "It's inevitable. It has been inevitable since the moment I found you again."

She turned in his embrace then, tilting her head back to gaze up at him. His face was stark, as if he had been fighting his feelings and could do so no longer. As if he'd surrendered to something bigger than himself.

And she knew what it was. Desire. Lust. Need. Complete and total, as she'd never felt before.

Except that wasn't true, she realized. She had felt it before. For him. For Adan.

She ran her palms up his bare chest, glorying in the feel of hot naked skin, of the hard smooth planes of muscle and the shuddering tension coiled there.

He wrapped his arms around her body and pulled her in tight, his head lowering to claim her lips with his own.

Isabella sighed with the pure pleasure of his kiss. His tongue tangled with hers as if it had done so a thousand times. His hands came up to cup her face, and then he deepened the kiss. She responded immediately, instinctually, though she had no conscious knowledge of what to do.

Or did she?

She dropped one hand down his torso, slid her fingers along the waistband of his shorts. She was rewarded with a growl of pleasure. A rush of pure feminine power went to her head.

How many times had they kissed like this? How many times had she touched him exactly as she just had?

"We need to go inside," he said, lifting his head. "I am not prepared."

It took her a moment to figure out his meaning. "I'm on the pill," she replied. And then she almost wished she hadn't when he stiffened beneath her fingertips. "My cycles were irregular. The doctor said it would help regulate them."

She thought he might walk away then and there, but he hesitated only a moment before bending to kiss her again. Then he caught the bottom of her tank top in his fingers and slid it upward. She hadn't put on a bra to come out here, so when he reached the naked flesh of her breasts, he groaned before breaking the kiss and whipping the shirt over her head.

His broad hands wrapped around the soft mounds, his fingers tweaking her nipples gently. Isabella's breath caught at the riot of sensations streaking through her. She clutched his forearms to steady herself.

"You are beautiful, Isabella. Just as I remembered," he said. There was an edge to his voice, a sharp slice of—*something*—that called out to her and made her body flood with heat and moisture.

She was so ready for him. Ready for whatever he wanted from her.

"Adan," she gasped as his head dropped and he took one pouting nipple in his mouth. Her head fell back as he suckled her, his lips and teeth and tongue knowing exactly what to do in order to make that excruciating connection between her breast and her aching core. Every pull of his mouth on her nipple created an answering spike of pleasure in the wet crease between her legs. She ached for him, for his possession, in ways she hadn't ever dreamed were possible before now.

He stopped, and she cried out, reaching for him to keep him from stopping.

Adan laughed, a low, satisfied male sound that made her nerve endings prickle with heat. "Do not fear, Isabella. I'm nowhere near finished with you yet."

He made quick work of the zipper on her jeans, sliding them from her body and turning to place them on the ground with her top. Then he slipped out of his shorts and spread them out, as well.

Isabella's breath caught at the sight of him naked in the moonlight. His body was magnificent, every line and shadow of him hard and perfectly formed. His erection jutted from his body proudly, and she found herself aching to touch him. To take him inside her and know what it felt like to make love with him.

She went into his arms without hesitation, and he lowered her to the grass, placing her on top of the clothing. Around them, the hedges shut them in from prying eyes. Over top of them, stars blazoned across the sky in the billions while the moon gently lit the curves and hollows of their bodies.

Adan kissed her again, and she put her arms around him, holding him close as he slipped a hand between her legs and found her wet center.

His groan made her heart leap with joy. And then she couldn't think because his thumb slid over her clitoris. Again and again while her body tautened like a bow beneath his fingers.

When he stopped what he was doing, she murmured a protest, but he only laughed.

"It will get better, I promise," he said, and then he was kissing his way down her neck, her collarbone. He took his time with her breasts, licking and sucking until she was panting his name—and then he swiped his tongue down the center of her belly, dipping into the hollow of her belly button before teasing her bikini line with kisses.

Isabella held her breath as he parted her soft folds. They were slick and swollen and so sensitive that she trembled with the slightest caress of his breath across her skin.

And then his tongue dipped into her moistness and she arched off the ground in ecstasy.

"We've hardly begun," he murmured against her flesh. He slid his tongue the length of her, broadside, and then teased her clitoris with soft swirls that didn't quite do what she wanted.

But then he did do what she wanted, what she craved, as he licked and sucked and nibbled her until she flew apart much too quickly with a harsh cry. A single hot tear slipped down her cheek as she gasped with pleasure and surprise at the intensity of her release.

Had it always been like this between them? She wanted desperately to remember, and yet she couldn't. A trickle of memory here and there was all she'd been allowed, when what she wanted was for the floodgates to open and everything to come back.

He moved up her body then, his mouth tangling with hers once more as he gripped her buttocks in a broad hand and positioned her beneath him. She wrapped her legs around his waist, her whole body shaking as he began to push inside her.

"You must tell me if I hurt you," he said, his muscles corded with the tension of taking his time.

Isabella swallowed a gulp of fear. She wanted him so desperately, in spite of her release a few moments ago, and yet she was frightened of him, too. Frightened of what this would mean.

"I don't really know what to do," she confessed shamefully. "I'm trying."

He kissed her again. "You're doing everything right, *habibti*. Everything."

He moved forward relentlessly, and for a moment she thought he would be too much for her, that she would have to tell him to stop. Her fingers curled into his arms, her nails digging into him as he filled her.

And then her body opened to him as if it had always done so, and he slid the rest of the way home with a groan. He was so deeply inside her she could feel the pulse-beat of his body within hers.

He didn't move, and she gazed up at him in wonder and shock. Had it always felt this way? The amazing sense of fullness and anticipation sent little electrical charges across her skin until she was dying for him to move, to take her even higher.

How could she feel so much pleasure when he'd done nothing more than enter her body?

The look on his face was equally awed and bewildered. It was as if time stopped while they stared into each other's eyes, as if the world ceased to turn, and no one existed except the two of them.

I love you echoed inside her heart—but her head insisted it wasn't true. How could you love a man you'd forgotten, a man you hadn't yet gotten to know again?

You couldn't. It was simply the overwhelming emotions she felt at being joined with him this way.

"Isabella," he said softly, and his voice held a kind of amazement that she recognized. As if he too were blown away by feelings he couldn't explain.

Another tear dropped down her cheek. He caught it with a finger.

"It would be the hardest thing I have ever done, but if this hurts you, we can stop," he told her. "Pain should not be a part of this. Ever."

She couldn't tell him that pain was a part of it for her, but not physical pain. Never physical pain.

"No," she said quickly. "Oh, no. Don't stop, Adan. Please don't stop."

With a soft exclamation, he began to move inside her. He took his time at first. Her body instinctively knew his, knew the rhythm, and she rose to meet him as he withdrew again and again, his thrusts gaining power each time they met.

It didn't take long for their lovemaking to slip into the danger zone, to become something so hot and intense that they were no longer in control of it. At some point, their hands twined together on the ground above her head. Though it was cool in the garden, sweat slicked their bodies as they tangled together in the center of the labyrinth.

Everything Adan did, she realized, was designed to spin out her pleasure for as long as he could make it last. But it was inevitable that it had to end. Isabella caught the fine edge of the wave, and then plunged into the depths of a shattering release that had her sobbing his name as she shoved her hips upward to meet him.

Adan gripped her bottom in both hands, lifting her to him as he made her pleasure last and last and last. By the time it was over, she was wrung out, spun out, shattered beyond repair. She would never be the same again.

"Look at me, Isabella," he said.

Her eyes snapped open.

"I want to watch you come for me."

"I can't possibly—"

"Believe me, you can." And then he began to move again. For the barest second, she wanted to beg him to stop—it was too much, too intense, and she would never survive it a second time. When he'd brought her to orgasm with his mouth, it had been amazing and wonderful.

But this...this was earth-shattering not only to her body, but also to her soul.

And then, just like that, the feeling caught again, spinning up inside her in one long pleasurable wave that she could no more deny than she could stop breathing.

This time when she shattered, he went with her. He gripped her hips, holding her to him, and plunged deeply into her body, shuddering inside her with such force that he cried out sharply as he came.

Eventually he rolled to his side, taking her with him until he was on his back and she was lying on top of him. She laid her head against his damp chest, breathing harder than she would have believed possible, and closed her eyes.

His fingers traced up and down her spine, softly, rhythmically, until she felt herself drifting. They stayed like that until their bodies cooled and the night air sent a shiver tiptoeing across her.

"We should go in," Adan said. His voice sounded sleepy, as if he, too, had been drifting.

Isabella pushed herself up, yawning. "I need my clothes."

Adan got to his feet and helped her up. "Forget the clothes," he said. And then he swung her into his arms and carried her into the house.

CHAPTER NINE

ADAN woke sometime around dawn and reached for the woman in his bed. She came to him instantly, opened to him, and then he was stroking into her body and losing his sense of place, his sense of self, as he got lost inside her lush sensuality. He thrust into her with more force, more rawness, than he ever had before.

She'd been so naive and sweet when he'd married her. He would not have considered making love to her like this, riding her body hard, glorying in the answering urgency of her need. She drove him to this, drove him to want to possess her again and again.

He hadn't intended to take her to his bed. Hell, he hadn't intended to make love to her at all. When he'd gone outside earlier, it had been more out of curiosity than anything else. He hadn't thought they would end up naked and making frantic love in the center of the labyrinth.

But they had. And when it was time to come inside, he'd thought they would part ways when he carried her to her bed and left her there.

Except that he'd gone straight to his room instead. Once there, he'd been delighted when she'd wrapped her hand around him and let him know she was ready for another round. He'd lain on his back and thrust up inside her while she ground her hips against him, her beautiful breasts bouncing in the moonlight, her glorious hair tickling his chest when she leaned forward to suck one of his nipples.

Now, her breathy moans filled his ears, made him crazy. He took her lips, caught her moans in his mouth and gave them back to her when he exploded inside her a short time later.

Adan fell asleep again, his arms wrapped around the quivering, sighing woman beside him. When he awoke much later, light was streaming through the windows and across the bed—and he was alone.

He sat up, half wondering if it had all been a dream. But, no, his body could attest to the fact it had not. He showered and dressed, then went in search of food, coffee and Isabella.

He found her in the kitchen with Rafiq and Kalila. She carried Rafiq on her hip as she floated around the kitchen island, gathering ingredients from the refrigerator, and pots and pans from the hanging rack above. She looked beautiful, radiant, her entire body glowing with that special look of a well-pleasured woman.

She smiled when she looked up and saw him. "Look, Rafi, there's your daddy. Say hi to Daddy."

"Dada," Rafiq yelled.

Adan's heart twisted. He loved Rafiq so much, and yet he couldn't help the twinge of jealousy that stabbed into him while Isabella held their son. He should be pleased the boy liked her, and yet, part of him was not.

Adan stepped forward and held out his arms, gratified when Rafiq went straight into them. It was petty of him, he knew, and yet he was delighted his boy wanted him more than he wanted to stay with Isabella.

When he caught her eye, he was surprised to see that she didn't seem disappointed. In fact, she was smiling at him as if they shared a secret.

Which, he supposed, they did. She crooked an eyebrow, and he found himself thinking of last night—of her lips, her sighs, the catch in her throat, the feel of her sex surrounding him, of that warm, wet, amazing place he wanted to spend hours exploring.

He broke eye contact with her and kissed his son on the cheek. He needed to stop thinking about Isabella before he grew hard in the middle of the kitchen. Before he handed Rafiq to Kalila and dragged his wife—*his wife*—back to his bed for the rest of the morning.

"Did you sleep well, Your Excellency?" Isabella said teasingly.

"Not as well as I would've liked."

"I'm sorry to hear that. Perhaps you should get a new mattress or something."

"The mattress is fine," he said. "It just needs to be broken in a bit more. Rigorous bouncing might do it."

Her eyes widened as she looked at him. She glanced at Kalila, who seemed oblivious to the undercurrents as she worked a puzzle in a magazine. Adan grinned as Isabella cut her gaze back to him.

Rafiq bounced in his arms then. "Bell!" he exclaimed. "Bell, Bell, Bell!"

Bell indeed, Adan thought.

"Yes, baby boy?" Isabella said.

"Bell!"

Isabella laughed, the sound as sweet and pure as spring water. "I'm sorry to hear you did not sleep well,

Your Excellency. Perhaps you should return to bed and catch up on your rest. We wouldn't want you to be unable to, um…keep up, as it were…"

"I think I can manage," he said, shooting her a grin. "Especially if I get some breakfast. Who's in charge of cooking around here?"

Isabella smiled. "The cook is shopping at the local market for a few things. I am making breakfast."

"You can cook?"

Her green eyes were filled with humor. "I had to learn a thing or two recently. Cooking was one of them."

He was doubtful, but she set about scrambling eggs and making toast. Before he knew it, she'd plopped plates of food in front of him and Kalila. Kalila looked at the blackened edges of toast doubtfully.

"It's American," Adan said helpfully. Kalila cut her eyes at him while Isabella's back was turned. Adan shrugged. Then he picked up a fork and dug into the eggs. Kalila followed suit, though she looked apprehensive.

Isabella came around and took Rafiq, placing him in his high chair and giving him a plate of food, as well.

Adan popped the eggs into his mouth. His taste buds rebelled instantly. He would have spat the eggs out, but Isabella was watching him hopefully.

"Good, right?"

"Um…yes," he replied. The eggs weren't inedible so much as overcooked. Any moisture had been leached out of them a while ago. They clung to his tongue like dust. Salty dust.

"The toast got a little burned, but I scraped it off," she said. "You won't even notice, I promise."

Kalila put her fork down as Rafiq spat out the eggs

and started banging on his tray. "He wants his usual, Your Highness," she said by way of explanation.

Isabella's expression fell. "I can get it for him. What does he want?"

"It's okay," Kalila said, hurrying to the pantry and grabbing the baby cereal Rafiq preferred. Within a few moments, she'd set a bowl in front of him and handed him a spoon. Somehow, Kalila found a way to busy herself without returning to her plate.

Adan took another bite while Isabella smiled and fixed her own plate. Then she stood across from him and lifted a forkful of eggs to her mouth. Her frown was immediate.

"I overcooked them," she said, dropping the fork onto the plate and setting it on the counter.

"They're fine," Adan replied. "Just a bit dry."

She reached across the island and gripped his wrist. "Don't, I beg you. If you keep eating, you'll get a stomachache. And then your imperial guard, or whatever you call them, will be marching me off to jail for an attempted assassination."

Adan set his fork on the plate. "You aren't used to this stove," he offered helpfully. "Or the toaster."

She sighed. "Yes, I'm sure that's it. Or maybe I just can't cook as well as I thought I could. I didn't do it that often, actually. I ate takeout quite a lot, in truth."

Adan stood. "Come, let us go out onto the terrace. Kalila will whip something up in no time."

Isabella sighed her disappointment. "Can I help you, Kalila?" she asked.

Kalila shook her head. "Go, Your Highness. This will take me ten minutes. It is very simple. I will be pleased to teach you later, if you like."

"Thank you," Isabella said before following Adan to the terrace. He pulled a chair out for her and she sat heavily.

"I can do nothing right," she said.

Adan grinned as he took the seat across from her. "I don't know about that. I can think of a few things you do exceedingly well."

She didn't seem mollified. "I hate that Kalila has to fix breakfast now. She has enough to do."

"Yes," Adan said, his heart twisting with the familiar grief and love for his old nanny. "This is not too much for her, though. It will be fine."

Her green eyes searched his face then. "You love her, don't you? I thought she was a bit old to be Rafiq's nanny, but then it occurred to me that she must have been yours."

"She is the mother I never had," he replied truthfully, stunning even himself with the admission.

"Your mother died when you were young?"

Adan's laugh wasn't humorous. "Oh, no. She is still very much alive, holding court in her magnificent house, and telling all her friends how proud she is that her son is a king. If she could trot me out for them and pinch my cheeks, she'd be even prouder."

"I'm sorry, Adan," she said softly, frowning.

He shrugged self-consciously. "Her children were prizes. Possessions to be displayed for others to admire. Children made her nervous, so she preferred to see us when we were at our best. And to send us away again once we'd made an impression."

"So Kalila raised you."

"Yes. She was the constant in our lives, the one who held our hands, patched our scrapes and hugged us when we needed it." He sighed. "She should be enjoying her retirement, but there was no one else...."

He broke off when she looked away and pressed a hand to her mouth. When she turned to him again, her eyes were glistening, but she did not cry. Her smile wavered at the corners.

"I did tell you I can't do anything right," she said. "Maybe it would have been better if you hadn't found me after all."

It wasn't so long ago he'd thought that, too, but he wasn't about to say it. He'd been angry for so many things, but he was tired of being angry.

"Why don't we worry about the present, *habibti?* The past cannot be changed."

"Are you truly that forgiving?" she asked, arching an eyebrow. "Or are you just enjoying the fringe benefits?"

In spite of his wish otherwise, a skein of anger began to unwind inside him. And guilt, because he *was* enjoying the sex. Too much, perhaps.

"We've spent one night together, Isabella," he said. "Don't start redecorating everything to your taste just yet."

Isabella didn't know why she'd pushed him. Why hadn't she just gone with the flow and enjoyed breakfast and the sensual afterglow of a night of amazing lovemaking?

Because she was frightened, she admitted to herself. Frightened of what was happening between them, and frightened of her feelings for him and their son. Already, she felt as if leaving would rip her heart from her chest. She'd been attempting, in her own stupid way, to interject reality into the situation.

The reality was that they'd had sex. Mind-blowing sex, but still just sex. One night of pleasure, even if he had been celibate for the past almost three years, was not enough to make him want her to stay forever.

She knew it, but she'd needed to hear it in real terms. She'd needed his censure instead of his warmth so that she could keep her feet firmly grounded. This man was not about to fall in love with her and beg her to stay. He hadn't been in love with her before, so why would he fall now?

If sex were the magic potion, then it would have worked on him years ago. Besides, she was a different person than she had been when they'd married. She didn't need his love. She only needed to be in her son's life. She knew what it was like to grow up without a mother, and she didn't want her son to experience the same. Nor did she want him to be shuffled between parents who used him as a pawn in their relationship.

She would do anything to prevent it.

"I wouldn't dream of redecorating a thing," she said crisply. "I—"

Kalila emerged with a tray just then and Adan shot to his feet to help her. He took the tray from her gnarled hands, admonishing her for not sending one of the serving girls.

"They were busy, Your Excellency," she said. "And it is no problem."

"Adan," he said firmly. "You promised."

The old woman glanced at Isabella, then nodded. "I did. Now be a good husband, Adan, and serve your wife," she said before rambling back into the house.

Isabella bit the inside of her lip as he turned. She wondered if he knew how much emotion showed on his face when he talked to Kalila. She could see it all written there: the love, the guilt, the pain, the frustration.

Her heart throbbed as he came back to her and set the tray down. She wanted to rise to her feet and put her arms around him. To hug him tight and let him know it would all be right. He was a man with so many burdens, and she felt guilty for adding to them.

The food was simple but filling. A copper pot held hot coffee, and Isabella took the handle and poured into two cups. They ate in silence. Isabella looked out over the garden as she chewed. The labyrinth in daylight was a far different place than it had been last night. Less magical, more ordinary.

She thought of their clothes, probably still spread out in the center, and found herself blushing at the memory. Not only that, but a shiver pulsed through her. A pleasurable shiver.

She'd tried not to think too much about what had happened between them—and yet, in truth, she'd hardly thought of anything else. The memories had been playing in the back of her head like a movie reel since she'd awakened this morning. All she could see was Adan's naked body covering hers. All she could feel was the incredible heat and emotion of their lovemaking.

Every stroke of his body into hers had been a revelation. Every kiss, every sigh, every caress. How had she lived each day without knowing that kind of simple joy?

And how had she committed the colossal mistake of allowing last night to happen? It would have been far better had she not. Except that she'd had no will to resist when she'd turned to him in the labyrinth. No will to do anything but see where her feelings took her.

Was that what she'd done two years ago, at her father's house? Followed her feelings to some dark, terrible place that separated her from her baby and her husband? Would she ever know what had truly happened?

"You said that your mother was relieved when you moved out of her house after your recovery," Adan suddenly said, startling her. "Why was that?"

Isabella spread jam on a piece of bread. It had always been hard to think about the many ways in which her relationship with her mother had gone wrong. But perhaps she owed him, since he'd shared his past with her.

"My parents divorced when I was eleven," she said. "I saw my mother rarely after that. My father wouldn't let me go to the States, and my mother wouldn't come to Jahfar. She called frequently at first, but then the calls tapered off. Eventually, she was more like an occasional pen pal than a mother."

"Staying with her was awkward."

"Yes. We were so different by then. I think I appalled her." She chewed the bread. It went down like a lump of sand, flavorless and gritty in her throat.

"Why do you think that?"

"Because she's so independent. And I was too Jahfaran, too traditional. I don't think she liked what my father had made me into." She'd been waiting, in those early days in her mother's house, for someone to tell her what to do. Thinking back on it now, the knowledge filled her with disgust. She'd got over her conditioning, but it hadn't been easy.

"You don't like talking of this," he said.

She shook her head. "I don't, but I probably need to. Maybe I'd remember more if I could face some of the more difficult parts of my life."

His brows drew together. "How do you mean difficult?"

Isabella shrugged. "I was an only child. You know that. And I always felt like such a disappointment to my parents. My father wanted a boy. My mother wanted to please my father. They divorced because of me."

"No one ever divorces because of a child. It's not your fault."

She looked at him in disbelief. "Do they not? Why do you wish to divorce me, then?"

His expression grew fierce. Troubled maybe. "That's different, Isabella."

"But you do intend to divorce me," she insisted. "Nothing has changed in that regard."

He tossed his napkin on the table. "It's a little premature to be discussing our future after only one night, don't you think?"

Isabella's heart throbbed. "You've had a long time to think of your future. I feel like I'm playing catch-up. Like I'm a dog chained to a tree and I can only go so far before the chain snaps me back again."

"What do you want from me, Isabella?" he asked, his eyes flashing in his handsome face. "I'm giving you this time with us. It's all I can promise right now. Because Rafiq comes first, and I will do nothing to compromise his happiness."

Why was she pushing him? Now wasn't the time, and yet she felt so hurt, so lost and alone, that she couldn't seem to help herself. She wanted, just once, for someone to say it would be okay.

And yet she knew that wasn't going to happen. Adan might have enjoyed her body, but he wasn't here to soothe her bruised soul.

The sudden lump in her throat made eating impossible. She pushed her plate away.

"I don't particularly like auditioning for a role in your life, you know." She got to her feet, her hands clenching at her sides. "I didn't come here to do so, either. Because you're right, this *is* about Rafiq. So I'd like to keep the focus where it belongs, if you don't mind."

"And what do you mean by that?" he asked dangerously.

She tilted her chin up. *Courage, Isabella.* "I mean that last night was a mistake I will not be repeating. If you want me in your bed, then you'll have to accept me into your life."

"Are you threatening me, *habibti?*"

She laughed without humor. "As if I could possibly do so. No, I'm telling you that I won't sleep with a man who refuses to give me more than vague promises about my role in my son's life. We don't have to remain together as a couple, Adan, but I *will* be Rafiq's mother until the day I die."

The following week would have been idyllic if not for the tension between her and Adan. He spent a lot of time in his office, on the phone, attending to affairs of state, but he often found time to stop and come to wherever she was sitting and playing with Rafiq. His face remained carefully blank when their eyes met, though when he gazed at Rafiq, the love that showed on his handsome features pierced her heart with its sweetness.

He had not once attempted to touch her or kiss her since her declaration to him.

And she had to admit that she missed the physical contact between them. It had been thrilling, intense and

terrifying all at once. She'd thought she would feel more
settled, less overwhelmed, if they went back to being
strangers to one another.

But nothing could be farther from the truth.

She craved him, craved his heat and scent and passion. One night with him had been the biggest mistake
she'd made; because it haunted the rest of her nights and
made sleep difficult.

Isabella firmly shoved Adan from her mind as she
got dressed and prepared for her day with Rafiq and
Kalila. Today, they were going into town to visit the
souq. It would be their first outing together and she
looked forward to it very much.

She met Kalila and Rafiq in the entry, and they
walked out to the waiting cars and got inside. Isabella
settled Rafiq in his car seat, and then they were rolling toward the small desert town. Rafiq chattered the
whole way about things he saw outside the window.
Before long, they were in town and Isabella was pushing
Rafiq through the *souq* in his stroller. Kalila had said
she could do it, but Isabella told her to enjoy the shops
instead.

A security detail ranged both behind them and
in front of them in order to make sure there were no
threats to their safety. It was disconcerting at first, but
Isabella soon forgot they were there as she let herself
enjoy the outing. The *souq* was colorful, the stalls
jammed together haphazardly to create a warren of
pathways. There were vendors selling spices, cloth, gold,
carpets, copper, clothes and hundreds of other things.
Isabella sighed happily. She'd missed this, though she
hadn't been allowed to attend the *souq* very often growing up.

Too dangerous, her father had said, when what he really meant was that he didn't have time to take her.

Rafiq stared wide-eyed at the motion and color all around them. Isabella stopped and bought him a honey cake at one of the stalls. She put it on the stroller tray and he dug into the sticky mess with relish.

"His father loved honey cakes at that age, too," Kalila said. "I used to make a special one on his birthday."

Isabella smiled. In the few days she'd spent time with Kalila, the woman had always been so formal and reserved. This was the first time she'd spoken of something personal.

"Was he a handful growing up?" Isabella asked, thinking that he was certainly a handful now.

Kalila laughed. "He was, as you say, a handful," she replied. "But a very loving boy nonetheless. He always regretted starting trouble, though I know he did it for attention."

"His mother's attention?"

Kalila frowned. "And his father's. Mostly his father's, I think. He learned early that his mother was not interested."

"Does he see her often now?"

Kalila shook her head. "Rarely. He ignores her calls. In his own way, I suppose he's paying her back."

Isabella glanced down at Rafiq's dark head. She couldn't imagine her own son feeling that way about her. A wave of love and sadness flooded her. If she had her way, he would never have reason to.

"He is a good man," Kalila continued. "You will need to be patient with him, but he will see what is best."

Isabella drew in a shuddering breath. "I hope you're right, Kalila."

The other woman patted her hand where it rested on the stroller, and they continued their way through the *souq*. The air was hot, and as midmorning approached, it became still and humid.

"We should go back," Isabella decreed after they'd been exploring for nearly an hour. The *abaya* she wore clung to her skin damply, and the headscarf was no longer doing so good a job of keeping the sun out. She'd long ago put up the hood of the stroller so that Rafiq was covered.

She glanced over at Kalila, frowning at her red face. The old woman wore black, which had to be so hot, but she wasn't sweating.

"Yes, we should go," Kalila said.

"Are you feeling well?" Isabella asked as they turned and headed in the direction of the cars.

Kalila waved a hand. Her gait was slow, but steady. "I am fine, Highness."

Isabella handed her a bottle of water from the bag she'd stuffed in the back of the stroller. "Here, drink this."

"You drink it. I can wait."

"No, I insist," Isabella said, twisting off the cap and giving it to Kalila. "Besides, I have more."

It wasn't until ten minutes later, when they were sitting in the car with the cool air blowing, that Kalila cried out. And then she sank in a heap against the seat.

CHAPTER TEN

HEART attack were the only two words he heard when Isabella phoned and said they had taken Kalila to the hospital. Adan ran out the door and hopped into one of the Land Rovers, gunning the engine and speeding out of the driveway before waiting for a driver or security. He made it to the small local hospital in record time, tossing the keys to a startled man in a white coat before dashing into the stark waiting room and demanding to be shown to Kalila's room.

Isabella was sitting on a bench in the hall. She stood as he approached, her face pale and drawn. Anger and fear pierced the veil of his emotions.

"Where is Rafiq?" he demanded before she could speak. First Kalila was ill—and now his son was missing. What was this woman thinking?

Her hands were clasped in front of her body. "There is a playroom nearby. He is there, with a nurse. And he has a bodyguard, never fear."

Guilt rippled through him, but he could not voice it. Instead, he turned to the door of Kalila's room.

"Before you go in—" Isabella said behind him.

He turned, one eyebrow lifted in question.

"The doctor is with her, but he won't tell you this in

front of her. She can't work anymore, Adan. She can't
take care of Rafiq. Her heart is weak. She's on medication, but it can't make up for her advancing age."

"And that suits you just fine, doesn't it?" he snapped.
"If you think this is your lucky opportunity, Isabella,
think again."

She looked as if he'd slapped her. The guilt washing
through him turned into a wave.

"I'll forgive you for that because I know how much
you love her," she said quietly. "You're scared and hitting
out at me. I understand that. But don't you dare think I
would ever take joy in someone else's pain. That's not
fair."

He ground his teeth together.

"You're right," he said. And then he turned and entered Kalila's room.

After another two hours, Isabella took Rafiq home. It
was time for his dinner and there was nothing more
they could do at the hospital. Kalila was in a private
room, receiving the best care money could buy, and
Adan was with her. She was weak and tired, but the
doctors seemed to think she would recover.

She just wouldn't be allowed to take care of growing
boys anymore. She needed rest, relaxation and someone
to take care of her for a change. Her husband had died
several years ago, and she had no children of her own.
She'd been living with her sister's family when Adan
brought her back to the palace to care for Rafiq, and
Isabella supposed that was where she would return.

It made her sad to think of Kalila leaving her son.
Rafiq was attached to her, and no matter what Adan
had said, Isabella did not rejoice in the fact that Rafiq's

care would fall to her with Kalila gone. She wanted to be a mother to her boy, but not at anyone's expense.

Worse, she felt as if Kalila's attack had been her fault. If she hadn't wanted to go to the *souq,* if Kalila hadn't insisted on walking with her—if, if, *if*...

There were too many ifs, and she knew it wasn't right to blame herself. The doctor had told her that Kalila's heart was weak and an attack had been inevitable.

Still...

Isabella shook herself from her reverie. She had the cook prepare dinner for her and Rafiq, then took her son to his room and let him play for a little while before bathing him and putting him to bed. He was fussy, missing Kalila, but she stood over his crib and sang until he began to drift. Once he was asleep, she bent and gave him a kiss, then retreated to her own room, taking the monitor that Kalila relied upon to tell her if Rafiq was awake.

The sun was just setting when she heard a car pull up outside. Doors slammed and then slammed again as Adan entered the palace. She waited a few minutes before going in search of him. He'd been gone so long, and she was worried that maybe something had changed with Kalila's condition.

She found him in his office, sitting in the darkening room and gazing out the window. His computer wasn't on, so she knew he wasn't working.

"Adan? Is everything all right?"

He didn't turn. "She will recover," he said. "But she's very tired tonight."

"Yes, I imagine she would be." Isabella bit her lip. "Do you need anything?"

He sighed and shoved a hand through his hair. "It's my fault," he said. "All my fault."

Isabella's heart cracked in two. "Adan, no." She went to him and put a hand on his shoulder. Squeezed. "It's not your fault. It's no one's fault." She swallowed a raft of tears. "And if you want to play the blame game, I'll say that I think it's *my* fault. I took her to the *souq,* and I kept her out in the heat too long…"

A sob welled in her chest and she stuffed her fist against her mouth to keep it from coming out. This was about him, not her. About his feelings and fears, not about her insecurities. Damn her, why couldn't she just comfort him and not make it about *her* for once?

Adan turned the chair and wrapped his arms around her waist, stunning her with the motion. He buried his head against her chest, his breathing coming faster and harder now, as if he, too, was working not to lose control. A tremor slid from his body to hers, and she put her arms around him and squeezed tight.

She didn't know how long they stayed that way, but the light in the sky had died away completely when his grip finally eased. She couldn't stop herself from cupping his jaw, from bending and pressing her lips to his forehead.

His hands slid to her buttocks, and a thrill of anticipation snapped over her nerve endings. She threaded her fingers in his hair, lowered her lips to his and drank him in.

They didn't speak because words weren't needed. They each knew what the other wanted. What they needed.

He undressed her with quick hands while she did the same for him. Soon, they were naked and pressed

together, their skin hot, their hands seeking, their sighs
and moans and kisses only the beginning. He set her
on the desk and stepped between her legs. Then he was
deep inside her and they were both gasping and groaning
with the incredible sensation. Papers fell to the floor as
he took her hard, but he didn't seem to care.

Isabella wrapped her legs tightly around his waist,
lifted herself to him, and let her head fall back as he
took her body to heights she'd been dreaming of for the
past week.

It was so good. So right.

Tears slipped down her cheeks unchecked. She was
glad it was so dark, because she was afraid of what he
would think if he saw her crying. Would he know she
cried because he'd ripped her heart out of her chest and
claimed it for his own? Would he know that, in spite of
herself, she'd managed to fall for him? That she saw
through him, through the facade of the harsh desert
lord to the soft, inner core of the man who loved his old
nanny so much he would shed silent tears for her?

She cried for herself, too. For the naive, stupid girl she
must have been. And for the woman she was now—the
woman who would have her heart shattered if this man
decided to let her go at the end of their two weeks.

She'd come to Jahfar to find out the truth. She'd found
something much more precious.

She didn't know what had happened between them
two years ago, or why she'd walked into the desert and
been lost, but she knew that *right now,* she loved this
man. She loved him and their child so much she would
do anything for them.

Soon, she forgot her tears as her body wound so tight
that she knew she was about to explode.

"Yes, Adan, oh yes," she gasped as he lifted her hips from the desk and ground into her, forcing her into a shattering orgasm that caused black spots to appear behind her eyes. He continued to drive into her—and then his release hit him and he groaned her name as his body stiffened and shuddered.

A few moments later, he gathered her to him and kissed her softly. They held each other for several minutes, not speaking, just breathing.

"Spend the night with me," he whispered in her ear.

A shiver skated down her spine. "Yes," she said simply.

Isabella was awakened in the night by Rafiq's cries. She stumbled from the bed where Adan was sleeping so soundly, the covers shoved down to reveal his naked body in all its magnificence. He lay on his back, one leg bent, an arm thrown casually over his head.

He stirred as she moved, then came awake as if a switch had been thrown inside him.

"Where are you going, *habibti?*" he asked.

"Rafiq," she whispered, holding up the monitor. "He's crying."

She went into the nursery and found her son standing in his crib. It took her a while to figure out that he had a messy diaper, but she managed to change it without too much trouble. Then she sang him to sleep again. When she turned to leave, Adan was standing in the door, watching her. He'd pulled on a pair of shorts, but his chest was bare, gleaming in the tiny night-light illuminating the room. His hair was mussed, and he shoved a hand through it, yawning.

"He's sleeping," Isabella whispered as she came over to him.

"You did a good job with him," Adan whispered back. "He's comfortable with you."

She felt ridiculously pleased at that. "I'm learning. But he's very patient with me."

Adan smiled. "Patient? I'd never have called our son patient. He's too much like me."

Isabella didn't miss his use of the plural. Hope blossomed in her soul. *Careful, Isabella. It doesn't mean anything, except that he's tired and stressed.*

He put his arm around her and they walked back to his room in silence. Once there, he stripped the robe from her body and kissed his way across her skin, taking his time, until she was writhing on the bed and aching for his possession.

He made love to her again, tenderly, drawing out the pleasure between them until there was nothing else that existed in this world but the two of them. Isabella came apart beneath him, and then slowly pieced herself back together.

Melancholy set in as they lay together afterward. She was no closer to remembering her life with him than she ever had been. She'd remembered pieces, but not the whole. And she hadn't yet remembered a thing about her baby.

She didn't want this time together to end, but she also wanted to see her father. She had to know what had happened and why he'd lied about it to her. Part of her worried that it was something horrible. Something devastating from which she would never recover if she knew the truth.

And part of her *had* to know the truth if she was to

move forward and build a life with Adan and her son. Adan hadn't said anything, but the way he touched her, the way he made love to her and held her—surely he'd decided they would stay together and parent their son as a couple?

He could not be so cruel as to give her false hope, could he? If he truly intended to send her away, would he have asked her to sleep with him tonight? It had not been about sex at that moment. They'd gone to his bed and fallen asleep in each other's arms until Rafiq's cries awoke them.

Now, Adan's fingers were stroking up and down her arm. Softly, rhythmically.

"I'm sorry for what I said to you earlier. About Kalila." His voice startled her, and she turned on her side to face him, spread her hand over his chest and delighted in the feel of smooth hot skin and hard muscle. A sensual shiver slid across her. She wasn't interested in sex right now, but touching him made her body stretch and come to life in places that should be too sated to do so.

"I know, Adan. You were scared for her. We both were."

"I shouldn't have brought her out of retirement," he said. "But there was no one else I trusted."

Isabella sighed wistfully. "She wouldn't have come had she not wanted to."

"Yes, but I shouldn't have asked. I should have searched harder for someone else. I should have married sooner."

Isabella felt a pinprick of anxiety. But what else could he say? He hadn't known she was alive then, she reminded herself. "You probably should have," she said. "And yet I'm glad you did not."

He turned his head on the pillow. "You have complicated my life, *habibti,* but I find I am not sorry for it. You love Rafiq very much, and this makes me happy."

I love you very much, too, she wanted to say. But she didn't. It was too soon, too fresh, and she was still frightened of it. Frightened of how vulnerable it made her. When she'd been alone in Hawaii, she'd known something was missing from her life. But she hadn't known what that was. Now that she did, the thought of losing it again terrified her.

And if she didn't quite know how she'd lost it the first time, how could she prevent it happening a second time?

"He's amazing," she said. "I can't believe we made him together. It astounds me every time I look at him. He has so much of you in him, and yet I see me, too."

"I must find another nanny for him," Adan said on a sigh.

Her stomach flipped, but then she told herself not to read too much into it. A nanny was not unusual in the least, especially for the son of a king.

"Can Kalila recommend someone?" she asked.

He nodded slowly. "I had not thought of it before, but yes, I will ask her once she's feeling better."

"How will you break it to her that she can no longer care for him?"

She could see the gleam of his teeth as he smiled in the darkness. "Kalila would never refuse an order from her king. I plan to buy her a house in Port Jahfar, on the coast, and fill it with servants to take care of her. I should have done this in the first place, but I admit I did

not think of it. I was a teen when she left my parents'
employ, and though I saw her from time to time, it wasn't
frequent enough that I wondered what she was doing in
her retirement."

Her heart squeezed. "You are very good to her, Adan.
She's lucky to have you."

"No," he said. "It is I who am lucky to have her.
And I want her to know it for as long as she lives.
Between me and my siblings, she will never want for
company. We will visit her often, and I will bring her
to the palace as frequently as she desires, provided her
doctor approves."

"I'm so glad she's going to be all right," Isabella
said, shivering as she remembered the way Kalila had
collapsed on the seat. Her eyes had rolled back in her
head, and Isabella had thought she was dead.

He squeezed her hand where it lay on his chest. "You
aren't to blame, you know. The doctor said it was lucky
someone was with her when it happened. If she'd been
in her bed, she would have died before we found her.
The heat in the *souq* exacerbated her condition, but it
did not cause it."

Isabella shivered again. "Then I'm glad it happened
the way it did, even if she frightened me half to death. I
was certain that if anything happened to her, you would
never forgive me. Nor would I forgive myself," she admitted. "Kalila has been kind to me. She's never once
made me feel as if I don't belong."

"Maybe it's because you do," he said softly.

They stayed at the Butterfly Palace for two more days
before packing everything up and returning to Port
Jahfar. Though the trip had been cut short, Adan felt

as if he'd learned all he needed to know. Now he had to get back to the capital and continue the process of governing his nation.

Kalila was being airlifted to the finest hospital in Port Jahfar, where she would continue to receive care from the best heart specialist in the country.

Adan worked on his laptop and took calls while they traveled, but he hadn't been able to take a separate vehicle from Isabella and Rafiq. He should have, perhaps, but he hadn't wanted to.

His gaze kept straying to his wife. She was beautiful, radiant and so much more confident and self-aware than he'd ever given her credit for in the past. He'd said she was a different person, and perhaps in some ways she was, but this luminous woman had always been there.

He just hadn't been able to see her.

She looked up from where she sat playing a simple game with Rafiq and caught his eye. Then she smiled at him, that lovely, secretive smile that sent blood pooling low in his groin. Always, he wanted her. This feeling hadn't abated since he'd taken her in the labyrinth over a week ago.

If anything, it had grown stronger.

This morning, they'd made frantic love against the marble-tiled wall of the shower, him holding her up and thrusting into her tight, wet body while she clasped him around the waist and rode him with abandon. Last night, he'd taken her from behind as she knelt on all fours in the center of the bed. He'd wrapped his hands in her glorious hair and lost himself in the heat and wonder of her.

And still he wanted more. Had he wanted her this much when they'd married? He didn't remember it being so overwhelming, this compulsion. He did remember enjoying her body very much, though he hadn't enjoyed her in quite so many earthy and raw ways.

She was his match in bed. His equal. And he was beginning to believe she was his equal outside of it, as well. She wasn't Jasmine Shadi. She wasn't quiet or meek or easily cowed. She wouldn't agree with him on everything. And she wouldn't tell him what he wanted to hear just to keep peace between them.

Adan frowned. He still didn't know why she'd left, why she'd abandoned her baby son, and that bothered him a great deal. If he kept her, was he endangering Rafiq's happiness? Was she only playing the good mother now because she wanted to be a queen? At the first sign of trouble, would she hand Rafiq off to a nanny and claim that he was too much for her nerves?

No. To the depths of his soul, he knew the answer to that question. Isabella was not like his mother. She would not ignore her child. His mother couldn't have faked deep love for her children for any amount of money. She'd loved them in her own way, but her way was twisted to suit her own purposes. They were a means to an end, a possession to be proud of. They weren't meant to be hugged and kissed and loved.

Isabella wasn't like that. He'd watched her changing Rafiq's diaper when she hadn't known he was there. Other than not quite knowing what to do, she hadn't acted like a woman who would rather be anywhere but where she was. She loved Rafiq. He couldn't be more certain of it if it were written in indelible ink across her forehead.

She *loved* their child. And he found he didn't mind so

much sharing Rafiq with her after all. It seemed natural to do so.

Still, he spent the journey weighing the pros and cons. By the time they reached Port Jahfar, Adan knew what he was going to do. There was only one decision he could make. One decision that was right for them all.

He stepped from the car, and Mahmoud, who had returned earlier in the day, bowed deeply. "Your Excellency. Welcome home."

"Thank you, Mahmoud."

Around them, servants hurried forward to gather luggage while his security team fanned out to oversee the procedure.

Mahmoud shot a glance at Isabella. Then he gave Adan a meaningful look.

"There is a *gentleman* here to see you, Excellency. A gentleman you have been desiring to see since your return from America."

CHAPTER ELEVEN

ISABELLA had just put Rafiq down for his afternoon nap. She closed the door to his room and settled into the living area that connected Rafiq's nursery to Adan's suite. A television flashed silent pictures on the screen. She didn't bother to pick up the remote and turn on the sound. Instead, she opened up a laptop computer that was sitting on a side table and surfed the web. She hadn't been on a computer since she'd arrived in Jahfar nearly two weeks ago. Her email was overrun, but she set about methodically answering her friends back on Maui.

The band wanted to know when she was coming back. They'd hired a temporary singer, but they needed her dreadfully. She laughed at the number of exclamation points that Kurt, the guitarist, put in his email.

A knock sounded on the door. She waited, expecting a servant to enter, but when no one did, she got up and opened it.

"Daddy?"

"Isabella," he said, his plump face creased in a frown. There was sorrow on that face. And fear. But fear for what? For her?

Her heart pounded with worry—and just as quickly, the worry changed to anger. He'd lied to her. Whatever had happened to her, he'd *lied*. She stepped back to let him in, folding her arms around her like a shield.

"Does Adan know you're here?"

"I have just been to see him," he said, taking a handkerchief from his pocket and mopping the sheen of sweat that glistened on his brow.

"And did you tell him what he wanted to know?" she asked, proud of how her voice didn't betray her cold fury.

"I told him enough."

"Then perhaps you can tell me what the hell really happened to me," she said very precisely, the words like razor blades in her throat.

He looked at her in surprise. She expected a sharp correction any second, but he did nothing of the sort. Good, because she would never be meek and dutiful ever again.

"I wanted to protect you," he said. "I did it to protect you."

"Protect me from what? And don't you dare lie to me now, not after what I've been through."

He took out a cheroot and lit it with shaking hands. She moved away, not caring for the smoke, yet realizing he needed it to calm down. Adan must have taken him to task for his deception. The thought satisfied her immensely.

"You were sick, Isabella," he said when he'd drawn in a lungful of smoke and let it out again. "You weren't yourself after the baby came."

A chill skated over her. She spun to face him. "Not myself? How do you mean?"

"You were depressed. Postnatal depression, the doctor

said. You were distant, uninvolved with the baby. And you talked of suicide."

"I don't believe you," she whispered past the huge lump in her throat. How could that be possible?

His face twisted. "Believe it, Isabella. Do you think I went through what I did for you just because it seemed like a fun idea?"

She swallowed. Hard. "Adan's never said anything to me about being depressed. Why not? Wouldn't he have known?"

"He didn't know because I didn't want him to know," her father snapped. "I couldn't afford for him to know. He would have had you declared insane, Isabella. And then he would have divorced you."

Fear wrapped around her heart and squeezed. Insane? Would Adan have done that? She shook her head. No, he would have helped her, not hurt her. He would have wanted her to get well.

"So you believed it was better he thought I was dead?" Anger—and fear—was a living thing inside her belly, twisting and turning and lashing her with its claws.

"It was better for everyone."

Horror permeated her bones as she stared at him. How could he have done it? How could he have been more concerned about his station and his business interests than about her?

Because she knew what had motivated him as surely as if he'd blazoned it across the sky. *I couldn't afford for him to know...*

If a prince had divorced his daughter for being suicidal and depressed, then he would lose respect. His business would suffer.

Prince Weds Daughter of Prominent Businessman

would have become Prince Divorces Insane Daughter of Prominent Businessman.

"How did you do it? How did you make everyone think I'd died?" she said, her lip trembling. She needed to hear it. Needed to hear to what lengths her father had gone to "protect" her.

To protect himself. Because, once more, she'd managed to disappoint him, hadn't she? He'd wed her to a prince, and she'd ruined everything.

He finished the cheroot and stubbed it out. "You really did walk into the desert, Isabella. We couldn't find you. It was two weeks before I got word that a woman resembling you had been taken to a hospital in Oman. You were found by British tourists who kept you alive long enough to get you there."

Her eyes were flooding with tears. "Why can't I remember any of this?"

"Because you were near death, because you blocked it from your mind—I don't know! When I realized you didn't know you had a child or a husband, I had you examined by a psychiatrist. He said you were repressing memories that were painful to you."

Painful memories? About Adan and Rafiq?

"But why didn't you tell Adan? I might have remembered if he'd come for me. I'd have been with my baby for these past two years instead of living somewhere else and believing the lies you told me."

He shook his head. "You would not have magically remembered, Isabella. And Adan wouldn't have let you near Rafiq once he realized you were so unstable."

He came over to her, put his hands on her shoulders. She wanted to shrug away from him, but she was too numb to do so.

"I know you don't believe this, but I did what I thought was best for you. You're my only child, and I love you. I would have sooner had you living somewhere else and not knowing about your past than to have you committed to an institution. It was a blessing that you had forgotten."

"You don't know that he would have done that."

"He is an Al Dhakir, Isabella, and he bears a great responsibility. More so now than before. He could not have afforded the attention. He most definitely cannot do so now."

A chill skated over her. "What do you mean by that? It's over. I'm back, and though I don't remember, I'm fine."

"For now," he said, his eyes full of sadness as he gazed at her. "But what if you were to get pregnant again?"

She shook him off. "I don't remember any of what you're saying. I can't just believe what you tell me when I don't know the truth!"

"I'm telling you the truth, child. You were depressed once—it's possible you could be so again. And who knows what you will do next time?"

She swiped at her eyes with trembling hands. "They make medication for depression. It won't happen again."

"You were on medication the last time, though I made sure your husband didn't know about it. But you didn't take it, Isabella, and look what happened. Do you want to take that chance again? Do you want to embarrass your husband, your nation, by trying to harm yourself or your baby? What if you succeed the next time? What then?"

She wanted to put her hands over her ears, like a recalcitrant child, and shut him out. She wanted to lock out the painful words and pretend she'd never heard them. How could she have done such a thing? What was *wrong* with her? Why couldn't she be normal, like any other woman who'd just had a baby?

Why wasn't she normal?

"What are you suggesting I do?" she asked. Part of her was gibbering in fear and the other part, the rational part, had locked on to cool, disconnected control. The only way to get through this was to not feel anything.

He sank onto one of the couches and steepled his hands beneath his chin. "Go back to the States, Isabella. Go back and forget any of this happened."

Tears dropped down her cheeks though she tried not to let them. "I can't do that," she said. "I won't do it. I'm not leaving my baby ever again."

He sighed and got to his feet once more. "You may not have a choice. Adan knows everything now. And he may not be willing to give you another chance."

She waited hours for Adan to come. The sun passed high overhead, then slowly sank into the sea, and still he did not come. He had to come eventually, because she was still in his apartments and Rafiq was still with her. She sat on the couch in the living area, a home-improvement program on the television while Rafiq played with a set of building blocks on the floor.

The people on television were so happy, fixing up their modest home with new curtains, paint and furniture. Newlyweds with a baby on the way, the host helpfully informed her.

Isabella splayed her fingers across her stomach. Had

she ever been that happy? Had she made plans with her husband for their home and their new baby, or had she simply done what she'd been told and not asked questions or dared to have an opinion?

She was very afraid she knew the correct answer.

Was that why she'd forgotten everything? Had she been so miserable that she simply couldn't face it? Was she that *weak* that she couldn't face her own past?

Angrily, she tossed the remote onto the couch. She was so wound up she wanted to punch something. She would have hauled off and socked the cushion off the couch, but it would make a noise and Rafiq would jump since he was so engrossed in his play. And she didn't want to frighten him. He was her precious, precious child. Her chest hurt with all the love she felt for him. How could she have ever dreamed of harming him?

Stop. She couldn't go there. She simply couldn't think it. Besides, she didn't know if it was even remotely true. She'd tried to harm herself, not him. She might not remember what had happened then, but she knew in her bones she could never harm her child.

Another hour passed and she put Rafiq to bed, then returned to the living area. She couldn't go to the rooms she'd been given when she'd arrived, because that would mean leaving Rafiq alone. And she couldn't go and lie down in Adan's bed since she was no longer certain he would want her there.

She fell asleep on the couch finally, curled up in a ball with the remote in her fist. When she woke again, the only light in the room was the glow of the television. She pushed herself up, yawning—

And squeaked as she realized she wasn't alone.

Adan sat in a chair across from her. He was watching

her, waiting—for what? For her to go crazy before his eyes?

She wouldn't give him the satisfaction.

"You talked to my father, I take it," she said. What sense in delaying the inevitable?

"I did."

"And so now you know."

"How are you, Isabella?"

The question made her angry. As if he was now worried about her sanity and needed to treat her with kid gloves. "Other than wanting to clap tinfoil on my head to keep the aliens from finding me, I feel just fine," she retorted.

He didn't crack a smile. "Did anything he said jog your memory?"

She crossed her arms. "No. I walked into the desert and nearly died. People found me. I woke up with a big gaping hole in my memory where you and Rafiq should have been. End of story."

She suddenly deflated, pulling her knees up to her chest and wrapping her arms around them. "It's frightening not to remember what happened to you, especially when people tell you things you said or did and you just don't remember any of it. It's like it happened to someone else, or maybe it's just a movie someone tells you about. Because it can't be you. If it were, you would remember."

He turned his head toward the closed door to Rafiq's room. "How has he been today, without Kalila?"

She shoved a stray lock of hair behind her ear. He didn't want to talk about it, of course. The moment they got to the difficult parts, he was done. Could she blame him? It was creepy, in a way.

"He fussed a bit, but he's been fine. He asks where she is. I told him she was sick and she had to go away to feel better."

"Do you think that's wise?"

"Yes," she said firmly. "He can't understand the full truth, but he doesn't need to be lied to, either. When I was five, my dog died. My parents couldn't tell me the truth—" Here she paused and shook her head. "Oh God, of course they couldn't." A bitter laugh erupted from her throat before she stuffed it down again. "They told me he ran away. For years I kept hoping he would come home again, wondering if I'd done something wrong to make him leave. It was harder when I learned what really happened, years after the fact."

He was looking at her with sympathy. She almost hated it, almost hated the way he seemed to see her as a fragile creature when only a few hours before he'd treated her like an equal. She didn't delude herself that he'd fallen in love with her, but she'd thought he was beginning to care. How could he ever care about someone as broken as she was? He'd always be wondering when she was going to crack again.

"Then I guess you were right to tell him."

"What happens now, Adan?" she asked. Because she just didn't feel like beating around the bush.

He stood. "It's late. We should probably go to bed."

Disappointment ate at her. She *was* tired, but she'd hoped he would say more. That he would tell her he'd been thinking about what came next. That he would say something about what her father had said, other than to ask if she was all right. She wanted to know how *he* felt about it.

But he wasn't going to tell her. Not tonight anyway.

"I had you moved closer," he said. "Your room is across from Rafiq's now."

Her room. He didn't even want to sleep with her anymore.

"Great," she said. Because what else was she going to say?

He walked over to a door and opened it for her. "Get some sleep, Isabella. We'll talk in the morning."

She paused in the doorway. Her hands itched to reach out to him. She wanted to wrap her arms around him, wanted him to wrap his around her and squeeze her tight. She wanted comfort and connection.

But he wanted away from her. Away from his crazy wife. Her heart hurt.

She wrapped her arms around herself to keep from touching him.

"Good night, Adan," she said. And then she went inside and closed the door.

Adan lay in his big, lonely bed and longed for Isabella. She'd seemed so tired, so fragile and worn-out, and he'd known he couldn't ask anything of her. He'd thought of taking her to his bed and just holding her, but he hadn't trusted himself to keep from doing anything else once he had her in his arms.

She'd had a lot to process this afternoon.

So had he.

He was still so angry with Hassan Maro that the man was lucky he wasn't sitting in the bottom of Port Jahfar's darkest prison cell at the moment. After he'd spoken with Maro, he'd gained access to the rest of Isabella's medical records. The doctor he'd had talk to her upon their arrival had examined everything and called him back immediately, confirming the findings.

Isabella had been suffering from postnatal depression, as he'd earlier thought, and she'd nearly died in the desert. Further, she'd chosen to block certain memories of her life as a coping mechanism for the emotions that had driven her out there in the first place.

Adan turned over and punched the pillow, his body aching. But his heart ached more. He'd thought back to the early days of their marriage and tried to remember what had happened between them. Not much, he had to admit. He'd taken her virginity, got her pregnant and left her to her own devices while he ran his businesses and waited for the birth of their child.

They had not been close.

She'd bored him, mostly. She'd done everything she was supposed to do as his wife, but she hadn't challenged him or made him long to come home at the end of the day. She hadn't even sung for him—and singing was such a part of her that she was constantly singing or humming something. How had he never realized that before?

Oddly enough, as much as she'd angered him when he'd found her again, she'd also electrified him. She'd made his blood hum with anticipation, and she hadn't stopped since the moment he'd kissed her in the back room of that seedy little bar in Hawaii.

Guilt was his constant companion now. Was it his fault she'd been so miserable two years ago? Why hadn't he paid her closer attention after Rafiq's birth? Why hadn't he known she was suffering?

Damn Hassan Maro for hiding it from him!

Had he caused her to feel so hopeless that she'd tried

to take her own life? The doctor had said it had nothing to do with him and everything to do with the hormones raging through her body, but why had she blocked her memories of him specifically?

He couldn't figure it out. And he knew he wouldn't figure it out even if he lay here for an entire month of sleepless nights. He would simply go round and round with feelings of guilt and anger and helplessness.

What he had to think about now was the future. Their future. He sighed heavily. Nothing was as he'd planned it.

He'd wanted to marry Jasmine because she was a friend, and because she was kind and gentle and would be a good mother to Rafiq and any other children they had.

But he couldn't do it. As he'd lain in bed with Isabella the night of Kalila's attack, he'd known the truth.

He couldn't take another woman to his bed, couldn't make love to her, when all he would be able to think about was Isabella. Somewhere over the past few days, Isabella had become vital to him. She made his blood sing, his heart pound and his body ache.

But it was more than that. She was so vibrant to him, so alive and beautiful, and she loved their son completely. He couldn't imagine his life without her in it.

Was that love? He didn't know, but he knew he wanted to find out. When he looked at Rafiq, he was overwhelmed with love—but it was different than what he felt when he looked at Isabella. What he felt for her was strong, but was it based on attraction or on something deeper?

He wasn't sure. How could he be sure?

And now, on top of everything else, he was worried about her. Could he give her what she needed, or were they doomed to repeat this cycle again? Could he make her happy, or was he incapable of doing so?

He wanted to fix it, wanted to make everything right again, and yet he did not know how.

He was a king, with a nation to lead and people to govern, and he couldn't even figure out his personal life. What did that say about him?

CHAPTER TWELVE

SOMETHING had changed between them. Isabella concentrated on the breakfast they'd been served beneath the Moorish arches of the inner courtyard, which adjoined the royal apartments. The food tasted like ash on her tongue.

She tried to read the same article in *Al-Arab Jahfar* for the twentieth time that morning, and for the twentieth time she couldn't get past the first paragraph without her mind wandering.

Adan sat across from her, his attention firmly on the folder of papers that Mahmoud had brought to him as they'd sat down to eat. He'd barely spoken to her since.

Not that she was surprised. He was horrified, no doubt, by what her father had told him. And he was merely tolerating her until he could find someone he trusted to replace Kalila. Or until he could divorce her and marry the woman he'd been planning to wed when he'd found her in Hawaii.

The thought made her stomach cramp. How could he have made love to her so passionately only yesterday morning if he'd still been planning to marry someone else? Not only that, but what about the things they'd shared with each other? It hadn't been just about sex, she was certain.

For her, it was about love. Her heart hurt with all the love she felt for him. Had it been this way before? Was she getting a taste of what it had felt like to be with him before she'd walked into the desert? She very much feared she was. Not only that, but she was also getting a taste of what it was like to be the only one whose heart was on the line.

Last night, she'd asked him what happened next. She'd been tired and heartbroken and she'd wanted to know. Now, she was too scared to repeat the question.

He'd given her a reprieve last night. He'd pitied her, no doubt, and he'd wanted to spare her feelings.

But today? Today he would tell her the bald truth. And she just wasn't ready to hear it.

Later, she would face facts, but for now she wanted to pretend everything was as it had been before. She wanted a few hours to remember what it had been like before her father had interjected the ugly truth of what had really happened to her.

She wanted to remember that she'd been building something precious with Adan and her son. Something she might never get back again.

"I am going to visit Kalila this morning," Adan said, startling her with the sound of his voice after so much silence. "I will ask her for recommendations about a nanny."

Isabella hooked her finger into her coffee cup, willing it not to tremble.

And so it began.

"That's probably a good idea," she said. "It will take time to find someone good."

"Yes," he said. "There is much to do in the coming weeks. It would be nice to have a new nanny in place to make everything go as smoothly as possible."

Isabella was proud of herself that she took a sip of her coffee without spilling any. "You're right. The sooner, the better."

She thought he looked at her oddly, but it was gone so fast she wasn't certain.

"What do you intend to do today, Isabella?" he asked. Clearly, he wanted to move on to small talk now that they'd gotten that out of the way.

She shrugged. "I was thinking of taking Rafiq to the pool."

"That's good," Adan said. "Rafiq loves to swim."

"And what about you?" she asked. "What will you do after you visit Kalila?"

His fingers drummed on the folder he'd laid on the table. He was so distant now, so polite, and it frustrated her. Where was the man who'd held her close in the night? The man who'd shared his darkest secrets with her?

"I have many things to attend to," he said. He looked at her then, his dark eyes piercing to her soul. "I don't know when I'll be done this evening."

Her heart sank a little. "So we should eat without you?"

He inclined his head. That dark, handsome head she wanted to cup between her hands while her fingers combed through his crisp curls.

"It would probably be best. In fact," he said, rising, "I should go now or I will never get through the day's tasks."

Isabella waited, for what she didn't know. Their eyes

met for a long minute, and her pulse kicked up higher and higher with each passing second. *Say something, Adan. Say you missed me last night. Say you want me tonight. Say it.*

But he didn't say anything. He simply turned and walked away.

Isabella took Rafiq to the kiddie pool where he splashed and played while she sat on the edge and watched him. The pool was partially shaded, but the weather was hot and she didn't drink enough water, even though someone continually brought her a fresh glass whenever the ice melted. She knew she was spending too much time fretting about the past, the future—and the present—but she couldn't seem to stop.

Two weeks ago, before Adan had crashed into her life again, she'd been happy enough—if a bit lonely and empty. She'd thought it was simply melancholy.

Today she had so much more to lose—and it terrified her. Which, in turn, made her angry. Since when had she reverted to the man-pleasing mind-set she'd grown up with? What did it matter if he didn't want her? She didn't have to let it control her life. Not everyone was lucky in love, after all.

People had their hearts broken all the time. People survived. She would, too.

When Rafiq started to get fussy, she took him back to his room and put him down for a nap. By then she had a headache, so she took some of the migraine medicine that Adan had got for her, closed the shutters to keep out the sun and lay on the bed in the darkened room, hoping the headache would soon abate.

She drifted in and out of sleep, her mind working on

so many things that at first she didn't quite realize what the scenes and emotions trickling into her head were. It began as a memory here or there, a snippet of life, until finally she sat bolt upright with a gasp.

Her heart thundered in her ears: she'd remembered her life with Adan.

They weren't the kind of memories where everything suddenly returned with such clarity and force that she could point to a moment in time and say, "This is when it happened. This is what caused it."

Instead, it was a body of knowledge downloaded into her head almost randomly, but nonetheless completely— or as completely as it would ever be. It was the emotion that slammed into her first, the helpless knowledge of what it was like to be in love with a man who did not love you. Or, worse, respect you.

Humiliation beat down on her. She'd tried everything to be a good wife to him. But after he'd got her pregnant, he'd become uninterested. Politely uninterested, just like this morning. She'd rearranged everything for him, suppressed her likes and dislikes to make sure he was comfortable and happy.

They took meals together often at first, and then rarely. He stopped coming to her bed. He did not make it to doctor's appointments, and he was often out of town.

She recalled growing big with child, recalled the sickness—the never-ending sickness that even now caused a pang of nausea to roll through her in sympathy—and her terror when the time came to give birth.

Adan had not been there. No one had been there, except for a servant. Her father was out of the country, and of course her mother was in America. Adan's mother was a stranger, a woman she'd met at the wedding and a handful of times since, who'd struck her as a cold, self-centered woman. She'd met his brothers, and his sister, but they were strangers to her, as well.

She'd given birth in a sterile hospital room, her closest friend the obstetrician who'd seen her through the pregnancy.

A drop of water splashed onto her breast, surprising her. She ran a hand across her cheeks, realized she was crying.

Of course she was crying. The memories were desolate, lonely. It's no wonder she had forgotten.

She ran through Rafiq's birth, remembering the agony of the contractions, the relief of the epidural and the moment when they'd handed her her child. She remembered feeling numb. She hadn't known what to do, and she'd only wanted to cry when someone insisted she put the baby to her breast. She'd wanted to escape. She remembered that clearly.

Shame and guilt hammered into her. She remembered feeling so strange, so disconnected, and she remembered not wanting to hold her baby. She remembered resenting Rafiq for imprisoning her in a routine that required her to subordinate even more of her self than she already had. Yet another male demanding that she change for him, that she be the perfect ideal of what a wife and mother should be.

Sorrow pounded through her in waves.

Oh God, she was every bit as horrible as Adan had thought she was. She hadn't wanted her baby. She'd wanted to escape, to be someone else.

She'd certainly tried to escape, hadn't she? For a time, she'd succeeded.

Except that she'd given up the one thing that was the most important thing in the world to her: her son. She'd asked herself for the past two weeks how she could have done such a thing. Now she knew, and the knowledge crushed her soul.

Isabella buried her face in the pillow and cried. She screamed and punched the pillow and kicked the bed until she was spent, until she had no energy left. She was a terrible person. She was damaged and sick, and she didn't deserve to be forgiven for anything.

She allowed herself to lie there wallowing in self-pity until the moment she heard a tiny cry on the monitor. Then she swung herself from the bed, sniffling, and took a deep breath to calm herself.

Whatever had happened in the past, she was Rafiq's mother now. She loved him. She would do anything for him, including sacrifice her happiness for his. She would never be that helpless, sad creature she'd been two years ago ever again.

She went and got Rafiq from his crib, then combed her hair and fixed her face before changing into a dress and a pair of low heels. She wanted to see Adan, wanted to tell him that she'd remembered. She didn't know why it was important, but it seemed as if she should tell him.

She picked Rafiq up, remembering to grab his favorite toy bear. A servant told her where to find the administrative wing as she left the royal apartments. She hummed to Rafiq on the way. He twisted a lock of her hair around his fingers, his bear clutched in the other hand.

Thinking of everything she'd remembered about his birth and the aftermath, she squeezed him a little too tightly. He started to fuss so she eased her grip again and smiled as she sang a song about an octopus.

As she turned into the administrative wing of the palace, she thought she caught sight of Adan. He was strolling down the hallway with a woman. A tall, dark-haired woman who had her arm looped in his. The woman laughed at something he said. They stopped and turned to face each other, and her heart lodged in her throat.

It was definitely Adan. He was so handsome in his white *dishdasha,* so exotic. She would know him anywhere.

He lifted his hand to the woman's face, stroked his fingers along her jaw while she smiled at him. And then he bent to kiss her on the cheek. Isabella's breath stopped in her chest as she watched him move his mouth to the woman's ear. Any second, he would kiss her on the mouth, whenever he ceased whispering whatever soft endearments he was whispering.

She couldn't look. She simply couldn't deal with having her heart ground beneath his custom loafers as she watched him kiss another woman, as she imagined him taking this woman to a bed with cool satin sheets and making love to her all afternoon long.

The way he'd made love to her not so long ago.

She'd been so stupid. So naive. She'd fallen for him. And, just like the last time, he didn't care one bit. His interest in her was tied to his desire to bed her. Once that was gone, so was he. Isabella whirled and fled back the way she'd come.

Adan spent the day in meetings with his cabinet, in phone calls with other heads of state and in going over the details for his coronation next week. He'd told Isabella he would be late, but he'd managed to finish earlier than he thought he would. Now he gathered the papers that Mahmoud had left for him and prepared to return to his private quarters.

He'd handled the situation badly this morning. But he hadn't known what to say. He hadn't known how to comfort her.

Everything he thought of saying sounded lame or trite. He was a man and a king, not a counselor. He understood action, not feelings. He understood how to make her body sing beneath his touch, but he didn't know how to soothe her soul.

He had to learn, however. If they were going to make this work—and he was determined they would for Rafiq's sake—he had to learn how to be a better husband.

The chef was preparing dinner when he arrived. He set the folder of papers down on a side table and followed the sound of voices to the courtyard. Rafiq was riding a toy car around the cobbled courtyard. Isabella sat at the table and clapped as he made his rounds.

She looked up as Adan stepped outside. The light in her eyes died—and then her gaze darted away. Inexplicably, a hard weight settled in his chest and refused to lift.

"We didn't expect you so early," she said.

"I didn't have as much to do as I thought."

"Of course," she replied, waving a hand airily. "You are your own boss, after all. If you wished to take an entire afternoon off, who would stop you?"

"Too many afternoons off and nothing would get done," he said mildly. "Though I expect things will settle into a predictable routine once the initial difficulties of transferring power to a new king are completed. My uncle never seemed to lack for family time, after all."

She pushed a lock of hair behind her ear. That glorious hair that he wanted to wrap his hands in as he made love to her in his bed. *Their* bed.

"And how was your day?" she asked. "Did anything interesting happen?"

"Interesting? Not especially."

She still hadn't looked at him. A tingle of alarm sounded in the back of his head.

She stood. "Well, I should take Rafiq for his bath."

He caught her wrist as she started to walk away. Her gaze fixed on his fingers where they encircled her.

"I'm sorry I'm not better at this," he said.

Her chin tilted up then. The full power of those green eyes turned on him—and he knew that something was wrong before she spoke.

"I remembered, Adan," she said softly. "I remembered what it was like. Our marriage, I mean."

His hand dropped away. He'd feared this even while he'd hoped for it. If she remembered, they could move forward. But if she remembered, she might not want to.

Right now he wasn't sure which side of the fence she'd come down on. Or why it mattered so damn much to him. She was still his wife, regardless. She couldn't do anything he didn't want her to do.

"When did this happen?" he asked, concentrating on the facts rather than the emotional impact.

"I had a headache this afternoon. I lay down for a while. It happened then."

Her voice sounded small, as if she were hurting so

much and trying to shrink from it. Guilt speared him. He had done that to her.

"Did you remember everything? The desert?"

She shook her head. "The doctor said I would probably never remember the days immediately before and after the accident." She swallowed. A laugh escaped her. Except that it wasn't really a laugh. "I still call it an accident," she said, "because I can't quite make myself name it what it is."

He blew out a rough breath. "It's not your fault, Isabella. Postnatal depression is a medical condition. There's no way of knowing who will get it and who won't."

He'd looked that up today when he'd had a chance. Aside from women with a history of depression in the family, one particular fact had leaped out at him: women who had stressful home lives and little or no support from their families were more susceptible than those who had more normal lives and relationships.

"It's terrifying to realize you weren't in control of yourself." She sucked in a breath. "I remembered when they handed him to me. I was overwhelmed, but not in a good way. He was like an alien to me, another being demanding my attention—someone else who wouldn't give me anything in return."

His throat hurt. He wanted to reach for her, but he didn't think she would appreciate it if he did. So he stood there with his hands hanging impotently at his sides.

"I suppose that shocks you," she said. "You'll think you were right to question my ability to be a good mother."

"I think you were overwhelmed by hormones. And by the fact you were alone."

She gave her head a tiny shake. "Women give birth alone all the time, Adan. Husbands go out of town on business or can't make it to the hospital in time. Those women don't have a problem bonding with their babies."

"I don't know what you want me to say to you."

"I don't think there's anything you can say," she replied.

"I can say I'm sorry."

Her head snapped up, her eyes flashing. "For what? For not being there? Or for not caring enough to notice something was wrong?" She ground her teeth together. Swore. "My father noticed, and look what he decided to do about it. Because he thought you would commit me, Adan. Even my father could see you didn't care about me."

He wanted to tell her she was wrong, of course he'd cared—but it wouldn't be the truth. He'd thought of his wife as another possession, someone who would be there to fill his bed, bear his children and run his household. He'd cared the way he would care about any living thing he was responsible for.

But that hadn't been enough. And he couldn't stand here and lie and say it was.

"I can't take back the past, Isabella. I can't change what happened."

A tear slipped down her cheek. She angrily swiped it away. "I saw you today, Adan."

He blinked. "You came to see me?"

"You were with a woman. You kissed her."

"I have kissed no woman but you," he said.

Rafiq kept zooming around the courtyard, squealing happily, but all Adan could see was the woman before him. The pain and anger on her face. The disenchantment.

"My God, you are unbelievable," she spat. "I saw you. And now I wonder if you lied to me at the Butterfly Palace, too. If you told me I was the only woman you'd been with in three years because you knew it would flatter me, make me more receptive—"

She broke off then, swallowed, and he knew she was fighting her tears.

"I did not lie, Isabella," he said stiffly. Fury whipped through him in waves. "I told you the truth because it *was* the truth. And you wanted me as much as I wanted you, regardless of how many women I might have slept with."

She stiffened as if he'd insulted her. "Well, you can rest assured that's not the case now. Because I don't want you anymore, Adan. I don't want you ever again."

CHAPTER THIRTEEN

HE was looking at her as if she'd grown two heads. But she'd been thinking a lot since she'd seen him with that woman today, and she'd come to a conclusion. She would not ever be pitiful again. She refused to love a man who couldn't love her, a man who cared so little about her that he could push her from his bed as easily as changing his shirt.

She was not a supplicant to the almighty King Adan ibn Najib Al Dhakir. She'd given up the job of supplication forever. She was the mother of his child, and she was going to be that for the rest of their lives.

But she would not live with him. She couldn't.

She loved him, and though it hurt her to imagine her life separate from him, she would not be a second thought to him—or anyone else—ever again.

"What do you want, then?" he asked, his jaw grinding.

He was annoyed, then. Good. Because she didn't need to be the only person affected, did she?

"A house nearby with a pool for Rafiq, and a small yard where he can play. It doesn't need to be anything grand."

"You want to live in a house near the palace?"

"Yes. And I want joint custody, Adan. I want Rafiq to know, starting right now, that I am his mother."

He'd gone slightly pale beneath his tan. Or maybe she'd just imagined it. "You want the divorce to proceed." It wasn't a question.

Her heart throbbed. Her breath sawed into her lungs painfully. "I think it's probably best. You've a wedding planned anyway. I assume the woman today was your bride-to-be."

He didn't answer at first. Then he nodded. "Jasmine. Yes."

Isabella was relieved that he was no longer denying he'd been with someone. At least he respected her enough to tell the truth now. Or maybe he just knew he'd been caught and saw no further need to prevaricate.

"How soon can this be done?" Because she couldn't stay here with him for a moment longer than she had to. She'd leave tonight if she could, but it was out of the question. Nothing could be accomplished that fast.

His brows drew down. She knew then that he'd got over the surprise and moved on to cold fury. Good, because she could deal with that better. If he were angry, she could be angry, too. It was far better than feeling hurt and love and sadness all at once.

"Do you truly want to do this to Rafiq?" he demanded. "Your parents were divorced, and you were torn between them."

She crossed her arms, as if it would somehow help to ward off the doubts that kept assailing her. "My mother went back to America. I'm not going anywhere. Besides, listening to them argue while they were still together didn't help much, either. It's better if we split, Adan, because there won't be any bitter feelings then. You can marry your new queen, and I can be our son's mother. When you have more children with her, you'll be grateful that I'm around to care for Rafiq."

"You've thought this all out, I see." His voice was so cold. So remote. If she touched him, would he feel like ice?

But no, she wasn't going to touch him. Not ever again. Her heart wept at the thought, but she stamped the feeling down deep. Rafiq was what mattered. She would endure what she had to for her son.

Seeing Adan with his new wife would kill her, but she would survive. In the long run, it would be better for her anyway. She could stop loving him and find someone who would really be good for her. Someone who loved her as much as she loved him.

And then, maybe, she would risk another child. If she knew her husband had her back no matter what happened, she would take the risk.

"I've had a lot of time to think today."

"Is this because of your memories? Or because of Jasmine?"

"It's everything, Adan. If you hadn't found me two weeks ago, we'd still be going on with our lives as they were. I'm grateful you found me, for Rafiq's sake, but everything else has been so hard to deal with. I don't think it does either of us any good to try and rebuild what was never really there in the first place."

He took a step closer to her then. Heat radiated from him in waves. "And what about the nights, Isabella? Can you so easily dismiss those, too?"

She moved a few steps away. He messed with her head, her heart, and she had to put distance between them or be pulled to him like filings to a magnet. She would be strong. She would not give in.

"The nights were amazing, Adan. You know that. And maybe they were necessary, in a way, though I don't know how you're going to explain them to your fiancée." She laughed then, the sound bordering on hysterical. "Of course you aren't going to explain them. Silly me. And she won't question you, because she's probably a perfect Jahfaran bride. Something I can never be again."

"You seem to know me so well," he said, his voice like ice chips pelting into her bruised heart. "Tell me—what else am I going to do? I'd like to know. It would make life so much easier."

"Don't make this any harder than it already is," she said.

"Why is it hard, Isabella? You've decreed this is the wisest, best outcome for everyone involved. So why is it difficult?"

Tears filled her eyes, made her vision swim. Damn it, she would *not* cry. "You know why," she declared. "I was starting to care for you again, Adan. But you've killed that, so don't worry that I'll change my mind. This is what's best for all of us. So divorce me and be done with it."

He looked so remote, so tall and handsome and regal as he stared at her with dark, glittering eyes. So alone. But he wasn't alone, not really. He never had been. She was the one who'd needed him, not the other way around.

But she was finished needing him. Whether it killed her or not, she was finished needing him.

"You have only to agree to it and we will be divorced."

Her heart stuttered in her chest. "Me? Why do I need to do anything?"

"Because we had a contract, Isabella, and I cannot set you aside without your agreement."

Her blood froze in her veins. "Is that why you took me to the Butterfly Palace? To get me to agree to a divorce?"

He bared his teeth in a cruel smile. "Precisely."

She could only gape at him. When she'd thought of a divorce as something only he could do, she'd felt as if it was out of her hands. As if there was nothing she could do or say to either proceed with or prevent it from happening. In a way, that had been a comfort.

But now? Now the responsibility was hers. The dissolution of their marriage lay on her shoulders. With a simple yes, the process would begin.

"You are despicable," she growled. "You didn't want to give me time with our son because it was the right thing to do. You wanted me to fail, and you wanted me to agree to divorce you once I had."

A muscle in his jaw ticked. "That was my intention, yes."

"And if it didn't happen the way you thought? What then?"

"Your agreement was meant to speed up the process. It would not have prevented it."

She could only stare at him, her heart breaking again and again. "And then you slept with me. My God, how could you do it? How could you be so cruel?"

"It wasn't my intention. It just happened."

She would have walked over and slapped him if not for their son still happily playing in the courtyard.

She would never, ever let her child see how much she despised his father at that moment.

"But I changed my mind about divorcing you, Isabella," he said. "Does that count for anything in this perfect little world you've devised?"

A tear spilled down her cheek in spite of her wish not to cry in front of him. He looked anguished, but she shook her head, certain it was a trick of her blurry vision. "No, not really. Because I'm sure it was for logical reasons that had nothing to do with what was best for me, and everything to do with what you thought best for you and Rafiq."

He swore softly in Arabic then. "You don't think much of me, do you?"

"Does it matter what I think, Adan? Do you really care?"

"Tell me you want the divorce, Isabella. Tell me, and it will be done."

She sucked in a trembling breath. Bowed her head. Swore six ways to Sunday that she wouldn't cry. That she would be strong and do this. "Yes," she managed. "I want a divorce."

He stood very, very still. And then he said, so quietly that she had to strain to hear it, "Then it will be done."

It took another two days before the papers were in his hands. Adan stared at the legal documents the solicitor had sent over, the words flowing together as nonsensically as if they were written in another language. He blinked, focused, and they coalesced again.

Divorce.

It was all there. All he had to do was sign it and then

have it sent to Isabella for her signature. They would no longer be married, and he could proceed with the wedding to Jasmine.

Except that he'd spoken with Jasmine two days ago when she'd come to the palace and told her that he'd decided not to divorce Isabella after all. She'd seemed so happy for him, smiling and giving him a big hug.

"I knew it would work out."

"You were right, as always," he'd said. And then he'd walked her down the hall to the entry, where he'd given her a kiss on the cheek and told her that she was a very special woman who deserved to find love rather than marry an old friend in order to help him out.

He'd said those words to her, but now, if he granted Isabella's wish, he would have to ask for Jasmine's help once more. At least until he was crowned next week.

He threw down the pen that he'd been holding. It had hovered over the line requiring his signature, but he'd been unable to form the words.

He wanted Isabella, and not simply because it would be easier.

He didn't want Jasmine, or any other woman. He wanted his wife. The woman who'd given him a son.

He wanted the woman he loved. Adan propped his elbows on the desk and put his head in his hands. He deserved everything that had happened.

Because as he'd stood there listening to her calmly telling him she didn't want him, that she wanted to live separately from him because he'd killed whatever feelings she'd had for him, he'd realized that his skin felt as if it had been turned inside out so that all his nerves were exposed. His heart pounded in his head, his throat, his stomach, until he felt sick with the throbbing, until he realized why it wasn't going away.

Why it would never go away.

He was in love with his wife. He'd wanted nothing more than to gather her to him and hold her tight, to tell her he loved her not only with words, but also with his body, with every breath he ever took.

But she hated him. In that moment, she hated him, and he'd known there was nothing he could do about it.

He deserved it. He'd taken her for granted when they'd wed. He'd ignored her, discounted her and failed her when she'd needed him the most. He didn't deserve her love then or now.

So he'd stood there and let her censure rain down on him. And when the first lone tear slid down her cheek, he'd hated himself for making her cry. He'd given her the truth because it was the only thing she'd wanted from him then, though it hurt her and made her think worse of him than she already did.

Adan shoved back from the desk and snatched up the divorce papers. He would not be a coward. He would give her what she wanted. But he wasn't going to be the first one to sign.

He strode out of his office, ignoring Mahmoud's surprised expression. There was an ambassador waiting, and a trade agreement on the line, but he didn't care right now. He would fix everything later. First he had to see Isabella.

He stalked down the hallway, took a shortcut through another wing to the royal apartments and burst through the door. He knew he would find her here because he'd not yet managed to locate a suitable house in town.

In truth, he hadn't tried very hard. He would, but he just hadn't wanted to let her go yet.

She shot to her feet as he entered her room without knocking. She was dressed in a pair of her Hawaiian shorts and a tank top, and his groin tightened at the display of so much gorgeous skin. Skin he wanted to worship.

Her hair was wild, as always. God, how he loved her hair. It suited her so much more than the sleek, false style she'd once worn to please him ever had.

She looked vulnerable, but then her expression hardened as she crossed her arms and leveled him with a green stare.

"Since when is it okay to burst into someone's room without knocking?"

He thrust the papers at her. "I've brought you something," he said, keeping his anguish tightly leashed. His voice sounded hard, cold, but he couldn't help it. It was the only way he could do this.

She held out her hand and took the papers. When she looked up at him again, her eyes were huge in her face. A tiny flame of hope kindled in his belly. He snuffed it out again. He would not seek hope where there was none.

She hated him. She would be glad to be rid of him. But she was going to sign first. She would be the one who ended it, not him.

"What am I supposed to do with this?" she asked. She bit her bottom lip and he nearly groaned.

"Sign it. It's what you wanted."

She looked down at the papers in her hand again. "You haven't signed."

"You first."

She walked over to a table and laid the papers down, smoothing them. "I need a pen," she said, not looking at him.

He growled as he spun and went into another room. He snatched a pen from a desk in the living area, then returned and held it out to her.

She hesitated, but then took it. Their skin brushed and he felt the jolt to his toes.

She uncapped the pen, then poised it over the paper. He could see her chest rising and falling, could see how the tempo increased as she stood there, hesitating.

Then the pen touched the paper. With a growl, he snatched the documents away. She squeaked as he ripped them in two.

Then he tossed them on the floor and grabbed her by the arms. "I don't want this," he said. The words felt as if they'd been ripped from his chest. "I don't deserve you, I know I don't—but I want you, Isabella. I need you."

She blinked. And then she shuddered in his grip. "I can't do this, Adan. Please don't keep touching me."

"I know you hate me. I know I deserve it. But give me a chance, Isabella. Give me a chance..."

A sob burst from her then and he let her go, though it tore him apart to do so. But he couldn't cause her any more pain than he already had.

"Why are you doing this?" she asked. "Why can't you just let me go?"

"I love you," he said, his throat aching with the words. "I can't let you go because I love you."

She sagged against the arm of the couch and buried her face in her hands. And then she was sobbing uncontrollably, her shoulders shaking, her tears like knife thrusts to his heart.

"I'm sorry," he said, tears welling in his eyes. "I'm sorry. I'll go. I'll get another set of papers and I will sign them. I will let you go, Isabella, if it's what you want."

He turned blindly. He had to get out of there before he did something stupid, like sink to his knees and beg.

"Adan," she said, and he stopped. "I'm scared."

And that was it, the moment of surrender. Hope blossomed inside again, but this time it wouldn't be crushed. He crossed to her as she straightened, and then he was holding her tight, his fists curled in her hair as he bent his head to inhale her scent.

"I'm scared, too," he admitted. "I never expected to feel this way."

She slipped her arms around his waist and squeezed him tight. "It'll be all right. It has to be all right if we're both scared."

He tilted her head back and gazed down into her glorious eyes. "I'm sorry for all the pain I've ever caused you, *habibti*. I'll do everything in my power to make it up to you, I swear. One day, you will fall in love with me again. And then I will deserve it."

She smiled through her tears. "My God, for a man who bears the responsibility for an entire nation, you certainly are dense."

He searched her gaze—and then he saw it. Love, shining through for him. His heart soared. "You love me," he said in wonder.

"Yes," she said simply. "I do."

"I want to question this good fortune," he said, "but I will not. I'm never giving you a reason to think twice about why you love me."

And then, to make sure she couldn't think at all, he took her to bed and spent the rest of the afternoon making sure she knew how thoroughly he loved every inch of her—body and soul.

EPILOGUE

ISABELLA rolled over in the blankets and discovered she was alone. She opened her eyes and stretched languorously. Just then, the tent flap drew back and a man in traditional garb entered.

"Well, hello, my desert lord and master," she purred. "Where have you been?"

Adan came over to where she lay on the king-size bed that occupied center stage in the tent. Lush pillows were piled around her, and a thick coverlet hid her body from view.

His fingers caught the edge of the cover and began to ease it down.

"This is not just a pleasure trip, my love," he said. "Some of us have work to do."

"Mmm, thankfully, not me."

He bent and took her mouth. She wrapped her arms around his neck and arched up into him as he uncovered her breasts.

"You are very naughty, Your Majesty," he said. "And very spoiled."

"But you love me."

"I do. Utterly and completely." He kissed her again,

and then ripped the covers from her naked body. A shiver of anticipation tingled through her.

"Now get up, Your Laziness. The day awaits us."

Isabella pouted. "Get up? Since when does the great King Adan ibn Najib Al Dhakir gaze upon his wife's naked body and not want sex?"

"Oh, he definitely wants it," he purred. "But I have a meeting with tribal chieftains to attend. Later, I will remember this conversation and make you pay accordingly."

Isabella laughed. "Make me pay? Who's the naughty one now, Adan?"

His eyes were hot. "We'll have to find that out, won't we?"

She reached for her robe and slipped it on as she stepped from the bed. Then she went into his arms.

"I like the way you think," she said before she gave him a long, lingering kiss.

"You make me want to be late," he said when she pulled back.

"It's not good form to be late."

He laughed. "You are not only naughty, you're also a tease."

"I'm building suspense for later," she said, grinning. "Have you seen the children this morning?"

"Rafiq wants to go horseback-riding. Little Kalila wants to know when we can go home—because the sand, she informs me, gets into everything. And the twins want to swim in the sea."

Isabella sighed. "Then I had better get dressed, hadn't I?"

He gave her a smack on the rear. "This is what I have

said, *habibti*." Then he kissed her again, swiftly. "But tonight you are mine."

"With pleasure, my lord."

"That is certainly my intention," he purred. He had reached the tent flap when he stopped and shook his head. Then he turned around and stalked back over to her.

"I'm the king," he said, slipping the robe from her shoulders. "I can be late if I want."

Isabella laughed. "I do love a man who knows what he wants. And who will do anything to get it."

Like flying halfway around the world to collect his runaway wife. Like ripping up divorce papers before she could sign them. Like this, now, when he showed her once more with words and caresses just how much he adored her.

Oh, yes, there was something to be said for a man who knew what he wanted.

* * * * *

DESERT DOCTOR, SECRET SHEIKH

MEREDITH WEBBER

Meredith Webber says of herself, 'Some ten years ago, I read an article which suggested that Mills & Boon were looking for new Medical Romance™ authors. I had one of those "I can do that" moments and gave it a try. What began as a challenge has become an obsession—though I do temper the "butt on seat" career of writing with dirty but healthy outdoor pursuits, fossicking through the Australian Outback in search of gold or opals. Having had some success in all of these endeavours, I now consider I've found the perfect lifestyle.'

CHAPTER ONE

JEN lifted the almost weightless child onto her hip and turned towards the car approaching them, hoping the driver would stop before he reached the tents so the cloud of gritty sand the vehicle was kicking up would settle outside rather than inside her makeshift hospital.

He did stop. The battered four-wheel-drive pulled up some twenty metres from where she stood, but a perverse drift of wind lifted the trailing red cloud and carried it in her direction, so she had to step backwards in order not to be engulfed in its dust. She put her hand over the little girl's nose and mouth, and scowled at the man stepping out from behind the wheel.

Unexpected visitors usually meant trouble. Most of the small states in this area had moved quickly into the twentieth century and then the twenty-first, with modern cities, wonderful facilities and the best of medical care, but in Zaheer, the ruling sheikh did not agree with modern ways and though he himself was rarely seen, his minions made the presence of even essential aid services uncomfortable.

The man who disembarked wore rather tattered jeans and a T-shirt, not the flowing robes of the usual official sent to ask what they were doing and to be shown around, suspicion of the organisation's aims bristling in the air.

This man was very different, though why Jen had that impression she couldn't say.

Was he a traveller lost in the desert, or something else?

Some instinct she'd never felt before warned her to be wary but she dismissed this vague unease with a sharp, unspoken *Nonsense!* Beneath the dust on the vehicle there appeared to be some kind of logo, so maybe he *was* an official, or an aid worker from another organisation.

She wanted to ignore him, to turn away, tired of the battles she fought with red tape, but with more refugees arriving at the camp every day she needed all the help she could get, and he might just be helpful to her.

She stood her ground.

But she didn't smile.

Which was probably just as well, she realised as the man stepped out of his dust cloud and she caught her first good look at the tall, well-built figure, the tanned skin, the dark, dark hair and—surely not green eyes?

She looked again as he came closer—they *were* green, pale, translucent almost, and so compelling she knew she was staring.

But all in all he was a man women would stare at automatically, and smile at as well—probably to cover the fluttering in the region of their hearts.

Not that she did heart flutters over men—not since David...

'Dr Stapleton?'

The visitor's voice was deep, but with a huskiness that suggested he might have a cold or sore throat, or that he might have cultivated it—a bedroom voice, practised for seduction...

Seduction? Where had that thought sprung from?

'Yes!' she managed, nodding to reinforce the spoken confirmation, knowing the fleeting thought of danger was nonsensical.

'I'm Kam Rahman,' the stranger said, stepping closer and offering his hand. 'Head office of Aid for All heard you were in trouble—trying to look after the medical needs of the people in the camp as well as run the TB programme—and sent me along to look into setting up a medical clinic here and to investigate the needs of the refugees.'

'You're a doctor?' Jen asked, taking in the threadbare jeans and the T-shirt that looked older than she was, once again trying not to be distracted by the blatant maleness of the body inside them.

'Trained in London,' he said, bowing deeply. 'But my father was an official of sorts in this country so I grew up here and speak the language, which is why Aid for All thought I'd be more useful here than in South America, where my language skills would be useless. Although, given the way the world works, it's a wonder I didn't end up there.'

He smiled, perhaps in the hope she'd enjoyed his little joke, but the smile made the sense of danger stronger and Jen found herself taking a backward step and shifting Rosana so the child was between her and the stranger.

Not that the man noticed her movement, or registered that she hadn't taken his proffered hand. He was too busy looking around, his keen eyes scanning the tent city that spread outward from the end of the road.

'You're more than welcome,' Jen told him, although inside she didn't feel at all welcoming. Inside she felt disturbed, which, she supposed, wasn't all that unbelievable because the man, with his erect carriage, his strong body, high cheekbones, the slightly hooded but miss-nothing green eyes, oozed sex appeal.

Startled by the directions of her thoughts, she realised it had been a long time since she'd noticed a man as a man, let alone considered whether he was sexy or not.

But there was something else about him that diverted her from personal reactions, something in his bearing…

Authority?

Now, why would she think that?

'So, are you going to show me around?'

The same authority in his voice, and it *was* authority—of that she had no doubt.

He'd thrust his hands into his jeans pockets, making the fabric tight around his butt as he turned, the better to see the extent of the camp, and Jen was distracted again.

Aware she should be thinking about the reason the man was here, not whether or not he had a good backside, Jen dragged her mind back into order.

'You're really an Aid for All worker—really a doctor?'

He turned back to her and smiled, which didn't help the disturbance in her body, then he crossed to the dirty vehicle and rubbed his hand across the passenger door to clear the dust from the logo.

'See, same as yours.' He nodded towards the equally dusty vehicle she and her team used. 'I don't have my framed medical graduation certificate with me—hard to hang things on the walls of tents—but I do have some ID.'

He plunged his hand into his pocket and pulled out a plastic-covered tag similar to the one Jen wore around her neck.

'There, we match,' he said, slipping the cord over his head.

Kam with a K, she noticed, but the ID looked genuine.

So why did she still feel wary about this man?

Because he was so handsome?

Well, if that was the case, she'd better get over it. The people in the camp needed all the help they could get.

'Come on, I'll show you around,' she said, as Rosana wriggled in her arms.

Jen looked down at the little mite, dark eyes huge in her thin face, stick legs bent with rickets, stomach distended from starvation. 'There isn't much to see, well, not in the medical tent. It's very basic. If you're setting up a general medicine clinic, maybe we can get another tent for it so we're not tripping over each other.'

She looked hopefully at the newcomer.

'I don't suppose you brought a tent?'

He was frowning at her—frowning angrily—as he shook his head, although she couldn't think why he should be angry.

Until he spoke.

'Weren't tents supplied by the government? Tents for the refugees as well as tents for the people helping them? Didn't I hear that somewhere?'

Jen shrugged.

'I don't know, although I have heard that the old sheikh has been ill for a very long time so maybe the country isn't running as well as it should be. And Aid for All certainly had a battle getting permission to test for and treat TB in the camp, so once we received the permission we weren't going to push our luck by asking for more. The tent we use was housing a family when we arrived, and they moved out so we could have it.'

Kamid Rahman al'Kawali, heir to the sheikhdom but travelling incognito through his country, shook his head as he looked around at the tent village. Things were far worse than he and his twin brother Arun had imagined. And they had to take at least part of the responsibility, for they'd pretended not to notice what was happening in Zaheer, throwing themselves into their hospital duties, telling themselves their medical work was more important than disputes between government officials, changing what they could change at the hospital where they worked, but slowly and cautiously. They'd been constantly frustrated in their endeavours because, even ill, their father had been strong enough to refuse to hand over any authority to his sons.

So they'd worked, and learnt, attending conferences and courses all over the world, finding good excuses to not visit their father until the last possible moment when they'd come out of duty to their mother, not out of concern for an irascible old man who had made their childhoods a misery, and who had refused to move with his country into the twenty-first century.

He had despised the city that had grown where the old capital had been, the new city built by foreign oil barons made richer by the oil they pumped from beneath the desert sands, and by foreign hotel chains who had built luxury housing for the oil barons.

He had objected to the idea of his country becoming a democracy, although when he realised it was inevitable he had made sure his brothers and their sons had stood as candidates and been elected to look after the interests of the family. Then he'd hidden himself away in the fastness of his winter palace, the hereditary, but not ruling, ruler, allowing those in the far-off city to do as they wished. That aim seemed to be to make the city more prosperous, not to mention glamorous enough to be attractive to foreigners, and to ignore the fate of the rest of the country.

Which was why a foreign aid organisation was now testing for TB in a tent in this refugee camp near the border of the neighbouring country, while in the city, in nearly new hospitals, first-class surgeons recruited from around the world were performing face lifts and tummy tucks not only on women but on men who had become soft and flabby from indulging in their wealth.

Foreign aid! How could this have happened when the whole basis for the tribal life of his people was looking after their own? And the people in this refugee camp, although they may have come in from over the border, were still their own, descendants of the same tribes that had roamed the desert for centuries.

Kam sighed and looked at the woman in front of him. The smooth skin of her face, framed by a dark scarf, was lightly tanned and sprinkled with freckles that had a look of casually scattered gold dust to them, while her eyes were a darker gold, brown, he supposed they'd be called, but so flecked with golden lights the brown was hardly noticeable. Pink, shapely but unpainted lips, slightly chapped—had no one told her the dry desert air could suck all moisture out of you in a few hours?—were pursed by worry or concern…

And why was he suddenly so observant?

With so much to learn and so much to do to right the wrongs of the past, this was no time to be noticing a pretty woman…

'I can get tents,' he said.

'Just like that? You can get tents?' Jen demanded. 'I've been sending messages to the city for months now, saying we need more help— Oh!'

She lifted her hand and held it to her mouth—to stop herself putting her foot further into it?

'You *are* more help,' she muttered, then smiled tentatively at him. 'I'm sorry I haven't been more welcoming. But tents?'

Kam returned the smile.

'Influence in the city—I grew up here, remember.'

He was fascinated by the freckles but knew he shouldn't stare, so he let his gaze rove casually over her, then smiled once more to cover the fact that his attention had been so easily diverted.

Again!

'Tents are easy.'

Jen didn't miss his casual scan of her body, but she refused to blush, although she was only too aware of what a sight she must present, her Western garb of jeans and a long-sleeved shirt covered by a long, all-enveloping grey tunic, red desert sand coating it and probably her face as well, and turning her blonde plait, beneath her headscarf, a dried-out, gingery colour.

But his inspection of her apparel—and his apparent dismissal of it, although she had attempted to adapt her clothing to meet the customs of the land—had annoyed her sufficiently to go on the attack

'Good, and if you've that much influence, I'll make a list of other things we need.'

He held up his hand.

'Best if I work it out for myself,' he said. 'After all, I know these people and can assess what will suit them, while you might be imposing Western needs on them.'

'I would think clean water and sanitation would be basic needs for anyone,' Jen muttered, but she suspected he was right as far as details were concerned.

'Of course, and these things, too, can be provided,' he assured her.

'And perhaps better housing before the worst of winter blows along the valley,' Jen suggested hopefully.

He looked around and Jenny tried to see the camp through his eyes—the motley collection of patched and tattered tents, the tethered goats, the children running down the alleys between the dwellings, a small flock of ragged-looking sheep grazing on the lower hillside, while two hobbled camels slept nearby.

He shook his head.

'Housing? I don't think so. These people are refugees from across the border, this isn't their country. If we build them houses, aren't we telling them that they will never return to their own lands? Wouldn't we be taking away their hope?'

He was extraordinarily good-looking and it was distracting her, and the distraction made her snippy. Although she could see where he was coming from, she wasn't ready to give in too easily.

'You don't want these people who have lost everything to have some comfort and a proper place where they can be treated while they are ill?' she demanded.

'I would love them to have comfortable homes and a hospital as well, but back where they belong—back where they grew up and where their families have roamed for generations. Back in the places of their hearts! Here, surely, if we build something resembling a permanent camp, they will feel even more lost, displaced and stateless. It's like saying to them, "Give up all hope because the war will never end in your country so you'll just have to sit here on the edge of ours and live on whatever charity can provide." I doubt there are people anywhere in the world who could accept that, let alone these fiercely proud desert inhabitants.'

'Well, you obviously know best,' Jen said, turning away

from him towards the big tent and adding under her breath, 'Or think you do!'

An anger she couldn't understand was simmering deep inside her, although she didn't know what had caused it— surely not this man pointing out something she should have known herself? And surely not the passion that had crept into his words as if he truly understood, and possibly felt, these people's yearnings for their home?

No, passion was to be admired, but there was something about the man himself that stirred her anger, an air of—could it possibly be arrogance?

Kam turned away to speak to a man walking past and Jen took the opportunity to check him out again.

A number of doctors, like a number of professionals in any field, were arrogant, but they usually weren't dressed in well-worn jeans and tattered T-shirts. They were more the three-piece-suit brigade.

She sighed. She hated generalising and here she was doing it about a stranger—and about other members of her profession.

And why was she thinking of him as a man—noting his looks and manner—when she hadn't thought that way about a man since the accident—hadn't ever expected to think about a man that way again?

She reached the opening at the front of the tent, and turned to wait for him to catch up, while once again a sense of danger assailed her.

'This is where we work and where I live. You can have a look in here then I'll find someone to show you around the camp so you can get your bearings.'

He looked as if he was about to argue, but in the end did no more than nod and follow her into the tent.

She led the way, still holding Rosana on her hip, trying to see the place that was clinic, hospital and home through his eyes. Various bits of it were partitioned off by bright woven rugs she'd bought from the traders who came regularly to the camp, determined to get whatever money they could from the desperate refugees.

In the clinic corner, the morning ritual of TB testing was going on, men, women and children all coughing obligingly into tiny plastic cups, while one of Jen's local helpers spread the sputum onto a slide and labelled it with the patient's name.

'As you probably know, the refugees are mostly mountain people,' she explained to her visitor, 'driven out by the warring tribes across the border, and by starvation because with the war going on they can't plant their crops or take their live-stock to good pastures.'

Her guest—or should she start thinking of him as her colleague?—nodded.

'I imagine in these overcrowded conditions diseases like TB can spread quickly, and with complications like AIDS in some cases, your first priority must be to complete this eradi-cation programme.'

Maybe she *could* think of him as a colleague.

It would certainly be easier than thinking of him as a man…

'Except that things happen, of course, to get us off track,' she explained. 'A child gets too close to a fire and is burned, a woman goes into labour—naturally we have to tend them. In these people's eyes—and in reality, I suppose—we're a medical team, so they come to us for help.'

And though still wary of him—of the person, not the doctor, she decided—she gave him the welcome she should have offered in the first place.

'For that reason it's great to have you on board. You can do the normal medical stuff and we'll get on with the TB programme.'

'TB treatment involves a period of nine months.' He interrupted her so firmly she took a step back. 'You intend being here that long?'

He spoke with a hint of sceptical suspicion that fired the simmering embers of the anger she didn't understand to glowing life.

'What do you think? That I'm playing at being a volunteer? That I came here for some kind of thrill, or maybe kudos—so people would see what a wonderful person I am?'

She scowled at him.

'Of course I'm here for the duration of the testing and treatment, although it might not be a full nine months, but then again, with more people coming into the camp all the time, it might be longer than that.'

He was obviously unaffected by scowls, or scorn, or anger. He waited until she'd finished speaking, then asked, 'Why not a full nine months?'

'Because we've cut treatment time to six months through a selection of different medication,' she told him, tilting her chin so she could look him in the eyes. 'Once someone is on the programme it's mainly a matter of supervision to make sure they take their medication. Isolation would be good, if there was somewhere we could send those with the disease, but then again, to take these people from the few family they have left would add to their problems. We treat the physical things as we can, but the mental burden they carry—the sadness—we can do nothing for that.'

The visitor stared at her as if she'd suddenly begun to speak in tongues.

'And you care?' he asked.

Jen stared at him in disbelief.

'Of course I care. Why wouldn't I care? I presume you're here because you care, too, or is this some ruse? Are you some kind of government spy sent here to see what's happening in the camp, or an Aid for All spy, checking I'm not selling the TB drugs on the side? Is that why you're here?'

'I've told you why I'm here,' he replied, all cool arrogance again. Maybe it was the voice—so very English.

Rich English.

Was his father a foreign oil baron that Kam had grown up here? Or, in spite of that English voice, did the blood of a long line of desert warriors run through his veins? She'd learnt enough of the local people to know they were a proud race.

Although the questions kept popping up in her head, or maybe because of them, Jen ignored him, setting Rosana down on a mat on the floor and nodding to one of the women helping with the TB testing to keep an eye on the child. She was about to show him the layout of the tent when she became aware of approaching excitement, the shrieks and wails and general hysteria coming closer and closer.

Stepping past her visitor, she was heading out of the tent when he pulled her back, pushing her behind him and telling her to stay there.

As if she would! She moved up to his shoulder so they exited the tent together, and saw the excited crowd, a body held between a number of men, women shrieking lament behind them.

'He was thrown over the fence. Men on horses threw him. It is Lia's husband. They have beaten him with whips.'

Mahmoud, one of many men in the camp who spoke a little

English, explained this as the group moved closer, and as Jen stepped to one side and waved to the men carrying the patient to bring him inside, she heard her visitor cursing quietly beside her.

But cursing didn't help. She led the men behind a partition in the tent and indicated they should put their burden down on a plastic-covered mattress on the floor. Then she knelt beside the man and saw the blood-soaked, tattered remnants of his gown, in places sticking to his skin, on others torn right off. They turned him on his side, as the wounds were on the front and the back of his chest and on his calves. Jen found a couple of cushions she could prop behind his knees to keep him in that position.

The man was moaning piteously, but when the stranger spoke to him in his own language he found the strength to answer.

Jen, meanwhile, was wondering where to begin.

'Pain relief before we start to examine him, I think.' Her colleague answered her unspoken question, kneeling on the other side of the man but looking across him at Jen. 'What do you have?'

Jen did a quick mental scan of her precious drugs.

'I've a small supply of pethidine but we should run it through fluid in an IV for it to work faster.'

Fluid—she had so little in the way of fluid replacement, a couple of bags of isotonic saline solution and a couple of bags of five percent dextrose in water, which was also isotonic. The man had bled a lot and both would help restore plasma levels and though she hated using up what few supplies she had, she knew she would.

Was she frowning that her colleague, who'd been taking stock of the patient's injuries, now turned his attention to her?

'You *do* have some fluid?' he asked, and she nodded and stood up, asking one her assistants, Aisha, to bring a basin of water and cloths to bathe the man, before heading for the little partitioned-off section of the tent that was her bedroom and digging into the sand in one corner where she'd buried this treasure.

'You bury it?'

She turned to see Kam standing near the rug she'd hung to provide a little privacy to this area, and now *he* was frowning, although she was the one disturbed to have him in her space.

'To keep it safe from thieves.'

He shook his head and walked away.

Tubing, cannulas and catheters were buried in another part of the area she looked on as her room, and she dug them up and dusted sand off the plastic bags in which she'd buried them.

'I don't have much IV fluid replacement,' she said, when she joined him by the patient. She was angry with herself for sounding apologetic, but he merely shook his head, though he frowned again as he saw the sand dropping from the bundle she was unwrapping.

If frowns were any indication, he was one angry man…

'And what you have you must hide? Isn't that overdoing things? Do you feel you can't trust these people? How can you help them if distrust is in the air all the time?'

Anger sharpened the demands.

'I don't hide things from the people in the camp,' Jen told him, defending the refugees, although she knew some of them might steal from need. 'But raiders come from time to time. Even if they don't need medicines themselves, they can sell them. It's one of the reasons drug-resistant TB has spread so widely. People steal the medicine, sell it to unsuspecting locals in the souk, and never tell the buyers they need to take far more than one box of tablets in order to be cured.'

She knelt beside the patient, opening the small trunk that held their most used medical needs, like antiseptic and swabs and small sutures. She found what she needed and first bathed the man's left hand then swabbed it, before bringing up a vein and inserting a cannula into it.

Marij, Jen's other assistant, had passed a blood-pressure cuff and small monitor to Kam, who was now checking the man's BP and pulse, while Marij and Aisha were cutting off the tattered remnants of the man's robe, leaving pieces that were stuck to open wounds, which would be removed later.

Jen set up a drip, pulling a wooden box that had once contained TB drugs close to the man so she could sit the bag of fluid on it, then she broke open the ampoule of pethidine, drew the contents into a syringe and injected it into the fluid, adjusting the flow so their patient would receive it slowly over a prolonged period of time.

But as more and more of the man's clothing was cut away and Jen saw the depth of some of the wounds, she began to wonder if they would be able to help him.

'How could anyone do this to someone else?' she whispered, awed by the ferocity of the attack.

'They must have taken him for a thief or, worse, a spy,' Kam said, his voice grim.

'But—'

Once glance at his stern, set face stopped further protest and she reminded herself she was there to help, not to judge. She concentrated on their patient.

'I suppose we can only do what we can,' she said, thinking how little that might be—what if there were internal wounds they wouldn't know about until too late? Although now she had someone with whom she could work, maybe they *could* save this patient.

The visitor nodded.

'I know you're a TB clinic but would you have surgical instruments? I think if we can debride some of the damaged skin, there'll be less likelihood of infection.'

Jen thought of the odds and ends of instruments she'd acquired over the last three years, now packed in among her underwear in the battered suitcase in her makeshift bedroom.

'I'll get what I have,' she said, but as she rose to her feet she wondered why Kam Rahman didn't have all this equipment himself. If he *was* from Aid for All and coming here to run a medical clinic in conjunction with the TB clinic, surely he'd have brought supplies and equipment with him.

She glanced his way but the badge he'd shown her was now tucked inside the T-shirt. Later she'd take a closer look at the logo on his vehicle—better by far than thinking about digging under the T-shirt for his ID…

CHAPTER TWO

WHY was she suspicious of him? Because he was far too good-looking to be an aid worker? Did she have preconceived ideas that they all had to be long-haired and wear sandals and not speak like an English prince? As she considered these questions, she stacked all the instruments, sterilised by boiling and now wrapped in paper, on a battered metal tray and carried it out to put it beside the stranger, then suggested Marij empty the bowls of water and bring fresh.

'That's some collection,' Kam said, as Jen unwrapped her treasured instruments and set them on the tray where they could both reach them.

'Three years of humble begging,' she joked, but from the way his lips tightened he didn't think it was at all funny.

Which it probably wasn't but, then, there wasn't much to laugh about here, so the man had better loosen up and get used to feeble humour or he'd frown his way into a deep depression.

'Sutures?' he asked.

They were in the chest with the dressings—and fortunately she had plenty of them, mainly because they were the first things people pressed on her back at home when she visited hospitals or surgeries, asking for donations.

'Now, how are we going to work this? Do you want to cut and swab and I'll stitch or would you prefer to stitch?'

Jen stared in horror at the damage that had been done, not only to the man's back but to his chest as well. In places the lash, or whatever had been used, had bitten so deeply into his flesh she could see the grey-white bone beneath it.

'I'll cut and clean,' she said, and heard something of the horror she was feeling in the tightly squeezed-out words.

'He'll be all right,' her colleague said, his voice gentle as if he knew she was upset. 'It looks far, far worse than it really is. And with me to stitch him up, there'll barely be a scar.'

'Surgeon, are you?' Jen teased, though it was unlikely a specialist would be deployed to somewhere like this camp.

'And why not?' he parried, leaving Jen to wonder…

He spoke again, but this time to the patient, the slightly guttural words of the local language rolling off his tongue. The man opened bleary eyes then closed them again, and Kam nodded as if satisfied the drug was working.

'Let's go,' he said, and Jen started at the neck and began to cut away the cloth that was embedded in the wounds, preserving what skin she could but needing to debride it where it was too torn to take a suture. Desert sand encrusted the wounds and the blood-hardened fabric, so the job was slow, but piece by piece she removed the foreign material, leaving a clean wound for Kam to stitch.

From there she moved to the wounds just above his buttocks, so she and Kam weren't jostling each other as they worked, and slowly, painstakingly, they cleansed and cut and stitched until the man's back resembled a piece of patchwork, sutures criss-crossing it in all directions.

Jen squatted back on her heels and Kam raised his head,

tilting it from side to side, shrugging impressively broad shoulders to relieve tension in his neck. For a minute the green eyes met hers but she couldn't read whatever message they might hold. Pity? Horror? Regret?

Emotion certainly, and she felt a little more kindly towards him. So many doctors, surgeons in particular—and she was pretty sure he must be one—could remain detached from the work they did, believing it was better for all concerned for them to be emotionally uninvolved.

'Do you want to swap jobs?' Jen suggested, as Kam roughly taped a huge dressing to the man's back then tilted him so he was lying on it. They both watched the patient to see if there was any reaction, but as he remained seemingly asleep, they assumed the pethidine was working and he couldn't feel the pain of the wounds on his back.

'You've been bent over there for over an hour. I can at least move around,' Jen added.

He glanced at her again.

'You like sewing?' he asked.

'Not really,' Jen said, wondering how he could make her feel so uncomfortable. He was, after all, just a colleague.

Problem was, of course, she'd never had a colleague who looked like this one…

Or felt any physical reaction to a man for a long time…

She hauled her attention back to the subject under discussion. 'But I've done most of my hospital work in A and E, so I've had plenty of practice.'

She was sounding snappish again and knew it was because it niggled her that this man could get so easily under her skin.

Because she was physically attracted to him?

Balderdash! Of course she wasn't.

'I'm sure you'd do as good a job as I, but now I've begun I'll finish it.'

And finish it he did, Jen cutting and cleaning, Kam sewing, until all the deepest wounds on the man's back, chest and legs were stitched, while the less deep ones were neatly dressed.

Jen, finishing first, checked their patient's blood pressure and pulse again, then studied the readout with trepidation.

'His blood pressure's dropping. I saw you examining him all over earlier—there were no deep wounds we've missed?'

Kam shook his head.

'But there's extensive bruising to his lower back and abdomen, which suggests he might have been kicked. There could be damage to his spleen or kidneys and internal bleeding, which we won't find without an X-ray or ultrasound.'

'Do you have a radio in your car? Do you know enough about the health services available locally to know if we could radio for a helicopter to take him out?'

Kam shook his head.

'I imagine you drove in, camping out in the desert for one night on the way. That's not because we—I mean the locals— want to put aid workers to as much hardship as they can, but because of the mountains around here. They have temperamental updraughts and downdraughts that can cause tremendous problems to the rotors on a helicopter, so they don't fly here. Fixed-wing aircraft are a different matter, they fly higher so aren't affected, but, of course, there's no handy airfield for even a light plane to use!'

He studied her as if to gauge her reaction to his explanation, but when he spoke again she realised he'd gone back further than the helicopters.

'You asked about a radio in my car—yes, I do have one,

but so should you. One in the car and one for your office or wherever you want to keep it—they're listed on the inventory you're given with your supplies.'

Jen smiled at him.

'The one in the car disappeared within two days of our arrival and the other one a couple of days after that. You can't dig a hole and bury radios. No matter how well you wrap them, you can't seal them completely and they tend to stop working when sand gets into their bits.'

She was smiling at him, but Kam couldn't return the smile, too angered by the artless conversation. He couldn't believe that things had got so bad people were stealing from an aid organisation, although he imagined these refugees had so little, he could hardly blame them for the thefts.

But how to fix this? How to redress the balance in his country? Could he and his twin achieve what needed to be done in a lifetime? Arun was working in the city, talking to the people there, seeking information about the government and whether, as their father's influence slipped, corruption had crept in.

Or had the people elected into positions of power only seen the city as their responsibility, ignoring what was happening in the country, ignorant of this camp on the border?

As he and Arun had been, he reminded himself with a feeling of deep shame. He couldn't speak for his twin, but nothing—neither work and study programmes, nor his father's orders to keep his nose out of the ruler's business— excused the way he, as heir, had allowed neglect to hurt his people. And nothing would stop his drive to fix this hurt.

Nothing!

Their patient groaned and Kam brought his mind sharply back to the job in hand.

'A drop in blood pressure certainly suggests he's bleeding somewhere. If you're short of fluid, we should consider whole blood.'

The woman he'd been surprised to find in this place nodded. He'd known she was here, of course, but he'd expected...

What?

Some dowdy female?

OK, not some dowdy female, but definitely not a beauty like this golden woman was. He checked the dusting of freckles again and even in the dimmer light of the tent saw the colour of them.

'Sorry?' Checking out her freckles, he'd seen her lips moving and realised she was talking to him.

'I was just offering to take some blood from him and test it, then maybe find some volunteers willing to be tested,' Jen suggested.

'His friends will surely volunteer. Take some blood. You can test it here? You have a kit?'

She nodded.

'Good,' Kam said, pleased his mind was back on the job, though the greater job still awaited him. 'We've got him this far, let's see if we can finish the job. Internal bleeding will sometimes stop, leaking vessels sealing themselves off, but if it doesn't, without an ultrasound I'd have to open him up and have a look. He's suffered so much already I wouldn't like to risk it until he's much stronger, so let's wait and see. We'll have to monitor him closely, of course.'

We'll have to monitor him? The words echoed in Jen's head.

The stranger intended staying?

Here?

In her tent?

Of course he intended staying—he was another aid worker, one who was sorely needed, and right now there wasn't another tent to house him or his clinic.

Unease fluttered like panicking moths in her stomach—or maybe that was hunger, it was well past lunchtime.

She turned her attention back to the job she was supposed to be doing—taking blood.

Marij had returned, having belatedly finished the morning's TB testing.

'Can I help?' she asked, in her soft, gentle voice.

'Would you type this blood for me?' Jen asked her, handing her the vial.

'Of course,' Marij replied, adding, 'And then you'll want volunteers—I will ask around and begin typing them as well.'

Jen turned her attention back to the patient.

'Shall we ease him back onto his side? And what about antibiotics? I have some but they're in tablet form. For a start at least, he should be getting them through his drip. And tetanus? Who knows if he's ever had a tetanus shot, but if it was a horse whip he was hit with, he'll need one.'

He helped her move the patient back onto his side, propping cushions gently against his injured back to keep him from rolling over.

'I've stuff like that in the car,' Kam said. 'Not much because this visit was more a recce to see what was needed, but I'll go and get what I have.'

Once again suspicion fluttered in Jen's chest. Would he really undertake a two-day drive just to see what was happening? And then drive back to the city to get what was needed and drive up here again? Six days going back and forth across desert roads that could swallow a car whole?

Or was the flutter discomfort at the thought of the man moving his things in here—moving in himself?

So close that if she woke in the night she might hear him shifting in his sleep, hear him breathing?

But where else could he stay? Until they had another tent, and she'd believe he could muster one when she saw it, he'd have to live and work here. If she put up another rug across the far corner...

She shook her head at her own folly. Whatever it was about this man that was affecting her, it wasn't going to be stopped by a brightly woven rug hung down between them. The way they blew when the tent sides were rolled up to allow cool air in, another rug would barely provide privacy.

She checked her patient, then looked up as a shadow fell across them. The cause of her concern was standing over them, a large cardboard box in his hands.

Was she staring that he offered a half smile?

The flutters she felt were definitely not suspicion, and all the more worrying because of that.

'I have some more pethidine,' he said, such an ordinary conversation, 'and antibiotics. The blood test?'

'Marij is checking now.'

Jen climbed carefully to her feet, but even with care she stumbled when she put her weight on a foot that had gone to sleep.

Kam's hand reached out to steady her, his grip surprisingly strong. She turned to thank him, but the words wouldn't come, held captive in her throat by something she couldn't explain.

She stamped her unresponsive foot, and caught his lips curving into a smile.

'That's not a sign of a tantrum,' she assured him, with a tentative smile of her own. 'The darned thing's gone to sleep. And so's my brain. I know you introduced yourself earlier, but did I? My name's Jenny.'

She held out her hand and watched him take it—saw the tanned skin of his fingers against her own pale flesh, felt warmth and something else—something she didn't want to put a name to.

'I knew the Jennifer part, but wondered if you shortened it.'

Jenny removed her hand from his, and tucked it in the pocket of her tunic, out of danger's way.

'Jen, Jenny, even, hey, you—I answer to them all,' she said, trying desperately to sound casual and light-hearted, although her arm where he had touched it, and the fingers he'd briefly held, burned as if they'd been branded.

The patient's name, they learned, was Akbar, and his blood group was B.

'Mine's B,' Jenny told Kam, who was sitting, cross-legged, by their patient, talking quietly to Lia, Akbar's wife. 'Let's do a cross-match and see if it's OK for him to have mine.'

Kam studied her for a moment, wondering about this woman he'd found on the border of his country. Wondering if she was the first fair-haired Westerner to ever tread these particular desert sands.

Wondering if he should take her blood…

Take *her*, as his ancestors might have…

The sudden heat in his body shocked him back to the matter in hand. Of all the times to be distracted by a woman…

'You need your strength for your job,' he objected.

It was a token protest and she took it that way.

'The loss of a couple of pints of blood won't hurt me,' she

insisted, handing him a syringe with a needle attached so he could draw blood from her forearm for cross-matching. She had pulled off her soiled tunic and now rolled up the sleeve of her shirt so he could access a vein, yet he felt strangely reluctant to move closer to her—to touch her.

He *had* to move closer—how else could he withdraw some blood?—and if their patient was bleeding internally, and his blood pressure drop suggested he was, he would need blood.

Kam crossed the distance between them in one long stride and took her arm, seeing as he did so pale scars like snail tracks, paler than the lightly tanned skin and puckered here and there.

Without regard to the intrusiveness of the gesture, he ran his forefinger lightly down the longest of them, then looked up into her eyes, knowing she'd read the question in his own.

Defiance was his answer, as clear as if it was written on a whiteboard. Ask me if you dare, she was saying, and though Kam knew he shouldn't, he couldn't help himself.

'Accident?'

She nodded briefly then swabbed the spot where a vein showed blue beneath the fine skin of her inner elbow.

Take the blood, she was saying with the gesture—take the blood and mind your own business. But Kam's mind was already racing off along a tangent—did the scars explain why such a beautiful woman, and she *was* beautiful in her golden, glowing way, would hide herself away in a refugee camp on the edge of a little-known country?

Was she hiding only these surface scars or were there deeper ones?

Had she lost someone she loved, leaving scars on her heart?

'Was it bad?'

She stared at him as if she didn't understand his question, but a shadow had crossed her face and he had his answer.

Very bad, that shadow told him, while the set of her lips again warned him off further questions.

But his sympathy for her made him gentle as he held her arm and eased the needle into the vein. He watched the vial fill with dark blood, trying to keep his mind on the job—on their patient and what might lie ahead for him, and for himself and Jenny as his doctors—not on snail-track-like scars on a woman's arm, or the dark shadow that had crossed her face.

Fortunately, the woman—Jenny—recovered her composure and her sensible conversation brought him back to the present.

'If it works in a cross-match, you can take it directly from me to him, although you'll have to keep an eye on him for any transfusion reaction because I'll be lying beside him.'

She smiled as if this were a little joke at her expense, but Kam couldn't return the smile, his thoughts veering back to the puzzle of why this woman was willing to do so much for people she didn't know, in an inhospitable place, and with no friends or family to support her.

Had she come to escape her memories?

Her pain?

'Well?' she prompted. 'Are you going to do a cross-match or should I?'

With his mind back on the job, Kam took another vial and drew a little blood from their patient, Jenny acting as nurse, tightening the tourniquet on the man's arm to bring up a vein then taping a dressing over the small wound. Kam mixed the contents of the two vials, watching anxiously for any sign of clotting, which would tell them the blood samples were not compatible. But the blood didn't clot and the intrepid woman who puzzled him now produced a cannula and loop of tubing.

'Let's go,' she said, sitting down beside Akbar while one of the nurses who worked with her explained to Akbar's wife what was happening.

Lia shifted to sit beside Jenny and hold her hand, babbling her thanks for the gift of blood—the gift of life.

'You need to be higher,' Kam told the unexpected donor. 'Are you all right to sit up if we stack pillows behind you?'

'I've two bedrolls behind the partition,' Jenny told him. 'I can sit with those behind me to prop me up and that way my arm is higher than Akbar's and it will feed down into him.'

She half smiled, while the nurse, Aisha, fetched the bedrolls.

'It will be up to you to check the blood's going the right way. I don't want to be taking more of it from the poor man.'

Not only was she here in this desperate situation but she was joking about it. Kam thought back to the women he had studied with, both women from his own land and Western women, but none of them had been anything like this particular female doctor. No fuss, no nonsense, just get on with the job.

Although there *was* one problem now he thought about it…

'I don't think we should run it direct into Akbar. We should measure the amount—both for your sake as a donor and his as the recipient,' he said, trying to be as efficient as she was at getting on with the job. 'Do you have a container?'

'The fluid bag is nearly empty. What if we run my blood into it, a pint at a time, then transfer it across to Akbar? We could fill something else, but at least we know the bag is sterile. And we can time it, so we know how long it takes to fill a bag then do away with that middle stage when he needs more.'

Kam realised he should have thought of these things. Had

he become too used to have everything he needed for his work right at his fingertips—too used to modern medical practices—to think laterally?

Setting the questions aside, he did as she'd advised, siting the cannula carefully into Jenny's arm, feeling the slight resistance as he pushed the needle through her skin then withdrew it carefully from the cannula, leaving the tube in place. He let this fill with blood before closing off the fluid running into Akbar and replacing that tube with the one through which Jenny's blood was running.

He switched the tubes again and began running the precious red liquid far more slowly into the patient. And he *did* watch for a reaction, feeling Akbar's skin, already hot with the beginnings of a fever, probably caused by infection, seeking other signs of transfusion reaction like violent shivering. But Akbar's body gave no indication that the stranger's blood was upsetting him. He lay still and barely conscious and hopefully would remain that way for some time, below the level of pain, while antibiotics and the body's natural defences began to heal his wounds.

'As if such wounds could ever heal!' Kam muttered to himself, but his second patient had heard him. 'To be beaten must be the height of humiliation,' he added, to explain his thoughts.

'We can only do so much,' Jen reminded him, as they sat and watched in case there was a delayed reaction. 'We can get him physically well, then hope that love and support and his own determination will get him the rest of the way.'

This was too much altogether for Kam—the woman was too good to be true. There had to be a catch, some reason she'd hidden herself out here, hiding her body under all-enveloping clothes and her golden hair under a scarf.

Surely this was taking escape too far!

'Why *are* you here?'

In this, his land, such a question was extremely rude, but Kam asked it anyway, wanting to know, although uncomfortable with his curiosity.

'To run a TB eradication programme,' she replied, a tiny smile flickering about her lips. 'We've covered that.'

'But why *here?* There must be people in your own land who need medical help. Your accent says you're Australian—isn't that right?'

She nodded, but her gold-brown eyes looked preoccupied, as if she'd never really thought about answers to his questions before that moment.

'I do work in the outback at home as well,' she finally told him. 'One placement at home, then one overseas.'

She paused, studying him for a moment as if deciding whether she'd elaborate on this answer or not.

What had she seen that she spoke again?

'I actually like the foreign placements better. At home, I feel a sense of helplessness that I will never be able to do enough, as if my efforts are nothing more than one grain of sand in a wide desert—scarcely seen or felt, and certainly of no significance. But here, and in other places I've been—in Africa, in Colombia—I feel whatever I do is helping, even if it's only in a very small way. And I do particular projects, like this TB programme, that have a beginning and an end.'

This time her smile was wider, and her eyes gleamed as if in offering him a confidence she was conferring a present on him.

'I look on these trips as my reward.'

Kam saw the smile but her eyes, not her lips, had caught,

and held, his attention. Hadn't someone once said that the eyes were the mirror of the soul? In this woman's eyes he'd seen compassion, and pain for their patient, and now a gleam that suggested a sense of humour.

Which she'd certainly need out here.

But still he was intrigued. 'So, working, moving on— that's what you like. Is it the freedom? The lack of ties to one particular place or person?'

She studied him for a moment, then she nodded.

'It's what I like,' she confirmed.

'You are a very strange woman.'

Her smile broadened.

'A very ordinary woman,' she corrected him. 'Some people see the things I do as noble or self-sacrificing but, in fact, it's totally selfish, because I love doing it—love the adventure of going somewhere different, the challenge of meeting goals under sometimes trying circumstances, the fun of learning about another culture, meeting people I would never have met if I'd stayed at home, tucked safely away in a GP practice, seeing people a hundred other doctors could see and listen to and treat.'

Kam was checking Akbar's pulse as Jenny explained this, but his disbelief registered in a quick shake of his head.

'And is there no one left behind you who is harmed by your adventures? No one left to worry?'

He turned to look at her, certain she would tell the truth but wanting to watch her face where, he was sure, he'd read hesitation if she chose to avoid his question.

'My parents are both GPs, in a safe practice, one I might one day join, but although they wouldn't choose to do what I have done, they live vicariously through my travels. They support me and scrounge equipment and drugs for me, and take in strangers I send to them, people from distant lands who need more medical attention than I can provide. They had a Guatemalan family live with them for six months while local reconstructive surgeons fixed their daughter's face. She'd been born with a double hare lip and cleft palate.'

Kam shook his head again, unable to find the words to express his surprise, although his own people would take in those in trouble just as easily. But he'd always considered that the way of the desert, born out of need when the support of others might make a difference between life and death.

'Let's see if the blood is doing any good. I'll check his blood pressure.'

The woman's practical suggestion jolted him as his mind had wandered far from his patient.

'I keep forgetting we don't have monitors doing these things for us all the time,' he admitted

Jenny smiled and shook her head.

'No such luck. But before they had all these fancy things, doctors managed and so will we.'

Kam returned her smile.

'Of course we will.'

He watched as she inflated the blood-pressure cuff and they both watched the readout on the small screen of the machine. Akbar's blood pressure hadn't dropped any further, but neither had it risen.

'Let's give it an hour,' Kam suggested. 'Are you feeling all right? Would you like a break from this tent before you give the second pint? A walk or, better still, a cup of tea? What eating arrangements do you have? It seems a long time since I had breakfast at my campsite.'

'A cup of tea and something to eat is easily fixed,' Jen said as he put out a hand to help her to her feet.

She took the offered hand reluctantly, no doubt because of the uneasiness and flutters, but she was grateful for it as he steadied her.

'This way.'

Telling Aisha where she'd be, she led Kam towards the food tent, squaring her shoulders and walking straighter as she recalled his upright posture and the slightly arrogant tilt of his head, wondering again about the blood of desert warriors...

The food tent was set up by a different volunteer aid organisation and stocked with tinned and dried foodstuffs. Most of the refugees collected food from the canteen but cooked and ate within their family groups, but those who had no families now ran the tent as a kind of cafeteria, providing hot water for tea and coffee and meals three times a day.

'Smells good,' Kam said as he entered.

'Stew,' Jenny explained. 'Not made with goat but with canned corned beef and dried vegetables. It tastes much better than it sounds.'

'Or you get very hungry out here in the desert and would eat anything,' her companion said, and Jen suspected he was teasing her. But would he tease, this stranger with the profile that could have been used as a model for an artist to etch an emperor's face on an ancient coin?

She had no idea and was slightly concerned that she'd even considered it because teasing, even gentle teasing, felt like personal attention...

The women tending the big kettles and stew pots handed them small glasses of tea and indicated they should sit while the bowls were filled with food.

Jenny lowered herself easily, used by now to this custom of sitting on one leg while the other was propped in front of her to use as an arm rest as she ate.

'You adapt quickly to local customs?' Kam said, half-teasing again as he nodded at the position she'd taken up.

'These people have had thousands of years to work out the best way to sit while eating—why would I want to do otherwise?'

She sipped her strong, sweet tea—the sugar was added as the water boiled—and watched the shadow of a smile pass across his face, then he too sipped at the steaming liquid, raising his head to speak in another tongue to the woman who was putting food in front of him. Jenny knew they were words of thanks and praise because, rather than the guttural sounds of everyday talk, they had the soft, musical notes that, to Jen, always sounded more like spoken poetry than day-to-day language.

'I may be able to sit properly,' Jen told him, 'but no matter how hard I try, I can't get my "Thank you" to sound like you make it sound. I think it would take a lifetime to learn the Arabic language.'

'And another lifetime, or two or three, to learn different tribal variations of it,' Kam told her. 'I can probably make myself understood to the people of the camp, but every tribe has words that are common only to it. Do you know that in Arabic there are eight hundred words for sword, three hundred for camel and two hundred for snake?'

'Putting the sword—an instrument of death—at the top of the most useful word list?'

He studied her for a moment then smiled a real smile, one that lit up his rather stern face and revealed strong, even white teeth.

'Definitely not. They have even more words for love.'

The huskiness was back in his voice, and Jen shivered as a strange sensation feathered down her spine.

She glanced at her companion, hoping her reaction hadn't been obvious to him, and was pleased to see he'd turned his attention to the woman serving their meals, speaking again, perhaps telling her how good the food smelt.

Another of the women set a bowl of food in front of Jenny and handed her a thin round of bread.

'Eat,' she said, then smiled shyly, as if embarrassed by showing off the English word.

Jen returned the compliment by thanking her in Arabic, although she knew her pronunciation was hopeless—especially after hearing Kam's fluid, rhythmic use of the same words.

They ate, Jen now adept at scooping up the food with her bread, holding it always in her right hand and using pieces of it as easily as she'd use cutlery at home. But as she ate uneasiness crept in, born of not knowing what to make of the stranger who already seemed so at home in the camp.

'We shall check on our patient then sit outside for a while,' he decreed, as if picking up on vibes she hadn't realised she was giving out. 'Today's experience has probably made you think of other things that a proper medical clinic will need.'

'I refuse to think about work while I'm eating,' Jenny said, wiping the bread around her bowl to soak up the last bits of gravy. 'Especially as we haven't had dessert yet.'

As she spoke one of the women approached, a big metal dish of sheep's milk yoghurt in her arms. She scooped some into Jenny's bowl, handed her a spoon, then passed her a tin of golden syrup, a carton of which had somehow found its way into the camp's supplies.

'Best dessert in the world,' Jen told Kam, scooping golden

syrup onto her yoghurt. 'Sweet and sour and very yummy. The women here think I'm mad!'

He watched her eat, shaking his head when the woman offered him yoghurt and Jenny urged the golden syrup on him, but she'd only taken a couple of mouthfuls when Rosana appeared, crawling across the floor of the tent and settling herself into Jenny's lap. Now Jenny shared, spooning most of the treat into Rosana's mouth, cuddling the little girl and talking to her all the time, although she knew Rosana didn't understand a word she said.

'She has no family?' Kam asked as they left the tent, Rosana once again perched on Jenny's hip.

'Not that we can find. In fact, I think she might belong to one of the warring tribes or clans across the border.'

She paused, stopping beneath a spindly juniper tree, knowing questions could be considered rude but intrigued enough to ask anyway.

'Having lived here, grown up here, do you know enough about these countries to understand the war that is going on over there?'

CHAPTER THREE

'SUCH a simple question,' Kam replied, 'but it's like asking me to tell you the history of the Bedouin in a couple of sentences. You know they are the nomadic tribes that roamed the deserts of the Arabian peninsula and north Africa, although in Africa there were Tuareg as well.'

His listener nodded, but it was the intensity in her eyes—her genuine interest and what seemed like a need to know—that spurred him on.

'Originally people think there were three main tribes, but over the years these divided into many clans. Clans and tribes were headed by sheikhs, who were appointed by the elders of the tribe, although members of the one family were usually the ones chosen so in a way leadership was hereditary.'

'And have they always fought or is it only recently that wars like the one over the border have been going on?'

Kam smiled at the ingenuousness of the question.

'They've always fought,' he admitted. 'Often against invaders, especially infidels, but also against each other, one tribe sending hundreds of men on camels and on foot to raid another tribe's camels. But the fighting had strict rules. You never attacked at night because Bedouin believe a man's soul leaves his body at night and to attack then would be to attack a dead man. So they would attack early in the morning, which gave the men who'd lost the camels all day to give chase and maybe recapture their own stock.'

'Giving them a sporting chance? It sounds more like a game than serious warfare,' Jenny said, smiling at him.

To encourage him to keep talking?

Or because she was relaxed and happy in his company?

He gave a long inward sigh that he should even think such a thing. The problem was, he'd been too long without a woman, not wanting, since he'd returned to practice in Zaheer, to have the complications of a love affair while establishing himself at the hospital. Then there'd been his father's illness and the suspicion that all was not well throughout the land, although until their father's death, he and Arun had been unable to do anything about it.

Now they could, but first they had to know what needed to be done, hence his decision to visit the more remote areas. Once they had a clear picture of what was happening, they could plan for the future, and do what they could to right past wrongs and bring better conditions to the whole country, not just the city.

Another smothered sigh, because thinking of Arun had reminded Kam that between them they had to work out the succession. It would probably have to be him, he knew this in his heart. As well as being the elder, he doubted Arun would ever marry again, and children were important to their people and to the succession.

Very important!

Arun's first wife, the gentle and beautiful Hussa, had died from complications of a burst appendix. Arun had been in the city, and his bride had been too shy and ill at ease in her new home in the family compound in the country to mention to anyone that she felt ill.

Arun had been devastated, but once over the loss had become a playboy, courting and escorting beautiful women of every nationality, determined to enjoy life his way but equally determined to remain unmarried, no matter how the women he bedded used their wiles.

But he, Kam, was talking warfare, not women, although thinking of Arun and Hussa and the succession had reminded him of another matter he had to sort out—that of finding a wife. As Zaheer's ruler it was his duty to marry, and though he'd once dreamed of marrying for love, love had never found him, so now his mother was actively pursuing a wife search on his behalf…

Definitely better to think of history and camels and raiding parties than wives and marriage—besides which, Jenny was looking at him as if puzzled by the lengthy pause in his explanation.

What had he been saying?

Battles…

Camels…

'It *was* serious, because camels were a tribe's wealth, but it became more serious when the tribes began to give up their nomadic lifestyle and settle in one place. In the past, tribes usually had a set pattern in their wanderings, spending summer months in one place and winter months in another, roaming from area to area, but within certain boundaries, to find grazing for their camels.'

'And sheep and goats?'

'Sheep and goats? My dear woman, the true Bedouin acknowledged only camels and horses. He might buy a goat from a village where goats were raised, and cook it up for a special feast—the birth of a son, for instance—but camels were their stock, providing all they needed—meat and milk, hair for making clothes and tents. You have seen women spinning camel hair?'

The woman shook her head and the moonlight caught the paleness of her plait as it shifted with the movement, catching his eye as well, making him wonder what the hair looked like unbound...

Was it because right now he should be sitting with his mother, discussing his requirements for a wife and checking the list of candidates, that he was distracted by the sight of pale hair?

'Where was I?' he asked, and even to his own ears it sounded like a demand, but Jenny stood her ground.

'The nomadic tribes settling in one place.'

Her face displayed her interest—a strong, intelligent face—but he wasn't going to be distracted again.

'Of course,' he continued smoothly. 'Across the border here you have two clans, both of the same tribe, both claiming to own the land where they want to settle. It is an impossibility to grant rights to one or the other because ownership of land has never been part of Bedouin history. The people here in the camp are from a different tribe, and the only thing the clans across the border agree on is that this particular tribe shouldn't be there, although, in fact, they have had their camps in the area for many hundreds of years and recently many of them have settled in the area, breeding sheep and goats.'

'So how will it be resolved?'

'Men from other clans within that tribe are already talking to the leaders. They need to settle the dispute soon because like all wars it means no one's planting crops or keeping herds and soon there'll be an even worse famine in the area. I understand people have already tried to mediate, but at the moment no one is listening.'

He paused, looking at the little girl who was perched on Jenny's hip, her head resting trustingly on the woman's shoulder, her eyes closed in sleep.

'As you said, she probably belongs to one of the clans across the border. The family would have known she was sick and that she would be better cared for here.'

Jenny brushed her fingers across the soft dark hair.

'Poor wee mite! But she's a favourite with everyone so she's never short of people to take care of her. She probably eats better than anyone else in the camp, although as you can see that hasn't always been the case.'

'Yet she comes to you at night? Is it wise that she should become dependent on you? Learn to love you? And you, if you love her, then leave…'

Jen stopped and breathed deeply, relishing the feel of the cool night air entering her lungs, enjoying the smell of the desert—of sand, and dust, and flowers she couldn't name, and goat and camel and juniper trees.

But tonight there was another dimension to the magic, and try as she may to deny it, it was to do with a man in jeans and ancient T-shirt…

A man who spoke of love…

'Is it ever wise to love? Yet we all do it,' Jen replied, dropping a kiss on the child's dark hair. 'Opening ourselves up to the vulnerability it brings with it, and to the hurt and anguish when it ends. You must know that, for when you spoke of the history of the Bedouins and the tribes just now, you spoke with passion. Growing up here, learning the history, it's obvious you grew to love this place.'

He was walking again, and she followed, realising he was heading towards a flat rock ledge where she often sat herself at night, looking out at the desert, purple in the darkness, the waves of the dunes reaching all the way to the horizon like the ocean on a windless day. Here she enjoyed the wide, star-bright sky and the wash of the cooling night wind over her skin. Here she felt, if not happiness then at least something that was very close to it.

He turned as he reached it.

'So you are an expert on love in all its manifestations?'

The question was so unexpected Jenny waited until she'd sat down to consider it.

Not that it took much consideration.

'Definitely not,' she said. 'I doubt anyone is. Although if you've experienced romantic love, then you might think you know about it. As for the other kind, love for each other, that's easier, although there are always people you come in contact with whom you can't love, even though some are people that your friends and family might find extremely lovable. But an expert, no way! What triggers love within us is a mystery to me.'

Was she really sitting here, looking out over the vast sandy desert, talking about love with a stranger?

'With romance, it's physical attraction, surely,' her companion said, not looking at her as he spoke so she had a moonlit view of his profile.

'Maybe that's what brings people together to start off with, but it doesn't always turn to love,' Jen argued. 'Look at all the marriages that break up, the affairs that end. Maybe love should come before the physical attraction—start with common interests and friendship and let love grow from that, not from over-heated hormones or a rush of testosterone to the brain.'

She saw him smile but he didn't answer for a moment, and when he turned towards her the smile was gone.

'So maybe the ways of the people here are wise, in that a bride is chosen based on suitability, not attraction. In olden times a bridegroom rarely met his bride before the wedding day—or days as it used to be—although he may have known her as a child, because marriages were made within the tribes and clans so she could have been a cousin he'd played with when he was young.'

Jen knew he was explaining more of the local customs and history for her benefit, yet she heard a note of…sadness, or perhaps inevitability in his voice.

'You speak as if you're not sure if you approve or disapprove of that particular custom,' she said, hoping for another smile, but all she got in answer was a shrug of broad shoulders before he turned back towards the desert stretched out in front of them.

Discomfited by the silence, Jen turned the conversation back to their patient.

'Getting right off love for the moment, if Akbar has internal bleeding, what's it most likely to be? Spleen?'

Kam looked at her and nodded as if agreeing with the change of conversation, or at least accepting it.

'I would think that's the most likely. It's easily damaged and will bleed a lot but on the good side it will often cure itself or, worst case scenario, he can live without it.'

Jen couldn't hold back her gasp of horror.

'You'd operate on him here? Remove his spleen? Under these conditions?'

Once again she had his attention and once again he was smiling.

'Wasn't it you who pointed out that doctors in days that are not so distant managed all these things without all the modern equipment we have on hand today.'

'They patched people up and hoped they'd live,' Jen protested.

'Which is what we'll do if we have to,' Kam said, his voice brooking no argument. 'What do you know about him?' he added, just in case she intended disobeying the warning in his voice. '*Did* he go to commit robbery that he was so severely beaten?'

'I'm guessing he went to find his son, although he may not have told his captors that, fearing for the safety of the child,' Jen explained. 'I know Lia has been distraught about the loss of their little boy. Apparently he was playing at a friend's house when they fled and they thought their friends would also flee and bring young Hamid, but when they arrived neither the boy nor their neighbours appeared.'

'They could all have been killed in the first raid,' Kam murmured.

Jen shook her head.

'Apparently not. The neighbour's wife was from a different tribe—from the tribe that is now in control of that area— so custom suggests she'd be spared and no doubt the boy is still with her.'

'Women and children have always been spared,' Kam told her.

'Or so men say,' Jen reminded him. 'But are they spared, left at home while their husbands and sons go out to fight? What are they spared? Physical injury, which is all very well, but line that up against mental anguish. I don't think they're spared much.'

Kam Rahman turned towards her, something like a scowl marring the stern symmetry of his features.

'You are the most argumentative woman I have ever met,' he said, and she had to laugh.

'That's not arguing,' Jen protested. 'That's nothing more than not agreeing with you! Have you reached such lofty heights in your career that lesser minions in the hospital bow and scrape to you? People often do to surgeons.'

But if he *was* a top surgeon, or even a middle-ranking one, what was he doing here?

Suspicion once again seeped beneath Jen's skin and she studied the man who sat looking out at the desert.

'You're right,' he said, surprising her by agreeing. 'The women do suffer. I wonder if that's why they are more superstitious than men, believing in amulets and written words that can ward off the evil eye.'

'Ah!' Jen said. 'I've wondered about that. Some of the women ask Marij or Aisha to write a word or words on a piece of paper and it is then tucked into a leather bag they wear around their necks. I thought they must be prayers.'

'They are,' Kam said, 'because who better to protect them than their God, whatever name he uses?'

But he wasn't thinking about amulets or prayers but that the women in the camp could not write. For whatever reason they were here, on the edge of his country, they should be being helped, and taught, a school set up for the children and perhaps informal lessons for the women.

Could he achieve all that was needed? How much could one man—two if he counted Arun—do to right perhaps not wrongs but certainly neglect? And how quickly could he set things up? The urgency of the situation struck him and with it came the knowledge that he couldn't afford to be distracted by his attraction to this chance-met stranger.

'I can understand their prayers, when they have so little,' Jenny said, breaking into his thoughts of what might lie ahead. 'Yet they do seem to have hope. I can't explain it in words but it seems to me that all these people hold hope in their hearts. Hope that soon they can return to the lands they know—to their summer camp in the wadi where the dates grow, or their winter camp where the cliffs are honeycombed with caves carved out by their ancestors over centuries. Those with English talk about it all the time and you don't have to be here long before you begin to feel this longing, or hunger, or need, all around you.'

But Kam already understood. Deep in his own Bedouin blood were the urges of migration, the need to feel the desert sands beneath his feet and to roam the lands his ancestors had called their own.

He frowned at his companion. His family had been settled for many generations now, and in spite of his father's intransigence about moving into the modern world, all his children and his brothers' children had been sent overseas to study, to become modern men and women.

Look at him—a doctor, a specialist surgeon!

So how could this woman stir a longing for the desert in his blood? How could she make him wonder if he needed an amulet or a word written on paper in a bag around his neck to protect him from her wiles?

Yet they weren't feminine wiles she practised...

Or were they?

He studied her, sitting so still on the rock, the child cradled in her arms. Just so had men and women sat all through the ages, he imagined, in this place—on this rock—but they would be a family, man, woman, child, so this was nothing but an illusion.

Yet it was an illusion he found unsettling…

As he found the woman unsettling.

He thought back to the list he'd given his mother—a list of the attributes she would look for in his wife—quiet, gentle, amiable, supportive, home-loving, a good housekeeper, equable and attractive had headed the list, and although he'd added intelligent and educated, both he and his mother had wondered if such additions were necessary. This woman would qualify for the last two, and was more than attractive, even when coated in desert dust, but as for the rest…

He shook his head in answer to his own question. This was a woman with wanderlust in her blood and a longing to keep moving on.

The silence didn't bother Jen for she loved looking out over the desert sands, but the peace she usually found at these times eluded her. Tonight the cool air brought tension with it, brushing new sensations against her skin and making her feel edgy, twitchy, uptight…

She tried to analyse these feelings, hoping that naming them might make them go away. But dissatisfaction was the closest she could come and she knew that must be wrong. She was in a magical place, doing a job she loved, so where would dissatisfaction come in?

Rosana grew heavy in her arms, and Jen shifted.

'I must take her in and put her to bed, then check our patient,' she said, and was surprised when Kam rose first, stepping towards her and lifting the sleeping child out of her arms.

'Sit there a while. It will do you good. I'll give the child to Marij or Aisha to put to bed and check our patient for you.'

Jen stared at him, trying to read whatever thoughts his face might reveal in the clear light of the moon. But as she hadn't been able to read it by daylight, trying now was futile, though as he bent to lift Rosana from her arms he was close enough for her to see the strong bones in his cheeks and the high dome of his forehead—the dark eyebrows above the unexpected eyes, and the smooth, tanned skin that was wrinkled at the corners of his eyes. From smiles and laughter, or from growing up in the strong sunlight of this country, squinting in the desert sun?

He took the child and Jenny watched him walk away. She'd seen little evidence of smiles and not heard laughter from him, so maybe they *were* sun-squints!

She propped her back against a rock and looked out at the rolling dunes, trying to think of things she needed for the camp that this man might provide, but his image kept rising up in her mind and she couldn't push it far enough to one side for her brain to work on practical problems.

Although she *had* written a wish list not long after she'd arrived. She'd concentrate on that—picture the words on paper. A well—that was the first item on her list. She knew from her reading that many wells had been drilled in the desert—water wells to provide a permanent water supply for the Bedouin who still roamed the land.

But would an Aid for All worker know influential enough people to have a well drilled at the camp?

He was walking back towards her, so now would be a good time to find out. Better to talk about wells and a new clinic than to sit in silence, surrounded by the magic of the desert, and allow this man's presence to move towards her on the breeze and stroke her skin and send shivers down her spine

'Do you think it would be possible to get someone, the government maybe, to drill a well to provide a permanent supply of water for the camp? At present we get big bladders of water trucked in and we ration it, but we're not always sure where it comes from and some bladders seem to be less clean than others. Everyone knows they should boil it before using it, but whether they do…'

He frowned down at her, then sank down in one easy motion to sit, cross-legged, on the rock.

The silence chafed Jenny's nerves, forcing her into more conversation.

'Of course, there mightn't be underground water so drilling a well could be useless.'

A deeper frown, clearly visible in the moonlight.

'There should be water,' he finally replied. 'Underground rivers run from the mountains—the wadis where the dates grow are fed by them. In the wadis the water is closer to the surface and easier to get to.'

There ended the conversation, no agreement or otherwise to asking someone to drill for a well. In fact, it seemed to Jenny that he'd moved far away from the fairly trivial conversation and was now lost in contemplation of things she couldn't guess at.

She studied his face as he looked out over the desert. She read sadness in it, but resolve as well, then she shook her head. Who did she think she was, judging a man's feelings from his facial expression—especially a man she didn't know and whose expression was verging on impassive?

But her thoughts had broken the magic of the evening so she broke the silence, pushing him on the subject they'd been discussing.

'Well?' she prompted, then had to smile that she'd used the

word in another sense, but if he saw anything amusing in it he certainly wasn't showing it, still frowning at her.

'You are sitting here with so much beauty all around you and thinking of wells?'

'We were talking earlier of what was needed in the camp,' she reminded him, although she couldn't remember if they had been talking about it or if she'd introduced the topic to distract herself from personal thoughts and feelings.

He waved a hand in her direction.

'The well is negligible—it will be done.'

He shrugged as if he could have a team of well-drillers here by morning, so insignificant he considered it, but it made Jenny even more suspicious of him. There was something going on here that she didn't like, but she couldn't work out what was bothering her.

Apart, of course, from the attraction she was feeling for this man—attraction she'd thought she'd never feel again.

'And if you wish to spoil the beauty of the evening with practicalities, I have been thinking we could ask for a couple of portable buildings—the ones that look like shipping containers. The oil companies use them for the workers living on site when new oil wells are being drilled. The buildings are shifted on trucks. We could ask one of the companies to give us one to use as a clinic-hospital.'

'Just like that?' she said, stunned by the size of the project he was suggesting. 'Aid for All practically had to beg to be allowed in to the country to do the TB programme with the refugees, and now you're confident enough of local support to produce a mobile clinic?'

She stared at him, again trying to read what he was thinking in his face, although she knew she was only guessing.

But he did look sad—it had to be sadness, making the corners of his well-shaped mouth droop slightly at the corners and the skin between his eyebrows deepen into a black frown.

'The old ruler has died,' he said. 'Things are changing.'

'Well. I'm glad to hear that, but will they change fast enough for us to get a well and the clinic?'

'They will change,' he repeated, and it seemed to Jenny that the words were a vow of some kind.

But, then again, it could be the magic of the moonlight on the desert creating fancies in her head, or the spell of the man to whom she felt attraction, weaving words about her, snaring her, though unaware of the disruption his arrival had caused in her usually placid life.

She had to get away—from him and the beauty and the moonlight—had to collect herself and her thoughts and get back to being sensible, practical Jenny Stapleton, doctor and aid worker...

'I'll check on Akbar,' she said, standing up and walking away before Kam could argue. She ducked into the tent, which seemed very dim after the moonlight, although it was lit by a couple of bright gas lanterns. Kneeling beside the patient, Jen nodded to Lia who sat so patiently by his side, wiping his brow and face with a damp cloth and whispering little prayers or words of love.

And as she examined him, Jen told Lia what she was doing, although she knew the other woman would understand very few of the words. But how else to communicate? She usually managed through hand signs and smiles, often leading to laughter, but with Akbar so badly injured only the most reassuring of smiles had any place in the strange conversation.

He seemed feverish, and tossed uneasily in his sleep, but

with pain relief and antibiotics flowing into him, there was nothing more they could do. Except refill his bag of blood, which was nearly empty.

She took his blood pressure and found it had dropped further. There *had* to be internal bleeding, although his pulse was good. Low blood pressure from internal bleeding was usually accompanied by tachycardia, a rapid pulse, which made the two signs she was reading contradictory.

Would they have to have a look?

Jen shuddered as she imagined even attempting to operate under these conditions. And if they had to, would it be better to do it now, before he lost more blood?

A sound behind her made her turn to see Kam had followed her in. Jenny stood up and spoke her thoughts out loud, glad she had someone with whom to share her worries.

But Kam was having none of it, turning it back on her.

'If I wasn't here, what would you do?' he asked, and she tried to think, although thinking was hard when he was so distractingly close.

'I doubt I'd operate, not right now, and that's not entirely because I'm not proficient at surgery or that it seems ridiculous to even attempt it in these circumstances, but because sometimes waiting and watching is better than rushing in. Maybe whatever it is will fix itself. There's no distension of his abdomen, although I know he'd have to lose a lot of blood for that to happen, but there seems to be little tenderness either. I pressed my hands against each quadrant and though he murmured when I touched where deep wounds were, he didn't flinch away at any stage.'

Kam nodded his agreement. He'd like to examine the man himself but if he did it would look as if he didn't trust Jenny's judgement and he didn't want to hurt her feelings.

'I'd like to give him more blood, though,' she said, 'and see if that helps his BP.'

She paused, then smiled at him.

'And your fingers are itching to examine him, aren't they?' Her smile broadened, making Kam think of things far removed from medicine. 'Go right ahead, I've always believed in getting second opinions. Also, you can examine bits of him I wouldn't like to, not out of any prudishness but for fear of upsetting Lia, and Akbar himself if he became aware of it.'

He took her at her word and repeated the examination he was sure she'd done quite competently, in the end agreeing with her decision to do nothing yet. If Akbar's condition deteriorated further during the night, then they could and would operate, but the old medical adage of 'First do no harm' kept ringing in his head.

Was she pleased he agreed with her? He couldn't tell, maybe because she was fussing with the bedrolls and organising herself to give more blood.

So practical for such a beautiful woman, or was that a sexist thought?

But as Kam bent over her to uncap the cannula he'd inserted earlier and fit a tube to it, he couldn't help but wonder again what had brought her here.

Wonder also if she felt any of the attraction he could feel simmering in the air between them, or if it was all one-way— she attracting him.

If she knew that, or felt anything, then she was hiding it well, treating him with polite consideration, tinged with just a hint of suspicion, as if his explanation for his sudden arrival at the refugee camp didn't sit well with her.

CHAPTER FOUR

JEN settled back against the bedrolls, once again wishing Aisha or Marij had been here to take the blood, but Aisha had gone to her own quarters earlier, and when Jen had returned to the tent, she'd sent Marij off to bed, telling the nurse she would watch Akbar overnight.

So she had Kam, kneeling so close to her she could feel the heat of his body, and a tiny flare of inner heat she didn't want to think about…

'It is best it goes more slowly into him than it comes out of you,' he said. 'So we will fill the bag again, then you, too, will go to bed. He will be my patient for the night.'

'I can watch him for a couple of hours,' Jen replied. 'I have to check the TB samples and also put out the medications for tomorrow.'

'Now?' Kam asked, surprised by the woman's complacency when faced with another few hours' work after she'd given a second pint of blood.

He started the blood feeding into the empty bag, resting it on a mat on the floor so the flow wasn't compromised.

'Of course now,' she said. 'Well, as soon as this is finished. It's why we're here. For testing we take samples on three consecutive mornings then, if they're found to be positive, we start the patients on the drug regime. Because we can only test about thirty people a day, the camp is divided into sections. In Section One, all those with active TB have been on medication for a couple of months, while we're still testing people in Section Seven, which is where new refugees come in.'

Kam considered the logistics of this. The camp, from what he'd learned, had close to a thousand people in it.

'How many are you treating? How prevalent is it?'

'About two hundred and eighty at the moment. Some are at the beginning of their treatment, when we give them streptomycin for two months as well as the three drugs usually used for treatment, while others are four months in and only have another two months to go.'

'You use isoniazid, rifampicin and pyrazinamide?'

Jen nodded.

'We give them the lot daily for two months then cut back to twice-weekly doses of isoniazid and rifampicin for another four months. It's more expensive than just giving the isoniazid and rifampicin for nine months, but it cuts the time of the treatment to six months and it's easier to monitor the drugs over six months.'

'Because you have fewer people dropping out of the treatment over the shorter period of time?'

'That's the theory, but we still get dropouts.'

Was he really interested or just making conversation?

And why did it matter?

Jen couldn't answer that one but she knew it did matter.

Was it because of that tiny niggle of suspicion she felt towards him, or because she was attracted to him?

She didn't think she'd like the answer to either question.

'Dropouts?' the attractive but suspicious man prompted.

'I'm sorry, I was thinking of something else. What did you ask?'

'I wondered if the dropouts remained in the camp or if you have people going back across the border.'

'I think some go back, although maybe what's happened to Akbar today will put a stop to that for a while. But some join up with the traders and go down to the city on this side of the border.' She hesitated then added, 'Oh, dear, I suppose that makes them illegal immigrants. I shouldn't have betrayed them like that.'

Kam smiled at her.

'In these parts, the lines that make this our country and the other side someone else's were drawn on maps made of paper, but it's far harder to draw a line in sand. I would think the locals recognise boundaries for business purposes, but people are people and should be able to travel freely wherever they wish, especially the real nomads of the desert.'

'I couldn't agree more,' Jen said, liking him again, seeing his deep and genuine regard for the desert people and his common-sense approach to boundaries. 'And now the bag's full, isn't it? I'd better get to work.'

He detached the tubing and reattached the drip to Akbar while Jenny stretched and climbed back to her feet.

She walked across to the far side of the tent where another small gas light was shining on the wide bench where she'd examine that morning's slides, then make patient notes and write out the drug list for the following day. Marij and Aisha distributed the drugs, using a group of young boys to run around the camp to find anyone who failed to come in.

'What about contagion?'

She turned to see Kam had followed her.

'In crowded situations like this, is it not spreading faster than you can cure it?'

'I don't have any scientific proof, but it doesn't seem to spread once treatment's under way. We are inoculating people we know for certain don't have it as we go, so eventually it should be wiped out, in this community at least.'

'Eventually? Will you stay that long? Will you see this happen?'

Jen shook her head.

'I'll stay through all the testing and initiation of treatment, checking for adverse drug reactions in people starting treatment and finding other drugs for them if it proves necessary, but once everyone's been tested and checked, probably in another month, I'll leave Aisha and Marij to oversee the distribution of the drugs and move on to something else—somewhere else.'

'Always moving? You are running from something perhaps? A broken heart? A failed marriage?'

Jen turned to face him, angry that he should accuse her of such things.

Even if they might, in part, be true…

Surely not, not after all this time. It had been five years since the accident, five years since she'd lost David and their unborn child and she'd thought her world had ended…

'No. I'm running towards something,' she said firmly. 'This is work I love, work I do well, and while I can I will continue to do it. It gives me all I need, with adventure, challenge and fun, not to mention satisfaction. Later, as I grow older, I might become less effective and that will be the time to reconsider this lifestyle.'

She tilted her chin in case he hadn't heard the defiance in her voice. He was shaking his head, as if he didn't believe her, but which bit didn't he believe—that she loved the work, the challenge, the adventure, or that she would continue to do it?

Deciding she'd never know, and it was best to ignore him anyway, she worked her way through the slides and set out lists of drugs to be dispensed the following morning. Because the drug regimen changed after two months and also because the patients were at different levels of treatment, the lists were important.

She felt, rather than saw, Kam move closer, leaning over her shoulder as she checked and rechecked the lists.

'You number the patients?'

Was he criticising this method? She swung around to look at him.

'Aisha and Marij give out the medication, and they use the person's name, but it is too easy for someone like me, who doesn't understand the subtleties of the language to make a mistake, calling a man Mahmoud when his name is Mahood, or something else that to me seems similar. It could lead to disaster. We have another list of names and numbers for the nurses, but after a few weeks they know all the names.'

Jenny considered this a rational explanation, so why didn't the man move away? Surely he couldn't be fascinated by sputum slides?

But whatever was keeping him so close didn't matter— what mattered was how his presence was making her feel. Out on the ledge above the desert, she'd blamed the air—the cooling breeze—for the discomfort she had felt in his presence, but here, in the tent, there was no breeze.

'You do this every night? Write down the medication lists?'

'Of course. I'm responsible so it's right I should do it. The numbers make it easy for me as well, because we started with one so the patients who have early numbers are well into their treatment. By the time I leave, these early numbered patients will be finished, and that in itself is a reward.'

Now surely he would move away.

He did, but not very far, pulling a stool over to the desk and settling next to her.

'I'll do the slides,' he said. 'I'm looking for acid-fast bacilli, am I?'

Jen turned towards him.

'You don't have to do this,' she said. 'It doesn't take me long.'

'And you don't trust me enough that you won't check them after me? Isn't that what you're saying?'

He was sitting so close she could see the shadow of his beard beneath his skin, so close she could smell the desert and the wind on his clothes.

'I will check them again,' she said, 'not because I don't trust you, but because it's the way I work. We take three specimens because one doesn't always show bacilli, and I compare all three. If there are three clear slides we cross that person off, inoculate them against TB and that's the last we see of them. When we find infection the person gets a number and the drug regimen begins. So tonight I have to take these slides and compare them against the ones from previous specimens and although this table might not look as if it's organised, it is.'

She reached over in front of him and lifted a slide that had a dab of yellow paint on one corner.

'Yellow is the third day, so I find this patient's first and second day slides—red and blue—and put them all together.

Once all three have been checked they get tossed into a drum of antiseptic and later will be boiled up to be reused.'

She was talking too much, explaining things that didn't need explaining and really were nothing to do with him, but the uneasiness she'd felt since the man had first appeared was growing and her body was turning wayward on her yet again, responding to something he was giving out—unconsciously, Jen was sure.

She kept explaining.

Kam listened to her talk, not because the testing and treatment of TB patients held an irresistible attraction for him but because he found he enjoyed listening to her voice.

Was he, as his American friends would say, losing the plot here?

He'd come to check out what was happening on the far edge of his country and to see what could be done to help.

He'd also come because he had been inexplicably angry and not a little ashamed to find out a foreign aid organisation was at work out here, when surely his people should be looking after the refugees in the way desert tribes had cared for each other right down through the centuries.

Now, when there was so much to be done—and not only here—he was distracted…

By a woman…

He shifted back a little so as not to be so close—not to feel her warmth and smell the woman smell of her.

Which gave her room to move!

'Well, that's done. I'm off to bed.'

She stood up and turned towards him.

'Are you sure you want to watch our patient overnight? I can share the duty—with two of us, we won't have to do long shifts.'

'No, I will watch him,' Kam assured her. 'I sleep lightly so I can doze beside him. I think his wife, too, will wish to be close. Between us we will ensure he continues to be stable. But before that, can I do anything for you? The camp is quiet so I assume all your helpers have retired to their beds. Do you need water for washing? Can I fetch it for you?'

She turned towards him, a frown pleating her forehead.

'You don't have to do that, neither do my helpers. I know my skin's a different colour to that of the people I treat, but I do try to respect their customs of dress and behaviour so that they don't think of me as too different or outlandish. Women here are the water-carriers. I'm a woman and I fetch my own water.'

She paused then smiled.

'Although now and then a small boy will do it for me—or maybe not for me but for the lollies I give him as a reward.'

Kam didn't like the smile. Not the smile as such, for it was a very charming smile. What he didn't like was the effect it had on him. It made him feel warm, and stirred more longing in his blood, only this longing was not for the desert sands…

He should walk away—swiftly—but instead found himself speaking once again.

'Just this once, can you not think of me as a small boy? I won't even ask for lollies. You have a bucket or a drum? And the water…'

She smiled again, her lips twisting upward in a teasing kind of delight.

'I doubt even the most vivid of imaginations could put you into the small-boy category. We'll go together,' she suggested. 'Maybe that way my reputation as a woman won't be totally destroyed by having a man fetch my water.'

She slipped away, returning with a plastic container so big he wondered how she—or small boys—ever carried it.

He took it from her, his fingers brushing hers, and knew this was probably the most stupid thing he had ever done in his entire life. This woman, foreign, argumentative and stubborn as she was, had already cast some kind of spell over him but as yet it wasn't strong enough to hold him captive. Now every instinct told him that to walk out of the tent with her, to stand in the moonlight once again, would tighten the invisible bounds, perhaps inescapably.

Something had happened back there in the tent. Jenny wasn't sure what it was, but she could feel it in every cell in her body. It was as if their conversation about TB and drug regimens had only floated on the surface of their minds while beneath it some unspoken dialogue had been going on.

But what?

She didn't have a clue.

She suspected that it had to do with the flutters she didn't want to admit to, and the butterflies in her stomach, and the shivery sensation that kept running up and down her spine, although it was far too scary to admit that, even to herself.

But as they ducked out the entrance to the tent and stood again in the moonlight, she could feel—what? Magic? Hardly, but something indefinable in the air, as if this man's presence in the camp—and right now by her side—was changing the very essence of her life.

'How ridiculous!'

'Ridiculous?' he echoed, and she realised, to her embarrassment, that the words had burst from her uncensored.

'Well, not ridiculous.' She struggled to cover up. 'More unimaginable. Here I am on the edge of a desert country, surrounded by Bedouin tents, and goats and sheep, walking to fetch water with a stranger by my side. It's like all the fairy-tales I read as a child rolled into one. Weird!'

'Until we reach the waterhole and instead of it being a lovely oasis in which you can see your fair reflection, or a well from which pure spring water gushes, it's a black balloon that's dusty and leaking and probably full of bacteria. The well will come before long. I promise you.'

He sounded angry and she wondered if she'd upset him with her silly talk of fairy-tales, but as he filled the drum with water she sensed his anger was dissipating and as they walked back to the big tent he pointed out the constellations, naming the groups of stars that were foreign to her, here in the northern skies.

Kam carried the water back to the tent, following her behind the hanging rug into the area where she apparently lived. He was appalled by the poverty of it—not poverty in a monetary sense but the lack of facilities for a woman such as she.

'You don't have a bed, a table, or a chair?'

The words burst from his lips and, as she lit a small lamp and hung it on a long metal hook that dangled from the centre of the space, she smiled at him.

'Neither do the refugees in their tents,' she reminded him. 'But I have my bedroll…' she waved her hand towards the larger of the bedrolls which she'd used as pillows earlier '…my suitcase full of clothes, a box of books, a basin to wash in and my drums for water. What else would I need?'

Kam thought of his brother's women, and some women he himself had enjoyed in the past—considered their sumptuous, scented bedrooms and racks of clothes and shelves of beauty products. Even his mother, who was old-fashioned in many ways, had an ensuite bathroom off her room and a fantastic array of perfume bottles ranged along its shelves.

'You can live so simply?'

His voice betrayed his thoughts and the woman smiled.

'I've learned to,' she said. 'And learned to appreciate the simplicity of a life with few encumbrances, although,' she added, and he heard a trace of wistfulness in her voice, 'I sometimes hanker for a real bath—to lie back in the hot water, preferably with lots of bubbles breaking against my skin. In fact, it's the first thing I do when I get back to civilisation—I insist my hotel bathroom has a proper bath, not just a shower, and I indulge myself.'

To Kam's dismay an image of this woman in a bath popped up in his head and although he'd never seen her naked, he could picture her quite clearly, tall, lithe and lean, the bubbles she spoke of rising from the water, adding luminescence to her pale skin...

'Thanks!' she said, and he stared at her, sure she couldn't be thanking him for thinking of her naked. 'For the water,' she said patiently, reaching out to take the drum from his hand.

He dropped it to the ground, unwilling to let her fingers brush against his yet again, and left the room, if it could be called a room. But he couldn't escape the tent altogether for Lia was sleeping by her husband's side, and he, Kam, had promised to keep watch over the patient. So he settled himself on the mat beside the injured man and tried not to listen to the sounds of water being poured into the basin, or the soft, sloughing noises that suggested clothes being removed.

A scent, so subtle he didn't at first register it as something different, mixed with the smell of antiseptic. Did she have enough vanity to bring perfume with her after all? he wondered.

He glanced towards the hanging rug and saw her silhouette, as tall, slim and lithe as he'd expected, then shame crashed down on him and he turned away, unable to believe he'd betrayed her trust in such a way, but at the same time wondering how to suggest she change the place she hung the lamp. She might have other men in the hospital some time…

Jen pulled on the long, silky, dark blue, all-enveloping shift she wore to bed and unrolled her bedroll, then she sat on the mat beside it and unplaited her hair. She covered it with a scarf by day partly out of deference to the custom of the land but also because it was so difficult to wash it, out here in the desert, with the limited water supply. So, to keep some of the dust out and also to hide it when it badly needed washing, she was happy to cover it. But every night she brushed it, dragging out the tangles, getting rid of a lot of the sand it had collected during the day.

If she had one jot of sense she'd keep it short, but although she was willing to go anywhere Aid for All might send her, she couldn't bring herself to cut her hair.

Pride and vanity, she knew that's all she kept it for, but wasn't a woman entitled to a few of these vices? Like the rose-scented soap she carried with her to foreign lands. She might be bathing in dirty water, but the soap kept her feeling feminine.

Like her hair…

She brushed and brushed, not counting strokes but enjoying the relaxation the rhythmic motions provided.

Movements beyond the hanging rug reminded her she had company in the tent. A patient, his wife and a man she didn't want to think about, a man who, all too easily, had reminded her she was a woman.

Not that he had flirted with her in any way, but being near

him, talking with him, feeling the maleness of him brush across her skin, had stirred up sensations she'd thought she'd never feel again.

And brushing her hair was making things worse—it was such a feminine thing to do—

The cry was one of anguish and she forgot about hair and femininity and feelings she didn't want to acknowledge, reacting automatically, rising to her feet and hurrying into the front part of the tent, her hands twisting her hair into a coil and tucking it into a knot at the back of her head.

Akbar was tossing and turning, crying out words Jenny didn't understand. Kam knelt over him, holding him down, talking to him in a soothing voice that seemed to be doing little to lessen the patient's distress.'

'I have some pethidine in that box I brought in. Can you find another ampoule of it for me?' Kam asked Jenny as she dropped to her knees beside him. 'There are some there, they should be near the top. And draw it up to give him subcutane-ously, which will work faster than an intramuscular injection. Once we have him back on fluid I can put the next dose, should he need it, in that.'

Jenny found the drug and thanked heaven Kam had appeared when he had, because without this narcotic analgesic to dull the pain and send Akbar back to sleep the man would be in agony.

She slid the injection into his arm, while Lia, who'd been woken up by her husband's cries, helped Kam restrain the angry, injured man.

Angry?

Was he remembering the beating? Jen wondered, squatting back on her heels as she waited for the drug to take effect.

Remembering the shame of it? Or was it just the pain that was upsetting him so much?

She glanced at Kam, wanting to ask him but knowing she couldn't—not right now.

But among the man's ravings she heard one word, repeated again and again—the man was crying not from pain but for his son.

A giant hand reached in and squeezed Jenny's heart, pain of loss remembered, pain she knew no narcotic, but only time, would heal…

Lia held her husband, tears streaming down her face, but she chattered on to him in a sing-song voice, trying desperately to calm the man she loved.

'Was it just pain upsetting him or is it the loss of his son? I heard him call the boy's name,' Jenny said to Kam, when Akbar had settled back into a drug-induced slumber and Lia once again lay quietly but vigilantly beside him. Kam had walked to the entrance of the tent and Jenny had followed him, needing to talk about the man's obvious distress.

Hoping it was pain, not loss!

Kam shook his head.

'It is being alive that's upset him,' he said quietly. 'He sees himself as a failure because he didn't find his son. He should have died, he was shouting, we should have let him die. He has no son, what is a man to do?'

'Are sons so very important?' Jen asked.

Kam looked surprised by the question.

'Of course. Every family needs a son to take care of the women should the father die. These days that might seem wrong, but the desire to sire a son is bred deep in the hearts and bones and blood of desert people.'

He paused and his face darkened.

'But in truth I believe Akbar feels a deep love for his son. Not all fathers are like that. For some the fact of siring a son or sons is enough.'

Was it thought of his own father that caused the flash of pain in his eyes? She found herself wanting to reach out and touch him, to comfort him, but right now the issue was Akbar, not of Kam's mysterious past.

'But if Akbar's feeling like that—as if he doesn't want to live—will we be able to save him? We need him fighting with us, not against us. Without his help, it will be harder to pull him through.' Now she was feeling Akbar's despair and knew Kam would hear it in her voice, but she couldn't hide it away behind empty platitudes or assurances.

'We have to get the boy,' she said. 'We haven't got Akbar this far to lose him because of despair.'

Kam turned towards the woman who'd spoken with so much determination. She was wearing a long, all-concealing gown yet he could imagine the shape of her body beneath it, while her hair, still golden in the moonlight, was sliding out of its knot and hanging in tendrils around her face.

Was she aware of her beauty? She must be. Surely no woman could be so devoid of vanity she'd not see how lovely she was.

'Negotiate some way. Do you know if they might need anything—the warring tribes? Food or water, maybe medicines? I wouldn't give them guns, but surely there's something we could offer for the boy.'

'I'm sorry, I was distracted.' Putting it mildly! 'You're not suggesting we meet with these people? The same people who have just beaten that man to within an inch of his life?'

'I'm not saying *we* as in you and I should, but you said

some tribal leaders were already talking to them in an attempt to stop the fighting, so maybe we could contact those people. Or I could go as a representative of—'

'Forget it!' Kam told her, sounding admirably calm considering how angry that final, ridiculous suggestion had made him feel. 'There is no way you are setting one toe across that border. I'm not saying those men are savages, but they consider themselves at war, and war doesn't permit a lot of niceties, neither does it have moral boundaries.'

He put his hands on her shoulders and turned her so she was facing him—so he could look down into her face and watch it and her eyes as he spoke.

'You will not go,' he said. 'Understand me?'

The cheeky grin that greeted this order raised his anger another notch.

'Understood, sir!' she said, and snapped a salute in his direction.

He was a man of the desert—he understood about straws and camels' backs—and that cocky gesture was one straw too many.

'You'd call me sir, would you?' he said softly, his body swaying closer to hers, into her space so she'd have to back away if she felt the threat implicit in his movement. 'And give me cheek, yet go on planning and plotting to get that boy back.'

He reached out and touched her cheek.

'You're thinking even now—will this work, will that?'

His fingers slid into the knot of hair and the whole arrangement came loose, sending the golden, silken threads cascading down her back.

'Will you use your beauty to beguile me? To include me in your plan? Is that the way you work, Dr Stapleton?'

He was close enough to see the golden flecks in her brown

eyes, and to see the rise and fall of her chest beneath her gown as she breathed in and out, in and out, perhaps a little fast.

'Will you offer me a kiss as payment?' Kam continued, sliding his hands beneath the heavy fall of her hair and lifting it to spread it around her shoulders. 'Will that work, do you think?'

Was she bewitched, Jen wondered, that she was held captive by his voice? Although witches did bewitching, not moonlight and strangers. In the desert there were peris, fairy-like creatures she suspected worked their magic by the light of the moon. Maybe they did spells…

'Shall we try?'

Some part of her head knew this was when she should break away—if not from the spell, at least out of reach of his hands and lips—definitely out of reach of those lips which were strong and firm yet so beautifully moulded she'd been sneaking looks at them on and off all day.

But her feet remained rooted in the cooling sand, and the man's face came closer, blocking out the moon, and finally his lips touched hers, brushing across them as softly as a night breeze before resting more positively, snaring hers and holding them captive as his voice had held her captive earlier.

There *had* to be a peri working magic somewhere here, because as kisses went it *was* magic. Not too demanding, nor too harsh, just a gentle but very thorough exploration of her lips and then her mouth while all the time his hand rested lightly on her back, beneath her hair, so at any time she could have stepped away.

But she may as well try to pull iron filings from a magnet. She couldn't move, content to have him explore, content to do a little exploration of her own, while her body went through the entire maelstrom of feelings she'd thought she'd never feel again—the tingling awareness, the fluttery beat of her heart, the slight queasiness in her stomach as if love was something for which there should be an antidote.

Although this was kissing, not love, and, if you considered that only their lips were touching—apart from the light hand on her back—it was very modest kissing at that. But Kam's lips...those lips had kissed before and were very, very good at it, which really should have been enough to make her step away but, alas, his expertise was also the reason why she couldn't.

'Do I sense you're not quite with me in this kiss?' he murmured, pulling far enough away for her to see his face. 'Please, tell me you're at least thinking about it and not about some mad scheme to get over the border and rescue the boy.'

She couldn't lie, so smiled instead.

'No, I was thinking about kisses,' she admitted, and saw the quick frown gather between his brows.

'Whose kisses in particular?' he asked, so huskily demanding she felt a sense of power, although she knew this man who barely knew her couldn't possibly be jealous.

'Oh, no one's in particular,' she said blithely, as if she'd sampled dozens and dozens of men's kisses rather than just David's. 'Just kisses in general.'

Kam growled then kissed her again, but this time the exploration stopped and the plunder began. This time he took and gave such heat and fire she thought her feet would surely leave scorch marks in the sand, and when he moved away she had to reach out for his arm to steady herself while her knees got organised enough to hold her up.

'We'd better say goodnight,' he said, his voice rasping against her lips as he kissed her one last time.

'We had,' she agreed, and, stronger now, drew away.

Tomorrow she'd ask Marij or Aisha about the peris and their deeds, or maybe this desert had its own spirits. Didn't djinns hail from these parts? Djinns, she knew, caused mischief, and could take on human or animal form. Was Kam a djinn in disguise, causing mischief in her life...?

CHAPTER FIVE

SHE woke up to noises in the tent, not cries and yells again but voices, speaking quietly, hushed in fact, as if the people out there didn't want to disturb her.

Slipping out of bed, she washed and dressed, glad she had a clean tunic to put on over her jeans, as she'd left the soiled one soaking overnight. Then, hair braided and scarf in place, she ventured forth to find Akbar still looking feverish and very pale, staring blindly at the roof of the tent while his wife and Kam spoke quietly beside him.

Jenny nodded to them but kept walking. Akbar wasn't one of her TB patients so she didn't know him well, and he might be a man who didn't want a woman, apart from his wife, to see him in this weakened state.

It was also better, she decided, to not be too close to Kam until she'd sorted out in her head exactly what had happened last night.

Well, she knew what had happened—she'd replayed it in every waking moment in the night. She'd allowed a virtual stranger to kiss her—worse, she'd kissed him back.

Eventually...

Embarrassment quivered in her toes and the distance

from her corner to the outer doorway of the tent seemed a million miles.

Kam, however, foiled her attempt at escape, calling her to the man's bedside and motioning for her to kneel down.

'Let me introduce you to Dr Stapleton,' Kam said to Akbar, who nodded regally towards Jenny as she knelt beside the mattress on the ground, then turned his head away. 'She, too, will be looking after you.'

Kam spoke in English first, for her sake, Jenny assumed, then repeated his words in dialect.

Akbar didn't respond, but Jenny sensed he hated the idea of being dependent on a woman and wondered if she could persuade Mahmoud or one of her other male volunteer helpers to act as his nurse. She'd talk to Kam about it—

'Come,' he said, as if she'd already mentioned needing to discuss something. 'We'll go to breakfast.'

He stood first, reaching down and taking her elbow to help her to her feet, and all the physical reactions she'd promised herself she wouldn't feel by daylight sparked through her body.

He *had* to be a djinn in human form!

Perhaps that would explain why he wasn't feeling any of the embarrassment she was feeling about the kiss.

Perhaps he'd already forgotten the kiss or, man-like, had put it out of his mind. Jen knew she wasn't a once-kissed-never-forgotten kind of girl but she felt slightly peeved to think he might have forgotten.

Duh!

She should be slapping her hand across her head to get her mind back on track, but as that might look a trifle weird, she made do with work-related conversation. After all, if Kam didn't remember the kiss there was no way in this wide world she'd let him know she did!

'Will Akbar find it hard to have women caring for him?' she asked as she walked beside, but an almost safe distance apart from, Kam towards the food tent. 'Should I get some of the men to take turns in sitting with him?'

'His friends will want to care for him, and most of them will take notice of what we tell them needs to be done, but we still have to watch for signs of infection and internal bleeding. I can do that. You're right, he'd prefer men around him.'

Kam sounded distracted and was frowning slightly, and she wondered if there was something he hadn't told her.

Or if, perhaps, he *did* remember the kiss...

But the conversation was medical, the subject Akbar, so she held up her end of it.

'I guessed as much. Well, as long as there aren't twenty of them clogging up the space and they don't bring their water pipes and smoke in there, I suppose I can put up with it.'

They'd reached the food tent where the women were already rolling up the sides so whatever breeze there was would flow through, but Kam had stopped and was staring at Jen as if he couldn't understand her words.

'You are one strange woman,' he said, and stood back for her to enter the tent.

Oh, yes? Had that judgement been made because she'd kept her distance—hadn't mentioned the kiss, and flung herself on top of him for another—or because she didn't want bubbling water pipes in her clinic tent?

She turned her head so she was looking back over her shoulder at him.

'Is that better or worse than argumentative?'

Kam heard the question, but didn't answer, mesmerised by something in the tilt of her head which had brought back memories of the previous evening. Instead of the woman in a dull grey tunic in front of him, he saw the woman in dark blue silk, her hair a second silken garment, a cloak around her shoulders.

'Argumentative, strange and stubborn,' he said, mainly to remind himself of the attributes that weren't on his list of what he wanted in a wife, although why he should be thinking of his potential wife in this woman's presence, he didn't know.

And how he'd gone so far as to kiss her, he had no idea. It wouldn't happen again, that was certain, for all she'd tasted like roses and honey…

The very last thing he needed right now was the distraction of a woman…

The woman in question was now speaking to the women in the tent, accepting a glass of tea then moving to where, to Kam's amazement, an array of breakfast cereal packets were lined up on a table.

'All this?' he said, waving his hand towards the choices.

'A breakfast cereal company is one of our largest contributors,' Jenny explained with a smile. 'I do keep telling their high-and-mighties that the basic ingredients—wheat and oats and corn—would be more acceptable and useful donations and far cheaper for them than giving us manufactured products, but I suppose grains don't have the brand name and trade mark stamped on them, so they lose out in advertising.'

'Advertising? They'd want to advertise their products way out here where no one has money to buy them, even if there were a shop from which they could?'

'Come and see,' Jenny said, laughing at him now, but she

took his hand and led him out of the tent and up onto a little ridge behind the camp. 'Look down,' she said, and the first thing he noticed was a cardboard patch on one of the tents, with the brand name of the cereal company written in huge letters across it. He looked around and here and there throughout the camp were similar patches.

'News planes fly over and take photos and what does everyone in the Western world see on the front page as they eat their cereal? Who knows, the letters are big enough they can probably see it from outer space. Martians might eventually come and visit earth for breakfast cereal.'

Kam smiled at her glib remark but inside he wasn't smiling. This was his country, albeit a very distant part of it, yet he was learning more about it from this foreigner than he could have believed possible.

And none of it was reassuring. Especially as the touch of her hand as she'd led him up the hill had distracted him again and he felt torn between his duty and this sudden and inexplicable attraction…

They returned to the food tent where he took a glass of tea, and ate cereal and yoghurt for his breakfast, pleased the organisation had scrounged spoons from somewhere so he didn't have to eat it with his fingers. They were sitting near the edge of the tent to get the breeze and his companion ate in silence for a while, then looked up at him.

'About Akbar, I didn't ask, was his blood pressure better this morning?'

'Much better, so if there was internal bleeding it seems to have stopped.' Kam thought this good news but his companion was frowning.

'But should we still take him down to the city for an ultrasound? You said you're here to look around and see what's needed—would you take him when you leave?'

'Let's wait and see,' Kam suggested. 'I don't need to return immediately, and if we keep an eye on him…'

Kam knew it was his own voice he was hearing, but what was he saying?

That he could stay in the camp indefinitely?

Of course he couldn't—there was far too much to see and do.

And why would he be thinking it?

He was looking at one possible answer, who was looking back at him with a puzzled expression on her face.

'But the well? The clinic?'

Kam waved his hand to dismiss her worries—and his own reservations.

'I can radio someone about them. I have a brother in the city—he'll find the right people to talk to about these things.'

Jenny grinned at him.

'If you still have a radio,' she teased, and Kam realised that although he'd been out to the car to get some gear, he hadn't thought to check.

'It had better be there,' he muttered, while his companion continued to smile, which infuriated him.

'And you should have one, too,' he growled. 'It's stupid to just accept that they are stolen and do nothing about it. What if something happened and you needed a radio in an emergency?'

'I think if it was life and death, a radio might magically reappear. There is no way on earth I'd show a lack of trust in any of these people by asking if they know where the radios have gone, but I wouldn't be surprised if at least one of them is in the camp.'

'And you just accept that? Accept the people you are helping would steal from you?'

Her smiled widened, lighting up her eyes, though there was sadness in it as well as she explained, 'They have so little, Kam, and have lost so much. If having a radio hidden in the corner of their tent makes up for even a millionth of the unhappiness they've suffered, I'm pleased for it to be there.'

He shook his head—he seemed to be doing it all the time, but every new thing he learned about this woman generated disbelief, while every new thing he learned about his country added to his sense of shame and frustration.

Of course he couldn't stay here for long, there were other outposts he needed to visit, camps along the northern wadi, small villages and towns. He had to learn about *all* the problems of his country, not just this corner of it.

But his body was remembering the kiss, weakening his resolve, although he knew full well it couldn't happen again. The very last thing he needed right now was a distraction and this woman, he suspected, could prove to be the distraction to end all distractions.

'I'll go and check I've still got a radio then have a look around the camp,' he said, as the little girl, Rosana, crawled into the tent.

But although Jenny picked her up and gave her a kiss and a cuddle, she then handed her over to one of the women who ran the food tent.

'I'll come with you as far as the car. We might meet a couple of my little boys on the way, boys you could trust to keep an eye on the car for you. If you explained to them you need the radio to let the people in the city know what is needed in the camp, I'm sure word would get around not to steal it.'

They left the tent together, but once outside Jenny paused,

as she always did, looking towards the mountains that rose up behind the camp, rough red and gold and ochre rock contrasting so magically with the vivid blue of the sky. She had come to love this particular view, and to feel connected to the mountains, so these quiet moments at the beginning of each day had become precious to her.

She breathed deeply, filling her lungs with the crisp desert air, so clean and fresh and unpolluted it seemed a privilege to be able to breathe it. It was at times like this that she wondered if she could, perhaps, stop her wandering. If she could settle in a place of beauty and let beauty complete the healing process…

Kam had walked ahead, then had apparently realised he no longer had a companion and had turned back towards her.

'Are you coming?' he asked, breaking into her silent communion with the morning.

She hurried towards him, hoping he wouldn't ask what had kept her—she'd feel stupid explaining how she felt.

The little boys she knew joined them, appearing, as always, from nowhere. They greeted her by name and held her hands and danced around her, happy, trusting children whose lives had been ripped apart by war but who had adapted with the resilience of childhood to a different life where fun and happiness were still possible as they played with their friends.

Kam was talking to them, perhaps asking them to guard his car, and they listened and chattered to him, abandoning her now for the far more important male.

'I think you've got it sorted,' she said to Kam as he opened the door of the dusty vehicle then nodded to her to show the radio was still there. 'After you've radioed, a couple of the boys will be happy to show you around the camp—in fact, they'll probably fight for the privilege. I'll get back to the clinic.'

She turned away but heard something in his words 'I'll see you later?' that made her swing back to face him.

Not desperation but some emotion—not the usual casual, offhand remark.

Or was she reading too much into it—was she letting memories of the kiss affect her thinking?

'Hard to avoid it,' she said lightly, 'when we share a patient.'

Returning to the clinic tent, she was surprised to find only Lia in attendance on her husband, who was lying on his side, so his face was turned away from his wife. Thinking Akbar must be sleeping, Jen intended slipping quietly past him, heading for the corner where people were already lining up to have their TB tests or get their medication.

But even in the dim light in this 'hospital' corner, she picked up the sheen of tears on Lia's face. Angry with herself for not knowing the language, she hurried to the testing area and took Aisha to one side.

'Lia is crying—do you know what's wrong? Are Akbar's friends not willing to sit with him? Visit him?'

Aisha's dark eyes glanced towards the rug that separated off the area where Akbar lay.

'He doesn't want his friends, he wants to die,' she said quietly, virtually repeating what Kam had told her during the night, although she'd put Akbar's outburst during the night down to his pain and possibly the effects of the drugs. 'He is angry with his wife, and with the men who carried him back here—probably with you and the other doctor as well. He should be dead, he says.'

'He said this to you?' Jen asked, unable to believe Akbar still felt that way.

'No, he yelled it at his wife when you and the other doctor

went to breakfast. He yelled and yelled, told her not to bring his friends, he had no friends. He told her to let him die.'

Jen knew that cultural differences often created far wider chasms between nationalities than language difficulties.

'Do you understand this?' she asked Aisha.

She first shook her head, then answered with a rather vague, 'Maybe.'

'Maybe?' Jen prompted gently, guessing that Aisha might be embarrassed talking about the reason for Akbar's behaviour.

'Maybe he feels shamed that he didn't save his son. Maybe his—his value as a man is diminished by this failure, and he would not want to live that way.'

Aisha's dark eyes looked pleadingly into Jen's, as if the other woman was begging her to understand the situation without the need for more words.

Jen nodded her response to those pleading eyes. She thought she understood—at least some of it. The man was the strength of the family in this land, the guardian and protector, so it would be natural for Akbar to feel diminished by the loss of his son, and even more devastated by failing to get the boy back.

'We have to get him back,' she said, and Aisha frowned at her.

'Akbar?' she said.

'No, the boy. Hamid. We have to get him back. Surely there's some way—someone we could talk to who has contact with the tribes across the border. Do you know anyone?'

Aisha shook her head, while the shocked look on her pale face suggested she didn't want to know—not anyone or anything—about such a crazy scheme.

Not that Jen was so easily put off.

'Kam knows people in the city,' she said. 'Maybe he will know someone who can intercede for us.'

'Maybe,' Aisha said, repeating a word already used too often in this conversation, although this time when she said it, it was full of doubt.

But as Jen worked through the day, her determination to do something about getting the boy back grew, so when she met up with Kam much later, as she walked towards the rock where she went to watch the sun set over the desert, she couldn't help but bring up the subject.

'If you know people who can drill a well for water, surely you know people who could negotiate for the return of the Akbar's son,' she said, plunging straight into the subject that had been on her mind without a greeting or enquiry about his day. 'Akbar just lies there. His condition isn't critical, and the pain must be easing, yet he has no will to live. In fact, he looks very much as if he's trying to will himself to die.'

Kam studied her for a moment, then waved towards the setting sun.

'Doesn't this beauty steal all other thoughts from your head?' he asked.

Jen looked towards the west, where vermillion and lilac stripes shot through the orange glow.

'Usually it does,' she admitted. 'It's why I come here at this time. But seeing Akbar as he is, seeing Lia's grief at his condition, I can't help but think there has to be something someone can do. Surely a man's life takes precedence over sunsets.'

Kam came towards her and took her hand, leading her onto the flat rock then exerting gentle pressure as he said, 'Sit.'

Jen sat, as much to escape the touch of his hand as from obedience. Memories of their kiss fluttered uneasily in her body, and she clung desperately to thoughts of Akbar and the grieving Lia to keep those memories at bay.

'Now, breathe in the cooling night air and watch the sunset,' Kam ordered. 'Akbar isn't going to die in the next ten minutes, or even the next half-hour. Maybe when the beauty of the desert creeps into your soul, it will ease a little of the anguish you are feeling for the couple.'

I don't want the beauty of the desert creeping in, she wanted to say. It is too seductive, too all-encompassing.

Too romantic!

There, it was said, if only in her head, but it worried her that she'd sat here every night since she'd come to the camp and enjoyed the beauty without a thought of romance, although she'd often thought of David and wondered what he would think of the nomadic life she led now, so far removed from the house in the suburbs and the little family that they'd planned.

The Jenny whom David had known had been a very different person, not better, or less good, just different…

'You are still thinking of Akbar.'

Kam's accusation broke into her thoughts and she turned towards him, wondering why he thought that.

'Actually, I'm not,' she said, and thought that would be the end of it but, no, he was apparently a persistent man.

'Then why the frown?' he asked. 'A sunset cannot make you frown.'

Jen put her hands up and wiped them across her face, hoping to clear it of all expression.

She must have failed for his quiet 'Tell me,' was a command and suddenly Jen knew she would.

'I lost my husband in the accident I had, my husband and my unborn son. This agony of Akbar's brings it back, although his son is still alive…'

She felt him move so his arm drew her closer, easing them both into the shadow of the rock.

'Is this why you travel? Why you can't stay still?' He had slid her scarf back off her hair and was dropping kisses on the top of her head. 'Is it the pain of loss that keeps you moving?'

The kisses were more of a problem than the questions. In fact, the questions were easily answered.

'The pain goes away, you know,' she managed, 'in time. You don't forget but it doesn't hurt each time you breathe. Then it doesn't hurt when you look at happy couples, and finally you can hold a child in your arms and while there's a hollow deep inside, it's not an ache.'

How could such quiet words hurt *him* so badly? Kam wondered, tightening his arms around the woman while emotion squeezed his heart. It seemed natural to kiss her, to move his lips from hair, to cheek, to chin and then to lips, and if her fierce response was born in memory, at least he knew enough to tell she was responding to him, not to a ghost from the past.

His was the name that trembled on her lips as he lifted his head the better to see her face in the dusk light, his the name she whispered as she leaned into him and raised her mouth to his again.

He captured it, that mouth, with its lush lips, and explored its depth and hunger, marvelling that life should so unexpectedly provide him with such a sweet surprise. All thought of the work he had to do, the wrongs he had to put right, were washed from his mind by fascination and desire.

The kiss they shared was different to anything she'd ever experienced, Jen realised as she drew in a deep breath to replenish the air Kam had stolen. It was as elemental as the night and the desert that lay before them, man and woman giving and receiving pleasure, although the heat building inside her suggested kisses would soon not be enough for either of them, and with prayers finished she could hear people moving around the camp, quiet voices calling to each other.

She dragged herself out of Kam's strong embrace, putting a little space between them.

'We were talking about work,' she reminded him. 'About Akbar…'

Kam released her, but she thought his hands moved reluctantly off her shoulders.

'We were talking about you,' he reminded her, his voice so husky she wondered if he'd been as deeply affected by the kisses as she had.

Not that she could admit it…

She shook her head.

'Before that,' she reminded him. 'Akbar, our patient, and Hamid, his son.'

Kam turned away from her and she heard a deep sigh.

'OK, but I refuse to discuss it out here. Later, in the tent—in the hospital if we can think of it that way—there we will talk. For a start you do not know who has the child, which of the warring tribes. This isn't something you can go into—is the expression half-cocked?'

Jen nodded absently, more or less agreeing with what he was saying but thinking more that the beauty of the sunset *was* seeping into her soul and working the magic it usually worked, relieving the tensions of the day—the tensions of the kiss—and reminding her of all that was good and beautiful in the world.

She leaned back against the rock she considered her personal back-rest and stretched her legs out in front of her, relaxing as the dusk crept in, turning the desert sands from vivid orange to pink and blue and purple.

'Such a beautiful place,' she murmured, but even as she said it, some echo of Kam's conversation rattled in her head. *Is the expression half-cocked?* he'd asked. Why? Was it an Australian expression, not an English one?

Not that he'd said he was English, had he?

The suspicions she'd harboured the previous day about Kam being a spy had sneaked beneath her defences, worse now because she'd kissed him. But though she studied him in the dimming light, she didn't mention these sudden and disturbing doubts, asking instead about his day and what he'd seen.

'The boys took me everywhere,' he said, and maybe because of her reawakening suspicion she began to worry whether taking him 'everywhere' in the camp had been such a good idea. What if he *was* a spy, not for the government or Aid for All, but for one of the warring factions? What if he was checking out the camp to see the best way to attack it?

And she'd been kissing him!

Forget kissing. What if she'd put the refugees at risk by being so obliging to him?

The questions made her queasy, and she shifted against the rock. There was one way to find out, but would he tell the truth?

'Are you really working for Aid for All?' she asked, when the queasiness threatened to overcome her.

'Why wouldn't I be?' he parried, which increased both suspicion and queasiness a hundredfold.

'That's not an answer,' Jen snapped, remembering the kiss again. Had she kissed a traitor?

'But who else would I be working for?' he asked, still avoiding a straightforward yes or no.

'The government, the warring tribes, who knows? You could be a spy—even working for Aid for All you could be spying on me, Aisha and Marij, reporting back to someone. I don't know. It just seems strange that after all these months someone appears out of the blue to offer help and wells and clinics. You might be promising these things to distract us from what you're really doing here—how would we know?'

Kam stood up then reached out his hand, silently offering to help her to her feet.

'You have to trust,' he said, and she wasn't sure whether he meant trust in taking his hand or in believing him.

She didn't take his hand just in case, although that was more to do with the dangers of touching him than trust.

'I'll stay a little longer,' she said.

What had he said or done to make her so suspicious? Kam wondered as he made his way towards the clinic tent, intending to check on Akbar before going for his dinner. People were moving about the camp in the dusk, gowned figures flitting here and there, and he realised how easy it would be for the warring tribes to have spies here.

Though spying on what? What more could be taken from these poor, stateless people?

'I am here to see how things are running and what the needs are,' he told Jenny, meeting up with her later in the food tent. 'From both a government angle and as far as Aid for All is concerned. I'm here to see what's being done and what more needs to be done.'

He spoke flatly. The idea that she might not trust him had upset him more than it should have, and Akbar's condition made things worse as the man refused to speak to anyone, refused to eat or drink, and when he had felt strong enough to sit up, he'd begun picking out the stitches on his chest and legs, cutting through the sutures with a rusty razor-blade a friend must have provided for him. Kam had considered taking the razor blade off him, but knew Akbar would then tear the stitches out and create far worse wounds.

Did Jenny know this that she was so intent on getting the boy back?

He didn't like to ask in case she didn't know—finding out would make her more upset.

So he sat and ate, waiting to see if she would respond to his explanation or perhaps tell him why she doubted him.

'So, I know you would only get a very general idea of how things are from one walk through the camp, but what did you find today?'

Was she testing him?

Kam couldn't tell, for her head was bent and her face in shadow.

'Jenny.' He said her name, but quietly, then waited until she did look up, her eyes dark in the shadowy tent, the pale oval of her face framed by the dark scarf. 'You can trust me,' he said, 'in every way. The fate of these people as well as their comfort and health and welfare is as important to me as it is to you. Do you believe me?'

She studied him, tilting her head to one side as if that might give her a different perspective, but it was his motives, not his looks, she had to be considering.

'I would like to,' she said, 'because these people are so vulnerable.'

She put down her dish and held out her hands in a helpless kind of gesture.

'And even if you are some kind of spy, what can I do? I can ask you to have compassion in your heart. To see their plight and maybe report on it, but not make things worse for them. I could beg, I suppose, trade kisses that would have no meaning, but in the end it is between you and your conscience what you do.'

The trade-kisses part made Kam's heart race, but only until he realised just how demeaning a suggestion it had been, especially coming after the kisses they'd shared not long ago—kisses of passion and desire, he'd thought.

But he'd asked for it, daring her to trade a kiss last night, but now he hurt for her that she felt such doubt, yet he couldn't make things right.

Not yet!

Except as far as kisses went. He could sort that out.

'Your kisses are too valuable for any currency but love,' he said. 'What we shared this evening grew from attraction and perhaps a little from pain. I doubt you can deny the attraction, Jenny, and I certainly can't. But…'

She half smiled at him.

'There's always a but, isn't there?' she said, so much sadness and regret in her voice he wanted to hold her again—kiss her again.

Instead, he nodded.

'Yes, there's always a but,' he agreed. 'Another time, another place, we might have met and kissed and enjoyed the attraction that has sparked between us, but suspicion is a bad basis for such things, and right now my life is bounded by demands I can't explain. Right now, seizing the moment and enjoying the attraction would be all that could happen between us, and I doubt that, even without the suspicion, you would enjoy such a relationship.'

Jen sighed as the words ran through her mind, then ran through again—poetic words, and things he couldn't explain.

'So I remain suspicious and kisses are forbidden,' she said, speaking quietly, half-teasing, although the other half was sadness.

Then Kam smiled and she felt the flare of heat again.

'Oh, I don't know that we can't kiss again,' he murmured. 'As long as we both understand that's all they are. Just kisses, not currency, or promises…'

Just kisses?

The flare of heat spread through Jenny's body, sending tingling messages along her nerves.

Would it hurt?

Harm anyone?

'Just kisses?' she repeated, and saw him glance at his watch.

'We should check Akbar first, then perhaps a walk along the edge of the plateau? The moon should be full enough to light our way.'

The tingling messages turned to shivers of apprehension, but Jen knew she'd nod agreement. That she could still feel longing and desire had been a revelation, like a rebirth almost, so surely it would do no harm to see where such a rebirth would lead.

Where moonlit kisses would lead…

CHAPTER SIX

THEY walked back to the clinic tent together, saying nothing more about the proposed meeting, although to Jen the anticipation seemed to spark in the air around them.

Kam knelt by Akbar, who appeared to be sleeping, perhaps trying to persuade Lia to get some sleep as well. Jen went on into her private corner, thankful she'd got through all the slides and medication lists during the day so there was no work awaiting her.

She wanted desperately to wash and change into something prettier than jeans and shirt and a long grey tunic. But that would look stupid, as if she was going on a date...

Changing clothes would look stupid?

What on earth was she thinking?

What could be more stupid than walking in the moonlight and trading kisses with a man who'd already said quite clearly he wasn't interested in her? A man who hadn't denied he might be a spy? Was she nuts? Of course she couldn't do it!

She undid her braid and brushed her hair before pinning it into a loose knot on top of her head and was about to strip off her working clothes when a commotion outside led her back into the main part of the tent.

Three of the small boys she knew were standing in the doorway next to a man in a black robe so old the fabric looked rusty. He had a black scarf rolled into a rope and wound around his head so only his eyes and his lips were visible.

He spoke and Kam moved so swiftly, grabbing the man's arm and hurrying him further out of the tent, that Jen felt a flash of fear. Was the man a messenger for Kam? Did this prove he *was* a spy?

Jen followed—after all, this was *her* clinic, not his.

As she came out of the tent the man gesticulated towards her and spoke again, Kam slamming words at him, obviously not agreeing, but the man kept pointing at Jenny.

'Go back inside,' Kam ordered, sounding so furious Jen almost obeyed, but somehow she was caught up in this, and, with the unease of distrust between them, she wasn't going anywhere.

'What are they saying?' she asked the boys, wide-eyed on-lookers to the confrontation. She knew they didn't speak much English but they were picking up more each day.

'That man wants you to go with him to the chief because chief's wife having baby.'

The child who had explained this pointed to the stranger.

'Go where? What chief?' Jen asked, and Kam shot some kind of command at the boys which not only silenced them but made them step back into the shadows.

'Then *you* tell me what's happening,' Jen demanded of Kam. 'And tell me the truth—no lies or evasions, thank you!'

He looked at her and shook his head.

'You should have stayed inside,' he muttered, and she threw him a furious glare which he obviously understood because he then explained.

'The wife of the leader of one of the warring tribes, the one who has taken over the village where most of the refugees lived, has been in labour eighteen hours. The woman who acts as midwife has told the chief the baby won't come out. He wants you there to help. I imagine he knows about Caesareans and assumes you can do one. I have been trying to tell him I can do one, but he—'

'The chief doesn't want a man touching his wife,' Jen finished for him.

Kam gave a grim nod, though he did add, 'And if you hadn't come out of the tent I could have told him you were away and I'd have to go.'

'What nonsense,' Jen said. 'These people aren't barbarians.'

Images of Akbar's flayed and battered body flashed before her eyes, and after them images of Akbar's acute distress.

'But it's perfect,' Jen said, suddenly excited. 'Tell him I'll come but only on condition we bring back Akbar's son as payment.'

'You can't make conditions with these people,' Kam protested. 'You don't even know if you'll come back yourself.'

'If we make a pact they'll honour it—I've been here long enough to know that honour exists among the tribes. Once someone's word is given, it is kept.'

Kam gave her one last frown then turned and spoke to the messenger, whose dark eyes flashed between Kam and Jenny as Kam was speaking.

'I'll pack a bag with what I might need,' Jenny said, and slipped inside the tent, stopping beside Lia to ask if she had a photo of Hamid. Lia's English wasn't good but eventually she reached into the folds of her gown and produced a small picture of a little boy, then a picture of the three of them, parents and child, both pictures worn and grey, as if looking at them had drained them of their shininess.

Jen slipped them both into her bag, found a warm scarf to wrap around her head and shoulders. Would they be walking or driving? Please, don't let it be riding on a camel—she found the favoured beasts unstable to say the least.

Outside, Kam and the stranger were still arguing, and as she appeared the stranger stepped forward and grabbed her arm, using one English word. 'Come.'

Jen pulled away from him, taking a step backwards, although she knew she couldn't waste too much time as the lives of both the mother and the unborn infant could be in danger.

'Has he agreed?' she asked Kam, who shook his head.

Time for bluff.

'Then I don't go!' she said, and turned to walk back inside the tent.

'Come!' the man repeated, but it wasn't the order made her turn but Kam's quick gasp.

The man had produced a long and very dangerous-looking rifle from beneath his robes and was now pointing it at her.

She took a deep breath and remained right where she was, staring defiantly into the dark slit where his eyes were.

'Tell him if he shoots me, the woman and the child will die and his leader will be very angry with him.'

Kam said something, and Jen had to assume he was translating what she'd said. Slowly the stranger lowered the rifle until it was pointing at the ground.

Kam spoke to him again, and this time he nodded.

'OK,' Kam said, grabbing Jenny almost roughly by the arm, 'you've got your agreement, although that was the most damn stupid thing I've ever seen anyone do. What if he'd shot you?'

She turned and smiled at him, although the smile was to hide the fact her lips were probably trembling—every other bit of her was. She'd never been so terrified in her life but she'd known she had to hide it—to show strength and determination in front of the man with the gun.

Kam walked with her as she followed the dark-gowned figure through the camp, aware of whispering as they passed and hisses of fear or disgust rising into the night air.

'If I'm not back tomorrow, you'll have to carry on the testing,' she said to Kam. 'The girls know the system, it's just the slides you have to check and compare to the others.'

'If you're not back tomorrow, I won't be either,' he said. 'Surely you didn't think I'd let you go alone?'

She wanted to stop right there and argue with him, but the black-robed man was striding on ahead and she wasn't sure just how badly off the pregnant woman might be, so she kept walking, berating Kam as she went.

'You can't come with me—that's just stupid. What happens if they keep us both—what will happen to the clinic with no doctor? Besides, I thought the man said he didn't want you.'

'He didn't want me as a doctor but I told him you don't speak the language and I would need to be there to explain to the chief exactly what was happening with his wife. I did rather emphasise the fact that the chief would be extremely worried if he didn't know what was going on and if you couldn't ask him for permission to do an operation. I added a bit of medical drama to make a Caesar seem a bit worse than it is, and our friend up ahead was probably turning green under his turban and decided better me than him telling that kind of stuff to the chief.'

'It's still stupid!' Jen muttered, not willing to admit she felt far braver about this adventure now she knew Kam was coming, although a little sick in her stomach when she thought of something happening to him.

These were the people who had beaten up Akbar.

They had reached the outer limits of the camp and to her relief she saw a battered vehicle standing beyond the loose wire boundary. No camels!

'Make sure he understands we want safe passage back here and we want the boy,' Jen said to Kam before agreeing to climb in.

Kam spoke and the man held up his hand as if giving some kind of oath then hustled them both into the car and took off, speeding through the moonlit night. If they were on a road, it wasn't discernible to Jen, but she was in the back seat so maybe Kam could see it from the front. Not that the man seemed to need a road. The vehicle was twisting and turning around the dunes, heading around the base of the mountains before beginning to climb.

'I know this place,' Kam said. 'As a child I was sometimes brought here to these mountains. I think there's a way across them back to our camp, a track Akbar probably took, maybe ten miles long, from memory.'

The driver said something to him, the voice indicative of an order, and Kam shrugged his shoulders but stopped talking.

Ten miles wasn't far to walk, Jen decided, if they had to make their own way back to the camp. Though over the mountains? From the camp side the mountains looked steep and not at all user-friendly, but if there was a track...

An hour into their journey the driver slowed, and ahead Jenny could see lights.

So this was the village where most of their refugees had

lived. The houses up ahead had been their homes, the gentle mountain slopes their grazing land. By moonlight it was a pretty place, the houses built of stone or mortar mixed from sand hard up against the cliffs.

But there were tents here, too, the black Bedouin tents she now knew so well, and it was outside one of these their driver stopped.

Fear caught at Jenny's throat and she breathed deeply. For all they were at war and had driven the refugees out, she reminded herself, they were honourable people in their own way.

Their guide barked an order at Kam, who got out and opened the back door for Jenny, giving her shoulder a little squeeze and keeping close to her as they moved towards the open doorway of the big tent. That hand on her shoulder and the closeness of his body rebuilt her strength, and she wondered that she could feel such trust in a man she'd doubted.

But at the doorway another man held up his hand, barring Kam's way and speaking so quickly Jen knew Kam's knowledge of the language must be good for him to follow it.

'This is the women's tent,' he said to Jenny, this time taking her hand while he spoke. Guessing she was fearful and in need of support? 'Our friend and I will not be allowed in, but the chief is just outside around the back. We will go and talk to him, then I will talk to you through the walls. You'll be all right?'

He squeezed her fingers gently and his eyes scanned her face, but she couldn't let him know how apprehensive she was feeling. She nodded, then, hearing a cry of pain from within, quickly broke away, although she turned back at the last moment, fishing the two photos from her pocket.

'Hamid,' she said. 'Make them give you Hamid. He must be with you or I won't help the woman.'

Jen knew she was bluffing, and she was reasonably sure that Kam also knew she was bluffing, but would the chief know?

That was the risk they had to take.

A woman took Jenny's hand and led her deep into the tent, where a lamp lit up a scene that could have been repeated in tents all over the Arabian Peninsula down through thousands of years. A young woman, bundled in clothes, lay on a pile of mats and a palliasse in the middle of the tent, other women kneeling and sitting cross-legged around her, one bathing her face, others holding her hands, all of them talking in their sing-song voices very quietly and, Jen guessed, encouragingly.

The girl herself—and she was only a girl—was extraordinarily attractive, even though her face was grey with fatigue and almost black circles lay beneath her huge dark eyes.

And those eyes held fear—Jen could see it. She knelt beside the girl and took her hands, talking to her, saying words she wouldn't understand but hoping her tone might convey reassurance.

'I'm going to examine her now. I'd like to remove some of the clothes she's wearing so I can palpate her abdomen at the next contraction and I'd like someone to tell me exactly what's happened so far.'

Jen spoke loudly, hoping Kam was outside the right part of the tent, then she heard his voice, talking quietly but quite audibly, and one of the women, talking all the time, began to pull the blankets off the girl, finally revealing her swollen belly.

'The woman says the contractions grew weaker and weaker. She is obviously an experienced midwife and she says she could poke her finger quite deeply into the

patient's belly during a contraction at the end,' Kam translated, while the woman who had spoken demonstrated this
for Jenny then held her fingers apart to show how far the
cervix had dilated.

'I'm going to listen to the foetal heartbeat. I'll make do
with my stethoscope,' she said to Kam, who immediately
translated. Jenny was strengthened by his voice and by his
presence not far away. She went to work more steadily now,
letting her training take over.

'The FHR is slow, under a hundred. I would have thought
tachycardia would be indicative of a problem, but the brady-
cardia is a worry anyway if it goes on for more than ten
minutes. I'll check again later. Can you ask how long since
she had a contraction?'

The patient was getting agitated and the women had to hold
her shoulders down until Jen gently pushed them away and
helped the girl sit up. She cursed herself for not knowing the
language but she kept her arm around the girl and patted her
shoulder, smoothing back the sweaty, tangled hair from her
exhausted face.

'No contraction for half an hour and before that very weak,'
Kam said. 'Is the patient all right? Is that her crying out?'

'Yes. What's she saying? What does she want?'

'She wants her husband,' Kam translated, his voice
sounding very dubious.

'What's the man's name?' Jen demanded.

'Abdullah.'

Jen repeated it and her patient grabbed her hands and
looked pleadingly into Jen's face, repeating the name and
pointing to herself.

'Why can't he come in?' Jen asked Kam.

The answer was brief.

'Custom!'

'Oh, spare me,' Jen said. 'You tell him he's a modern man, a leader, and it's up to him to start and set new customs for his people. What sort of leader is he that he bows to ancient ways at a time like this? OK, some of them are good, but others must be tossed out. Say it any way you like, but tell that man to get his butt in here to reassure this poor woman. He needn't stay—in fact, I doubt he'd be much help during a Caesar—but she's so distressed she needs to see him and she needs to see him now.'

While Kam's voice rose and fell outside, Jen finished her examination. The contractions must have lost force early in the latent phase for the cervix hadn't reached four centimetres dilatation. After twenty hours this poor young girl was still in the first stage of labour.

Jen's admittedly basic physical examination suggested it was a problem with the girl's pelvis, the bones failing to open wide enough to allow the baby's descent.

Then voices at the doorway and a flutter of rearranging of scarves among the women suggested Kam might have persuaded the chief to enter the tent to see his wife.

Jen rearranged the rugs and clothing over the girl's belly and again pushed her limp hair back from her face.

A deep voice spoke and the women scattered like pigeons in a square, then a huge man appeared.

'I have got my butt in here!' he said, in a deep, guttural voice, and Jenny had to smile.

'How long would you have gone on letting my colleague translate?' she asked as he strode towards them, his eyes on his young wife on the bed.

'Perhaps for the whole time,' he said, 'for why would you believe you needed someone to translate?'

He knelt beside the bed and began to speak very gently to his wife, and once again the language sounded like poetry.

Jen let the two of them talk for a few minutes then she knelt on the other side.

'I brought my colleague in case you wouldn't come in, then he would have had to explain to your wife what we need to do. The labour has gone on too long. I think perhaps because your wife's pelvis won't allow the baby through.'

She pointed to her own pelvic region and used her hands to show how the pelvic bones usually opened.

'I think the baby is now getting distressed, and as you can see, your wife is exhausted. I would like to do a Caesarean and deliver the baby that way. You know what it means?'

'You cut her open and take out the baby. Will she live, my wife?'

Jen could have hugged him. So often people thought first of the child—would it live?—but this man must dearly love his wife for her to be the most important issue in his mind.

'She will, but she will have to take it easy for a few days— she should move her legs and walk a little but not move around too much or strain herself, just until the scars, both internal and external, heal. I can come back and see her every day if you wish.'

The man nodded then began to speak to his wife, who looked at him with her lovely eyes brimming tears, while her two hands clung to one of his.

He shook his head, and though Jen knew Kam could probably hear the conversation, he knew better than to interrupt whatever was passing between the two of them.

'She wants me to stay,' the big man said, looking pale himself now, as if he'd rather be facing a thousand fighting tribesmen than be present at his baby's birth.

'Men do it all the time in the West,' she told him. 'Even with a Caesarean birth. We can hang up a rug so you can sit at your wife's head and not have to see the operation. I will give her an anaesthetic so she won't know you're there, but I know you will honour your word. And if you are there, we can hand the newborn baby to you, and you can cut the umbilical cord if you wish, so you are part of this great occasion and will be the first to hold your child.'

The man took a deep breath, looked down at his pale child bride and nodded.

'I will do it,' he said, and began to give orders so the women came scurrying back, and in no time there was a rug hung above the woman's waist.

'I need my colleague to assist me,' Jen told the leader. 'It will be easier and safer if he is here. He can remain behind the rug with you, giving your wife the anaesthetic and oxygen to ensure she and the baby are all right. I will also need water and some clean cloth and something to wrap the baby in when it is born.'

More orders, then Kam appeared in the doorway. He took in the situation in a glance and made his way to the head of the makeshift bed and knelt on the other side of patient's head.

'I'm doing the anaesthetic?'

A smile for Jenny's benefit. She was thankful for it, aware her heart was racing with what ifs.

What if she botched the operation and the baby died?

The woman died?

'It's ether—you can use it?' Jen said, handing him a bottle

and a swab to pour some drops onto. 'She might feel nauseous after this anaesthetic,' she explained to the chief, 'but it is all we have.'

Jen rummaged around in her bag and produced the small canister of oxygen she'd dug up from a corner of her room and passed this with a mask and tubing to Kam. She set out the instruments she'd need—scalpel, retractors and small clamps being the most important. She didn't have any obstetric forceps but felt she could manage with her hands, although that might mean her patient would have a larger scar than was strictly necessary.

All these things rattled around in her head as she mentally rehearsed what she was about to do. Then, as a woman put down a basin of water and a pile of spotless-looking cloths beside her, Jen washed and soaped her hands, dried them and pulled on gloves.

The woman Jen had taken to be the midwife remained beside her and Jen was glad she had someone on hand to take the baby and see to it while she finished the operation.

'Ready,' she said to Kam.

'I'll tell you when,' he said, and although she couldn't see him, she knew he'd be pressing the ether-sprinkled pad to the patient's nose and counting slowly down.

'Ready,' he said, and Jen began, swabbing then cutting through the skin and outer flesh through the uterine wall, keeping the incisions as small as possible, feeling for the baby's head then gently easing him out—for it was a him.

'You have a fine son,' she said, handing it to the waiting woman, who used a tiny straw to suction out his nose and mouth. 'In a minute, when we know he's breathing real air and turning pink, you can hold him. Do you want to cut the cord?'

A strangled 'No' was the answer, so Jen cut and knotted it then motioned to the woman to pass the baby to his father.

The woman hung back so Jen took the baby, now a satisfactory pink, his eyes wide open as if to take in all he could of this new world. She held him close for a moment and thought of all that might have been, but the past was gone and with it other dreams and plans and happiness. This was now, and a new life was just beginning. She dropped a kiss on the cloth swaddled around the little head, then leaned around the rug to hand him to the man who sat there, still holding his wife's unresponsive hand.

Keeping his promise.

An honourable man.

He took the tiny child, a look of wonder akin to disbelief on his bearded face and tears in his dark eyes, but though he held the child, he turned his attention back to his unconscious wife. The deep love he felt for her was almost palpable.

Jen delivered the placenta and sewed up the wounds she'd made, checking for any signs of bleeding as she went.

'I'm putting a dressing on her now,' Jen said to Kam, knowing he would be watching the woman's eyes for signs of returning consciousness. 'Let's see how clever you were at judging dosage.'

'If you knew how long it was since I used ether,' he grumbled. 'In fact, I don't know that I've ever used it.'

'Everyone can use it,' Jen reminded him. 'Didn't dentists use it for a long time in the past?'

'She's coming round,' Kam said, and his voice told her how relieved he was. 'Have you any pain relief we can give her? The wound will hurt like hell.'

'She will forget her pain when she sees her son,' the chief said, but Jen wasn't so sure.

'I've got some tablets I will leave for her,' Jen said, speaking to the chief again. 'Do you have access to ice, or is that a stupid question?'

'We have power in the village and refrigerators. I can get ice,' he said, so Jen explained how wrapping ice in towels and holding it against the stomach might help reduce the pain.

'And make her take the painkillers—she can still breast-feed her baby without them affecting her milk.'

One look at Kam's face was enough to tell her that this was not the kind of conversation this desert chief was used to, but the man was holding up very well, mainly because most of his attention was back on the tiny being in his arms, who was wriggling now and then and gazing up at his bearded father as if taking in every detail of the man who held him.

The patient stirred and groaned, and Jenny wondered if she should give her something stronger than an oral analgesic until the maltreated parts of her body settled down, but then her husband bent towards her, tilting the baby so she could see his face, and wonder overtook the pain.

She reached out a tentative finger and touched a tightly clenched fist, then she looked up at her husband, the question—is he really ours?—obvious in her eyes.

Kam slipped away and Jen roughly washed her instruments, wrapped them in a clean cloth so she could take them home to sterilise them and moved towards the door, leaving the pair to examine their miracle together.

'Have you asked about Hamid?' she asked, joining Kam outside the doorway.

'They will get him when we are ready to leave,' Kam said, but something in his voice made her turn and look into his face.

'You don't believe him?'

'Oh, I believe him, it's the "when we are ready to leave" part that bothers me,' he said. 'Do you think that man will let you go when his wife still needs care? Do you know what it would have taken for a man like him to be present at the birth of his child? He is going against thousands of years of tradition, which tells me he must love her very, very much. Do you think he's not going to worry about her recovery? Not want a trained person taking care of her?'

'But I can't stay,' Jen protested. 'And he promised.'

Kam touched her arm, no doubt to calm her, although she was feeling far from calm.

'It wasn't he who promised,' Kam reminded her, 'but his lieutenant. Desert people are very wary about making promises because their word is their bond. So they will avoid giving it. They will procrastinate as long as possible or seek an out. In this man's case, the out is his lieutenant. He's the one who gave his word.'

'Well, it was that or shoot me, I suppose,' Jen said, and although she spoke lightly, she was feeling a great deal of disquiet.

'Don't worry,' Kam said. 'I'll find the man who promised and talk to him. He is obviously trusted by his chief that he was sent on the mission, so he must be important to the tribe. What if you write out exactly what must be done for your patient—when to give her painkillers and how many, when to check the dressing and change it if necessary? Have you enough dressings and antiseptic to leave some for them? I'll check the chief reads English as well as he speaks it and if not will translate your instructions. We'll set everything up then tell them we can come back—when? A week?'

Jenny thought about it, her imagination providing lists of things that could go wrong for the young mother.

'I don't know, Kam,' she finally said, and must have sounded so despairing he put his arm around her and gave her a hug. She nestled gratefully against him, drawing strength from his body. 'Not a week certainly. Imagine if infection set in!'

Comforting, that's what it was, to have his arm around her shoulders, and if it started little tremors of desire at the same time—well, she didn't have to acknowledge that part.

What she had to do was concentrate on the problem.

'It didn't take us that long to get here. What if we take Hamid back tonight and I promise to come over again each night to check on her?'

Kam gave a long, theatrical sigh.

'So much for kissing in the moonlight,' he said, squeezing her a little closer.

'That was never going to happen,' Jenny told him. 'I'd come to my senses just before the messenger arrived. As you said, this can go nowhere, so why…?'

She shrugged away the rest of the explanation and eased away from him before he felt the tremors in her body. Only this time they weren't just tremors of desire, they were tremors of disappointment as well.

But Kam must have felt something, for he moved away as quickly as if she'd pushed him.

'I'll find our guide,' he said, and disappeared into the shadows.

CHAPTER SEVEN

THE guide returned but his face was grim. He spoke to Kam, and now it was his turn to look grim.

And angry!

'Apparently the chief says we cannot go,' he translated, but something in his tone told Jen that wasn't right.

Although it wasn't hard to guess what bothered him.

'*We* cannot go?' she repeated, with just enough emphasis on the first word for him to understand she'd guessed the things he hadn't said.

'The chief wants you to stay. I have offered, and explained I can do whatever is necessary for the woman should things change. I said I could work through the midwife here, but the chief wants you.'

'And Hamid?'

'Our guide says Hamid is waiting for us—he has him safe.'

'Then you could take Hamid back and run the testing for a while. The two nurses know what to do—all you'd have to do is check the slides and put out the medication. I'll stay for another day and—'

Kam couldn't believe she'd be stupid enough to suggest such a thing, and his anger at her, and at the situation, made his abrupt 'No!' sound far too loud, too aggressive, too explosive.

'One goes, we all go,' he insisted. 'You've said you'll return. Why should your word be any less believable than theirs?'

Useless question. He knew why. For centuries these people—his people—had trusted no one but their own, often with good reason as waves of raiders and conquerors had swept across their lands.

He spoke to their guide, who was adamant Jenny could not leave the camp, although he seemed shamed to have to say that.

'Well, she needs to sleep. At least show us to somewhere we can sleep, and we want the boy with us—that was your promise.'

Their guide nodded and led the way to a small cave, hollowed out over the centuries by the nomads as shelter and home during their summer stays in the mountains. Inside, lit by the dim light of a tallow lamp, the little boy already lay asleep, the photos clutched tightly in his hands.

Jenny squatted beside him and watched him as he slept, then she looked up at Kam and smiled.

'So we've saved two children today,' she said softly, and in the words he heard an echo of the child she hadn't saved. That she could be so—so brave—about this situation affected him deeply, sparking anger deep inside.

'Saved him? Don't you realise the situation? We're far from saved, and neither is Hamid, and now we're at the mercy of the chief.'

Jen shook her head.

'Do you really believe he'll harm us?' she said, and Kam couldn't tell a lie.

'No, not harm us, but he could keep us here indefinitely.'

'Not us—me,' Jen argued. 'You can go, the guide will take

you back, you and Hamid, which will stop Akbar's self-destruction, and it will mean the testing can go on.'

'Forget the testing!' Kam all but yelled the words, remembering the sleeping child and stopping himself just in time. 'And forget about me going back and leaving you here, that is just not going to happen.'

But even as he spoke, he knew he had to do something. For a start, if Arun didn't hear from him for twenty-four hours, he would start to worry. The way the country was, they'd both known that Kam going out into the far reaches of it had been the most dangerous job, for if he was recognised by anyone against the hereditary regime, he could be captured or even killed.

And here, should someone recognise him, he'd make the perfect kidnap victim, held to ransom to finance the struggle going on between the tribes.

They had to get away.

Tonight!

'Did you write out the list of what to do for your patient?' he asked Jen.

'I left it there, but I can tell you what was on it if you want to write it in your language.'

She dug into her bag and brought out a pen and small pad, handing them to Kam then telling him what to write, taking her time as he was translating as he went.

'They must watch for signs of fever—I've left antibiotics for her to take and the chief understands she has to take them regularly until the course is finished, but if she starts to run a temperature, they should give her aspirin as well, and bathe her to keep her cool. When I come back I'll bring more antibiotics, stronger ones, just in case.'

He finished the care instructions then kept writing, the curvy script filling another page. Once done, he set it down on the ground and put a rock on it, with Jen's medical bag beside it, then indicated a pile of mats that would serve as their beds.

'Piled together they'll be softer, but I can split them so we have separate beds,' he suggested, watching Jen's face in the dim light, wondering if she'd dare to lie close to him.

And why was he suggesting it?

He wasn't sure, except he had this urgent need to keep her safe, and if she was wrapped in his arms, that would go some way towards achieving his aim.

Not that he intended sleeping for very long. He was going to get them out of here tonight—all three of them.

'I guess the pile of mats would be more comfortable,' Jen said, but so tentatively he wondered if he should forget the holding-her-in-his-arms idea. He could keep her safe if she slept against the wall of the cave and he slept between her and the door. Although, even in this tense and potentially deadly situation, his arms ached to hold her for other reasons.

'You're not happy about it?' he asked, and watched her face.

A tentative smile hovered around her lips and he was sure she was blushing beneath the golden freckles, although the dim light made it impossible to tell.

'With what we feel—the attraction—is it a good idea…?'

The hesitant phrases dropped so confusedly from her lips it was all he could do not to take her in his arms right then and there, to comfort and protect her. But he didn't want to make the situation more difficult than it already was, and his mind needed to be focussed on escape, not attraction.

'I'm being ridiculous, aren't I?' she said, turning so he could see her face in the lamplight. 'But it's been five years since David died. Five years since I've felt something even close to attraction to another man.' The halting confession faltered, then she lifted her chin and continued. 'It's not that I thought I'd never love again, although I did think that for a long time, but it's as if what we had was so special it couldn't be replicated. Now here I am, stuck in the desert with a very sexy man, feeling all kinds of things I've never felt before, and I'm confused.'

'Why?'

She smiled a real smile this time.

'I suppose because I think you're sexy, for a start. Because I noticed, and because I felt something I didn't expect to feel, and yet it's for a man who has no interest in a relationship, so it's something that has no future, and I honestly don't know that I can handle that kind of thing. With my husband, we met and fell in love and got married. I've had no practice at any other kind of relationship, but I do know when he died it nearly killed me, so I don't want to love like that again—to love and lose someone. Yet if I give in to this attraction and it leads to love, that's exactly what will happen.'

Kam stared at her.

'Is this the woman who travels all over the world, often to very unpleasant places, and exults in the challenge, the adventure, the fun? Can't you see that sexual relationships are all of those things? That they can be part of your life, and make it fuller and more exciting?'

Jen studied him for a moment.

'No, I can't see that. Oh, I know it works for some people. My best friend can handle love affairs but that's because she doesn't want any more than the fun and adventure and challenge as far as her liaisons are concerned. She's married to her career and she looks on a little fling with someone as relaxation. But me? I just know I'd make a mess of it, Kam.'

He reached out and drew her into his arms and held her close against his body.

'No kisses, then, I promise,' he said softly. 'But lie with me. That way I'll know you're safe.'

He led her to the pile of rugs and pushed her shoulders gently so she sat, then he knelt and took off her sandals, his hands warm against her skin, the little act of kindness so unexpectedly intimate Jen felt the desire she was fighting ripple through her once again.

But as she lay down on the pile of mats and Kam settled beside her, she glanced towards the sleeping child, and she wondered if they should draw him in, put him between them, not to keep herself safe from her own emotions but to keep him safe.

'Hamid?' she whispered to Kam.

'I will watch him—he'll be safe.'

'But you need to sleep yourself,' Jen protested, and she felt his arm wrap around her shoulder and draw her closer.

'When both of you are sleeping, I will doze,' he said. 'Now, go to sleep, Jenny Stapleton, before I forget I am here to protect you not make love to you.'

How could she sleep when his arm lay heavy on her shoulders and her body felt his warmth and wanted more of it?

How could she sleep when remembered delights of lovemaking were flickering not only in her body but in her mind?

How could she sleep—?

She'd think of Hamid, the child they'd saved, or would save. Kam had said so. She'd think about how they were both risking their lives to save a child for a man they hardly knew. She'd think of Kam…

Kam…

She snuggled closer…

'Jen, I want you to wake up but quietly.'

Kam held her, speaking into her ear, his hand ready to close over her mouth if she made a startled noise. He already had the child awake, sitting close beside the pile of mats, his big eyes even wider now Kam had explained what they were doing.

'Jen, can you hear me? I know you're tired, but I need you to wake up.'

She stirred and turned her head, and even in the dim light of the cave the golden hair made a glorious tangle all around it. She'd have to hide it in her scarf because the moonlight would give it a glow that could be seen for miles.

'Come on, we're leaving,' he whispered, helping her to sit up. 'Tie your hair up as best you can and put your scarf around it. I'll carry your sandals, we'll go barefoot at first. And we'll leave your bag. I've written in the note that we'll come back tomorrow, but if we leave the bag they'll know we mean it. I've also given them my radio call-sign so they can contact us if there is a problem sooner than evening.'

She seemed to understand for her hands were fighting with her hair, trying to get hanks of it, uncombed, to braid. Then she lifted her shawl and wound it around her head and across the lower part of her face, a clever woman working out that her pale skin might also gleam in the moonlight.

A clever woman, but was he leading her to her death?

Kam didn't know, but he knew he had to try to get her out of here. If he left her and by some ill-chance the young mother died then they would kill Jen as well, or hold *her* for ransom, trading her for guns to keep the killing going. That she, who only sought to do good, and who had already suffered so much, should be put in such a position…

They had to leave.

He walked to the door of the cave, checked the man who had been left to guard them was sleeping then, taking Hamid on his back, he motioned Jen to fall in behind him and led the way, guided only by his childhood memories, praying they were right and that he wasn't leading two innocent people into disaster.

They slipped like shadows through the sleeping village, tension coiling tighter with every slip on a stone or brush against a branch, noises almost silent but sounding loud in the still night air. He waited for an alarm, a cry from a sentry posted somewhere in the village, although he judged the chief was confident in this, his stronghold.

'Do you really know the way?' Jenny asked when they were far enough above the village for her whisper not to carry.

'Of course I do.' Such a confident lie, but what was the sense in both of them worrying? 'We're on a path—can't you see that?'

'On a path made by sheep and goats and herders going up to the higher slopes, I would say from the look of it.'

He turned back to look at her and saw that she was smiling. His heart tugged at its moorings in his chest. How could she smile, this woman in a foreign land, being led through the mountains by someone who might not know the way, a child they had to cherish between the two of them?

And how could he not admire her, even, given the tug, feel more than admiration?

Feel love?

'It branches off,' he said, because to tell her what he was thinking and feeling would make the thoughts and feelings real, and neither of them wanted that.

When love between them was impossible...

They walked swiftly but quietly, climbing ever higher, the little boy walking now, stoically silent although the climb through the thinning air must be taking a toll on his slight body.

'Ten miles you said?' Jen asked the question when they stopped to rest beside a spring and Kam cupped water in his hand and made them both drink. 'I don't know how long it takes to walk ten miles on flat ground, let alone climbing through mountains in the moonlight.'

Kam smiled at her.

'I doubt it takes longer in the moonlight. In fact, it might make the journey faster for we can see where we are going and the night is cool. Come on, if we rest too long you'll stiffen up.'

'Or someone following us might catch up,' Jen suggested.

'There's no one following, not yet,' Kam said, knowing he'd have heard any pursuit because he'd been listening intently for it.

They climbed higher and higher until it seemed they were right at the top of the world—seemed they could touch the stars that massed like sparkling crystals in the velvet dark sky above them—yet still another ridge would rise in front of them.

The track wound and twisted, in and out of moonlight and shadows, sometimes wide enough for them to walk abreast, sometimes in single file. It was so quiet and still it was easy to think they were the only people alive in the entire world.

Until suddenly, as they entered a patch of shadow, a figure rose up from the ground, tall, dark-robed, head swathed in a turban—threatening just to look at.

Jen gave a cry, quickly stifling it with her hand, but she knew it hadn't been quick enough. She pressed her hand to her chest where her heart thudded so hard she thought it might burst out, then Kam was speaking and the shadowy figure answered, before stepping forward and squatting down to take Hamid on his back.

'You can't let him take Hamid,' Jen protested, racing towards the man to snatch the child from him. 'Not now when we've got this far.'

Kam stopped her, his hand settling on her shoulder and bringing her momentum to a halt.

'It's our guide,' Kam said. 'He says he knew we'd try to leave and has come to help us, to show us the way and carry the child. He doesn't like it that his chief would not honour the word he gave so he will honour it himself.'

'And you believe him? If Akbar was whipped for crossing the border, imagine what the chief would do to this man for betrayal. Why should he lead us where he says? Why wouldn't he make us circle around so we'll be right back in the village once again?'

'He gave his word. I trust him,' Kam said, then added with a tinge of sarcasm, 'Although there's not a lot of trust around.'

Was he referring to her suspicions of him—her questions as to whether he was a spy?

Jen didn't know, any more than she knew the truth about Kam's presence in the camp or their guide's offer to lead them home. She sighed at all the things she didn't know and followed, trudging along in the footsteps of the guide, Kam right behind her, barely puffing, the ease with which he climbed making her even angrier.

The path levelled out and they walked between high rock

walls and along a narrow track with a steep drop to one side of it, then, barely noticeable at first, they began to drop lower, going downhill now, down and down until they rounded a corner and there, still a hundred or more feet below them, lay the refugee camp.

Their guide set Hamid back on his feet, spoke to Kam, then disappeared back in the direction from which they'd come.

'He must return to his home before dawn or the chief will be suspicious,' Kam explained to Jen, as he took over as leader on the downhill path. 'He'll meet us where the vehicle was parked at six this evening, so that way we can get back before it gets too late.'

If we get back, Jen thought, but she didn't want to go there, so she questioned instead how the man could return to the village so swiftly.

'Before dawn?' she echoed, nodding towards the east where the sky was already lightening.

'He will run, now we're not with him,' Kam explained, then he knelt and took Hamid on his back and they continued towards their temporary home.

'Four hours,' Kam announced when they finally reached the clinic tent and stopped outside while Hamid crept in to be reunited with his parents, the wailing and cries of delight telling them all was well. 'Not bad for a ten-mile hike over the mountains.'

'Tell my feet that,' Jen said, lifting one sandalled foot to inspect it for wear and tear.

'Come, there'll be hot water in the food tent—we'll get something to eat and drink.'

'A hot drink? Food? That sounds like bliss. Come on, feet, it's only a little further.'

She turned towards the tent but Kam was quicker, lifting her into his arms and striding with her towards the tent, already lit to welcome the early risers in the camp.

Despite her weight, he held her easily, carrying her as though she were a child like Hamid. And with his strong arms holding her and her body pressed against his rock-hard chest, a sense of security, so strong she tingled with it, washed through her body.

At least, she hoped it was security…

Once in the tent he sat her on a mat and spoke to the women who were preparing food and drinks. One came immediately, a basin in her hands, a towel over her arm, and knelt in front of Jenny.

Kam thanked her and sent her on her way, removing Jenny's sandals himself then lifting one pale, slim foot, washing it, drying it, massaging it gently, then examining it for cuts or blisters before setting it back on the ground, to take care of the other.

'You'll put some antiseptic on the cuts and blisters when you go back to your tent,' he told her, still looking at her feet so it wasn't until she made a little sound of pain or protest that he looked up into her face.

She was staring at him as if she'd never seen him before, the look on her face so incredulous he wondered if he'd changed from a human into a djinn.

'What?' he asked, puzzled by her expression, but all she'd do was shake her head. Although he thought a smile was on its way, quivering at the corners of her lips, it did no more than tantalise him by not fully revealing itself.

He turned his attention from lips to feet.

'Do you have some soft slippers you can wear today?'

He looked up at her again, but all suggestion of a smile had disappeared and she was now frowning at him.

Before he could question her again—this time about the frown—the woman returned, bringing a tray with hot sweet tea and small pancakes, freshly made, their spicy scent making his mouth water.

'I didn't realise how hungry I was,' Jenny said, taking one of them, folding it in quarters, then eating it with obvious enjoyment. She took a sip of tea, and sighed.

'This is good,' she said, then looked at Kam. 'All good— the foot care, the food, the tea, not to mention your rescue efforts bringing us home over the mountains. Did I thank you?'

None of which explained the frown.

'I don't want your thanks,' he said, wondering how to ask about the frown, but no words came so he ate a pancake and drank some tea, then, because she hadn't answered about soft slippers, he asked one of the serving women if there was anyone in the camp who could sew the slippers the women wore inside their homes during the winter. He had a thick shirt they could use for fabric…

He washed my feet!

Jen wasn't sure whether to laugh or cry because the gesture, as much as his gentle touch, had totally destroyed any barriers she had tried to build between this man and her heart. With that one simple act of kindness she had awoken once again to love.

This man could well have saved her life tonight, leading her over the mountains, and she hadn't fallen in love with him then.

But as he'd washed her feet…

He couldn't know, of course, and neither could she reveal it. But how to hide a feeling that was bubbling like a spring of delight, and excitement, and happiness inside her?

With practicality, of course…

And distance…

And pretence…

'Well, we have Hamid back with his parents, and for that reason alone the walk was worth it,' she said, taking another pancake from the stack, folding it carefully and this time dipping it in flavoured yoghurt before biting into it. 'But might we have angered the chief to the extent that he will be more careful in his guarding of us tonight?'

'You do not have to go back,' Kam told her, his voice stern. 'I can go. I can treat the woman.'

Jen shook her head.

'I gave my word. We expect them to keep their side of the bargain, so how could I not go? Besides, that young woman, she's barely more than a girl, Kam, she might be upset or frightened, and a strange man around would make that worse. In fact, you don't need to come at all now we know the chief has such good English. He can translate.'

'Translate things about post-partum bleeding to another woman in his tribe? I don't think so. And that *is* the type of thing you might have to discuss.'

Jen shook her head.

'The women there are capable and experienced. One of them at least is a competent midwife, I'm sure of that. She will have explained things to the young mother and she'll watch to see the baby feeds. It's just the risk of infection in the wound or internally that bothers me. I need to go to check for that, but you needn't come. In fact, I'm probably safer on my own, because if two go they can keep one of us as ransom for the other to return, as they intended doing with Hamid.'

Kam heard the words, even heard sense in some of them,

but if Jenny thought he'd let her go over that border alone, she was mistaken.

That was thought number one.

Thought number two was more a question—what lay behind this sudden rush of common-sense words from a thoroughly exhausted woman? Why was she discussing this at all when she should be finishing her breakfast then having a sleep before beginning, belatedly, her day's work?

He sensed something beneath the words, some hidden reason for them, but maybe that was because so much about him was also hidden. She'd talked of her suspicions of him, and he'd parried them, but now he wished with all his heart that he hadn't had to lie to her—or maybe not lie, but at the least conceal the truth. Especially now they'd talked so much of trust.

'OK, that's breakfast done,' she said, looking up at him and smiling, but it was an open friendly smile, not the hidden one he'd hoped to see earlier, peeping out almost shyly. 'I'm going to follow my cup of tea with a couple of belts of coffee and that way I'll get through to afternoon. I'll feel better tonight if I have a nap this afternoon.'

Kam didn't protest, although when she'd finished a small cup of coffee and bent over to put her sandals back on he stopped her.

'Wait.'

He looked towards the serving woman who told him her friend had gone to get the slippers.

'Wait for what? What's going on?' Jen asked, and Kam smiled at her, reminding her of the need for distance and pretence.

'You didn't answer me about soft slippers,' he said. 'Someone is making some for you.'

'Someone is making me slippers? Making slippers while I ate breakfast? That's impossible!'

But the other woman had returned and she now came towards Jen, shyly offering a pair of the prettiest slippers Jen had ever seen. A deep maroon, a colour she knew came from the dye of a local desert plant, and decorated with embroidered flowers.

Kam took them from the woman, exchanging words, then he slipped them on Jen's feet.

'They feel as smooth as velvet,' she whispered, wriggling her toes to luxuriate in the softness.

'They're made from felted camel hair,' Kam explained. 'I think young girls learn to make slippers almost as soon as they learn to walk, and there always seems to be someone making them in every camp.'

'They're beautiful,' Jen said, pointing her toes in front of her the better to admire them. 'Will you thank her for me, and thank whoever gave them to her? Should I offer to pay—to buy them?'

Kam smiled again, the smile slipping over the broken barriers around her heart and touching it with happiness.

'You'd insult them if you offered to pay and, of course, I thanked them. And now, Dr Stapleton, let's get you home— you can't walk across the sand with those pretty feet.'

He bent and lifted her again and although she wanted to protest—should protest, she could have worn her sandals across the sand between the tents—she didn't, content to steal a few minutes in his arms, impersonal though they may be.

He had to stop carrying her, Kam realised as he held her against his chest and felt his heart beating with desire. Oh, that he could be carrying her into his own tent, a beautiful woman he'd claimed as his!

Of course, he didn't have a tent, and this particular beautiful woman certainly wasn't his.

She couldn't be his, she of the wanderlust and he in need of a stay-at-home wife…

He set her down inside the big tent, and was pleased to see Lia and Akbar sitting with Hamid between them, the little boy prattling on about his adventures, the parents happy just to have him there.

When Akbar saw Kam he did nothing more than nod, but the nod said a thousand things that words could never have said. Kam nodded back, understanding between the two of them, though Lia had to put her thanks and happiness into words, a stream of them, until Akbar held up his hand for silence then announced he was moving back to his own tent now.

'He's leaving?' Jenny asked, as Lia helped her husband stand and a conversation she couldn't follow went on between the men.

'They want to be in their own tent,' Kam explained, and Jenny nodded.

'I can understand that. They want to be a family. You will tell him to call in each day so we can check his wounds.'

Kam smiled at the anxiety in her voice.

'I will,' he promised, not telling her he'd already given Akbar this advice, only he'd suggested every second day. Jenny was more anxious than he was, worrying that any adverse consequences in the camp might jeopardise her TB programme.

Jenny headed for her corner of the tent, knowing her hair must be like a bird's nest beneath the shawl still wrapped loosely around it, knowing her body needed a break from Kam's proximity while her heart needed to recover from his gift of slippers, for she knew he must have asked for them and probably would pay for them.

Wasn't there a bumper sticker back in the real world about senseless acts of kindness? That's all these were, she told herself. Washing her feet, finding slippers for them—it meant nothing more than kindness. It was her folly that they turned her heart to mush...

She dragged the brush through her tangled hair, letting it pull at the knots, thinking pain might help restore some common sense. It didn't work, her heart beating faster as she heard Kam talking to Marij or Aisha as they began the morning testing.

At least she'd got the knots out with her efforts, so now she could plait it, then a quick wash, a change of clothes and she'd be ready to start the day.

A deep sigh started way down near the pretty slippers and escaped in a rush of air. Had it only been twelve hours ago she'd stood here, washing, and wishing she could change into something pretty, worrying that her meeting with Kam on the rock would look too much like a date if she did?

Some date!

She washed, dressed then joined the two nurses, noticing as she passed that Kam had set up a kind of clinic near the doorway of the tent and was tending what looked like a deep cut on one of the small boys who hung around her most of the time.

Detouring towards them, she realised the rest of the boys were hanging back.

'What happened?' she asked Kam, as she drew closer and saw the jagged cut that slashed across the child's forearm.

Kam turned to her and smiled then motioned the other boys closer.

'Did you ever swear allegiance to a gang? Become a blood brother, or in your case a blood sister? Your boys have formed a—I suppose club is a better word than gang, and had to mingle blood to take their oath. Problem was, the only knife they had was a kitchen one and it was blunt, so they used the top of a tin can and Ahmed here went a little deep.'

Jen wasn't sure if smiling was the right response, but she was fond of the boys and they were now eyeing her warily, so she did smile, then said to Kam, 'It's not dangerous, this club, is it? I wouldn't like them to be swearing blood oaths to maim or kill or steal or do anything bad. Without school to attend, they could get up to all kinds of mischief.'

Kam finished winding a bandage around the now cleaned wound and sent the boys off with a warning to be careful, and it was only as they turned to go that she realised one of them was carrying Rosana on his back.

'You want to know what their blood oath was?' Kam asked, smiling so broadly Jen knew it wasn't bad, although the way the smile made her feel fitted the description only too well.

She nodded, and his smile became a chuckle.

'They've adopted Rosana,' he said. 'The oath was to protect her at all times, both now and all through her life. That little girl has got herself a family, even if they are all nine or ten. They'll grow up and so will she, and pity help any young man who might fancy her later on. He'll have to run the gauntlet of those boys, and really prove himself worthy— What's wrong?'

Jen shook her head, aware tears were seeping from her eyes and slipping down her cheeks but unable to stop them.

'They are so good—there is so much goodness,' she finally managed, swiping at the tears that still escaped her brimming eyes. 'Here in a place where people have so little, and where hope is close to dying, those little boys have pledged to help that child…'

Kam could not help himself. He pulled Jenny into his arms, steered her into the relative privacy of the space she called her bedroom and held her close, rocking her in his arms until he felt the tension ease out of her.

He tilted her chin and looked down at her face, using his handkerchief to wipe the dampness from her cheeks.

'How can you do this work when you feel the pain of others so strongly?' he asked, his voice gentle but bemused.

'How can I not do this work?' she replied, offering him a strained smile. 'When I see the problems other people have, how can I not do something, however small, to help?'

She kissed him lightly on the lips, readjusted her scarf and slipped away from him.

CHAPTER EIGHT

JENNY worked hard through the morning, uninterrupted by the usual requests for medical help as Kam was seeing those who felt sick or were injured in some way. She wanted the slides done and the medications put out by early afternoon, so she could have a sleep before returning to the rebel camp.

The thought brought a slightly grim smile to her lips. One night of adventure and she was considering this return to the other side of the border as calmly as she'd catch a train to the city back home in Brisbane.

Better than considering other consequences, she decided, although a slight tremor of apprehension in her abdomen suggested she didn't feel quite as blasé as she'd like to be. The chief *could* keep them there. Or he might be so angered by them leaving the previous night, he would kill them.

Somehow, Jenny thought not. Regardless of the cause of the fighting, the chief was intelligent enough to know they weren't part of it, and that making them part of it could bring retribution down not only on his head but on the heads of his people.

'No more patients, so I'll help with the slides.'

Kam settled himself beside her, causing consternation in her lungs and happy little leaps of delight in her heart.

She concentrated on the consternation.

'You didn't come to help me out but to check the needs of the place and start a medical clinic. Have you contacted your brother? Asked him about a tent for it? Mentioned a well?'

Kam took a group of red-marked slides and slid the first onto the plate of the microscope.

'I've spoken to my brother,' he said, knowing it wasn't the reply Jenny wanted but unwilling to tell her a lie and unable to tell her he'd done no more than say he was alive and his research was going more slowly than he'd expected.

Not exactly a lie but there was no way he could leave until Jenny's trips across the border had ceased.

Unless, of course, he could provide her with a suitable escort, but who?

And as far as the well and other things were concerned, he was aware that radio messages could be monitored easily and hadn't wanted to alert the rebels over the border to the fact that he might be a person of power. If he'd spoken of the camp's needs, Arun would immediately have got things moving, and the chief in the captured village might begin to wonder. And mention of their adventure of the previous evening would undoubtedly bring Arun rushing to the mountains, a complication Kam didn't want to think about.

Not least because his brother had a way with women, an ease about him that drew women in, so a mild flirtation led to something more very quickly…

Suffice it to say he didn't want his playboy brother anywhere in Jenny's vicinity. Not for selfish reasons, he told himself, but because he'd sensed a vulnerability in her from their first meeting, and now to know she'd lost her husband and unborn child…

'Have you gone to sleep there, or is there something on the slide I should know about?'

Jenny's question jerked him back to the present.

'No, this one's good. I put it where?'

She showed him and continued writing notes for medication, but working so close to her was distracting, while thinking of her crossing the border again tonight—

Gut-knotting—there was no other word for it.

'I think I'll check the boys,' he said, and stood up, knowing he couldn't stay beside her without trying to persuade her not to go. Yet he knew, short of tying her to a tent peg, there was no way to stop her.

Stubborn woman!

Beautiful woman…

'Thanks for all your help,' she said, as he eased away.

'Sarcastic woman!' he said aloud, then hurried from the tent.

Jen was glad he'd gone. Having him so close had been distracting, to say the least.

He'd washed her feet!

She *had* to stop that thought recurring in her mind. Surely if she wanted to think of his kindness she should be thinking of the way he'd sheltered her as she'd slept the previous night, his arm around her shoulders, the air between them zinging with the attraction they'd both now admitted, but him understanding her halting explanation of inexperience and honouring her wish to not take the attraction further.

'You go,' Marij said to her an hour later, when the daily medications had been given out and the testing finished. 'Aisha and I will do the rest. We can put the slides together and we know the medication plan as well as you do. You go and sleep.'

Aisha looked as worried as she sounded.

'I'm not that tired,' Jen told her. 'I think doctors get enough early training of sleepless nights to be able to handle them with ease.'

'I do not worry over your lack of sleep,' the nurse replied. 'I worry about you going back to that place again tonight. It is dangerous. It is stupid that you go. And that man who goes with you has not the sense of a rabbit that he lets you go. Look at what they did to Akbar.'

'They thought he was going to steal from them—he did not tell them about Hamid in case they hurt the boy. I suppose he was lucky he was only flogged, not dealt some far worse punishment.'

Aisha shuddered.

'You are right, although I think even over there they are no longer barbarians who would cut off the hand of a thief.'

Jen joined in the shuddering, but was quick to reassure Aisha that she'd be all right.

'They want me healthy and with both my hands,' Jen joked, 'so I can look after the new mother. Just pray there are no complications.'

'I will pray for you,' Aisha said, and Jen knew she would. 'Now, go and sleep.'

Jen obeyed the order this time, suddenly so tired it was the only thing to do. Who knew what mistakes she might have made if she'd stayed there?

She woke at five, her internal alarm in perfect working order, and found her water containers full and her wash basin already filled with water for her wash.

The little boys or Kam?

Deciding it didn't matter but thankful that she didn't have to fetch it herself, she stripped off, found a towel to stand on, then soaped herself all over. After three years with Aid for All, she was an expert at bird-baths, as she called her splash, soap and rinse routine, and now rinsed off all the soap and dried herself, pleased to know the rose scent of the soap lingered on her skin.

Now, what to wear? The long tunics she put over her jeans were fairly tight fitting, and the one she'd been wearing had hampered her as she'd climbed the mountain the previous night, but jeans on their own weren't the answer for a visit to the rebel camp. She opened her suitcase and dug to the bottom, pulling out a long full skirt she'd bought at a market in Colombia. It was black but a wide band around the bottom of it was decorated with beads and braid, making it a little festive.

A long-sleeved blouse, also black, would complete her outfit and with a scarf around her hair, she'd almost pass as a local. Well, not quite almost…

She dressed then brushed her hair, a refrain—should get it cut—accompanying each stroke. Not that she would, for her hair having grown it since the accident, was the symbol of her new life…

Kam was waiting outside, and for a moment she thought she saw admiration in his eyes, but he made no comment on her clothing, simply nodding to her then leading her swiftly through the camp towards the place where they were to meet their guide.

'I've some bread and water in my backpack,' he told her, 'but I think with us coming at this hour, they will offer us food.'

An idle conversation but there was something bothering him, so when he paused and looked around the camp and then up at the sky, she asked, 'What's wrong? Something other than us going back across the border? What else is worrying you?'

'There's a storm coming,' he said, then continued on his way, leaving Jen to follow.

Which she did, although she, too, looked up at the sky as she walked. No sign of clouds but, then, there was no sign of the sky either. A hazy greyness, so pale it was almost white, was all she could see.

'There are no clouds,' she pointed out, as she caught up with him again.

'But what do you see?' he asked.

'Haze? We get heat haze in the summer—is this the same?'

He shook his head.

'This haze is caused by dust—there's a sandstorm brewing.'

'I've heard of them, but does that matter? We'll be in a vehicle, we'll still be able to get there and back, won't we?'

This time he smiled as he shook his head.

'Windscreen wipers don't clear dust from the windscreen, and sand in a storm can strip a car of paint—that's how fierce these storms can be.'

Jen looked around again but the haze didn't seem any worse than it had minutes earlier. She was thinking of asking what was the worst that could happen if the storm did come when they rounded the last corner of the camp and saw the vehicle ahead of them.

'Oh, Kam, it's our same guide,' she said, grabbing her companion's arm to share her delight. 'I've been so worried he might be in trouble and been beaten or had his hands cut off or something.'

'Hands cut off?' Kam echoed, stopping to turn back and look at her.

'Something Aisha said,' Jen explained, aware her smile was growing broader by the second. 'Please, tell him how glad we are to see him and ask if he and his family are all well, so we know there've been no repercussions.'

Kam spoke to the man who bowed and smiled at Jenny then the conversation must have shifted to the possibly approaching storm for both men were looking upwards and pointing to the sky.

She climbed into the back seat of the vehicle while the men spoke, and settled the small bag she'd brought with her on her lap. Women all around the camp had heard about the baby's birth and had brought small presents for it, including a tiny pair of embroidered slippers.

She'd asked Marij why people would send gifts to the baby of tribesmen who had forced the refugees from their home, and Marij had smiled.

'The baby is a new life, innocent,' she said. 'The baby is not to blame for what has happened.'

And even thinking about the conversation made Jen's eyes water and her nose go snuffly. What was wrong with her that she was becoming sentimental over such small incidents?

Was it the baby?

She pressed her hand against her own belly, remembering it swollen and hard as a melon, eight months pregnant when the accident had taken not only David but their unborn son.

Maudlin—that's how she was getting, and she had to get over it.

Fast!

Kam and the driver had climbed into the front seats and to distract her mind from maudlin she tapped Kam on the shoulder.

'Was he in trouble with the chief?' she asked.

Kam shook his head.

'The chief thinks we made our way over the mountains on our own, possibly with Hamid guiding us.'

The chief didn't exactly think that, Kam knew, but didn't say so. The chief, according to their guide, was very suspicious and because he would know a foreign woman wouldn't find her way across the mountains, his suspicions undoubtedly rested on Kam.

However, suspicions, imagined or otherwise, were the least of everyone's problems right now. Their guide agreed that a sandstorm was on the way, and even as they drove Kam could feel the wind picking up, blowing sand against the car, dust settling on the windscreen.

By the time they reached the women's tent in the village, the wind was whistling and the sand keening as it swept across the desert's surface. Soon it would scream, Kam knew. Soon anyone outside would be lost and disoriented, unable to move until the storm subsided.

Which could take days...

They stopped outside the women's tent and Jenny got out. She hurried in, the sand and wind blustering about her, plucking at her skirt as though unseen hands were grabbing it.

'You have come.'

The chief was with his wife, Jenny's medical bag beside him, the women of the tent far back against the walls, which were all wound down and no doubt pegged because, although they ballooned in and out, they held fast.

'I said I'd come and I will come again. I have kept my word so I expect you to keep yours, and let me go when I have done my job. There may be no need for me to see her every day, but until her wound is healed I will keep coming.'

The chief nodded but, understanding more now about oaths and agreements, Jen knew this meant little. Until he shook hands there'd be no agreement he had to honour, and he probably wouldn't shake hands with a woman anyway. Jen would have to leave those negotiations to Kam.

But she did have something in the way of peace offerings. She knelt beside the woman who held her sleeping baby in her arms and began to undo the string on the small bag she'd carried.

'No!' the chief ordered, snatching the bag from her hands.

'Hey, it's OK. You should know I wouldn't harm your wife or your baby—or anyone's wife or baby, for that matter. The women from the camp have sent gifts for the baby. I was going to show them to your wife.'

The chief, who'd by now had time to examine the contents of Jenny's bag, had the grace to look embarrassed.

'They are kind and the gifts are thoughtful,' he admitted, then spoke to his wife, spreading out the gifts in front of her.

She touched each in turn, smiling and looking from them to the baby, then packed them back into the bag and set it beside her.

'How is your wife feeling?' Jen asked, trying to pretend everything was all right, although the chief's sudden, angry reaction earlier had frightened her.

'She is in pain but the tablets help, also the ice. This will take some time?'

'Like all wounds,' Jenny explained, 'it will take time to heal, both inside and outside.'

The man nodded then repeated Jenny's words to his wife.

'May I examine her?' Jen said. 'I need to check the wound to see there's no infection and to take her blood pressure, temperature and pulse to make sure everything is mending as it should.'

The man translated for his wife, then called a woman forward. It was the woman Jen had assumed was the midwife.

'I need to talk to her about women's medical matters,' Jen told the chief. 'Perhaps you would prefer it if my colleague translated these.'

The man looked from Jenny to his wife, then back to Jenny.

'He will remain outside the tent and I will wait with him. I could do the translation, you understand, but it would not be right for me to speak to a woman of my tribe of such matters.'

He spoke again to his wife, kissed her forehead then left the tent, leaving his little bride looking insecure and nervous again.

'Are you there, Kam?' Jen asked, and when he answered, she began, explaining first that she was going to examine the woman, beginning with the regular observations.

'Will you tell her this is normal and there's no need to be afraid? She's nervous and unsettled without her husband here, and I don't want to upset her more.'

Kam spoke, then the chief chimed in, and Jen hoped he was repeating the reassurances.

Smiling encouragingly at her patient, Jenny began the tests, pleased to see no elevated temperature, no raised pulse or irregularities in her blood pressure.

'All good,' she reported to Kam, then, with the help of the other woman, she unwrapped her patient and examined first her breasts for signs of soreness or milk fever.

'Will you ask the midwife if the baby is feeding from the breast and if the woman's milk has come in yet? It may be a bit early, but it's best to know so we can watch for any trouble.'

Kam and Jenny's helper conversed for quite a time, then Kam reported all was well and that they could be confident the midwife knew her job, having helped more than two hundred babies into the world and watched over the mothers and their infants for forty days and nights after the birth.

'It is a time the women spend with other women,' Kam explained. 'The chief being with his wife is an exception and he is only there to reassure her, leaving her to the women most of the time.'

'That's good,' Jen said, smiling at the new mother, who now looked slightly more confident.

Carefully, Jen undid the dressings on the wound, asking for more light so she could examine it more closely, seeking any signs of redness or weeping from infection. It looked clean and she asked Kam to check the woman was taking her antibiotics as well as painkillers.

'Of course she is,' the chief replied. 'I see to it she does. I do not want her sick.'

'The wound looks good,' Jen reported, and saw the midwife's smile as Kam repeated it. Then the woman spoke, words tripping off her tongue, while Jen applied new antiseptic to the wound and dressed it with clean dressings.

'She's asking if she can learn to do the operation. She said it looked easy and many women in the tribe have died because a doctor couldn't come and do it when a baby becomes stuck.'

Jen squatted back on her heels, straining to hear Kam's voice as the wind was now whipping against the tent walls and echoing around the camp with an eerie, wailing sound.

'I know a number of midwives back at home whom I would be happy to have do it, but there's the anaesthetic as well. Are there many tribal people in these parts on both sides of the border? Would it be possible to set up a course for the midwives to learn enough to do a Caesarean?'

'Boy, are you getting into delicate ground!' Kam said.

'You, a doctor, suggesting a nurse might be able to do doctor stuff as well as any doctor.'

'Or better,' Jenny told him. 'There's no reason why not. After all, we train paramedics to do emergency trauma work, so why not train midwives to do Caesars?'

'Why not indeed?' Kam said, and Jenny smiled as she heard him translating their conversation to the midwife. At least, that's what she thought he was doing.

Finished with her examination of the mother, she asked if she could look at the baby. Once the request was translated, the young mother displayed him proudly, unwrapping his swaddling garments so Jen could see him.

'He's beautiful,' she said, awed as ever by the miniature perfection of new life, saddened as ever by her own loss.

The girl-woman glowed with pride and happiness and held the infant to her breast where he nuzzled for a moment then began to feed.

Jen wanted to ask about the customs here, about feeding times and habits, but she knew the chief might find the conversation awkward if it was carried on in front of him so she assured him that all was well and packed her bag, ready to leave.

Kam met her outside the doorway of the tent, a worried frown warning her there was something very wrong.

'What is it?' she asked.

'Can't you see?'

She was still within the porch-like area at the entrance to the tent, outside the inner wall but still sheltered, but now she did look outside at the thick dust cloud swirling beyond the outer wall.

'The storm?'

'The storm!' Kam confirmed. 'We can't go back tonight.'

He didn't add that storms like this could last for days, because he didn't want Jen worrying. 'The chief has suggested we eat dinner with him then sleep again in the cave dwelling. He has had his men put some provisions in there and rugs across the entrance. They will keep out some of the dust, but in a storm like this it gets everywhere. You breathe it and eat it and sleep with it in your bed, no matter how hard you try to keep it out.'

He watched Jenny's face as she took this in, then drew her closer to adjust her scarf around her head so it also covered her face.

'Come,' he said, taking her hand in his. 'We're going to run. Stay close behind me.'

They ran, Kam regretting he hadn't taken the scarf the chief had offered him. Wound around his face, it would have prevented the stinging sand from burning his skin, but he feared that if he wore it he might be more recognisable than he was in a baseball cap.

A foolish fear, perhaps, but one he wasn't going to put to the test.

Once at the chief's meeting tent, he slipped off his shoes and helped Jenny off with her sandals, before leading her inside. Their guide was there and other men, already seated on rugs on the ground, helping themselves to food from a huge pot in the middle of the rug.

'You will eat,' the chief told them, and Kam served a dish of stew for Jenny, gave it to her with some bread, then helped himself as well. He was uneasy, the storm an unexpected complication. How long might they have to remain in this place?

Would Arun, hearing of the storm, accept that radio transmissions would be difficult and not come riding to his rescue?

Kam ate, but barely tasted his meal, and when he saw that

Jenny had finished hers, he excused himself to the chief and took Jen's arm to help her to her feet.

'You didn't want to stay and chat?' she teased, when they were putting their sandals back on in the entry-way and gathering strength to once again venture out into the swirling, dancing, deadly sand.

'I wanted to get you safely in the cave,' he told her, then his body leapt as the implications of the statement brought excitement to it.

Too bad! His body was used enough to celibacy to get over its excitement, though being stuck in a cave with Jenny Stapleton while a sandstorm whirled outside, possibly for days, would sorely tempt it.

Once again he adjusted Jenny's scarf, wishing he'd asked one of the women to find a shawl for her so he could better protect the tender skin on her face from the onslaught of the sand.

But something was better than nothing and when he was convinced he'd covered as much of her face as he safely could, he took her hand, told her to stay behind him and ventured out.

Jenny realised as soon as they stepped out of the lee of the tent that the storm had become much worse. She put a hand to her face to shield her eyes and followed close behind Kam.

The air was filled with red, gritty dust, whirling and eddying angrily all around them. She saw vague shapes she guessed were tents or houses and prayed Kam knew where they were going.

The ducked along alleyways, staying close to walls in the lee of the wind, but already sand drifts were building up against fences and walls in the way she imagined snow would build up against the walls of houses during a snowstorm.

'We're here,' Kam said, and held a rug a little to one side so she could duck inside the cave.

It was dark, but someone had left a lit lamp on a table at the back, beyond the mats where they'd slept for a short time the previous night.

Jen walked towards the light, feeling sand inside all her clothes, wishing she could take them off and shake them but shy in front of Kam.

'Oh!' she said, when she approached the table. There, set out for them, or maybe just for her, was a hairbrush, soap and a jar of what looked like face cream and smelt of roses, a clean robe she could wear to bed, and a selection of shawls and scarves.

At the other end of the table was a small spirit stove, a kettle, cups, flat bread wrapped in cloth and some canned goods, but most surprising of all were the teabags, a whole packet of them.

'There's water in those drums in the corner, a basin to wash in, a privy behind the curtain, and we're all set up to play house,' Kam said, coming to stand behind her and examine the supplies for himself.

'Play house,' Jen echoed, and turned towards him, unwinding her scarf from her face as she did so. 'Did you play house as a child?'

He half smiled and rubbed his hand across his chin, and she saw where wind and sand had burnt his skin.

'I don't remember being a child.'

It was such a bleak statement Jen gasped then turned to take him in her arms, to hold him to her body as if that might in some way make amends.

They were too close!

Kam's lips found hers, sand and grit forgotten as they gave

in to the attraction that had simmered between them since they'd first met.

Jen remembered her brave words of the night before, about not being able to handle an affair, but they'd been spoken before Kam had washed her feet.

Now she knew that kisses between them were never going to be enough!

Not only knew but was longing for whatever followed, with a desire so strong it was like a pain, both in her chest, and abdomen, and right down to the apex of her thighs, a pain that throbbed in time to the beating of her heart, a pain that could only be alleviated in one way…

CHAPTER NINE

KAM broke the embrace.

'We'll not rush into this,' he said, tilting her face so he could look into her eyes. 'You're sure?'

Jen nodded because a bald yes might have sounded too clinical somehow, and this, as far as she was concerned, was about love. Not that Kam would ever know it, but if her voice had trembled when she said yes he might wonder.

'So let's get the sand out of our clothes and off our bodies. Are you shy of me, Jenny? If so, I'll pour a basin of water for you and set it in the corner of the cave so you can wash in privacy, or I could help you undress and shake the sand from your clothes, and wash your back…'

He was giving her a choice. It was too much. Jen shook her head then nodded, and saw Kam smile.

'Let's start with the scarf, shall we?' he said gently, and he unwound the scarf he'd wrapped around her head. Then he slipped the band from the bottom of her plait and set it on the table, picking up the brush as he unwound her hair.

'If you only knew how often I've dreamt of doing this,' he whispered, beginning to brush her hair with long, firm strokes. 'It has tempted and tantalised me, that plait.'

Jen tingled from his ministrations but knew she had to get her emotions in some degree of order.

'It can't have been too often,' she reminded him. 'We've only known each other a couple of days.'

He smiled and kept on brushing.

'I daydream as well,' he said.

Eventually Kam was satisfied he'd rid her hair of most of the sand it had collected and he let her gather it and knot it on her head, then, his fingers shaking slightly, he undid the first button on her shirt, his eyes on her face to read her reaction, determined not to rush her if she showed the slightest hint of apprehension.

Her eyes met his and held them, so he continued to undo buttons, although he could feel her body trembling beneath the light cotton of her shirt, a trembling that increased as his fingers brushed against the swell of her breast. His own body was behaving badly, but he ignored it and kept going, eventually peeling the shirt off and taking it towards the door to give it a hard shake, then setting it on a ledge that ran along the side of the cave that had been dug out over centuries of summer visits from the tribes.

He turned back to find Jenny had taken off her skirt, without attempting to cover her body, although he guessed she must be longing to. She handed it to him to shake and set beside the shirt on the ledge.

Her bra and tiny bikini panties were both black, sensibly so considering the difficulties with laundry in a desert, yet they made her pale skin look even paler, and the sight of her, the swell of hips, the indentation of her slim waist, then her body swelling out again in full, heavy breasts, started a hunger so strong he had to hold himself back from taking her into his arms and tossing her on the pile of rugs that made up their bed.

'You are beautiful,' he managed, although the tightness in his throat strangled the words as they came out. 'Beautiful!'

She moved, taking the basin to the corner, filling it with water and, with her back to him, removing the rest of her clothes and soaping her scarf, using it to wash her body.

And even in the dim light Kam could see the fine tracings of the scars across her back, no doubt from the accident in which her husband had died.

So she'd suffered a double blow, and his heart ached for her, but heartache didn't stop the hunger...

He stripped off his jeans and shirt and picked up a towel and the jar of rose-scented cream. He came towards her slowly, as he would to a skittish horse unused to man's handling.

'Let me dry you,' he murmured, and although Jen started at his voice, when he touched her with the towel, she stood still. But rubbing cream into that pale skin, feeling her flesh beneath it and the curves and indentations of her body proved his undoing.

'If I keep this up, I'll shame myself,' he said, nodding towards his very obvious erection. 'You finish with the cream while I have a wash.'

Jen took the jar from his hands and moved across to the pile of rugs. The light was dim enough for her not to feel embarrassment, or was it because of the way she felt about Kam that such a negative emotion had no place in her mind?

She didn't know and neither did she waste thought on it for very long, contenting herself instead with rubbing the smooth, scented cream into the skin on her face and neck, enjoying the simple pleasure of pampering herself.

As for Kam...

She watched him as he washed, saw the strong shoulders

she knew he had because he'd carried her so easily, and the way his back tapered to a slim waist and hips, before swelling to a very attractive backside and strong, long legs.

Was it the unreality of the storm and the cave and the rebel camp that was making what lay ahead possible for her?

Or was it love?

She rather hoped it wasn't love pushing her into Kam's arms tonight. The love she felt for him should be separate to this. It would be far better for her peace of mind if she'd finally matured enough to take some pleasure from a chance meeting with a man to whom she felt attraction; if she'd matured enough to enjoy an affair and then forget it—or maybe not forget it but tuck the memory away somewhere safe—and move on with her life.

That way the love she felt for him could stay hidden in her heart, rather than leaking out and embarrassing both of them.

He turned towards her and she realised it was all academic anyway. She was about to make love—OK, have sex—with the most gorgeous man she'd ever seen, and her body was so excited it was a wonder he couldn't see her shaking from the other side of the cave.

But when he reached the pile of mats on which she sat, he lay down and propped himself on one elbow, frowning at her.

'What's wrong?' she said, reaching out her hand to take his and pull him down beside her.

He resisted her tug and continued frowning.

'I have no protection,' he muttered, as if both embarrassed and angered by this circumstance that had caught him in a cave in the desert in the middle of a sandstorm without a condom in his jeans pocket.

Jen squeezed his fingers, and tugged again.

'It's OK, I'm protected,' she told him, not adding what kind of protection—that of her inability to carry a child. The sadness of it hit her like it usually did, but not as strongly so she could let it pass. While it wasn't one hundred per cent certain, her doctors believed the internal injuries she'd suffered in the accident meant she would never conceive again.

'You are beautiful,' Kam repeated, finally sitting beside her and taking her into his arms, kissing her as he'd kissed her earlier, gently at first then with increasing passion until they were both shaking with the need to find the ultimate release.

Yet they held back, exploring with their hands, Jen rediscovering the delight of a hard male body, the contours of thick slabs of muscle, the smoothness of male skin. Kam's fingers traced her scars and he hissed beneath his breath, but the touch was so gentle it excited her more than it embarrassed her.

His hands roamed her body, touching it in secret places, setting it on fire, until she took the initiative and guided him inside her and they joined in a rhythm old as time itself and together found release, his gasp echoing her own cry of satisfaction as her body melted into a million quivering nerve cells before slowly reforming into human shape.

Sated, they lay together, silent by unspoken agreement, and finally Jen turned sleepily in Kam's arms and snuggled up against his body, letting sleep come, although the wailing of the wind outside and the splatter of sand against the mats was loud enough to wake the dead.

There was no night or day in the time that followed, just the crying of the wind, rising to shrieks and falling to moans, and the movement of the mats that formed their doorway, and desire, heating Jen's body and hammering in her heart. Was it the same for Kam?

She could only guess it was, for the simplest, slightest touch would have them back on the pile of mats that formed their bed, their bodies more familiar to each other now so pleasure came more easily, although held back at times so the ending would be all the sweeter.

'I can't believe this is happening,' she said, some time in what she thought might be their second night in the cave. 'All we do is make love and boil water for cups of tea.'

She was making a cup of tea as she spoke, naked as the day she'd been born and feeling no shame. It *had* to be because it was like a time out of life, a diversion from reality that would have no meaning in the future. What happened here in the cave would remain a secret held inside her, a memory to cherish and inspect from time to time, but never to regret.

'There's not much else to do in a sandstorm,' Kam told her, 'although I do need more sustenance than tea and bread. I think I'll open the cans and you can make us a nice stew from whatever's inside them.'

'Hey, I made the tea, you make the stew.'

He stared at her and Jen knew something had shifted between them.

'You can't make stew?' she said, hoping a light-hearted tease might shift things back again.

'I've never thought to do it,' he said, and somehow the distance grew even greater.

We've never talked about ourselves, Jen realised, the realisation bringing an icy shock. Apart from her mentioning David's death, they'd had no personal conversation. He could be married with five kids! What had she done? How could she have been so…uncaring?

Was this the way affairs worked?

She didn't know but wished she had her friend Melissa here—well, not right here but at the other end of a telephone—so she could ask.

But Melissa wasn't here and all the implications of not talking about personal things had struck her with a force that made her hands shake.

'We know nothing about each other,' she said, her voice strained as what ifs hammered in her head. 'What have I done? Is it because your wife cooks for you that you can't make a stew? Are you married, Kam? Have I been the cause of you being unfaithful to your wife? Or to someone who is important in your life? Why didn't I ask? How stupid could I be?'

He came towards her, his hands reaching out towards her, but she stepped back so he couldn't touch her, knowing his touch could make her forget her concerns—forget everything—and right now she needed answers, not oblivion.

She pulled on the gown that had been left for her to sleep in and, seeing the gesture, Kam wound the sarong he'd told her was called a *wezaar* around his waist.

The gestures—the covering of their bodies—said far more than words and emphasised the rift between them.

'I am not married and there's no one else in my life at the moment.' She could see his eyes, see the greenness, although the cave was dimly lit, and she read truth, but also something else in them.

Something else he wasn't long in revealing.

'Do you think so little of me you think I'd cheat on my wife? Or betray a special woman?'

Jen held out her hands.

'I don't know what to think, Kam,' she said helplessly.

'I've never been in this situation before, and things happened so quickly.'

This was the truth but not the whole truth. Inside Jen a tiny bud of hope had sprouted and was now swelling irrationally. He's not married, there's no one else, he washed my feet—could he not love me?

Couldn't love grow between us?

Stupid hope, she said mentally, determined to squelch it before it got too strong. Remember this is a time out of reality, a window into another world, open for a short space and soon to close again.

This isn't love.

Well, not on his side…

Kam had walked back to sit down on the mats, and all Jen wanted was for things to be right between them again.

But how to get from here to there?

With practicality, of course. And pretence. She would pretend she hadn't felt the shift, and that the marriage conversation hadn't happened. Go back to stew!

'Did you live at home when you were studying, that you never learnt to fend for yourself, shopping and cooking and such?'

'I studied first in London and then here. My family had a house in both cities and staff, of course, so, no, cooking for myself wasn't something I ever learnt.'

Staff, of course? Who had 'staff, of course' in this day and age?

Very, very, very wealthy people, that's who!

She stared at him as the little bud folded back on itself. Very rich people married other very rich people, not nobodies from Brisbane, Queensland, Australia.

Kam knew the time had come to tell Jenny the truth. How could he continue to lie—or if not to lie to deceive—a woman who had given herself so unselfishly and wholeheartedly to him, who had met his passion and matched it with her own, the little cries she'd uttered lingering at all times in his head? Memories of them were causing his body to stir even now when coolness lay between them.

'Come and sit beside me,' he said. 'I'll make do with tea and bread for now, then you can teach me to make stew.'

She came, handing him a cup of tea and a torn-off piece of now stale flat-bread.

'Maybe learn to make bread as well,' he joked, but she didn't smile, alerted by his tone that this was serious.

'Jen…' he began, then stalled.

How to tell her?

How to explain?

Should he begin with his father? With his illness and the gradual slide into decline his country had taken?

But he didn't want to blame his father, or blame anyone for his deceit, so…

'Jen,' he tried again, and this time found some of the words he needed. 'You were right to be suspicious of me.'

She got up so quickly her tea spilt.

'Sit!' he ordered. 'Let me explain.'

She sat again but she was trembling and he wanted to take her in his arms and hold her close until the trembling stopped, and then maybe for ever.

That last thought shocked him.

For ever meant love.

No way could he be in love with Jenny Stapleton—not now, with his country in turmoil, looking to the new ruler to make things right again. What would the people think of that new ruler marrying a foreigner? He'd lose all credibility. And on top of that, his mother was even now scouting for a suitable bride.

'So, are you going to explain?'

She'd stopped trembling and now sounded angry, angry enough for Kam to realise he'd been lost in his own thoughts for too long.

'I meant no harm, coming to the refugee camp as I did,' he began, 'and as for my name, it is somewhere near the truth because I've held a passport in the name of Kam Rahman since I was seven. That was how old I was when our father sent me and my twin brother Arun off to school in England. My full name is Kamid Rahman al'Kawali, so he simply shortened it. Arun's is pronounced the same as the English Aaron but spelt A-R-U-N, but for school he was Arun Rahman.'

'So, you're not who you said you were, but you've been this person you're not since you were seven?'

Kam turned to Jenny to see if she was teasing him, but no vestige of a smile flickered about her lips, and her eyes looked very stormy, golden glints darting like fire in the dim cave.

'Is that an excuse or an explanation?' she continued, her lovely lips, slightly swollen by their kisses, set in a thin, grim line.

'It's the beginning of an explanation,' Kam told her. 'My father changed our names because he feared we might be kidnapped if our real identity was known. Not that he'd have missed us, he was quite old by the time we were born and had little contact with us. But he'd worked his way through four wives in order to finally produce sons to ensure the succession, and for that reason he was wary.'

'Succession? Your father?' Jen pressed, and Kam understood the question.

'The hereditary ruler of our country—the one over the border—the sheikh who recently died.'

'So, let me get this straight,' Jen said, using the excuse of putting down her empty teacup to stand up then return and sit a little further apart from him. 'You're not Kam Rahman, but Kam something else—what comes after that?'

'Kamid Rahman al'Kawali,' Kam told her, wondering why his full name would matter.

Jen repeated the name in her head. It sounded nice. But the bud of hope had already withered on its stem. Even if he loved her—and there was not one single, solitary reason to think he might—he couldn't marry her. His marriage would be important to his country and his people, and apart from that, as the hereditary ruler he'd need to have children to carry on—sons doubtless. He'd already told her how important sons were…

Her heart ached with regrets she knew she shouldn't have, and certainly would have to hide.

Anger would help!

'And you couldn't tell me this right at the start? You had to be someone else. Was there a reason?'

Kam sighed.

'My father was ill for a long time, and things have deteriorated throughout the country. We are wealthy people, and always have been, even before oil was discovered here, having been successful traders from many centuries ago. And we've always prided ourselves on taking care of our own. So, imagine my surprise and disappointment when I discover there's a foreign aid organisation working in our country.'

'But you've been working here yourself, in the city, you said. Shouldn't you have known?'

Kam shook his head.

'I barely knew my father and, though ill, he kept control through his brothers and their sons. My father married four times, wanting sons but only having daughters until his last wife, my mother, produced male twins. Once we were born, that was enough for him. He went back to his favourite, his third wife. My mother was set up in her own house and we were raised by the women around her until he sent us to school in England. It could have been rebelling against him that made Arun and I decided to study medicine rather than go into businesses the family owned. That made relations between the two of us and our father even more strained so, although we worked here, it was as ordinary citizens, not as sheikhs or heirs to the old man.'

Jen thought of her own close family, without whose love and caring and support she'd never have recovered from the deaths of David and her unborn child. She remembered her childhood, filled with laughter and the confidence that came from knowing she was loved.

Her heart ached for the children the twins had been, for the childhood they'd never had…

'When our father died, both Arun and I would have preferred one of our uncles take over as ruler, but people came to us with disturbing reports that things were bad throughout the country. Someone told us of Aid for All, other reports were that government funds were being siphoned off to family members rather than being distributed evenly to the people. We didn't know if one uncle had gone bad or if all of them were in collusion, so how could we pass the succession to any of them?'

He paused, looking directly at Jenny, although the light was so dim she doubted he would see the despairing pity in her eyes.

'I came out here to see the work Aid for All is doing and to find out why we can't do it ourselves. After this camp I intended to travel through the other villages on or near the border so I could see for myself what was happening in the country, while Arun is checking what he can in the city.'

'Also incognito?'

Kam shook his head.

'He's too well known in the city—both of us are. And as well as that, the checking there needs influence—bankers and government officials—so his position is important for him to collect information. But out in the country people react differently to the ruler, particularly if they feel the family has been neglecting them. I wanted to see things for myself, and to work out ways to right genuine wrongs, not be told tales of woe by someone who might want nothing more than to make money out of an untenable situation.'

Jenny nodded, understanding all of this yet still feeling the deep hurt of betrayal. She had been suspicious of Kam and now knew her suspicions had been well founded.

So how much did it count that his reasons for deceit were good?

It didn't seem to help the pain she was feeling, or the devastation that had swamped her when she'd realised who Kam was, although the devastation, she knew, was to do with the shrivelling of the bud of hope that had sprouted from her love.

'Let's make some stew,' he suggested, standing up and offering his hand to help her up.

Jen didn't take it—couldn't—she was too confused, but as a child she'd played house as well as anyone, and a little make-believe might be what was needed to get them through until the sandstorm subsided and they could safely return to the camp.

She turned the wick on the lamp a little higher and set out the tins of food on the table.

'See, that's tinned corned beef, or that's what it looks like from the picture on the side,' she explained, putting the largest of the tins to one side. 'And there are tinned peas and tinned carrots and even tinned potatoes. An onion would be nice, and something to make gravy.'

Kam was studying the other tins, reading labels Jenny couldn't understand.

'This is soup, would that do?' he suggested. 'To make it into soup you add water so perhaps if we didn't add the water…'

He sounded so uncertain, this strong, confident man to whom uncertainty would surely be foreign, that Jenny longed to put her arms around him, to assure him that she understood why he had deceived her. But her own emotions were too raw to put on show, and touching him was likely to start the flaring heat between them, so she thanked him for finding the soup and set him to opening cans while she lit the little stove again.

With the cans opened, Kam then rummaged around at the back of the cave, muttering to himself about why the electricity wouldn't have been connected when the houses in the village all had it.

'I suppose because no one ever lived here permanently. It might have belonged to a family that only came in the summer,' Jenny suggested, chopping up the corned meat then putting it and the contents of the other tins into the saucepan and wondering what the resulting mess would taste like.

'Not too bad,' Kam announced when they finally sat down to eat. He'd found some flour and although Jen knew flour and water were the basic ingredients, she wasn't too sure about making flat-bread. But she'd tried and, though tough, the bread, cooked in a frying-pan that had been hanging on the back wall, didn't taste too bad.

'You don't suppose they've forgotten we're here,' she suggested, trying to make near to normal conversation in order to distract her thoughts from how good things had been between them during their first twenty-four hours in the cave.

'I don't think that's likely, but the wind has been so fierce no one would be venturing outside. It can blind a man, or push him over, so people shut themselves inside their tents or houses and wait it out. It won't last much longer. Already the keening of it is lessening, the sound less shrill, don't you think?'

Jen didn't answer, wanting to cry because the easy communion they'd enjoyed, the whispered endearments they'd shared as they'd made love, had been replaced by such banal conversation.

Conversation about the weather, of all things!

A touch would bridge the gap that had grown between them and have them back in bed within minutes, while conversation was widening the gap into a gully. But wasn't it better to let it widen—let it widen further from a gully to a gulch or even to a gorge?

She longed to touch him, but knew the parting would be harder if she did, and the parting was as inevitable as an ending to the storm.

'It was like a dream,' she said quietly. 'A very special dream, but like all dreams it had to come to an end.'

Kam didn't answer, couldn't...

He knew he'd lost her. He'd felt the shift in the closeness between them way back when she'd mentioned stew. Hard to believe that stew of all things—and a revolting stew at that—should have torn them apart.

Admittedly they had been due to be torn apart, or, if not torn, due to part. He had to move on to other places, she had work to finish in the camp. He had to sort out the succession and his country's problems and she lived for the adventure and fun and challenge of her work abroad.

But surely he could offer adventure, fun and challenge to her right here in his own country!

The thought startled him.

What was he thinking?

Marriage?

It certainly would have to be, because a woman like Jenny deserved no less.

There were precedents set in other Arab countries of a ruler marrying a foreigner, and in most cases that he knew of, the unions had been happy and successful.

'Would you marry me?' he asked, pushing away the rest of his stew and the almost inedible bread.

The idea had followed so closely on his previous thoughts he'd voiced the question without giving it much consideration. Until he saw the look of shock and disbelief on her face…

'What?' he demanded, not understanding either emotion.

'This all began back when I realised we didn't know each other, and we still don't—well, we don't know much about each other,' she grumbled. 'How can you possibly suggest marriage to someone you barely know, based solely on the grounds of good sex? And how could I even think about it when you've deceived me from the moment we met? What kind of a basis for marriage is that? Honestly, Kam, that was the most ridiculous suggestion I've ever heard. And who is the older of you two—you or your brother? It seems one of you will be the new ruler, so surely you'd need a wife from your own culture; surely that would be more acceptable to your people, especially if your father spent his last years alienating them.'

'I thought there had been more than good sex between us,' he replied, his chest hurting at the implications of that particular remark, while the other objections she'd brought up niggled at the edges of his mind with irritating insistence.

A shout from outside the cave broke into the strained atmosphere that had been worsening between them.

Kam went to the door to greet their guide and lead him inside.

He carried a covered cooking pot and the aroma rising from it suggested it was a tastier meal than the stew they'd just made.

'You will eat, then the woman will check the patient and I will take you back to the border. If the chief's wife is well and the baby, we will wait a few nights before we ask the doctor to come again.'

Kam agreed that this seemed very sensible but in a few nights he'd be gone, or should be. There was much to do and he'd already lingered too long.

But to let Jenny return here alone?

It was not only unthinkable but the thought caused him serious pain.

He took the cooking pot and set it on the table, assuring their guide they'd eat then go across to the women's tent.

The guide bowed to Jenny then departed while Kam translated what he'd said.

'If the mother's OK I could wait a week before returning,' Jen said, and Kam's stomach cramped a little harder. It *might* have been the canned soup stew, but Kam suspected it was fear for Jenny.

Fear?

Concern at least, but surely concern wasn't strong enough for stomach cramps.

So he was back to fear, but fear for a woman whom, as she had so succinctly pointed out, he barely knew?

Why?

Unless…

No, he wouldn't go there. Love had never been an issue in his life, maybe because he hadn't experienced it as a child. Not the warm, loving, laughing family type of love he'd read and heard about. He had friends, of course, but liking covered what he felt for them.

But love for other people, especially for a woman, wasn't something he'd thought much about, and he'd certainly never considered it could be a trigger for fear…

CHAPTER TEN

'I'LL get dressed and we'll go, shall we?' Jen suggested when they'd sat and looked at the stew pot for a while, and it had become obvious neither of them was going to eat.

She didn't wait for an answer, gathering up her clothes and taking them to the dark corner they had used as a bathroom, dressing as quickly as she could, pulling on her doctor persona with her clothes, hoping her mind would be strong enough to put all the side issues of Kam and sex and the end of love to one side while she examined the new mother and her baby.

He must have dressed while she had been dressing, for he now stood beside the hanging mats, ready to hold them for her as she left the cave.

But memories made her reluctant to just walk out, and her body ached with the knowledge that what they'd had was finished.

Over…

Done with…

Move on…

But her aching heart couldn't make the leap, and she could feel tears welling in her eyes and a lump in her throat.

'Do you think they'd mind if I took the cream?' she whispered, the lump in her throat making her voice so husky it was a wonder Kam heard her at all.

He cursed, long and fluently, and although she didn't understand the words, the crisp, almost bitter tone in which they had been uttered told her they weren't cries of delight. Then he took her in his arms and kissed her so savagely her knees went weak and only by clinging to his shoulders could she remain upright.

The magic worked again, her nipples peaking, breasts growing heavy, the newly sensitised place between her thighs tingling with anticipation. Her hands grasped him and held him tight and with the kiss she gave back to him she tried to tell him all she felt, tell him that she loved him and always would.

But who understood kisses?

And the one thing he shouldn't know was that she loved him...

They fell back on the bed, grappling with their clothes, not bothering to strip but finding each other and making love one final time, intense, passionate, mutually satisfying love.

Or was it sex?

Jen no longer knew or cared how Kam thought of it—to her it was an expression of her love, given freely and without remorse or regret. For this one brief time Kam was hers again...

Kam helped her fix her clothing, doing up her bra catch and buttoning her shirt. His fingers fumbled with the tasks.

Because he knew this was it?

This was the last time he would touch Jenny's clothes?

Touch Jenny?

Unless...

'Why wouldn't you marry me?' he asked when they were ready to leave, the jar of rose-scented cream clasped in Jenny's hands.

She smiled at him.

'There are probably as many reasons as there are grains of sand in this cave. First, there's your position in your country, and your duty to your country, and how your family would feel if you married a foreigner, and the fact that you don't love me and I wouldn't like a marriage without love, and so many more reasons that the baby in the women's tent would be a toddler before I finished listing them.'

Kam heard them all but took little notice, his mind having picked up on the 'you don't love me' reason, and halted there.

'How do you know I don't love you?' he demanded, and she had the hide to smile again.

'Do you?' she asked, and having deceived her once he couldn't do it again.

But he could dodge and weave a bit...

'I know so little about love,' he told her. 'I know I love my brother because we only had each other for a long time. We were ignored by our father, passed on to nurses and waiting women by our mother, then sent to boarding school in a cold, hard, foreign country from the age of seven. We clung to each other, and grew to think and act as one, facing life and all its challenges together, and probably, at the same time, shutting out friends we might have had, for a while at least.'

'But you do have friends?' Jen pressed, and he nodded.

'Good friends, and each of us have different sets of friends, but I'd say liking is what I feel for them, not love.'

'And women? Surely at some stage of your life there's been a woman who set your pulses racing, and made your chest hurt when you were apart, and made your heart do a little flip when you saw her again after being parted?'

Kam tried to think.

'Pulse racing, yes, but that's attraction and desire. I couldn't call what I've ever felt for a woman love.'

Jen stood on tiptoe to kiss him gently on the lips.

'Then I feel sorry for you, Kam, although love hurts and losing a loved one is probably the most painful, agonising, gut-wrenching, heart-slamming hurt of all. But without it in our lives there's an emptiness, a void, a space we try to fill with other things, like challenge and adventure and fun.'

There was a pause and then she added, 'Which works for a time, of course.'

She ducked out of the cave before he could answer and, afraid she might get lost, he followed.

What had she been saying?

What had that final remark meant?

That challenge, adventure and fun were no longer enough?

That she'd found love again?

That she loved him?

He reached out a hand to stop her before she walked into the women's tent, but it was too late. She'd slipped off her sandals at the entrance and was already greeting the women inside.

Kam trudged around the tent to the place where he was used to waiting, ready to translate anything too medical or female oriented for the chief to tackle. But the chief wasn't there.

'What's happening?' Kam asked the guide who waited in the chief's place.

'The chief is at a meeting. If there is any problem with his wife or child I am to get him, but if not, he is not to be interrupted. It seems the arrival of his son has made him reconsider his claims on this territory. They are holding peace talks in the tent, but he has a message for the woman doctor. If the war is settled, will her organisation test his people for TB as she is doing for the refugees? It would be bad for them to come back if some people here still have the disease.'

'I can guarantee a testing and treatment programme for you—tell him that,' Kam said, then, in case the guide might be suspicious of his ability to make such a promise, he added, 'I work for the same organisation.' That was true. A donation to Aid for All had ensured he could move around his country under their banner. 'But I am in a higher position.'

The guide and the chief would accept this happily, their own customs suggesting a man would always be in a higher position than a woman.

Jenny's voice stopped the conversation. She was asking Kam to tell the woman that all was well, her wound was healing beautifully, the baby doing well, and they wouldn't need to come back for a few days, when Jenny would take out the stitches.

'Could you also tell the midwife what a great job she has done in looking after the pair, and tell her that although we would love to work out a way to teach her about Caesareans, the difficulty would be the anaesthetic and also if there were complications during or after the operation, unexpected haemorrhage, for instance. Perhaps you could tell her that your country is setting up a new air medical service, with doctors from the hospitals in the city working by roster to take emergency trips out to the far reaches of the country, and neighbouring countries as well.'

Confused though he'd been feeling, especially as far as Jenny was concerned, Kam had to smile. Talk about getting her pound of flesh! Now she knew who he was and how fervently he and Arun wished to make amends to their countrymen, she'd no doubt be coming up with more schemes like that, although an air medical service *was* a good idea. It was easy enough to build runways in the desert.

Somewhat reassured by the idea that peace talks were under way and Jenny's return in a few days might be all the safer because of that, Kam made the arrangements, though determined, when he radioed Arun on his return to the camp, to ask him to send someone out who could act as interpreter but also guard her safety.

Someone with enough authority to see that she remained safe while in the rebel camp.

He couldn't think offhand of anyone he'd trust that far and the thought worried him, but Jenny was speaking again, saying she was finished and would he please say goodbye to the women for her.

'There are a couple more pregnant women here,' she told him when she met him at the door of the tent minutes later. 'So you might need that aerial medical service sooner than you think, although I'll be here for another month or so myself. Could you tell them that and tell them if they want me to come to see them, or want to come across to the clinic, I'd be only too happy to check on them?'

'You can't cross back and forth across the border,' Kam told her, the irrational anger he felt at her putting herself in danger seizing him again. 'Have you forgotten the danger? The way we were treated on our first visit?'

'Ah, but now we're friends,' Jen told him. 'The chief is a question mark, but his wife, the midwife and the other women have begun to trust me, and trust leads to friendship. I can't believe they have no say in the running of their lives and no influence with their menfolk. Their friendship will protect me.'

'You are too trusting for your own good,' Kam snapped at

her. 'I don't want you coming back and forth over the border, no matter how many women are pregnant.'

'Don't you, now?' she snapped right back. 'And I should care because?'

'Because I—'

He heard the words he was about to utter in a kind of practice in his head and caught them just in time, then as it dawned on him they were the stark, honest truth, he said them anyway.

'Because I love you,' he said, and though his heart was hammering with the emotion of the declaration and his body shivering with reaction, he still took in the look of shock imprinted on her lovely face.

'Oh, but, Kam, you can't,' she wailed, desperation seeding the words with misery.

'Why can't I?' he demanded, angered now he'd made his declaration and she'd deflected it. For answer she studied him in silence for a moment then she took his face between the palms of her hands and looked into his eyes.

'Because your country means so much to you, more even than I think you realise. And to do your duty to it, you must marry and have children.'

Then, oblivious of the people around them, she reached up and kissed him on the lips.

'I can't have children,' she whispered against his lips, then with a quick, final hug she released him.

But he was not ready to let go.

'Can't? The accident? You know for sure?'

'Ninety per cent sure,' she said gently, and turned to greet their guide, who'd come to take them back to the border.

Kam forced his numbed mind to work enough to give orders to his legs, moving like a robot behind the pair. Once beyond the light at the entrance to the women's tent, the dust still lingering in the air blocked out any moonlight or starlight, so they followed closely in the wake of the guide, their feet shuffling through drifts of sand and stumbling over piles of it in unexpected places.

Kam held the door for Jenny as she climbed into the car, but knew he couldn't talk to her about this until they were alone.

Which didn't stop him pondering the problem.

She'd lost a baby in the accident—what other damage might have been caused?

He felt his heart squeeze with pain at the thought—remembering Jenny with Rosana, remembering the love she felt for the little boys, her concern for Hamid. Jenny giving her love to other people's children...

The guide dropped them back at the border and they crossed into the camp, and even in the dim night light they could see the sand piled against the tents, in some places women sweeping at it, trying to move it away.

'It could make the whole camp disappear if it blew long enough,' Jenny murmured as they looked around.

Just like that—normal conversation. Love, attraction, sex, whatever it had been put behind them—as far as she was concerned.

But what about *him*? He had all the symptoms she'd mentioned. The racing pulse, the hurting chest and the little flip of his heart when he'd seen her putting on her sandals at the women's tent, although their time apart had only been a matter of minutes...

He wanted to talk about it, but she was pointing out the way the sand had built up against his vehicle and wondering if he'd be able to get it out.

'You'll be leaving, won't you?' Jen said, knowing he had a job to finish, hoping the sooner he left, the sooner her heart would start to heal.

Hoping the sooner he left, the less chance there was of revealing her feelings for him.

'Tomorrow—I should go tomorrow,' he told her, moving closer so she knew it wasn't a departure time he wanted to talk about, but personal things.

'That's for the best,' she told him, then turned towards him, looking up at him in the dim light, the moon nothing more than a suggestion in the still dusty air. 'It was wonderful, Kam, and I'll never forget what we had. Fun, challenge and adventure, all my desires rolled into one.'

'*All* your desires?'

'All I've wished for since David's death,' she said, which was the truth as far as it went, but a truth that had changed when she'd met Kam.

He grasped her shoulders and gave her a little shake.

'Not love? Have you banned love from your life because you lost one man you loved—because you suffered pain? Would you deny yourself the pleasure of it once again, just to avoid hurt? You talk to me of how empty my life must have been to have not loved, yet you've shut off *your* heart behind barriers, travelling the world, helping others, moving on, in case you become too attached to a particular place or person and in losing it or him or her, you'd hurt again. I thought you brave, courageous, but you're not— you're a coward, too afraid of the consequences to grasp at happiness.'

'I can't, Kam,' she said, keeping her voice steady with an effort. Knowing she couldn't say another word without breaking down, she walked into the big tent that was her home, clutching her arms across her chest to still her hammering, hurting heart.

Jen cradled Rosana in her arms as she watched the car approach, hoping as always it would stop before the tents so the dust that trailed it would not go into the clinic. Was it because she held Rosana again this morning that she remembered Kam's arrival? The child weighed more now and chattered cheerfully, her life with the boys as guardians obviously suiting her.

And was she, Jen, thinking of Rosana to stop herself thinking of Kam, arriving like this in a far less shiny car only a little over a week ago?

She wasn't going to answer that, mainly because thinking of Kam was a full-time occupation. They didn't interfere with her work, but the memories were always there in the back of her mind, memories of warmth and laughter and his gentle touch along her scars.

You couldn't see the new scars…

The dust settled and she realised this was a very different vehicle, splendidly large and shiny beneath its patina of dust. A figure emerged from the far side, a figure in a flowing white gown, hands upraised to secure the shiny black double braid that held his scarf in place.

Jen couldn't help but stare. This was an image from fairy stories and fancy magazines, the tall, strong desert warrior in his snowy robes—his stance, his presence casting awe on all who saw him.

She smiled at the thought for the little boys, who'd come running when they'd heard the car, now stood back, heads bowing, something akin to fear on their faces. Then the figure knelt and held out his hands and the boys moved closer, smiling now, shyly touching his robes.

Kam!

Heart thudding, Jen held Rosana closer, the urge to flee tingling in her legs.

But she wouldn't run away.

She and Kam were finished, they both understood that. Besides, another man had now emerged from the vehicle, a tall, tanned man who came closer, smiling at Jen, holding out his hand, his green eyes…

Had she been mistaken about the first man?

Had she got over Kam so quickly her heart didn't thud and her stomach didn't cramp and her breathing didn't hitch in her throat when he approached?

'You know I'm not him, don't you?' the man said.

Jenny whispered, 'Arun?'

He nodded but looked a little put out.

'I thought as you'd never seen him in his local gear you might not have known it was him. So why didn't you, Dr Jenny Stapleton? We're identical. Everyone mistakes us.'

Jen smiled at him.

'You didn't make my heart beat faster,' she admitted, feeling a weight lift off her shoulders as she spoke, knowing he would understand it as a declaration of her love. 'But if you tell Kam I said that, I'll deny it.'

She glanced across to where the man who did make her heart beat faster had last been, but he'd disappeared, although a few of the boys were still there by the car.

'I won't tell Kam but I did suspect you must love him. From all I've heard—and, believe me, I've heard plenty—I suspected you might feel the same way about him as he feels about you. So why, Jenny Stapleton, won't you marry him?'

Rosana was wriggling in her arms and the man who wasn't Kam reached out and took her, murmuring gentle words to the child, making her clap her hands and giggle with delight.

'He didn't tell you?

The little boys—the blood brothers—appeared and took Rosana, and Arun followed Jen into the tent.

The women in there fell about in their eagerness to serve him, and watching Arun charm them Jen was glad it was Kam she loved, not him. Charm came less easily to Kam, he used respect in all his dealings and earned it in return.

She watched as Arun was served his coffee, and little sweetmeats and cakes were offered on a tray, then as the women withdrew, Jen raised her coffee-cup towards him.

'Did you wear the full outfit today to impress the locals?'

'Ouch!' he said, and tried to look hurt, although his green eyes glinted with humour and she couldn't help but like him.

'Actually, it's the full outfit because I'm on official business. We both are. We have an engineer with us and he's going to check out the site for the best place to sink a well, then Kam and I are meeting with the chief across the border to discuss a trans-border arrangement for an aerial medical service and to work out a timetable for the refugees to return to their village.'

He paused, smiling at Jenny.

'I understand you had not a little to do with the medical service suggestion.'

Jen shook her head, unable to believe it might be happening so quickly.

'I didn't think he'd do anything about it—not right away

when he, and you, I suppose, have so many other pressing problems.'

Arun smiled again.

'I think any suggestion you made would be acted on immediately, Jenny. And, anyway, the other pressing problems have become less pressing. Kam has agreed to take over the succession, our uncles have stepped down from their positions and government workers from within the various departments will take over their—Jenny! What's wrong?'

She managed to put down her cup before the wooziness made her spill the contents, and she reached out for the ground to stop herself from fainting head first into the plate of cakes. Arun came swiftly to her side and steadied her, his strong arms holding her until the faintness passed.

'I'm all right,' she managed, but the words that had caused her faintness—*Kam has agreed to take over the succession*—echoed in her head, ripping out the last faint threads of hope she'd stupidly been clinging to.

'It was— I...'

No words would come, for nothing could explain the emptiness inside her.

'Tell me,' Arun said, and suddenly Jenny knew that all she felt could no longer be contained within her pounding head, or hidden in her hurting heart.

'Tell you what? That I love Kam? That's easy to tell, Arun, because I do. With all my heart and soul and being. I never expected to feel love like that again then, bang, love suddenly slammed into me like a train. But it was Kam Rahman that I loved and I even began to hope he might love me back—it was like a miracle. Then he wasn't Kam Rahman but had other names tacked on which made him heir to the throne of a sheikhdom, and that made everything impossible.'

She stopped, already having said more than she should have, worrying about Arun repeating it to Kam.

But Kam must surely know she loved him even if she hadn't said it...

'Go on,' Arun said, and she looked at him, frowning, wondering what more there was to say.

'Why impossible?' he prompted. 'And don't tell me it's because you're a foreigner, because foreigners have been marrying into our family for centuries—where did you think Kam's and my green eyes came from?'

'It wasn't just the foreigner thing,' Jen admitted, sensing Arun wasn't going to let it go and wanting to talk about it anyway. 'I was eight months pregnant when we had the accident that killed my husband. I lost the baby as well and the damage caused at the time means I can't have children.'

She tried a smile she knew was a bit wobbly on her lips.

'A foreigner might have been OK, but a foreigner who can't produce heirs? That would be impossible—I couldn't do it to him. Marrying Kam when he already has so many problems to sort out, and when he, and you, are trying so desperately to pull Zaheer together after years of neglect. No, he needs a wife of the people, someone who understands what has to be done and can help and support him—someone who speaks the language, for a start!'

She paused, then added bleakly, 'But most of all he needs someone who can give him sons!'

She shook her head and hoped the tears she knew were welling in her eyes didn't overflow and go streaming down her cheeks, but when Arun put his arms around her and drew her close against his body, so she felt it could be Kam who was holding her one last time, she couldn't hold them back.

But indulgence in such weakness couldn't be allowed to go on, so she pulled away within a minute, straightening up, sniffing back the tears, swallowing the sad lump in her throat and asking him if he'd like to see the camp or the testing programme before they met the guide at the border in an hour.

'I'd rather talk to you,' Arun told her, but she shook her head.

'I've already talked far too much,' she said. '*Far* too much! I'll get over Kam and he—if he really loves me—will get over me, especially as he has to juggle his new role as ruler and his medical work, and life will go on for both of us. I've been told of an AIDS testing programme in Africa I can join when I finish here. It's in place I've never been.'

'Adventure, challenge, fun!' Arun said, and Jen began to wonder just how much information brothers—twins—might share. Not all of it, she hoped...

'That's right,' she said. 'It's not for everyone, but it suits me.'

'Suits you to run away.'

Arun spoke so sternly Jen stared at him.

'I'm not running away,' she said. 'I'm moving on, as I always intended to.'

'You *are* running away. You're running away from love because it hurt you once before. You're using the excuse of being a foreigner and not being able to have a child, but basically it's because you're a coward.'

'You can't say that!' Jenny snapped, really annoyed with the man now. 'You don't even know me!'

'No, and I don't know that I want to, because I would have thought the woman Kam finally fell in love with had more guts.'

'Guts?' Jen echoed weakly, still annoyed but wondering what on earth Arun was getting at.

'The guts to fight for him—to fight for happiness for both of you. So what if you can't have children? In another fifty years—even thirty—inherited positions could well be a thing of the past.'

Jenny stared at Arun. Was he right? Was she gutless?

No! If Arun was right and Kam truly loved her, wouldn't he be here? Wouldn't she be talking to him rather than Arun? Wouldn't he have wanted, on arrival, to speak to her, touch her, at least to hold her hand?

The fact that he was walking through the camp in search of a site for a well told her all she needed to know—duty came first for him and, sadly, that was how it should be.

The little boys arrived to tell them the guide was waiting, and Jen was relieved to set aside her doubts and follow her little friends towards the border. She introduced Arun to the guide and saw the proud man bow his head towards Arun, then open the car door for him. Jen opened the back door for herself, recognising her place in the local scheme of things—one of relative unimportance.

At the village over the border Arun translated ably, and Jen removed the stitches and pronounced her patient well, the baby beautiful, and all the pregnant women in sound health. Arun spoke again, but in his own language, and soon the women clustered around Jenny, leading her to a mat where tea and coffee were laid out, and plates laden with dates and other fruit and sweets set in the middle.

'You will eat and enjoy the women's company,' a deep voice announced, and Jenny turned to see the chief in the doorway, Arun just beyond him. Another order was issued and the midwife took the baby to the chief who presented him proudly to Arun

It seemed for ever before she heard male voices approaching the women's tent and the chief appeared once again in the doorway.

'You are ready to return?'

Jenny nodded, getting to her feet, thanking the women who had entertained and fed her, using the few words of Arabic she knew and hoping they were the right words. Then she walked to the doorway of the tent where the men waited just beyond the entrance, the chief in his usual black robe, Arun contrasting in his white. She bent to fasten a sandal, wobbling slightly as she did so. A strong hand reached out to steady her, and awareness shot like an arc of electricity right through her body.

'Kam?' she whispered, turning towards the man in the white gown who now held her steady.

He *had* come!

The white-clad figure nodded, his green eyes looking deep into hers.

'Did you think I'd take your no and walk away?' he said. 'How could I when you'd taught me what love was like? I know you believe you'd do my position harm by marrying me, but have you thought what harm you'd do my heart? Do you know what the only valid reason for not marrying me would be? That you didn't love me.'

He turned her so he could study her face, and Jen realised the chief had moved away and they were alone.

'Can you tell me that? Look me in the eyes and say it? I don't think you can, Jenny, because I think you love me as much as I love you, and do you know how much that is? As boundless as the desert, that's my love, as strong as the storm that brought us such delights, as incalculable as the number of grains of sand on which we stand. Do you think I would prefer a wife I didn't love, or that I would not marry you because you couldn't produce an heir? I have a brother who can do that, and cousins should Arun not marry. It is not an issue, Jenny, when set against the love I feel for you.'

He paused, then bent his head and kissed her thoroughly, withdrawing only far enough to question her again.

'*Now* tell me you don't love me,' he whispered, and Jen stared at him in confusion.

'I *do* love you,' she managed, 'but it still seems wrong.'

'How could it be wrong if love lies between us, Jenny? Is it not said that love will find a way? Love will find our way, and light our path, and lead us wherever life is meant to take us. So marry me and share the journey, share the joy that love will bring us, without thoughts of other things or regrets for what might have been. Just love, Jen, and you and me.'

Jenny snuggled closer to him.

'You and me and however many thousands of people you rule over,' she teased.

'Well, yes, there's them, and my family, and your family— but at the heart of it all is us.'

'Us,' Jen echoed, and felt all the turmoil she'd been feeling in her heart and head ease into happiness. 'Us,' she whispered again, reaching up to kiss Kam on the lips.

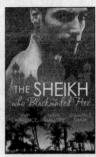